The Kinsman

A NOVEL

Cover artwork of "The Kinsman"painted by Madeleine McKay
11 inches by 14 inches · Oil on Canvas
WWW.MADELEINEMCKAY.COM

The Kinsman
A NOVEL

is published by
Shiptree Publications · Honolulu, HI 92822-5712 USA

.

Additional copies of this book may be ordered directly at
WWW.GARDNERMCKAY.NET

McKay, Gardner
  The Kinsman: A novel
    Shiptree Publications, ©2011.
    ISBN: 978-1-883684-32-7

First Edition published June 10, 2011
Printed in the United States of America

The Kinsman

A NOVEL

by

Gardner McKay

SHIPTREE

HONOLULU, HAWAII

OTHER PUBLISHED WORKS BY
Gardner McKay

Novel
Toyer: A Novel of Suspense

Memoir
Journey Without A Map

Short Stories
"Toyer"
"The Fortunes of Schlomo Khabout"
"One Summer in Charente"
"Into the Rose Garden"
"In Another Lifetime"

Plays
Sea Marks
Masters of the Sea
Me.
Toyer
In Order of Appearance

Teleplays
Untold Damage
Sea Marks

Screenplays
Toyer
Me.

Table of Contents

Introduction

Foreword

Part One
Rwanda

Part Two
Goodbye, America

Part Three
La Rochelle

Introduction

Gardner and I were at a Christmas party at a neighbor's house; I think it was 1998. Someone told a joke and that led to another, and then somehow it segued into titles of "The World's Slimmest Volumes."

A charming English lady friend with a wonderful laugh delivered the line, *"Negroes I've Enjoyed Talking with While Yachting."* Everyone chuckled.

Rwanda had been very much in the news at that time, the dreadful daily massacre of thousands, and Gardner was so disturbed by the events that he was moved to write something about it. That line at the party resonated with him, and the idea began to germinate. Gardner had never been to Rwanda, so he did most of his research through the local library and made contact with the Rwandan embassy and their consulate to verify certain details concerning events and the country.

Since 1995, Gardner had been writing short stories for his weekly radio program called "Stories on the Wind," which aired Sunday evenings on Hawaii Public Radio. When he began working on this book, he decided to read an abridged version of *The Kinsman* in weekly episodes, and it was well received. The book, as it is here, was completed in 1999.

I am eternally grateful to Don Davidson and his crew at The Peninsula Press on Cape Cod. Without their encouragement and guidance over the past two years, this book would not be published today. Don is the person who has made this possible by proofreading, advising and organizing the details to deliver Gardner's ideas. And while I'm sure Don will do everything in his power to see that this observation never makes it to print, his humor and self-deprecation and love of words are so congruent with Gardner's that his appearance at this juncture is nothing short of providential. This book is dedicated to him.

Madeleine McKay
Honolulu, Hawai'i
June 10, 2011

The Kinsman

No one goes to Rwanda in the summer. No one goes to Rwanda in the winter. There is no high season there, only a low season. It may look like a tropical Switzerland, but it's the opposite of a resort. Nobody goes there unless he wants to see black people hacked to death by machetes. Club Dead. Only my first impression, of course. I could be wrong.

Call me Jib, that's a baby nickname. Apparently during some dry spell in my babyhood I thought I was a puppy and, according to sources close to me, spoke gibberish. Now I'm twenty-six, and I don't do that anymore, but I'm still called Jib. I busted out of Yale for grades. I've never done drugs. I have no visible means of support. I'm a yachtsman. A wandering Protestant. I'm definitely the leading contender for black sheep of my rather austere family from Middletown, Rhode Island, all made up of aunts, uncles, and cousins who live behind walls of old money. My Aunt Pearl says I give *dilettantism* a bad name. I'll be okay. I'll just never run for the Senate.

This is my story. I really don't expect you to believe it. But you probably ought to, because it's true.

Part One
Rwanda

Rwanda

I was not having a good day.

A couple of weeks ago, I'd flown to Nairobi to meet Jocelyn Ortion for a safari. My fiancée. I missed her at Shambalah. I missed her at both game parks. I tried to catch up with her all through Kenya. We kept crossing paths; my fault, I guess. So, she left me a chilly note at Treetops and took off in my chartered plane to wait for me in Tanzania a few hundred miles south.

So that's how I found myself rattling along a dirt road in a discarded UN Land Rover en route to join her in Tanzania. It seemed like a good idea at the time, being driven through Rwanda in a recreational vehicle that had been sold for scrap to my driver, Leopold Asoferwa, a good soul, who had yet to discover that it had more than one gear. Things just developed that way, my non-safari, and anyhow, that's how I discovered Rwanda.

We entered Rwanda around dawn that first morning at Byumba. The border was guarded by fidgety nine-year-old soldiers who were shorter than their guns and asked if we had any chocolate. They couldn't decipher my passport. Did this eagle mean I was Egyptian? Sorry.

Leopold gave them a can of instant coffee and, in spite of not coming up with the chocolate, the kids allowed us to drive on. Leopold explained to me that this was the new regime. Youngish, I thought, and forgot about them until about twenty miles further south when we were stopped at a roadblock held by slightly older soldiers who didn't want chocolate or instant coffee, but smiled when I offered them some nice American dollars. They accepted them without knowing what they were. I wish I'd been carrying Lire, so many zeros. I asked Leopold who these men were, and he said they were the new government troops. The good guys. But he seemed nervous. In fact, he'd showed his anxiety the moment we entered the country, and he stayed edgy the whole time; he definitely did not want to be driving me through there. He said that he had a wife and children living next door in Kenya, and the only reason he was driving me through this *rataba* (he told me every so often, as if I had amnesia) was that he needed money to pay for his children's schools in Nairobi. I could only assume that a *rataba* was not a place he wanted to be.

Leopold's other name took some getting used to. *A-so-fer-wa,* and I said it slowly. As Leopold Asoferwa drove us through thicker overgrowth along the road, he constantly imagined Hutu rebels hiding in the tall grass around us. I had yet to see my first one, so I wasn't impressed.

Now it was late afternoon of the first day. I was bone-banged weary. We'd been driving over rutted roads, foot-by-foot. I'd been bounced and rattled into submission. I was played out and parched. It had taken all day to make maybe eighty miles, according to what I figured from a French survey map.

Leopold had bought this four-wheeled item from the UN for a very good price, he assured me. I bet he had, I told him. Every part of it had been individually condemned. And as if that weren't enough, suddenly it proved it by veering off the road. It had lost its steering.

A cable or something had broken. Who knows? I'm no mechanic, so I sat down in the grassy field beside the dirt road and the bargain Land Rover while Leopold crawled under it. As I sat there with evening settling upon the empty fields around us, I couldn't help noticing that it was quite beautiful. I got my camera and started snapping pictures of the mountains in the distance. After a few minutes of my doing that, he came over to me with a small piece of the car in his hand. He declared that we'd have to camp where we were overnight, an idea he regarded with cool alarm. Terror, actually. And I was not a big fan of the idea.

Without even putting the car in four-wheel drive, he gunned it, spinning its wheels out of the ditch onto level ground in the high grass, then turned the motor off. The fields surrounding us were silent. No birds singing, no roosters crowing, no dogs barking, no voices. The silence was kind of eerie in the emptiness of the area, the wide abandoned fields, especially because I'd be spending the night there.

He would sleep on top; I would sleep inside, he said. I wasn't frightened, but I couldn't get it out of my head that I was here entirely by mistake, that I had done this voluntarily.

He started chatting nervously, looking around at the high grass for Hutus. It had grown out of control because of the rain, he said. There'd been lots of rain, but it was also high because the fields had been abandoned by the farmers. They were very rich fields, he said, even richer than Kenya's, for growing tea, coffee, bananas, avocados, all sorts of grain, the works. He couldn't stop chattering. The farmers had run away. They were not there any more. And if they'd stayed, they would have been murdered.

But, he said, now things were being made better. Supposed to be anyway. The new regime had taken charge and the Inyenzi were beginning to come back. I asked him who the Inyenzi were and he told me an *inyenzi* was a cockroach, but the real name for them was Tutsis, which sounded pretty strange.

Without looking at the sky or anything, he said it would rain that night and that we should maybe try to look for better shelter. He pointed to a church we'd passed half-a-kilometer back. A little white wooden church that looked abandoned; the only building in sight. He said he thought we might be able to sleep in it and cook there. So, after watching him tinker with the car for a while, I decided to walk on over there. I took my camera. Rustic little white church, surrounded by pretty trees. Good.

That was where I got my first glimpse of the reason for Leopold's fear, and it became my own.

It was still light when I started down the wide grassy path. Halfway there, I waved to this little boy lying in the grass. A black boy, for sure, but still the way he was lying reminded me very much of my cousin Nick, because of the way Nick loved to lie under the sprinklers, summers in Rhode Island when we were kids, when we were six or eight. The little boy didn't wave back to me, so I called out, "Hello!" But he still didn't wave. So I figured he must have been asleep.

I couldn't see it until I walked closer, but his head had been detached from the rest of his body which was turned away from me. His face was toward me, eyes closed, and his skin had gone pale like the kind of papier-mâché mask we used to make at playschool. He had been dead a while. There were many flies, and I can't tell you how I felt. It was a sort of a seasickness in my face. I was in the presence of death for the first time since my freshman year at Yale, when a frosh had jumped from the bell tower.

Well, even worse, this was murder. I could see that this little boy had been slashed across the back. There was a deep maroon V cut on top of his head. And one of his hands was missing, nowhere in sight.

He was only this very little boy, but someone with a blade of some sort must have been so pissed off at him that he wanted to make sure he'd never grow up. Then, I saw the hand. His hand. I was practically standing on it. I wouldn't have known it was a hand; it was so tiny and black. Curled up, it looked more like a bird's foot.

I waved to Leopold. He walked over to me slowly, carrying a tire iron. He stared at the boy. I thought I was going to pass out.

"What happened to him?" I said.

"Machete-machete."

He pointed to something a distance away that I hadn't seen.

"There is another," he said. Buttocks in tall grass.

"Who did it?"

"Hutu." He waved his hand at the two bodies. "These are Inyenzi," he said. Before I could ask, he added, "They are Tutsi."

They used to be Tutsi, I thought. Now, they were refuse.

Leopold shook his long head, still looking at the bodies. "These Inyenzi are the clever ones. These cockroaches, they are the farmers who own the cows and the fields, and the Hutus are the stupid ones. But there are many, many more Hutus."

I couldn't think of anything to cover the boy with, so we walked down the path toward the church. Leopold's fingers were drumming on his legs. His eyes were everywhere. He was terrified, and I was learning why.

Halfway to the church, the wind changed and brought us a smell. The fields had smelled fresh green from the rain, but this new smell was sweet, like the odor of feces I had smelled earlier when we drove through a village called Melindi. But then it changed and got much stronger.

Leopold took my hand. His hand was hard as roots. We walked together the rest of the way toward the church hand-in-hand. We both knew we were smelling the smell of death.

Standing outside the church in a wooden shrine was a plaster cast of what must have been Jesus Christ holding his arms out, his palms open, in a gesture of welcome. Jesus had not done well. He had been decapitated, small chunks of him had been cut off, pieces of him lay among crusts of brittle flowers, strewn sacrifices at his feet.

The church door had been nailed shut. Leopold pried at it with the tire iron, and we pulled it open. The smell overcame me. Flies were everywhere. Inside was a full congregation. Dozens and dozens. More than a hundred men, women, and children crammed into its wooden pews. It was a horrible mess. The stench was outrageous, a hundred times worse than natural gas. All of them were twisted or curled or spread, and some were hanging onto each other; and all were dead and had been dead not very long, maybe for a few weeks. Some had gone pale like the boy outside, and some were blacker than lake bottoms. They had been trapped there in the church like bugs, and they all were dead, some in cowering positions, their hacked arms up in front of their heads. They had head cuts, arms and legs nearly cut off. Deep black wounds. Here and there, I saw a child who'd clung to a woman for protection and had been cut clear through. I had never seen so much anatomy.

"Machete," was all Leopold whispered. "Hutu."

I stood frozen with my hand over my nose, trying not to breathe. As if that would help.

It was a death these Tutsi surely would have seen coming toward them, and it must have been a loud death, too. Not loud in the way guns fired off indoors are loud, where they stun your ears. Here there would have been the screams and the sound of the machetes hitting bones. That was what they would have heard.

I stood there wondering what it would feel like to see death hacking its way toward me. Being innocent. Not even being a soldier. These dead were probably just poor people who had a bad life anyway. They did not ask to live there.

Then a baby's arm moved. But before I could do anything, I saw a rat under it. Then another. There were scuttling sounds as the rats resumed feeding. They didn't mind our presence; there was enough for everyone.

It blindsided my capacity to understand. I mean there I was standing in this wooden church with pews and little scattered books. I wasn't watching this on a screen. I was there. I've seen hundreds of pictures of terrible things, but pictures don't smell bad, and it was impossible not to smell it. I threw up; Leopold didn't.

Outside behind the church was a storage shed, and we opened the door. It was full of women mostly naked. I didn't need to be a gynecologist to see that they'd all been raped. Then hacked to death. These women must have been culled from the church, taken out back, raped, killed. Then they were hidden in the shed, maybe in some weird act of shame or contrition. Who knows? We are, after all, born of woman.

I closed the door. I stood outside breathing in gulps.

I was sick. Leopold was panting from fear. The sun slanted beautifully. We were standing in a magnificent field, mountains rising in the near distance. A perfect sunset.

I couldn't even speak. It was certainly my right to think anything I wanted to think and, in those moments, I didn't want to be in the world.

"Go fix the car now." I ordered Leopold. I was through being diplomatic. "Fix the fucking car now."

He trotted off toward the Land Rover leaving me with the dead. It would be dark soon. There was no flashlight, and he couldn't work long, not for more than an hour. I certainly didn't want to be standing in that stinking field any longer, but even before he got to the car I knew we were going to sleep in it that night, close to the dead.

We skipped dinner. I curled up on the back seat. Leopold climbed up on the roof and lay under the tarpaulin holding my hunting rifle. I guess he figured the Hutus wouldn't see him up there and they'd get to me first. As I lay there, my brain was rapidly churning; this wasn't summer stock. This was the whole world. I had heard of it.

I lay there spinning for an hour. Whenever there was even a slight breeze, the odor from the church muscled its way inside the car. Sick as I felt, I wasn't scared. I was detached. I just told myself that the Hutus didn't want me dead, that I wasn't Tutsi, and that I was safe from them. Except for robbery. And what do you know? The next day, my camera disappeared at a checkpoint further south. But without even knowing it, I had shot a full roll of film in the church, emptied the camera. I had the film.

As Leopold had predicted, that night the rains came, but he kept dry on the roof under the tarp. When it stopped and the skies cleared, the moon rose. Jesus, I won't even try to describe it. Just say that it was a huge perfect circle and that it was white. It was bright as day. I'd given up trying to sleep. It was so white, I think I expected something with more red in it. But it was different than any moon I'd ever seen. It lay there huge and took my mind away from me. I guess the moon can do that. It's so different from the sun. Try and stare at the sun. I can't. But I can stare at the moon, which is what I did. I couldn't stop. It made me look at it more and more. And after a while, it seemed to be working on me, making me think, as if it were a receptacle for my thoughts, asking me to pay attention to it, wanting me to answer it, to come up with an answer to something. An idea. It seemed to be witnessing me. The sky was clear, the land was bright, the moon was rising. I could see the little church that was also white, less than a quarter mile away through the window.

Bloodlines and/or religion, was that all this was? A cultural thing? Methods to deal with differences differed wildly. Why had the Hutus left their victims in plain sight? Babies, mothers, you know; no mass graves needed. As if it were okay. That everyone should know about them. Didn't this show that they had pride in their work? Everyone else tries to cover up genocide, burning and burying, but to the Hutus this just must have seemed to be an act of prejudice. It was their way to solve the snob thing. Jesus, I thought we Americans were snobs, but this was the ultimate snobbism. Then all those other snob things I'd read about started to look the same. The Serbs and the Russians were methodical, clumsy, messy, and they hid their victims in discrete graves. The Turks, the Japanese, Pol Pot were much more open about their genocide. The Argentinians pretended they didn't do it. Arabs relied on bombs in cars, planes, markets in their fifty-year snit with Israel. The Nazis had a neatness about them; poison gas, a dreadful grace. With *schadenfreude,* they filmed it in progress, and they would never have stopped filming if they hadn't been interrupted. All of them, just a bunch of deranged snobs.

The moon set, but the night went on and on, and it was a very long night.

In the morning, we drove past another body lying off the road in plain sight, like a chair with a broken leg. Then we passed what must have been a grave, trenches the length of our tennis courts, mounded high with good earth and sticks marking both ends. Then in a mile there was another grave and further on, another. What graves there were, were not yet dry and maybe they would never be, with the rains.

Leopold said that these Hutus had hacked to death one million souls in one hundred days. He called them souls. I asked him if he was religious. He wouldn't tell me. Many of the Tutsis fled to other countries across the borders, but one million did not. The ones that were hacked to death. There were thousands more left for dead among the dead who did not die and escaped with permanent wounds. Half-dead people. Some unable to speak, out of their minds, dismembered. The survivors. It is a country of old men, orphans, widows. He said "million" casually, as if he'd forgotten what it meant. He didn't expect me to believe him.

We passed an old woman dragging a bundle behind her on a stick. The remaining Inyenzi were returning home, Leopold said, to their land. I told him to stop the car.

"Ask her what those long graves are," I told him.

Leopold asked her a question. The woman was terrified to be spoken to. She put her hands to her mouth. She reached in her sack and held out a grubby index card with some typing and a photograph stapled to it.

"Tutsi," Leopold said. "She cannot speak."

I thanked her and told Leopold to offer her a ride. She was very tired, but she was too confused to say "yes". I handed her a pack of Marlboros that she carefully put into her bundle.

"Hutus would never bother to bury anyone," Leopold said after we'd driven away. "They are much too stupid. But the Tutsis do. They care. They bury their dead." It was a good sign. More and more, we encountered people on the road carrying possessions, the remainders of families walking back from their exile, in fragments, searching for each other, hoping to find them in the small cement houses that looked like burned-out sculptures, the house where they hoped to begin living again but would relive their tragedies.

By now, I had figured out that one million people divided by a hundred days was ten thousand a day. I did find that hard to believe.

"Is that gossip?" I said. "The one million."

He shook his head.

"You have to know how. They were trained by the French. They taught them they could kill one-thousand in twenty minutes. The Hutus learned how all right."

He said they also clubbed them to death. Had I noticed that the women in the shed had been clubbed to death? No, I hadn't, I said. Well, they had and sometimes they burned them, too.

"Parents hid their children in the tall grass, but when the children saw their parents being hacked to death they cried out and betrayed their hiding places and then they were killed, too."

"Why?" I asked. He knew I meant the whole damn thing.

He told me that the French wanted to keep a foothold in Africa and this was the way to maintain a one-party system in Rwanda. "The Hutus had a French-trained militia called the *Interahamwe*." Incredibly, had the French begun all of this? The training of a militia for this genocide? That's what he said. He shrugged. Take it or leave it. I tried to leave it.

On the flight home from Tanzania even though some images blurred, the hacked bodies did not abandon me. They clung to me like cats. The smell of death was in my clothes; the hunchback moon over the little white church, the crumbling statue of Jesus Christ, polished corpses floating in the river, the terrified mute old woman with the torn ID card, the dead boy's lost hand.

There was another image just before I left Rwanda. Something I imagined that I saw on a huge lake. Lake Kivu.

I changed planes at Heathrow Airport outside of London. The first newspaper I saw carried a front page picture of a dead Israeli soldier. I searched it for news of what I'd seen in Rwanda, any mention. Ten thousand a day for more than three months, one million killed. I couldn't find a word. I didn't know why that was. The story was over. The numbers had leveled off; the stacks of bodies had cured. The lone Israeli soldier dead on the front page was the only news, and one million chopped-up Rwandans lived only in my imagination. And the image I'd seen on Lake Kivu.

Newport

Middletown sweeps up the hill above Newport like the Potala Palace in Llasa, Tibet. My uncle's greathouse, Ledges. Lume swung open the glass-and-iron front door as he had ever since I was a little boy. He greeted me warmly. We didn't touch, of course; he was wearing dove gray gloves. Then, as always, there was the huge marble eagle reigning over the great entrance hall, my lifelong reminder to get it together.

"A pleasant trip to Africa, Master Charles?" He used the word *Africa* as if it were the Hamptons.

"Africa." I shrugged and smiled, "What can I tell you, Lume?"

Lume smiled; he understood about Africa. When we were kids we figured that Lume had come to earth from the planet Krypton.

Dinner. Table talk of Aunt Pearl's costume ball, closing the summer homes, planning the distant Christmas and, of course, my Uncle Rut's syndicate in the next America's Cup races, still a long way off.

It was good to be here, to be back at the end of summer. Ledges seemed boundless: the table long, lined with cousins and friends. My Uncle Rut sat at the head of the table; Aunt Pearl, at the foot. "The other head," as she put it. She owned her own great house, too, a half mile down the road: Rondelay, with my favorite room in her own palace given over to Bonnard, Pissaro, Magritte, Delvaux.

Ledges and Rondelay. They were not real estate. They were beyond the grasp of realtors. Mansions like these were never sold. They were clung to by genera-tions. Then, they might burn or something.

Both my cousins, Nick Routledge and Sack Smith, worked at the same firm on the Street. I had yet to find my niche, of course. Still, the bond between us was very strong. We three had sailed together aboard *Yankee* in the last America's Cup elimination in 1995 off San Diego. We were eliminated by *America3*. Outsailed. Period. We died of our own technology, and some of it was Uncle Rut's. He even had a spy on Los Carlos Hill transmitting wind data via satellite to us. Everyone on the afterguard was watching TV monitors; the skipper, helmsman, tactician, navigator, even Rut, everyone but a lawyer. No one looked at the water anymore. Then *America3* lost in four races to New Zealand, and the Cup went to Auckland.

Aboard *Yankee,* Nick and Sack had sailed on deck, and I'd been sewerman. That is, I spent all the races looking after the sails in what's called the *sewer* under the foredeck.

Now Uncle Rut was organizing a new *Yankee Doodle* syndicate to build a pair of challengers that would sail under the New York Yacht Club burgee and bring the Cup back to Newport, where it belongs. Where it all started in 1851.

"Dreams are nothing, Old Jib. You can't just let 'em lie there or they won't happen." God, don't get him started.

This time, I wanted to get the hell out of the sewer and get on deck onto a sheet or a grinder. That was my dream, and I said as much.

Uncle Rut leaned toward me down the table. He really enjoyed talking to me like I was still sewerman.

"You have to do something about 'em. Dreams are abstractions, piles of unpainted lumber and undyed fabric, unfinished half-assed ideas, bad art, boring surrealism, vague incentives. You follow me?"

I nodded. I was still coming off my twenty-four-hour flight, in the isolation booth of my jet lag. "Other than that," I said, "how do you feel about dreams?"

I got my laugh. Down the table, Nick and Sack gave me supportive chuckles. Nick had once told me to go for it, that the job of black sheep of the clan was wide open. That I was a finalist. "Someone's gotta do it," I'd said, and I was the best qualified.

Rut let it go. "I'm afraid I don't have the time for dreaming, Old Jib, but I do have one or two goals."

He frowned directly at me. He had a bull's head minus the horns. He was out to nail me. "What about you?"

"Pass," I said.

"Okay," Uncle Rut said, "goals. We'll go around the table. Nick?"

"Get the Cup back."

Rut smiled. "Attaboy! Sack?"

"Ditto."

"Good goal. Sally?"

Sally mentioned telemarketing, ground floors, whatever. I didn't get any of it. I wanted to shake Rut, yell something at him, but I didn't know what. I said, "What are your goals, Uncle Rut?"

Everyone stopped chewing. He took it fairly.

"That's an easy one," he leaned way back. "My next goal is to open a Seven-

Penny plant in Western Canada. To create a new market for internet soft-ware. That's a goal, Old Jib. It's not a dream."

"So we can assume you don't dream?"

Everyone stopped chewing again. Nick and Sack were looking down, trying not to crack up. Sack was closest to me. "Go get 'em, Jib," he whispered.

"I mean right now. What is your greatest goal in life?" I said.

"I just told you. To break into western Canada with Seven-Penny soft-ware."

"That's it?"

I had definitely closed in on the job of black sheep, so I may as well play out my hand. I could say anything I wanted from that position. In the rich silence that followed, Aunt Pearl (God bless her eyes) said, "May I tell you my goal, Rut?"

"Go ahead, Pearl," he said wearily.

"My goal is to finish eating my roulade of lamb without throwing a bun at you. Now would you kindly leave poor Jib alone?"

Uncle Rut laughed. Everyone relaxed. We all smiled at each other.

Pearl turned to me, "How was the flight?"

"Long flight."

"Was Africa fun?" Claire said *Africa* as if it was a country. It was my turn. My trip. My botched safari. I was glazed.

"Do you have any pictures?"

There were pictures, not printed yet. I told them about my camera being stolen. Anyway, I said, the only pictures I took were of corpses, not giraffes. Suddenly I didn't want to get into it. Someone chuckled. They were eating, pouring beer. I noticed Aunt Pearl listening.

Nick asked if there had been any fishing. He meant bluewater sportfishing, of course. I don't think Nick realized that Rwanda is not near any ocean. So, I told him that there was this huge lake, Lake Kivu, with tons of fish, but that . . . and I hesitated for a second. "You wouldn't want to fish there."

"Why not?"

"You wouldn't."

"Why?"

"Well, you don't want to eat the fish, because they've been feeding off . . ." Now, I wondered if should I say *bodies* or *corpses*. We were at the dinner table, after all.

I chose *corpses*.

"Bad vibes," Sack said.

"Not the greatest idea," Rut said.

"To say nothing of unsanitary," added my cousin Claire.

I was glazing over. About to mention that even though the Rwandans were starving, they considered it immoral to eat these fish, because they would be eating their relatives. But I had to stop talking. I felt a rock blocking the top of my throat and if I didn't stop talking, I'd choke. When I could speak properly, I said that there had been massacres up until pretty recently, but I might as well have said *carnivals*. Anyway, isn't this the sort of thing you could expect to find in Africa?

During the pause Uncle Rut said, "What else is new, Jibby?" The window on Africa slammed shut.

I liked Rut. He was okay. He was what he was. He put his money where his mouth was. Laurence George Routledge, past Commodore of the New York Yacht Club, in 1958 he came within a whisker of defending the America's Cup against Australia, but was beaten out by a friend, Briggs Cunningham.

I think that for years, inch-by-inch, Rut's world had been falling away from him without his knowing it. It was as if constant business development were the only answer. He couldn't dream, I guess. But, to be honest, no one had ever really paid much attention to my opinions anyway.

Tomorrow I would definitely have to get out on the water. Sail *Di*, my six-meter, out of Newport Harbor and let the Atlantic Ocean clear my head. That might do the job.

Aunt Pearl

After-dinner coffee, brandy, and whiskey were served in the dark library. The *Libe* we called it, with its massive height, brass-railed balcony, the perfume of books, rows of first editions, folios, pages uncut, Dickens and Stevenson. The essence of aged stability. The four men played billiards in the eerie glow above the blood-red baize, their glasses of whiskey along the rail. I sat on a leather Chesterfield so highly-polished that I had to grip my heels into the carpet to keep from sliding to the floor.

The brandy was Remy Martin's Louis XIII; the whiskey was single malt Laphroaig. I chose the whiskey over the Cognac. It was a tough call, but it felt good to be back at Ledges making these decisions. Pearl sat beside me. The air hissed out of her cushion.

"*Pardonez moi*," she smiled. "Have you forgiven me?"

"For what?"

"Not responding properly to your tale at the dinner table."

"Your brother responded properly."

"Oh, he does that. He loves you, Jib."

She set her demi-tasse on the table and brought out an enameled necessaire and began doing her cigarette.

"He never forgives me anything. Can't he get past Yale?" My flunking out.

She had picked out an unfiltered cigarette, and was tapping it to death against the necessaire. She mounted it into a simple holder.

"Well, he's trying to be proud of you."

"What's standing in his way?"

She nodded to the table. "I thought you liked billiards. Odd man out?"

"Just didn't feel up to hearing balls collide." I struck a match, she took three puffs, then stubbed it out in the ashtray. Doctor's orders.

"How's Jocelyn?"

"Who?"

"Oh, dear."

I made a French shrug and puffed out my cheeks.

"She has other fish to fry."

"Or another chef to fry them?" she tinkled her scotch. She had a wicked smile. She saw I wasn't amused.

"Nah, when I caught up with her in Tanzania I seemed a bit too grim for her. I called her a snotty brat."

"Which she is, of course."

"And other things."

"I didn't mean to make fun. Sorry."

She made me her charity face, a truly warm expression. She meant it, of course. She was sorry.

Outside the realm of her apostles in Newport and New York, Pearl's visage might have been considered diabolic. Claire said she reminded her of Mrs. Danvers in *Rebecca*. She had the nose of a weather vane. Her eyes had not always been hooded, but now they were. Still, they were deepest blue, and glinted playfully. Her hair was fierce, steely, upswept waves of slate; her grand manner was Delphian, one expected oracles. In England, they would have relieved her of any confusion by knighting her, making her a baronetess or a dame, or something, and draping her with a wide ribbon. But here in Newport, she had to get by on a smaller circle as an aristocrat in a village of aristocrats. She was definitely an aristocrat of the first water, and though she resembled a snob, she was not one. But who was I to judge snobs? Being one myself.

"I'm not sure, Pearl, Jocelyn may be moving to Chicago. If she does, I'll take it as a sign."

"That would be terribly perceptive of you, Jib."

My mind had wandered away from the room. "Did you listen to what I said at dinner?"

"I had to. You were holding forth."

"And?"

"Well, let me see: you had a dreadful trip, your camera was stolen, you have horrible pictures, you missed the safari, and Jocelyn flew home alone in a snit. Do I pass?"

"No."

"Why are you angry at us?"

"Do I seem to be?"

"You seem to be."

"Dunno. I seem to have moved from my body into my brain."

"That sounds *molto dr-r-ramatico*. What's happened to you, Jib?"

She brought out another stubby cigarette, a Lucky Strike or something, and began beating it around. "Three puffs, don't you feel sorry for me?"

"I do, Pearl" I said, "but not for that reason."

"Oh dear, will we be *mysterioso*? There is a vacant charm to this pointlessness,

Jib, I must say. Africa's Africa and it's made you exquisitely boring, which is a step backward. You used to be amusing."

"Come on, Aunty, what's yer point?"

"You've come back a better person who speaks in metaphors? Well, it won't wash, buster. You're twenty-six years old, you're set and you ain't gonna change. What would you do without your sky-blue Corvette and your toy boat out there in your bathtub?" She nodded toward Newport Harbor.

"I wonder."

"Africa. Do you really have time in your busy schedule for all that?"

"We don't reckon time the same way."

"Where is this bloody Rwanda?"

She had chosen the right adjective.

"Rwanda? It's in the middle. It's not on the way to anywhere. It's a little bigger than Connecticut and much more beautiful. It really is like a green Switzerland if you don't look at what's on the ground."

"At what?"

"One mustn't look at the details. They could haunt you."

She withdrew another short cigarette.

"A single dream is all you need, Pearl. It's breakfast for your life, because it only takes one dream to last you a lifetime."

"Oh, dear. I don't believe that you said that."

"I can't either, but I did, and it's exactly what I meant."

"Someone over there fed you a slice of human race pizza."

"A hot slice with extra pepperoni."

"Enjoying your Cognac, dear?"

I was thinking strange sounding things and, oddly enough, I was enjoying it, and my belief in them was starting to catch up to them. I was close to something important, and I didn't know what it was.

"Let's have no more talking in riddles, Jib. I know you too well. Please wear some protection on your head against the sun next time."

"Have you ever seen a little kid with his hand chopped off? A hand so tiny it could have been a squirrel's? Cut off so clean that the bone wasn't even shattered?"

Aunt Pearl was involved in dozens of charities, big ones, obscure ones, and they all gave balls. She had a charitable soul. And tons of money.

"We all do our good works, you know that. Rut does some fabulous things. He gives thousands every year to Alzheimer's, Heart, Cancer. He's a good man."

"All bystanders are guilty, Pearl."

"Who says?"

"I says."

She sipped her coffee. She had a threatening way of carrying her nose, as if she might attack you with it.

"Try to come up next weekend for the ball. I'm closing Rondelay for the winter." It was that time of the year.

I slept badly that night.

Aunt Pearl would cling to Rondelay forever, just as Rut would cling to Ledges. They were worth clinging to, made of New England granite, well-hewn. The sun and rain struck their balustrades as if they were paying them compliments.

⚑

Manhattan

There were yellow leaves blowing the next morning when I drove down to New York, back to the amusing debris of my life. My poor boy/rich boy charade. My fourth floor Village walk-up. I fed my cat, who was waiting on the fire escape. I still don't know his name. What was next? The next morning Aunt Pearl woke me.

"Jib?"

"Yes."

"It's Pearl, darling. Meet me at le Cirque. One sharp."

Women of power. What can I tell you? I'd planned to see the Claude Darrieux movie at the Museum, which suddenly seemed like a huge waste of time.

"Sure. What's up, Pearl?"

"I'll tell you when I see you. I beg you, don't you dare be late."

I wasn't; she was. She always was. A diva.

"I can't sleep, Jib, thanks to you."

She made a face that could heal cancer.

"Tell me, Jib. Tell me the story."

"What story?"

"What you wouldn't tell me last Saturday."

"I don't know what it is. And, anyway, you won't listen."

"I will. Tell."

Aunt Pearl had a tiny black key in one eye, her left, that must have fascinated men in earlier times. She'd had several husbands, and whenever she talked about them it was with affection. But she had a way of making them sound like breeds of dogs. Retrievers, setters, shepherds she had once owned and loved.

"I was in the poorest, saddest country on the face of this earth, and you know something? It's a seriously beautiful country. As beautiful as any place I've ever seen."

The waiter took away her plate. She twined her fingers into the tablecloth.

"So many killed. Not the way we kill people."

"Is there a difference?"

"A subtle one. We never see the people we kill anymore. These people were killed by hand, one at a time, with their eyes open. You know, chopped up the way we chop kindling wood. You know. Butchered."

She added, "Intimately."

Yes, that was the phrase for it all right. *Intimately butchered.* I told her about the huge white moon and the little church with all the intimately butchered people inside. I told her about the morning after, when Leopold had gotten the Land Rover going, down the road about fifty miles, what I'd seen when I'd gone away from the road to take a whiz in the river.

"There was this river; the Kagera, I think it was, a small river. I was taking a whiz. It was early morning. I stared out at floating logs. It was very misty. I could not see halfway across it, but they weren't logs. I could barely understand what I was watching, what it was. It wasn't driftwood. It was bodies, polished bodies, nudging each other, slowly bumping the shore, moving slowly downstream, heading south, long welts, hack marks, bodies floating face down, face up, bodies getting slowed down on the grass along the shore, getting stuck on roots, the body of a baby caught midstream on a stick, slowly bobbing up and down in the current. A body was caught on the bank not far from me. I wanted to free him to send him on his journey, but it made no sense. What journey? It would have been only a game I was playing."

"Poor Jib."

"Yeah, poor Jib. Jib wanted to free them. All of them, do something with them, not just let them go away. But what? I would have helped them if I could, but I couldn't."

"Of course, you wanted to. What a dreadful memory. You've always had a good heart."

"Not really."

"Well," she hesitated, maybe knowing to say it would be wrong. "You've always had a kindness for all dogs."

"This is my fellow man we're talking about, Pearl." I had never thought anything like these thoughts. She could see it in me.

"You've always been an outsider, Jib."

"You always called me a dilettante."

"Well, of course, darling, because Nick and Sack settled down and trundled ahead. You listen to no one. You sail your own boat, dear.

"My *Di.*"

"Yes and you're a better sailor than the lot of them. Look at all those regattas you won. You have a better touch than Rut, though he'd never tell you so."

"Sailing, sailing over the bounding main."

"I think I know what you're feeling now, darling, believe me, and it's quite simply that no man is an island."

"The hell he ain't no island, Aunt Pearl. We live on one. Newport. We have our goals. No dreams allowed."

"And you were always the daydreamer gazing out the window."

"You want to know the difference? Goals and dreams?"

"Tell."

"A goal you can see the end of, because it's exactly what you want it to be. A dream. Now, that's different. A dream you can never see the end of, because it's obscured by clouds or something and anyway there really isn't any end to it and you don't even know how you got into a dream and you can't imagine what it means or how to get out."

"Oddly enough, that makes very good sense to me."

She put her hand on my arm. The grip in her fingers. Unbelievably, I was sort of crying, feeling sorry for myself.

The French adore that sort of crap, men crying in restaurants, our waiter said to another waiter, "*Voyez, l'homme avec le creve coeur.*" I understood, "See the broken-hearted man." I wanted to tell him that it was his cousins who had broken my heart. His cousins got the ball rolling in Rwanda and all spoke flawless French.

But I ordered dessert instead. Chocolate decadence for me; strawberry ladyfinger tart for Pearl. I had something more to say.

"Before I left, I saw children singing, every one of them an orphan. All of them black, of course, but it was quite beautiful I must say. There were a few women singing with them. I don't know what they were singing, but they were singing together. They had come back to their villages and found nothing and they were starved, but they were singing."

"Sounds marvelous."

"But there was something else. I don't know how to tell you this."

"Just do."

"Yes." This was the final test. "I'll try, but here we are at le Cirque waiting for our desserts with the sun streaming through the windows, so go ahead and laugh. It's just that something very weird happened before I left."

"Tell." She nodded warily, waiting.

"Okay, right before I left, I stood at the base of Mount Kegara (it's a small hill) and stared down at Lake Kivu. That's their lake, Lake Kivu. It's huge: thirty, I don't know, forty, fifty miles. You can't even see across it. I couldn't take my eyes off the surface. The sun was behind it, and it was glinting like a trillion oyster shells. I stood there hypnotized when, all of a sudden, I was watching a pair of white, twelve-meters, *pure white*, tacking upwind away from me. I swear to God. A match race, this great duel was going on between them, sailing close-hauled toward a windward mark I couldn't see; beating upwind, tacking crossing each other. Lord, it was blowing! What a duel, each trying to outpoint the other, pinching higher and higher, then falling off, gaining speed, nearly touching, hip-to-hip, so close they could read each other's lips, their hundred-foot masts grazing their spreaders, inches apart, changing leads again and again on the final tack to lay the windward mark. I don't know how long I stood there. I was numb. It was racing at its best: the perfect match race."

"Sounds glorious. Nothing more breathless than a close match race is there? What seems so strange about that?"

"You weren't listening."

"I was. That's such a marvelous memory, Jib. I adored it."

"Pearl, there are no yachts in Rwanda."

"Don't be impudent."

"Well, there aren't any. Everyone's dead there. Don't you get it? If they're not dead, they want to be. Or they're psychotic, or starving, or their family's dead. They don't know what a yacht is. They don't play tennis either, or even golf."

I was talking too loud. Our waiter was enjoying me. Tears. *Un scene.*

"Darling, I'm trying to see your point."

"I just can't shake it. I watch those fantasy yachts every night now; those incredible twelve-meters. That fantastic lake surrounded by mountains, always in a strong breeze. There they are racing, tacking against each other. They help me sleep. Then I dream about those two great ladies, close-hauled, hip-to-hip, fighting their way to the weather mark. They always miss the floating bodies, never hit crocodiles, and always sail between them with their masts crossing, switching leads again and again. One boat ahead; then the other. It's the most bizarre sight. I can't get rid of it. It's not a nightmare."

I wiped my eyes with my napkin.

"Why are you crying, Jibby?"

"I wish someone could tell me what the hell it means."

"Well that's not so complicated, you love match racing. So you take it with you everywhere. Isn't that true?"

"Yeah, I do, but what about the bodies floating in the water, so shiny they look lacquered. The hacked bodies and the boats cutting through them in that miserable place, those incredible beautiful white boats surrounded by that incredible hatred."

"What do you want to do about it?"

"Not a clue."

"Well, darling you've got a choice, either put two boats on Lake Kivu or see a doctor. I know a very good woman."

Last year Aunt Pearl had become a sudden and extremely unwilling widow and told me she had gone to a psychiatrist for the first time in her life.

"I don't think either would work, Pearl. But I'll keep thinking about it."

"Well, I'm a blank, but you've got me intrigued. Let me know what comes of it. Now what do you suppose became of my strawberry ladyfinger tart?"

Rondelay

I didn't see Aunt Pearl again until the following weekend. As expected, we all gathered in Middletown to celebrate the end of summer. This was Pearl's perennial gala night, and we were told to wear costumes.

As always, it was at Rondelay, Pearl's greathouse, the last party of the summer, her costume ball. She wore a black, beaded gown from the 1920s. I wore a huge, tortilla flopped over my head with two eye holes punched out. I went as a burrito, but Nick told me I looked more like a giant sperm. So, I went as that and won the prize, a bottle of Champagne, for the Best Really Stupid Costume; Aunt Pearl called it a portobello mushroom. Instead of hiring a dance band from Boston, because of her endowment, she was able to obtain the entire Narragansett High School marching band to play. She gave them Cole Porter sheet music and told them to give it a whirl, and we tried to dance to it. It worked. None of us was drunk enough, but neither were we sober. And no one had to drive anywhere. So, when the band got in their bus and went home at midnight, we kept opening bottles. We played charades, a staple at Pearl's parties, and believe it or not, it was fun, in a falling down sort of way. Pearl really has a knack for making any party work.

Then later, at the very end, when we were really tired, but still didn't want to quit, we gathered in the Libe and sat around the dying fire in the huge French Renaissance hearth. There was a September chill. We played "slim volumes." You know, we each had to think up the title of a book with only about one page in it.

"All right, slim volumes," Pearl announced. "Ready? Let's go around the fire. Claire?"

Claire said, "*Great English Cuisine*," which was okay.

"Nick?"

Nick was funny, always ready. He thought for a moment. "*The Directory of Humble Parisians.*"

He'd just come back from Paris. We all laughed.

Then, Sack said, "*Deep Thoughts of Movie Stars.*" That was okay, too, a little wordy.

Then, it was my turn. I just said, "*Russian Table Manners.*" I don't know why. It wasn't especially funny, but we laughed anyway, because of the way I said it with a Russian accent. It went on like that.

When it got to be Aunt Pearl's turn, she got the biggest laugh. She said, "*Eight Hundred Years of German Humor.*"

But Uncle Rut claimed he'd heard that one before.

Pearl said, "Well? And what is yours going to be?"

He was always needling her; he was her big brother.

We waited. Then, he said very quietly, "*Negroes I Have Enjoyed Talking With While Yachting.*"

He barked with laughter, and so did we. What Negroes? It stopped me cold. It was certainly original. But what was really funny about it? Was it that I had never seen anyone with more than a deep tan in regattas racing yachts? It caught me wrong. Not because it was an ethnic slur; that wasn't a problem around Middletown. Blacks dominated other sports, but yacht racing? Was it funny or was it absurd? Was that the joke? It was absurd enough to be funny.

I didn't know it then, but something clicked on within me that night while sitting on the deep leather Chesterfield in front of the old embers. I had heard another voice, but what had it said? I didn't know. I felt a chill. A body chill. It was like trembling, only I couldn't see it and no one else did. I slipped away and headed for my room and to bed. I needed to be alone, but I bumped into Pearl on my way to the stairs. She had noticed it.

"Why do you care, Jib?"

"I don't know, Pearl. I'm trying not to, anyway."

"What does it mean?"

"Not a clue."

I knew it meant something. That night I was haunted by the Negroes I'd seen who were not yachtsmen, the shiny bodies floating and the stacked Rwandans with their toothy mouths open as if they'd been laughing hysterically just in time to die, their bald bones rising out of their hulls, human skins abandoned by life who had not asked to live in Rwanda or die there. Whose deaths were caused by only being themselves. These were the Negroes who were not yachtsmen.

⚑

The Cup

Sunday. I awoke with a thrilling flush. Something had happened to me in the night. Asleep, my mind had dealt me good cards, a full house. I was amazed by it. A complete plan. Everything fit. I didn't see why it wouldn't work. I realize I'm lazy, but if you happen to be lazy, your mind certainly takes good care of you. A lazy man is full of ideas. I went looking for Pearl. She was the only Routledge who seemed remotely interested in what was eating at me. The only one who still prayed. She might laugh or she might not, but she'd listen carefully.

Various breakfast courses of sausages, eggs, kippers, bacon, and potatoes were being warmed in silver chafing dishes on the sideboard along one wall of the empty dining room. I was alone. The rest were sleeping in. I poured coffee. I knew Pearl would be in the chapel.

A chapel was attached to Rondelay, a simple Gothic plan built of Maine sandstone that could seat about two dozen. Cool aged incense. There she was, head bowed. A priest, young enough to display facial eruptions, stood in front of a plain gold cross reading aloud from a prayer book that rested on a lectern.

I sat in the pew beside her and found the Psalm he was reading in the soft, red leather prayer book. There were three of us. I was still high from the night before and the stained-glass rosette caught the low morning sunlight and dazzled me. A bold window that played sun like music. Pearl had commissioned it from Matisse three years before his death, and he told her it had been inspired by the thirteenth-century stained-glass window at Chartres. I slipped under. When I came out of my trance, the priest was closing his service with the Lord's Prayer. She whispered to me, "I wish he'd go back to the original wording, not everything should be improved."

He was new. After he cleaned up his altar and covered the gold cross, he came by and sat in our pew. She handed him an envelope and said, "Paul, I beg you not to use the rewritten Lord's Prayer. I really don't care how popular it is. Kindly, don't."

She said this politely, and Father Paul was not offended. "Of course, Mrs. Hood." He smiled and promised.

He stood, faced the altar, and curtsied, then turned and clacked down the stone tiles and out of the tiny chapel.

Pearl had hung on to her last husband's name, Hood, the husband she would still be married to if he hadn't died. It was a strange case. Harry Hood was a man I'd expect to have been killed climbing Anapurna or been burned at Le Mans or rolled on by his hunter, but he died of an infection incurred while buttering bread.

He had used a kitchen knife wet with blood from a raw chicken, and he cut a fingernail. Three days later, in Saudi Arabia, he woke up with septicemia; by afternoon, he was in septic shock, then in a coma, and then it was over. It was the defining tragedy in Pearl's life.

She mourned Harry Hood for a year, and every day of it she wore black. Her turning point. It was understood that she would never marry again, even though swains gripping polo mallets appeared from as far away as Argentina. Clean, silver-haired men who looked well on yachts, still played tennis decently, loathed bridge, made arugula salads with dandelions, and put single, perfect roses on breakfast trays. Vaguely military men, some titled, who knew wine and how to amuse guests at dinner.

After Harry's death it was over. Pearl knew it. She turned to charity work and did little else. Their marriage had definitely not reached its zenith.

We were alone in the chapel. We held our prayer books, the sun streaming through the Matisse window's colors made the chapel stone come to life.

"I feel close to Harry." She meant here in the chapel. She once told me that on his grave she cleared the weeds and hoped for flowers. "If that absurd thing hadn't happened to him we would still be together." There had been no third act. Then, she added, "I pray for you, too, Jib. You know that, don't you?"

"Why?"

"I always have. I want you to find your place in life. Like the others."

I took a breath, then let it out. "I think your prayers have been answered, Aunt Pearl. I might have found my place."

She gave me a Sunday morning smile, eyebrows high.

"I had my dream again last night," I said.

"Refresh me."

"The twelve-meter match race on Lake Kivu. I know what it means, Pearl."

"Tell."

"It means . . . Hang on."

I took another breath, a huge one, and let it out slowly. This was going to be hard.

"It means that Rwanda can challenge for the next America's Cup."

"Why on earth would they want to do a thing like that?"

"Because they can."

"But darling, isn't it just a bit unexpected? They have no history of yachting. And, anyway, aren't they all black people?"

"Yes, but they don't need to be."

"Black or yachtsmen?"

"They don't need to have a history of yachting to win. The other isn't optional. They need to be black."

"Need?"

"To make any sense out of this."

"You're being impudent again and very mysterious, Jib. I know who they are and where they are. They're in the center of Africa. What would be the point?"

"The point would be, Pearl: Do you have any idea how many bucks the America's Cup races generated in San Diego last time out? They expected a billion, but they settled for nine hundred million. I mean it's on a par with the Olympics or the World Cup."

"But why is it such a good idea for Rwanda?"

"Because whatever country that wins the Cup becomes the host country next time, which is not like the Olympics or the World Cup. It's a given. New Zealand won it last time, and that's why we're all going to race in New Zealand. They earned that right. Good rule. I truly believe Rwanda could make a decent challenge, Pearl."

"But it's landlocked. How could that tiny little country even compete?"

"With lots and lots of courage. It would mean unifying a horribly divided country for the sake of all. The poverty's horrible. But they've got a new government that's determined to turn things around. They have a perfect lake to learn sailing on, and there's the Ivory Coast for heavier weather sea trials. The French are very much their big brother, so we might be able to use their military resources. We can put out a call for able-bodied men, and then introduce them to the conception of yacht racing."

"Jibby, calm down, dear. I've never seen anything like this in you."

"Neither have I. It's quite a departure, isn't it?"

She smiled.

"Now, what about my darling brother? I mean he's starting up his syndicate again. He'd say you were coming out against your family. But you always have, haven't you, in your way? I don't think he'd be drawn to this sort of behavior."

"Especially from me."

"More like the Civil War this time. And anyway weren't you supposed to crew on *Yankee Doodle*?"

"I know, I know. I was supposed to marry Jocelyn Ortion, too."

"Aren't you?"

"For the time being, no."

"Well, this is a day of surprises, although I never once thought you'd be right for each other."

"Thanks."

"I'm supposed to be an investor in the syndicate."

"You've already agreed?"

"It's just assumed."

"But unmentioned?"

"Some things don't need to be mentioned."

"Well, don't."

"He's my brother, Jib. Though Rondelay versus Ledges might be fun, it would truly split our family down the middle."

"Rwanda racing hell-bent for the Cup, with its all-Negro crew against the *Yankee* and the New York Yacht Club."

"Yes, that's all very ironic, and you know I've always been waiting for you to make some sort of effort in any direction. And I did promise I'd support whatever you chose to do, but this is . . ."

She fell short of using the word *absurd,* which she pronounced *abzurd.*

"Exactly why would we want to do this?"

"One billion reasons. Because they need help. Our government hasn't done zip. This billion dollars would become the greatest charity contribution ever made by anyone. Just think, you'd be in effect giving one billion dollars to a completely depressed nation where the annual wage is something like a dollar-ten, where children really do die of sorrow, where the people have lost the will to live, where they come home to nothing. They don't know what lies ahead. They suppose it must be life, but they don't even care." I loved what I was saying, but I could hardly believe it was me saying it. "I can answer that, Aunt Pearl. Do you understand?"

"I wish it could come true, Jib, but you must be serious. You can hardly dress yourself. How do you plan to organize such a huge enterprise by yourself."

"Thanks, but I can find people who can."

"Rut will be furious. He could use a lesson in humility, but this is absurd."

"Coming from me?"

"From anyone, dear, but especially coming from you," she said. "But *that,* I'm afraid, is what makes it too delicious. Was this in any way inspired by his slim volume about Negroes yachting?"

"A direct descendent."

She smiled. She loved the idea. It had it all. As a great charity, it crossed all lines: family lines, color lines, snob lines, money lines, tradition lines, yachting lines, Newport lines, international lines, sporting club lines. A real game breaker. It was racy. She wanted it. And Rwanda needed it. It was the most colossal underdog. David standing up to Goliath was a slight mismatch; this was alley cat versus lion.

"I'm going to call Forrester and Lourde Monday, and let's see what they say."

Saint Pierre Forrester looked after Pearl's investments and charities. Her Hood Foundation made her one of the richest women in America. Unfathomably rich. Saint Pierre was the kind of man whom Pearl would naturally gravitate toward, one of the very few she would listen to. He'd been a diplomat, assistant secretary of state, undersecretary of the navy. Not some barking WASP, but a mondial liberal. Harry Hood had been Saint Pierre's law partner.

"This what you mean by one of your dreams I take it."

"Quite." I was delighted. "It's a goal-orientated dream."

"Making it real will take a bit of thought, I suspect."

"Like turning a cobweb into gold."

⚑

Saint Pierre Forrester

Everyone in the room was named Morris, Morgan, or Jonathan; it was the same name, really. Except Pearl and me. We were waiting for the head partner of the firm, Saint Pierre Forrester.

"Sorry I'm late." Saint Pierre Forrester entered brusquely. He bent and kissed Pearl's hand making the act look completely natural. An easygoing kindness hung about him. He would never say why he was late. He could have been detained by a president or a slow taxi. It seemed as if he'd been built of cornerstones. He looked at Pearl with great affection, sat down behind his desk, and faced us. The sun behind him, highlighted his slicked-down gray hair, be-knighting his shoulders like blades.

"Pearl, Pearl, Pearl. Now do I understand you want to start a syndicate for the America's Cup?" He sounded sympathetic. "It's my duty to warn you. No more yachting. No more fun. No more nice guy. It's business. It's rough, tough and dirty, just like any dirty, old corporation. I can't imagine why you, of all people, would want to get involved."

"You mean someone of my age and comfortable status risking financial loss?"

"Exactly."

"Well, maybe I do."

"Lunacy. Pure lunacy, of course."

"Aside from that," Pearl said. "Let's let my nephew Jib explain it to you."

I did. Surprisingly, I was not nervous. It took me ten minutes. I was not boring. The Jonathans and Morgans hung on every word. Saint had smiled at the idea when Pearl had mentioned it, but now he looked more serious. When I was through, he paused and opened a box and held a cutter against the tip of a cigar. I could smell the scent of cedar and tobacco from where I sat. He cut the head off the cigar. When the execution had been completed, he opened a box of long wooden matches.

"You're not going to smoke that wicked thing are you?" It was Pearl, of course, who could say anything she wanted.

"I was considering that, Mrs Hood."

"Without offering me one?"

"Forgive me." He never seemed to be caught off-balance. He struck a great wood match. He handed the cigar he had cut to Pearl and held the flame low.

"I'll just take three puffs and give it back to you."

She took it and puffed away with pleasure. We all waited for her to cough, but she didn't. And when she had taken her three puffs and handed it back to Saint Pierre, he drew his own smoke, exhaled it upward, looked at me and said, "Please call me Saint if you like, Charles. You know something? I don't believe I've ever seen a Negro crewing on a sailboat have I?"

"Only in the West Indies."

"But not in a yacht."

"No, probably not. These are fishing boats."

"But there's no rule against it."

"No, it's just that they don't seem to be drawn to yachting."

"Well, they've certainly been drawn to golf and tennis."

"To say nothing of football and basketball."

"Well, I must say, Charles, I admire your gumption. I think you're mad, but in the best possible way. There's something to this idea of yours that I like. It would be startling, I must say, to see an all-Negro crew whizzing across the finish line in a Twelve. Wouldn't it?"

"It would, sir." Me again.

"It might give your Uncle Rut a cardiac arrest."

Silence.

"This is the first I've heard of your interest in yachting, Pearl."

"Jib's the sailor, Saint."

"I can see where gambling enters this scheme. It's hardly a business venture."

"What would you say if twenty million dollars purchased one billion dollars in charity? Wouldn't you consider that a good investment?"

"Bit of a good thing. Oh, my. Yes, I certainly would." Then, without thinking, he added, "That's a very good rate, five thousand percent interest."

"I want to take that gamble."

"Pearl." He chuckled. "Seriously, Pearl."

"Seriously, Saint. What I'd be investing would be five percent of my worth."

"Six."

"Anyway, it's not a business venture; it's a bloody philanthropy."

I was watching the most fabulous conversation I'd ever seen. And it was going my way. Saint Pierre went silent, smoking.

"Then no need to warn you, Pearl."

"No need, Saint Pierre."

There was another huge silence. He did not approve.

"What capital to get this started? What's the entrance fee?"

My cue. "Performance bond. We need to post a two-hundred-and fifty-thousand dollar performance bond to the race committee. By March."

"I'll need to see your proposed budget, Charles."

"I'll need to make one, then."

"Plus your starting up moneys."

"I'll rough it in. We'll need to free up a couple of million," I said to both of them.

Big talk from a little boat. I explained that all boat money would be spent outside the challenger's country, that we'd try to buy up a pair of Twelves from the last America's Cup and build a compound in Rwanda and construct our boat-yard on Lake Kivu from the ground up from local materials and resources. Saint nodded. He tapped his cigar. He buzzed for teas and coffees. This was getting good, and I was getting light-bottomed.

Finally, Saint Pierre stood and thanked the others and told them the meeting was over and that the rest would be family business. This part of the meeting was to be confidential. Saint waited until our drinks had arrived before he told us a shocker. By coincidence, he'd just learned that the CIA had definite evidence to implicate the French with the genocide in Rwanda. The CIA had obtained recorded transmissions from trucks deep in Rwandan forests made in French by officers in the French army. The trucks were never located, because they were constantly changing position and we weren't interested at the time. They had instigated it.

"But why the French?"

"This was a planned madness, of course. They needed a stronghold in central Africa; they picked Rwanda. Officially, they needed a one-party system in place there. Training men they called the knifemen. If what they did resembles the final solution, it should. But it was far less graceful. The French are no longer what I'd call a clever people. They are standing on the hems of their gowns. They pretend to be worldly, but they act more like shut-ins. Anyway, they have two assets: a great amnesia and a great past. France is the Egypt of Europe."

"What are you saying, Saint?"

"I'm calling my friend at State, then I shall be able to answer you."

"What would be the point?"

"You would have carte blanche in Rwanda to do as you please and perhaps financial help to make your entry official."

"About what?"

"About the possibility of blackmailing the French government into helping us. Without them working behind us, this endeavor might sink like a navy anchor." He looked at the both of us. I felt involved in conspiracy. A challenge might be possible, he was saying. Rwanda was their protectorate after all. For the moment, he'd accepted my idea in principle even though there were no existing facilities in Rwanda, probably the poorest country in the world, certainly no expertise in match racing, no knowledge of sailing, no body of water except one huge lake full of bodies and crocodiles bordered by a country not a lot bigger than Connecticut.

"I think we could add some muscle by mentioning it to the world press."

"Then your plan is to blackmail the entire French Government?"

"Yes, well, only their foreign office. I hope you're not a francophile, Pearl, because this could change their opinion of you."

"I've lost interest in the French, Saint. I mean look at the Citroen, for God's sake. It looks like a Dust Buster."

"I've never considered them to be a bright people. I respect their cleverness, however."

Saint's idea of threatening the French by offering the press some CIA recordings of their officers ordering the Hutu knifemen to massacre Tutsis would expose their government to the world. It was bold, shrewd, outrageous. He said he might be able to pull it off. Aunt Pearl was impressed. It worked for me.

"Shall we go ahead, then?" Saint asked Aunt Pearl. It was time to know.

She looked at me. I nodded.

"By all means," she said.

"I'll fly to Washington tonight," he said. "I'll talk to my friend at State. If it is unequivocally true, they owe the Rwandans a colossal debt, and I believe I can get their government to help repair some of the damage they caused given the fact that Rwanda's their protectorate. And they'll provide help to you if we show them that we can reveal their instigation of one million killings there." He looked directly at me. "The problems you face are surmountable. But without some help from the French, this whole thing might be called off."

Aunt Pearl called me the next afternoon. She was excited. Saint had come back from Washington convinced that the French had a large part in the massacres, and he planned to go to Paris for a conference with Francois Loeb, their assistant secretary of state.

"I knew I hated them," she told me. "They're worse than the Nazis, because they're not as bright. He even let me listen to a tape of a broadcast made from a truck being secretly driven around Rwanda by a French colonel, telling Hutus where to locate hidden Tutsis and commanding them to massacre men, women, and children. It is unforgettable. It's blood curdling. He has quite a few tapes. It's all there. I promise you."

Saint had asked Pearl to go along with him to Paris to attend the meeting. She had accepted; she was delighted. They were, in their own way, American royalty: Saint, because of his ambassadorships; Pearl, because of her fortune. Without uttering a word, she had presence.

They were back from Paris in three days. Pearl was glowing. They hadn't even trusted the phone line they were talking to me on, so the news came as a surprise.

They had not only been able to meet with Francois Loeb, the foreign secretary to Africa, but after two meetings they also met Cluny, their secretary of state, who decided to help them in any way he could for this endeavor.

"Saint really squeezed their escargots," she said. "Rwanda was their little African goat, and after he played them a tape they realized how much they cared for Rwanda's well-being. Her betterment they called it."

"It wasn't a matter of blackmailing," Saint smiled. "It was a matter of morality, and I hope you don't mind, Charles, but I suggested to Loeb that he accept credit for your idea. Is that alright?"

"Whatever it takes," I said.

"They need it. They're saying that this endeavor will put poor little Rwanda back on its feet. She was their favorite hobby."

"Don't the French have their own entry?" I said. "What about the official French Cup challenge?"

"It might have dried up."

"Good," I said. I was thinking of available twelve-meter hulls put up for sale by other syndicates. I couldn't tell anyone outside the room what we were up to, especially my fiancée, Jocelyn Ortion. If she knew, she would tell her mother. Word would get around. For what I was about to do, I would be despised by my entire family and their circle of friends, instead of being merely abhorred. To this bunch it would mean putting me in lifetime Coventry, a silence that would extend from the social world to the business world. I would be branded un-American. To me it sounded okay, something like setting fire to a house full of junk that I didn't have the guts to throw away. The ball was definitely in my court.

Suddenly, everything had meaning. Everything seemed important. Everything was terrifying. Anything I did from now on would lead to the Rwandan Cup challenge; every breath I took. And it was my secret. If it was up to me, Uncle Rut wouldn't find out until he saw us sailing down on him. My cobweb dream was coming true. But dreaming had been a snap compared to this. As Pearl had said, now I had to turn the cobweb into gold strong enough for us all to dance on. Her prayers for me had been answered, and my nightmare was beginning to ride.

Saint Pierre had asked me for a list of my needs. It took a while, two days of imaginings. Aside from my own expenses, I needed seed money to get things started: hiring and building, things I had never done before. I needed two mid-sized practice boats to introduce sailing to the men who had never sailed.

I saw advertised in a magazine, *Sail*, that there were two sloops available in Sweden, K-boats. I know the class: like Herreschoff S-Boats, thirty-five-footers, about twenty years old. Cheap. If we bought them and got them on a ship right away, they could be in Tanzania in a month. Then, by rail to Kigali, the capital of Rwanda; then, from Kigali to Lake Kivu, where I had seen my vision. God knows how. I was figuring this thing out. I needed to get at least thirty men together to build our facility by the lake; men who'd become the boat crew. Saint suggested paying them with coupons instead of cash. Coupons that could be cashed at the Central Bank. Salaries, food, building supplies, tools, materials. There could be robbery. No graft with coupons. He could set that up for me, he said.

Aunt Pearl whispered to me that we were turning my cobwebs into gold.

Part Two

Goodbye, America

Goodbye, America

I was on my own, and that was okay. I couldn't do anything more in New York. I needed to get back to Rwanda. There were still twenty-two months until the starting-gun blasted at Hauraki Gulf off Auckland, New Zealand, when the great ladies sailing under a dozen flags would fight it out for the privilege of meeting the Cup defender, New Zealand. I needed to organize my boat crew and start developing the men; that much I could start to do alone. I still had time to find a skipper, a navigator, a technician, and a helmsman. I needed to lease land on Lake Kivu, maybe buy it. I needed to find a local builder and make plans for the compound, the dormitory, dock, and boathouse. I was excited and worried; I'd never felt that way before. I had responsibilities, a new kind of rush. I guess I was stimulated.

I would leave in three days.

On the way home to my apartment, I stopped by for groceries at an upscale Greenwich Village market called Mrs. Grundy's, where she had needed to double-price to keep the ordinary grocery shopper away.

Waiting at the checkout counter, I saw my groceries laid out in a row before me. Three brook trout, a paperback book by Cormac McCarthy, red wine, bagels, cigars, tequila, Italian sausages, two months' supply of cat food. I looked at the array. If I had been someone else buying these things, I'd have known we'd get along, whoever the hell I was. I looked at it, and for the first time in my life I actually felt lucky. I grinned. This display of wonders was my recent biography. Not anyone else's. And I was going to a place where not one of them could be found.

"I am so fucking lucky," I said aloud. Too loudly. About six people turned and glared at me. The kid at the register smiled. He made it clear that whatever I was up on was alright with him. The act of talking to yourself in the city is okay, but smiling a lot is controversial.

I lived with a nameless, gray-black tiger cat who came and went through a panel door out to the fire escape. I met him by chance. I think I would have gotten a dog. I can talk to a dog, but I travel too much and he would have died of dehydration. So, when this tiger cat wandered in thirsty from the fire escape one afternoon, I gave him a bowl of milk, leftover salmon roe, and the key to the apartment. He was fixed for life. I cut out a panel door in my window: his private entrance from the fire escape so he could come and go as he wanted, no questions asked. I usually left a month's supply of cat food with the woman who lives below me, a concert violinist, but this time I left her two cases. The cat seemed to enjoy her playing, and she enjoyed serenading him. So, everyone's content. Plus, I think this woman was the only human being (including me) he'd ever envied.

That night I met Jocelyn Ortion for dinner. I'd been seeing her since I'd gotten home. My fiancée, the debutante emeritus. I knew better than to share my breakthrough ideas on luxury with her. But sitting across from her at Destine, chatting blindly over the last scallops and creamed caviar I'd see in a while, I cracked, "Hey, Jocelyn, don't you feel lucky?" It was a dumb thing to say.

"Lucky? How so?" She kissed the rim of her wineglass lightly looking at me over it.

"Lucky for what you have?"

"Which is?"

"To refresh your memory, anything you want."

"Ji-ib." She said it reproachfully. A frown crossed her clear brow. There was this long pause that eventually filled the entire restaurant. Was I serious?

"You have everything, Jocelyn, except your ability to know it."

"Ji-ib," she said again; then, "God." She was about to ask me to take her home when I told her I was kidding. She said she really hoped I was.

Just because I suddenly felt like needing what I had, I couldn't expect Jocelyn to suddenly need what she had. Or to learn anything except that I had probably become a dangerous element and would be defecting to the Third World. Which I was. But we never discussed Rwanda. I never mentioned my going back there for a few months. It was like that with us.

After dinner, we walked over to my place. For all of her arrogance, snobbism, and self-absorption, Jocelyn had absolutely no self-esteem. I've never known a girl with low self-esteem who was not capable of multiple orgasms. I didn't know why that was, but Jocelyn was certainly included in my survey. We separated before midnight. I would miss her in Africa.

So, I was leaving America without telling her. A day later, I packed the essentials: half-a-gallon of tequila, four pounds of Italian sausage, two dozen bagels, twenty-five Antony & Cleopatra Classicos, three bottles of Hennessy Four-Star, and the Cormac McCarthy book. It might last the two months I planned to stay, if I was careful. I hadn't seen anything even remotely resembling this kind of booty in Rwanda. The only booze I'd seen there was a barley wine made of sorghum the odor of piss. It didn't taste so bad considering that there was crud floating in it that could have been solid sewage. They did have a commercial carbonated water from Burundi called Spit, that seemed okay to drink. The beer was called Simba, with a picture of a roaring lion on the label. It was even okay warm. So my evenings were set.

I left late at night. I called Jocelyn and left a message.

"Hello, Mrs. Ortion, it's Jib. Would you please tell Jocelyn that I suddenly decided to go back to Africa for a few weeks?"

"You must have loved it there." I felt a chill. Jocelyn must have told her I was becoming no longer possible. Weird.

"I'll be sure to tell her when she gets back from Fisher's Island," where they had a house.

And so, I was gone.

⚑

⚑ Rwanda

I stayed in a village near Kigali that first night at a one-story, cinder block hotel. I awoke eager and early. In the morning, it was cool, sunny. I'd heard that the elevation was about a mile above sea level. Down the road there was an open kitchen with coffee, and I took half a bagel with me and asked them to toast it.

Everyone was on foot. There were some on bicycles. What cars were there were mostly French and very old. But there were too many amputees moving along by the roadside, too: men, women, children.

I took a bus into Kigali and walked to the American Embassy, a flat-headed, two-story, stone building with a U.S. Marine guard posted by the door. I showed him my passport, and he let me into a waiting room with bullet-proof glass. I waited in the hallway to speak to the ambassador, Lyle Andrews, who sat at a desk in an airless room, an uncomfortably warm man in a thin, white cotton shirt, who fanned himself rapidly throughout my visit. I confided my plan to him, which was a mistake, even though I cut the speech to three minutes. He blinked at me constantly, sweat in his eyes, waiting for it to be over so that he could smile sympathetically. When he regained control of his face, he told me that he couldn't offer me any help.

Saint Pierre had warned me not to bother with the American Embassy, that the CIA was their chief employer, and that they weren't too aware of the Rwandans' well-being, only their politics. I asked Mr. Andrews about renting a car, and he said maybe a Land Rover was available. It had been abused by the UN and was being sold for scrap metal. Another from the UN used car lot. I bought it on the spot and hired a man named Moses Mazimpaka, who spoke pretty good English and looked like he'd been constructed out of bent coat hangers. I told Moses I wanted to see Lake Kivu and to look for a flat piece of land to build a boathouse and dormitory on. He said there were no gas stations on the way, and we needed to fill two jerry cans with petrol, then chain them with a padlock to the back of the Land Rover.

But if the ambassador was amused by me, maybe the church could set me straight and help me line up a crew. So, I asked Moses where the church was.

"Which one?" he said. "Rwanda have Protestants and Catholics."

"The closest one," I said.

ß

Bishop Jean Demaseine

At St. Paul's church, I was told by a missionary that the bishop would be at home resting. Moses drove the three of us a quarter mile. The houses were off by themselves, each walled by dry hedges.

The bishop lived in a house of clay mixed with straw, baked bricks around the base walls, covered by a tile and sheet metal roof. Pretty nice. It had survived, of course. The Roman Catholic Church had always stood behind the Hutus. I knocked on the door and an old woman, a servant, told the missionary in Kinyarwandan that he was down the road fixing a parishioner's car. The missionary translated this to me and off we went.

We stopped at what must have once been a Volkswagen. There were bullet holes in the door. I could see legs sticking out from under the car with boots, no socks, and a black robe. The man standing beside the car said that the bishop was trying to re-connect an exhaust pipe that had fallen off. A car was a rare luxury.

"*Voila*," said the missionary. I thanked him, and he walked away.

I heard French curses coming from beneath the Volkswagen. The curses were modest ones. Moses said the bishop was calling the car a she-goat without milk. I liked the bishop even before I met him. He asked the car's owner to pull him out by his legs, which he did.

The bishop stood. He was my height, but broader, the face of a hippo. He looked strong enough to turn a twelve-meter grinder all by himself. His robe was grey with road dust and covered his shoes. On a leather thong hung a plain cross made of lignum vitae. The car's owner knelt in front of him and kissed his ring.

"Thank you, your Excellency," he said.

We watched as the man got into his car, started the motor, and drove away. Then he turned to me.

"Bishop Jean Demaseine." We shook hands. He smelled of crankcase oil. He had a bass baritone voice.

49

"Charley Routledge," I said, glad that no one knew me as Jib. "Pleased to meet you, Bishop Demaseine."

"Charley. You are Canadian?"

"I am American."

"That is no better," he said in French, but he was smiling. He had made a joke. I spoke enough French to answer him.

"If you say so, Bishop Demaseine," I sort of smiled back.

"Bishop Jean, please. Believe me, I mean no harm," he was having fun at my expense. He had spaces in his mouth where teeth had once been. Instead of eyes, he seemed to have a bunch of red spots. So many in Rwanda had un-named afflictions. He had vertical scars, three on each cheek. It was a face that could easily be made famous.

"What has brought you to my country? What has brought you to see me?"

We drove back to his house, and he invited me in. Moses waited outside. The living room was separated from the kitchen not by a wall, but by an orna-mented woven screen. He asked the woman for tea. So, while we sat and had mint tea (I think it was), I told him what the America's Cup was and how I thought it might be possible for Rwanda to put together a challenge. The races were still nearly two years away, I said, but I needed to find men now to begin training them and that soon we would have two sailboats to teach them and that we had to practice with until the actual challenger itself.

"Why?" he said.

He said *why* beautifully, as if we were playing a game he hadn't yet learned. He must have thought that I was half-clowning, half-serious, or out of my mind, which was alright in Rwanda.

"Do you care to know what I think?" he said without waiting for me to answer. "I think it is a very funny idea."

"No, no, Bishop. It's a serious idea. It will help your people."

"Charley, I believe it is foolish to expect that sailing will help our economy."

"It's an idea," I said. I was losing him. "Haven't they lived without hope long enough?"

"Yes, but this. I think this empty cup is as high over our heads as the clouds in the sky."

I told him that the cup will be filled with what is in everyone's dreams. He laughed. He liked that.

"I will do what I can." What he gave off was a volume of humanity, as if his knobs had been turned up and left up.

"Where will you do your teaching?"

"I will try to begin on Lake Kivu. The men will have good food and vita-mins, and they will pour concrete and hammer nails and construct a building for the boats, as well as one for themselves. They will also do hundreds of exercises every day."

"Murumba," he said. "It is the largest village on Lake Kivu, Murumba. It is the best place."

I'd seen it. I would try to locate a strip of land there to build the boathouse and also dormitories for the crew and the rest of the team. I needed room for a dock. I'd seen the lake water. It was smooth without the ocean surge that could wreck a twelve-meter tied to a dock.

Even though he had never heard of the America's Cup before that day, I think Bishop Jean was trying to understand how winning it would help his people and that it was a project built on the slimmest of hopes. It was an illogical equation. Faith would come in handy.

"You promise me that it will be more useful than kicking a soccer ball in the roads," he said.

"God, yes," I said. "Excuse me. It will be much more useful, but I will need to make the men understand that they are to be in a sailboat on the water and that they will need not only strong legs, but very strong arms to pull at the sails."

"Good," he said. He considered kicking a soccer ball a great loss of time and valuable energy in a country where there was little left. "Will you invite anyone into your crew?"

"What do you mean?"

"Will you invite Tutsis?"

"Yes, of course, Bishop Jean. It is one country, Rwanda. It is one flag. It is one boat."

He raised his chin and shook his hippo head. He seemed insulted by my stupidity. After a while, he said, "These are blood enemies. How can you be so frivolous?"

"I'm hoping this endeavor will be more important to them than their hatred. I need your help."

He brought out a clean handkerchief and hacked, then spat into it and examined what he had spat.

"You will have grave trouble. Can't you understand that? Grave trouble."

I knew he meant death.

"It is Hutu against Tutsi. Always that."

"Why does it have to be?"

"Sometimes hatred comes naturally. A cat hates a dog. Hundreds of years ago, Tutsi people down came here from the north with their goats and their long-horned cattle, but we were already here. Of course, you see the difference in us right away: they have straight noses and are very very black. I am Hutu." He held his chin up for me to see. "We are pure Negro and many not so tall as they. We are less smart, I'm afraid. We have the big bums. The storage of fat in our buttocks." He laughed.

Was I learning too much?

"But I will help you, Charley. You will need more than I can give you." Bishop Jean dropped his gaze to the floor. "If you put them side by side and turn your back on them for a minute, they will kill each other." He said it without changing his expression. "The anger is the bloodline."

"Of course," I said. "That is where I beg your help, Bishop Jean. They must be made to understand that what we will do will be for the good of both sides and will bring untold happiness and riches to this country."

"How is that possible?" He seemed worn out.

"Tourists will come," I said.

He raised his eyebrows and looked at me. "Tourists?" As if he had never heard the word. "Tourists," he said it again. He liked the word.

"Tourists are new people," I said. "They will come to see your country."

He looked at me like I was a bug.

"People will not come to look at my country, even if they are tourists," he explained. "I can assure you of that."

I said, "Yes, they will. You think of yourselves as the black sheep of Africa."

"What are sheep? There are no sheep here. There are only goats, and maybe we are not even the black goats."

I said that the weather is always gorgeous in Rwanda, and the mountains are breathtaking.

"If you say they will come, what would tourists do here?"

"They will look at your country. They will tour." I found myself speaking sort of the way he spoke. "They will sail on your lake and climb your mountains. They will take photographs. They will buy small handmade objects. That is what tourists do. They are a strange people, but they are only curious; they come to look. Some will play golf. Some will take walks, but they will all bring money. They mean no harm. They do not stay long."

It was unimaginable to him. The only tourists he had ever seen entering Rwanda were the Tutsis returning to burnt homes, carrying a pot, and trying to find their husband or their child alive. He gave me the first of several "you-don't-understand" speeches he would be giving me during those first few days.

"You don't understand," he said politely, but firmly,

I told him the Cup challenge would be perfect. Everyone would see beautiful pictures of our white yacht sailing on your beautiful Lake Kivu with Mount Kegara in the background, practicing for the races against the world.

"But we cannot be expected to beat the Americans who are so powerful and all the other boats in the world. How can we?"

"It is one boat against another boat, twelve men. Not one country against another country. Just twelve men against twelve men."

"But surely, we must lose."

Of course, I'd thought of that. "Bishop Jean, even if we don't win, we win." I said it slowly.

"No," he said. "If we don't win, we lose."

"No. Win or lose, thousands of tourists will come from miles away to admire your beautiful country. If we win, a million will come. Houses and hotels will need to be built to hold them. Businessmen will start businesses. Stores. People from America will buy your crops of coffee and tea. They will advertise your country in magazines. They will say, "For something new? Think Rwanda!" Rwanda will be as famous as France. Money will grow in your pockets; food will cook on your stoves. Your church will be full."

I don't know where I was getting this from, but it was pouring out of me like a born again zealot. It seemed right, and I guess I believed it. "Anything can happen."

"But we cannot win," Bishop Jean said with finality. "It is simply not possible."

"It won't happen by itself and not with that attitude," I said. "Where's your faith, Bishop? I don't want to lose. But win or lose, our attempt will be seen by the entire world as noble and daring, and it will have many times the power that the challenges from rich countries with nuclear capabilities, such as Japan and Australia, will have."

"To say nothing of your country."

"Or your continent. Your country will be the only African country in history ever to compete."

"And it is the smallest," he said. "God loves the smallest dog."

"Then God will love your country even more than the others." I could sell men's clothing. "You will be the truest underdog." He liked that.

"Where should I begin?" I asked.

"Well, why don't you ask for the soccer players to step forward. Such a stupid game kicking a ball, but you will get the fittest men."

It was a brilliant idea. "I will do that," I told him. "The fittest men in the country."

"You will be sure to find two-legged men as well. Because one-legged men cannot play soccer. But be careful," he said. "There are many strong soccer players with only one arm, but there can be no one-armed sailors. It is a boat, after all, and sails must be pulled."

"I will try to find a place for everyone," I promised. "But I agree, sadly. On the boat we cannot have one-armed sailors."

Late that afternoon when I left him, he was smiling, but it was a sympathetic smile.

Bishop John Pennis

Moses drove me to the Protestant church. I found the bishop in the nave standing alone above an aluminum tub baptizing a very black child the size of a kitten who seemed to be asleep. It awoke briefly when the water struck its forehead, but slipped back in silence. It was very sad. After the baptism, in the vestry, I asked for a few minutes of the bishop's time.

"I watched the baptism," I said.

"Oh, yes," he said in a Scot's accent, "the wee one died." It was a fact.

A Protestant Bishop, a Scotsman, Church of England, not a tall man, strong-looking, a Greco-Roman wrestler, he later told me. He wasn't in great physical shape: there were red blemishes on his face, his hands trembled, and he walked with a long cane. His toupée must have just come in the mail. It was crisp, reddish, parted down the middle. I could see its little white label.

His name was Pennis. Normally, I would have said something like, "Pennis? Any problems with that name in school?" But I skipped over it and explained to him as quickly as I could the purpose of my visit.

He interrupted. "A sport, laddy?" He was angry. "These people don't want a sport. These people are deeply scarred. They are exhausted. Isn't sport a luxury of the rich? Here they beg in the streets. What about life? They pray for a day of corn."

I nodded while he was speaking.

"It is naive of you to come here from your America and expect that five hundred years of rivalry can suddenly cease because you bring to them a sail-boat race."

Said that way, it sounded even more absurd.

"May I speak?"

He nodded.

"Has the killing stopped?"

"Last week, mind you, I was driving to a parishioner's hut, a Tutsi. By the road, a Hutu waved at me. I slowed down, but I didn't stop. He lowered his spear and ran it clear through an old man who fell dead by the road. Then, he waved again in a friendly way. It was done in an instant and for my benefit."

He spoke about it easily, as if it had been a domestic fight. It meant nothing.

"The problem is so complex, laddy. It has nothing to do with your common sense."

Bishop Pennis cranked his head sideways with a boys-will-be-boys kind of smile.

"You want to shout at them, 'Look around you at what God has given you! A land where everything grows, a land of perpetual springtime. Rain forests, lakes, rivers. A small country, indeed the smallest in Africa, but an abundant one.' But no, they would rather go down their path of destruction. They have even forgotten why they hate each other, the blood is so old. Ask a child, 'Why do you hate?' He'll answer you, 'My father told me to hate.' That's all it is, believe me, the memory of hate. It is no deeper than that, but it is very, very old."

He told me what Bishop Jean had said, that the Hutu were here first. They came east from the Congo a thousand years ago. The Tutsi were Nile-otic, which means they came from the Nile and that they came south from Ethiopia some five hundred years ago and dominated the Hutu because they were smarter.

"Then we came here a hundred years ago," he said. The white people. He seemed racially impervious, a wise choice considering the neighborhood.

"Even though the Catholic Church was behind the first bout of 'ethnic cleansing,' as the massacres of twenty years ago were called. They no longer sanction it. Thank God."

I told him that this sport, this sailing race, had the power to bring them together. That the America's Cup was no longer really even a sport, but had taken on vast economic proportions. And if it came to Rwanda, the recovery could begin.

"Of course, everything takes time," he said, but he barely understood.

I told him I needed a team to run everything, and I needed a boat crew of a dozen men.

He told me what I had already seen: that Rwandan people were small and generally weak, that we could find men who were willing to do anything for food, but that we would need to nourish them and provide for their families as well.

"What if we advertised for a professional soccer team?"

"Brilliant game," Bishop Pennis said. "I know some grand footballers. How many do you need?"

"Thirty or thirty-five."

"Will you pay them?"

"Yes, of course."

"How much?"

"I'm not sure. Does four hundred francs a month seem reasonable?"

"Four hundred Rwandan francs."

"Yes."

He could see I was serious. One Rwandan franc was equal to thirty cents.

"Would you like my opinion, laddy?"

"Of course, your Excellency."

"Please, just call me Bishop."

"And, please, call me Charley."

"Well, Charley, I believe I'd start them off at two-hundred francs a month."
Seventy dollars.

"Did you speak with Bishop Demaseine about this?" he asked.

"Getting the soccer players was his idea."

"He has a good mind, but he does not like football." He smiled and shook his head. "He feels that football is an affliction of the soul. 'Anything to give them hope,' he once told me, and I believed him."

I could sense no jealousy. I heard later that John Pennis had been given the chance to return to England to live as a priest in his own parish house in Surrey, but that he'd stayed on here to help the people. He was consecrated bishop here. Some considered him a saint. I also heard that he was dying of monkey fever.

"I can help you make recruiting signs. I have paint and wood from crates. We shall need to submit all of your recruits to medical exams."

"Why?"

"The virus of AIDS is very strong here." He looked at me sadly. "Did you know that?"

⚑

The Crew

The next morning in Bishop Pennis' rectory, a one-story cinder-block building, under the luminous fiberglass roof, we made the signs that we were going to put up. We painted my signs in French and Kinyarwandan with exclamation points, here and there. They read:

ATTENTION SPORTSMEN!
MAKE MONEY!
RWANDA NEEDS <u>YOU</u>
FOOTBALL SOCCER PLAYERS
NO KIDDIES

We loaded them in my Land Rover and carried them on the road to Kigali and nailed them to buildings. And on trees along the roads. In a place of complete desolation, a call for sport seemed like black comedy, but I needed to start somewhere, and this was it: today, now.

That night I went to see Bishop Jean Demaseine and asked him if we could pick him up in the morning and drive him to Murumba with Bishop Pennis to see what the signs had brought to us.

In the morning, Moses drove the two bishops and me to a flatland I'd found by the Lake Kivu. The mist had not yet risen; the lake was huge and still. In the near distance, I could see the nostrils of a crocodile barely breaking the surface and leaving behind a pigtail of ripples, nothing more.

"They don't bother you," Moses said. "They like to eat other flesh but ours; maybe sometimes a baby, you know, but there's plenty for them, plenty fish."

"And bodies?"

"Not many more, I think," he said.

No one showed up. The bishops waited in the shade of a small shower tree. They would do the explaining.

Finally, nearly at midday, when the mist had risen and the sun was warm, one man came, a Tutsi. He had a missing-in-ceremony hand that had been

57

replaced with a wooden one. His name was Ba'ale. He had a small narrow face, a narrow nose, and was so black his eyes shone. He sat in the shade of an acacia tree not far from where the bishops sat.

Then another came, walking carefully. A Hutu. Mungo. He was not tall. He had a wide nose, and his skin was the color of fine Italian leather. He sat under another tree.

It was nearly one when the third one came.

Then others started coming, warily, walking barefoot. Some on bicycle. All in rags and expecting danger, maybe to be killed, but unable to resist the lure of our signs. A dozen men. They came one at a time. They were furtive, suspicious of a trap. They were barely comfortable and did not understand, but when they saw the bishops they settled down and sat patiently waiting. They were small and stood apart from each other, separated by bloodlines sometimes I couldn't see. There had been intermarrying, and now some of the Tutsi closely resembled the Hutu. Most stood apart, but there were a few tall midnight blue Tutsis with long thin noses who looked different than the stockier wider Hutus with their brown skin and flattened noses. Otherwise, I couldn't tell the difference between them. It was as silly as any other mindless religious hatred.

We waited together. The day grew hot. I was starving. By two, twenty-six men had gathered and now stood or sat in various stances in a vague circle a hundred feet around on the ground that was to be become our compound.

Three Tutsis were one-handed, and another was without an arm. Bishop Pennis told me that he knew them and that these were good men and would train with us and his cook would teach them to cook and guard and clean. Maybe at less pay because they were crippled. I said they should all be paid the same. It would be easier to calculate. One man; one salary. He nodded.

A particularly angry-looking Hutu arrived carrying a machete. The only one who came armed. Bishop Jean, his great hippo face smiling at the man, said to him, "I am Hutu. Let me keep this cutlass for you, my friend." The man hesitated, but Bishop Jean relieved him of his machete.

The Hutus stood with the Hutus; the Tutsis with the Tutsis. Some had been there four hours squatting, edgy, watching us with fear. When the bishops spoke, it was nearly evening. They drew the men closer together. It was uncomfortable not knowing what might happen. Bishop Pennis spoke first and told them that we would embark together on an endeavor that would stretch far into the future. Everyone would be paid, but there would be rules. And if these rules were broken, then that person would no longer be a part of the endeavor and would be sent home.

"We will begin here in Murumba." With his cane, Bishop Pennis marked the dirt on the lake shore. This is where we will build the house for you to sleep in and your dock for the boats. And this is where we will eat and cook. And this is where we will exercise. Each man will need to be strong. Each capable man will be paid two hundred Rwandan francs every month, and for that he will be expected to build a boathouse, a dormitory and a dock, as well as to exercise for one hour every morning and one hour every evening and pretty soon learn the art of sailing. He will live here five days a week," Bishop Jean said.

"You will be paid in coupons with your name on them that can be traded one day at a time at the Banque Central for not more than twenty francs in one day. It is understood that this money is for your family needs. You will eat here and sleep here. You will have no expenses here during the week. You will not be able to leave at night." He added, "For this rather generous sum you will be expected to obey these orders. You will behave well to one another, or you will leave without your coupons." He looked toward a group of Hutus. "There will be no more killing," he growled. Then he looked toward a group of Tutsis, "And there will be no revenge. Is that understood?"

No one spoke.

He struck his cane against the tree. "Is that understood?" He was growling.

Eventually, all the men nodded that it was understood. From that first day, the bishops were on hand each morning on in a show of solidarity; every day they would visit the camp. I obtained good, simple plans from a builder that Bishop Pennis knew. The men built their dormitory house in ten days, still segregated under supervision, occasionally a Hutu holding a nail for his enemy's hammer, one holding a plank for his blood enemy's saw.

The men worked hard, as men do, I guess, who appreciate the privilege. They were young and strong and had amazing stamina, but they were not yet strong enough for the winches they would be grinding and the lines they would be spinning around the big coffee grinders on the deck of the twelve-meter. They were taking doses of vitamins and eating better than they ever had. In one month I saw a change. They had all gained an average of six pounds and none of it was fat.

They built the long, one-room dormitory, and when thirty hammocks had all been hung, the men moved in. Out of these, I had to pick a crew of twelve and an alternate crew of twelve. There'd be injuries, sickness, defections. But for those who stayed and didn't break the rules, they'd have a secure future. The dozen men who were not training to be on the boat's crew learned to cook, and every evening they made stews. They were welcome. I kept a bottle of tiger sauce, a spice, but it was actually water mixed with a sedative called Rhopinal to make sure that the men got a good night's sleep and that there was no sleepwalking.

They were locked in during the night. There were two guards posted outside. Inside, it was never to be dark. There'd be a priest from Bishop Pennis' parish, or a nun from Bishop Jean's, and every evening after supper, one of the bishops came to talk with the men and listen to them. They were in so much pain. The memory of the massacres had not aged. Every one of the Tutsis had been devastated in some way and so had a few of the Hutus.

The bishops listened to every one of the men. They had nightmares, and their nightmares were similar. The more they talked, the more they learned that they were not alone and that the men who had killed their families were guided by forces even they did not understand. Within a few weeks, the bishops had some of the Hutus holding hands with the Tutsis. And enemies were sleeping peacefully side-by-side without the help of Rhophinal.

⚑

The K-Boats

We had finished building the dock and were building the boathouse when our two training boats arrived from Sweden. They came by ship docked in Tanzania and were loaded on flatbed railroad cars, then unloaded at the station in Kigali. The men were getting used to each other. So, after we'd towed the boats on trailers behind the Land Rover, we slowly dragged them off the road and down to Lake Kivu on wooden sleds. Hutu, Tutsi and mules all tugged together to the edge of the lake, where we launched them. The men were very excited. It was better than a christening. They had never seen such pretty boats, they kept saying.

We stepped the masts from the new dock, rigged the stays and booms. They were tiller boats, sloops, K-boats, twenty-years old, not bad, thirty-five feet long, two-ton keels, half the length of our eventual twelve-meter Cup challengers, but good enough to get the men starting to learn how to set sails and steer and accustom their bare feet to the angles of a deck.

We'd wait for the two Twelves. I still didn't know where they were coming from. The cutting edge, the technology, the digital meters to gauge the wind, the boat speed, wind angles, direction, velocity, the tiny cameras that monitor the wind streams on the sails. There'd be time to answer questions that no one yet knew to ask.

I lived not far away from the compound, maybe half-a-mile, in a two-room cement block house I rented from the Protestant church. It had been abandoned. The owners had disappeared. The family was not known to be either alive, or dead. I hoped that they had simply run away, but I felt that they would never come back. I could walk along the lake to our compound each morning and come home the same way. There was no need for the Land Rover.

But I was getting edgy. I wanted us to get out on the water and get our feet wet and see what we had.

The Killing

It had to happen.

"*Heywe! Heywe!*" Moses woke me. *Heywe* was one of the first Kinyarwandan words I had learned – *Come see! Come see!*

I stumbled through my house and stood outside blinking. It was just getting light.

"What is it?"

Moses already had started running back toward the compound ahead of me. I trotted after him shouting questions along the way. I couldn't understand him. He shook his head hard. It was something very bad. When we got to the new dock he stood facing the two sloops moored to it. They were simply called A and B. He pointed toward B.

"What?" I said.

"Go on the boat." He nodded to the B boat. I jumped across to it from the dock. It dipped slowly and rose. The hull was steady, a deep-keel thirty-five-footer. He pointed to the bow. I went forward. I opened the hatch to the sail locker and looked down into it. It was dark in there, but I could see it. There it was. I felt white as the sails. Curled up among the sails, a man lay surrounded by his blood. I couldn't tell who it was, but I knew by his blue jersey that he was one of us.

"Bujumbura," Moses said in a very quiet voice from the dock alongside. Bujumbura. One of our most promising crewmen. A Tutsi.

Judging by the amount of dried blood I now saw on the deck, I could tell he'd been killed somewhere else, then had been dragged onto the boat and for some reason been dumped onto the sails. They were made of Dacron, and his blood remained unabsorbed in dried lakes among their rumples.

Bujumbura had been hacked to death with a machete. Like all the others. I stood staring down. All I could see were those bodies piled in the church and floating down the river. Bloodlines bloodlines bloodlines was all I could think. Bishop Jean. The hatred will never be over. Even if they kill everyone they hate, and then they all kill themselves, the hatred will survive.

And then I saw that Bujumbura's death was due to me. It was my fault. If I hadn't come along from my granite tower and invented this crazy scheme, Bujumbura would still be alive and starving to death and living in despair along with his sister's family and the rest of the country. Anyhow, for six weeks I'd given him a future to live for that had meant a lot to him.

The challenge was over now. Officially, this morning. The killing had come to us, and our crew would never be able to get rid of it and sail together. The bishops had been right: I'd been frivolous, as Bishop Pennis said. It was over.

When Uncle Rut ever found out about this I'd take my lumps. I can hear him now. "Slim volumes: *Jib Routledge's Directory of Negro Yachtsmen.*" And he'd use his word, *fiasco.* And maybe he should. I wonder if he'd still offer me my berth on his challenger.

"Moses, call the police." My voice was shaky.

Call? On what?

Then I said, "Moses, run. Fetch the police. Get the Land Rover. Be quick, I will wait right here. Don't be long."

Naturally, because Bujumbura was a Tutsi, and the policeman who eventually showed up was a Tutsi, and a mean Tutsi gendarme, he only interviewed the Hutus. I was lucky enough to witness the interrogations.

"Josue Valence. Did you kill this man?"

"I did not! Why would you think I did kill him?"

"You are a Hutu, after all, and he is a Tutsi."

"Yes, that is true, but he is my sailing partner."

"Ha-ha-ha!" The tall Tutsi gendarme laughed, "Get out of my sight, Valence. Go."

"You are a fool," Valence told the gendarme before he walked away.

With this sort of candor, I knew we'd never get the killer. No one was going to step forward. The victim was Tutsi; the killer was Hutu. You could wait around all year, but no Hutu was going to step forward. And it was probably a Hutu member of our crew who had done it.

It was tense in the hours after the discovery of Bujumbura's body. The men were on guard. There was no talk, not even between friends. They did their cleaning chores in silence and waited for night and the revenge killing. The sloops stood waiting at the dock, rising and falling on the slight surge. The challenge was over, and we had never once taken them out.

In the hours following the discovery of Bujumbura's body I set my sights on getting drunk that night, an easy target, not a noble one. But before that happened, I wanted to call Aunt Pearl.

It was five in the afternoon when I drove up to the American embassy, a two-story French colonial building. High ceilings. They let me use the phone in what they called their quiet room, no listening devices. They told me to put my credit card away. We all knew the embassy was no more than a CIA station, so I guessed it was the CIA's party. I reached Pearl at her town house in Manhattan. I woke her.

"Jibby, what time is it?"

"I don't know, late afternoon. I guess."

"Well, it's dawn here. Where are you?"

"Rwanda. To refresh your memory."

"Don't be impudent. What time did you say it was?"

"Evening. Now that we've established the time of day."

"Tell me why you don't sound happy."

"It's over, Aunt Pearl." I went on to tell her what had happened. That this was the first killing, that there would be others.

"Are you in danger, Jib?"

"No. Only the Hutus are in danger now."

I told her that the Tutsis would need to retaliate, and then the Hutus would need to retaliate, and everybody knew it. So it was only the beginning of a process. And all night long they would be planning the next killing. Waiting. I asked her to tell Saint I saw no way out and that I'd be coming home soon. "It was always a fiasco," I said.

"How dare you call it that." I could see her mouth shape the *dare*.

"What would you call it?"

"A brave idea. It was a good investment."

"That could never work. Look, Pearl, we were trying to shove a Third World country into the First World."

"You utter snob. After all I've gone through," she had a wonderful anger. "We're the country who behaved like a Third World country when they needed us. Not them. That is the most pompous thing I have ever heard in my life. How dare you make such a pronouncement?"

"Okay okay, Pearl, go back to sleep, I just called to tell you it's over. Don't make it harder on me than it already is. I'm very depressed"

"Really over?"

"Really. These bloodline things never heal, and the hatred is so old it's genetic and no longer a matter of control. So, please tell Saint he'll need to pull your money out of Le Banque Central after this month's pay day. I'll donate the two K-boats to the Coast Guard."

"But Rwanda's doesn't have a coast."

"I guess that's why they don't have any Coast Guard boats."

No one laughed.

"There's something else, Jib. You've got to call your Uncle Rut. I hate to tell you, but he knows."

"How did he find out?"

"You know Rut. It might have been a leak in Saint's office, or Jocelyn's mama. I swear, that woman. Gossip is pocket money to her. Anyway, he knows."

"Must I call him? Why bother? He'll only laugh at me."

"He's not laughing, Jib. He compared you to Benedict Arnold. He mentioned your trust."

That would be my inheritance. Before he died, my father named Uncle Rut as executor of his will.

"He just feels betrayed and bewildered by my pathetic challenge against his attempt to bring the Cup back to Newport Harbor so you all could watch the races from your balcony."

"He's livid."

"It's over."

"I think he's willing to welcome you back to the boat. Call the office and Marie will patch you through."

We said goodbye and, in less than a minute, I could hear Uncle Rut's voice barking into the phone.

"Hey, Champ!"

Champ was what he called me at odd times whenever I screwed up.

"Hey, Uncle Rut." I called him Uncle out of deference.

"Where are you, Champ?" His voice was rising sharp and clear through the phone.

"Rwanda."

"Tell me it's not true."

"It's very true." I couldn't admit to him it was over.

He began to say something about his goddamned goals. I being the dreamer, of course. But I couldn't hear most of it. His words were lost in a rush of hissing.

"Can't hear you, Rut. What's that horrible noise?"

"Flames," he shouted.

Flames. I needed to think for a moment. I took a wild guess.

"You're in a balloon."

"Of course, I'm in a balloon." Uncle Rut was a sportsman. "Did you think I was calling from a burning house?"

"Why are you in your balloon?"

"We're setting a record, I hope."

"So where are you?"

"Africa."

"Oh, like me. What country?"

"Buttfuck, for all I know. Do we need to know what country I'm drifting over to discuss your betrayal?"

Betrayal. There it was.

Before I could answer, he said, "Do I believe this crapola about your own syndicate with Saint Pierre and Pearl."

I told him he should believe the crapola.

"Is that why you turned the family against itself and wasted my money on a hair-brained scheme?"

"Pearl's money," I said.

"My money. Her money was headed straight into the *Yankee Doodle* pot." That was the name of his challenger.

"My men deserve a shot, Uncle Rut."

"From that little outhouse of a country? This is the America's Cup. Tell me I'm wrong. "

"You are wrong, Rut. It's a beautiful country, a hell of a lot more beautiful than Rhode Island."

"I don't care if it's Bali. They do not deserve a shot. They do not belong in the race. They have no tradition of yachting. They don't even have a coastline. Where did you plan to hold the races should Rwanda have won and been the host country?"

"I haven't decided. Maybe Lake Tanganyika, although Lake Kivu might be better."

"If this is one of your dreams, it is the worst one I have ever heard, bar none."

"It is definitely a dream." Our voices were fading.

"How did you ever come up with it?"

"Remember the night last fall when we played Slim Volumes?"

"What?" He hadn't heard me.

"Have you ever missed two meals in a row?" I said. "One?"

"What?"

Maybe he had heard me. I could imagine him skimming along the desert, a quarter-mile up, setting a record.

"We're a family of individuals, Jib, bound together by simple tradition and mutual goals. And our goal is to beat the ass off the New Zealand boat in two years. You're trying to contaminate the historic tradition of the sport."

I didn't have the guts to tell him I was no longer trying to contaminate it.

"If Rwanda wins, it would mean a *billion* dollars to them. Just think."

"You can still crew on *Yankee Doodle*. Not too late. I forgive you. Holding a spot for you on the foredeck as bowman."

It was the berth that I'd always dreamed of: bowman on an Cup challenger.

"I can't Uncle Rut. Rwanda needs the Cup more than America." The first time I'd ever spoken those words aloud. It was simple treason.

His answer was lost in a whoosh of gaseous air being set to flame. I hung up. Now my job was to get drunk.

It wasn't until two days later when the balloon was forced to land in India that we spoke again. Things had changed for the better at my end. I could laugh at the Benedict Arnold business.

One thing I never feared was the unknown. In fact, I looked forward to it; I trusted it. It was the known that I was suspicious of. It bored the hell out of me. Knowing what was coming. Doing what was expected of me. I felt very comfortable not knowing what was next. Give me a wide empty field anytime. As a kid, by not caring what came next, I dismissed my family's expectations of me.

That night I chose a village bar I'd driven past a few times on the road to Kigali, a suave establishment with a couple of tables in the dirt out back. The Top Hat.

I had hoped for the best. The men who followed me into this scheme were good men. They had a childlike trust in me and somehow their trust hadn't been fulfilled. And tomorrow morning I would have to tell them it was over and send them home.

I was doing pretty well, drinking local banana wine that smelled like cologne and chasing it with Simba Biere. I sat there holding my plastic cup in one hand and my bottle in the other. This would be an easy project.

Another American was standing inside at the bar. Jacket and a tie. I'd seen him around. He seemed to be in Rwanda without purpose. Anyhow, I watched him slowly get into a fight with a Frenchmen. So, I stood up and went in and hit somebody, then so did he and everyone sat down again. I didn't want to know who this American was, but now I would have to, forced into it by my patriotism, my flag over the reality that my countryman was a jerk.

His name was Carter. He was in Rwanda promoting, of all things, a religion. It had a fresh new name, Church of Hope, that I didn't recognize. He called himself an entrepreneur, and I'm sure he was. But he was just a guest as far as I could see. He clung to me; I was buying. We'd forged a bond. He actually told me that he believed God had sent me to look after him. It was very dark out that night. I do remember Moses driving me home to my cement house and Carter, the entrepreneur, ending up asleep on the floor. God had sent him that, too. I hardly remember Moses saying that he was going to lock us in for our own protection and that he'd sleep in the hammock that hung under the ramada outside. I remember listening to the rain attacking the tin roof. My last thought just before I passed out was that patriotism would eventually wipe out the human race.

The Announcement

Very early the next morning, I got up and knocked on the door to my house. Moses unlocked it and let me out so I could take a piss. On the way back in, I kicked Carter in the ribs. He screamed. He'd been sleeping on the floor and was now wide awake. I'd forgotten all about him. I told him to get out, that I had a rough morning ahead of me. I never knew how many francs he had slipped out of my wallet. It was empty.

Moses brought me coffee and a mango. He fried me a fish, but wouldn't tell me where it had come from, so I didn't eat it. The smell gave me a queasy feeling that was probably the smell of failure. No more Cup challenge. I dreaded what I had to tell the men this morning. They'd understand it, of course, but it would send them back to where they came from, which was hunger and misery, followed by death.

I told Moses to take the Land Rover and pick up Bishop Jean and Bishop Pennis. I needed them to come down to the compound. I had something important to tell the men.

I put off the walk to the compound as long as I could, until nine, stalling over my coffee and mango. The men had turned to me for sustenance. They'd expected it to last forever, but forever in Rwanda is temporary.

Then, at nine I trudged (that's the only word for it) I trudged along the sandy shore to the compound, toward the two masts with a sense of doom.

When I got there, it had changed. The men had separated. They'd cooked their corn meal and eaten fruit and put their breakfast fires out and were being led in exercises by Ba'ale, one of the Tutsis who had one hand. When he saw me coming, he picked up the pace.

"UN-DOO-DWA, UN-DOO-DWA, UN-DOO-DWA," Ba'ale shouted out to them as they stretched their limbs toward the sky, then toward the earth, then back up toward the sky. It made me sadder to see them exercising. It seemed pretty hopeless to get in shape for a project that was never going to be, but I watched them and let them go on. They'd be paid through the month. I sat by the coals and poured coffee into an enameled metal cup. The Rwandan coffee was amazing, as good as any French or Italian I had ever drunk, and now the world would never know about it. The race would have changed everything. It would have gotten their coffee exported.

I watched the men exercising. The differences between the Newport Yacht Club and our yacht club were the strict by-laws. In Newport, necktie for dinner, no smoking in the club house; in ours, one murder and you're out.

I watched the men, all of them wiry. They were so willing. When the boats had first been launched and the masts had been stepped, I had forgotten all about reeving the halyards, and there was no boatswain's chair to haul a man up. So, I told the men we'd need to unstep the masts. When one of the men who'd been watching me figured out what I wanted, he took the line in his teeth, then walked right up the mast and reeved it through the masthead block.

I liked these men. Different from anyone else. I cannot always tell Tutsi from Hutu, but that morning was easy, because they had segregated themselves. I never had a clue as to what they were talking about, but I know they liked me. The money had helped. Now they had corn and flour for their families. They had tea, as well as sugar to put in it. It had been a good period. They were buying goats and thinking about buying cows.

They didn't know what I was made out of at first. They could only take me at face value, and I didn't have a good first impression. I looked about sixteen with all that unregulated hair. It was the way I stood, too. I was always sort of leaning on an imaginary post, like I didn't care, even when I did. I *looked* rich. No matter what clothes I wore, I *looked* rich, leaning on things. I smiled more than I should have. I seemed to be untroubled, because I usually was untroubled. Except that morning.

The bishops arrived with Moses. I called a stop. They had no idea what was coming. Somehow, Carter had gotten a ride with them. America's guest. What did he want?

The exercise hour was over. Some of the men straggled down into the lake to cool down. Others sat and stared at us. I told the bishops what I needed to do.

Then, an amazing sight.

Josue Valence, the one who'd called the Tutsi gendarme a fool, walked into the compound dragging a rope with a body or something large tied on the end. It was a badly bruised herdsman being dragged through the dust, feet first. Josue put one foot on him and spat. The man was in no condition to spit back. I immediately recognized the herdsman as Hutu.

"Moses, go back. Get Officer Abdai, quick."

When the tall Tutsi gendarme arrived, Valence said to him, "Here is the killer of Bujumbura. Ask him did he do it. He is a Hutu as I am a Hutu. I told you once that Bujumbura was my sailing partner, and you laughed at me.

Now, I tell you again, you are a fool." He tossed the rope-end directly in the gendarme's face, knocking his hat to the ground. "Now laugh at me, fool." He walked away.

When Officer Abdai had taken the Hutu herdsman away, Bishop Jean stood with his arm around Josue Valence, talking quietly to him. Then, he said to me, "What are you going to call our challenger, Charles?"

"You mean the Cup challenger boat that we don't have yet?"

"Yes, yes, yes."

"It has no name."

"May I have the honor?"

"Of course you can, Bishop Jean. Give it a shot. You have real optimism. I like to see that in a bishop."

He laughed widely. "We call people of our race our kinsmen, blood relatives, but you see now everyone here is our kinsman. You must call our boat *Kinsman*."

We didn't have a boat, but we had a name for it.

It was on again. What Josue Valence had done was so strong that the effect spread. I could sense that it was going to work. The bishops both agreed. There would be no announcement.

⚑

Training

There were nights before I fell asleep when I lay looking up at the shaky shadows on the ceiling that I would imagine the ceiling of my Greenwich Village apartment, my fourth-floor walk-up: the wide plank floors, the summer heat, the open windows with the tops painted shut, my nameless cat on the fire escape, the common street sounds, the violin being played on the floor below, the sidewalk shouts, the house quarrels, either love or anger. My retreat from the inconvenient world.

I would try to imagine what it must have been like there now in the Village: the dawn vegetable stalls, the sweet-smelling pickle factory on the next block, the Village where it would have been morning, down the block for coffee, maybe breakfast. Then, suddenly I would be back in my cinder-block house, a light rain falling on the roof. I would marvel how it all began, and how I had gotten there. Then, I'd know what I was doing there.

I am a college dropout in a family of honor business graduates. While I was in school, my parents prayed for me to be average. I was always told that I was incompetent. Worse. That I would amount to zero. That never bothered me. Making no appearance was better than a half-assed one. Zero was okay.

But all that had happened to me that fall and was happening now in Rwanda made me begin to wonder who I really was: that the measurements they took of me in school and the measurements they took of me at my first job were the wrong measurements and so maybe what they called "success" was not what I called "success." I've always been a simple man, and there I was in Rwanda leading simple men. And for the first time in my life, it felt right. I felt right.

The morning after Josue Valence's great act, I woke up edgy. It was time to get on the water. I told the men we would be going out that afternoon. First, they would watch me sail back and forth, and then in crews of four, everyone would get a chance to go out and get the feel of the boat close-hauled under sail. While Bujumbura's blood was being scrubbed off the deck of K-boat B, we began to bend the sails on the spars of K-boat A.

Sailing is easy; racing is pretty mindless stuff. You make your boat go faster through the water than the other boat; you get ahead and stay ahead. It's an instinct. It's an emotion. It requires very little research. A match race is a duel; your hull is your saber. It was something I knew how to do. I was a born sailor, born with a tiller in my right hand. All of us Routledges were. Nick and Sack and Claire all sailed boats long before they could drive a car. Everything I knew about driving came from sailing. I'd always been the best sailor in the family. Even Uncle Rut knew that.

The breeze freshened-up about two, and I took the A boat out and, on a reach, made pass after pass, skimming the dock where the men stood. Moses was on board with me as lookout, spotting crocodiles so I wouldn't ram one. They were too heavy, he said. He translated to the men on the dock:

"Watch his hands. Now, watch. He trims sail. See where wind is. Watch how he turn boat up to wind. Watch now. He tack away from the wind. See how tight he keeps boat sails."

Up close, the boat charged by them, lee rail down. They could see the speed I was generating by sail trim: the sails taut as blades, the spoon bow clicking along through the chop.

Every man got out on the water that afternoon. Even the dismembered men. Each man got his hand on the wheel. They took to it gratefully. This was so much better than anything they'd been doing. There was a lot of laughter, especially when one of them fell overboard, and I had to jibe around and pick him up. They seemed to enjoy falling overboard. Then the men started falling overboard two at a time, and it became a nuisance. Moses reassured me that the crocodiles were not interested in them, and apparently they weren't. But just to be safe, I wasn't about to offer my own alabaster New England body to them. That week I'd be ready to choose a helmsman to break in, to follow me in the practice races.

It was a fantastic first day, the best day we'd had as a team. We laughed all afternoon. The men loved it. I saw no jealousy. That evening I drove up to the embassy and called Aunt Pearl to tell her the good news. I woke her again. She was still depressed.

"Don't be," I said. And when I told her the story of the small miracle and that the challenge was back on, she was as elated as she'd been before. She laughed heartily when I told her about the men jumping off the boat into crocodile-infested waters. I asked her if she had spoken to Saint. No, she said, they'd both left messages for each other. He had left one for her saying that the Italian syndicate had folded and that their famous red boat, *Il Moro*, known as the fastest challenger ever, was being put up for sale along with her stable mate and that we had officially put in a bid for them.

But what had happened that day had happened by itself. I couldn't possibly have done it. Something mystical had gone on, something to do with God.

And nothing to do with religion. It's not that something had been broken and repaired. It was as if Bujumbura's death, and what Josue Valence did, had been necessary. As if Bujumbura had needed to die to show us that we could be made well between the bloodlines.

Sometimes you can see it on a very old wall that had once been badly cracked and repaired. You can see where the weather has worn away the bricks, rounding them in, and where the mortar binding them has been stronger than the bricks. And it is the mortar that sticks out, because it has not been worn down at all. That was how it seemed to be with us. The crack was made stronger than our wall. Our mortar was stronger than our bricks. The men had been given something better than hatred.

Was I making something out of nothing? It was the best feeling I'd ever had. Sack Smith may spend his life trading bonds at Dunlop Dalton and never for one moment have what I had then, what I was feeling. I felt I'd learned something there over those first four months. I'd learned to say "yes" and then do something about it.

I was in charge. I knew more than anyone. They had heard of nothing; what I told them was new. Everything I said was true. Thirty men looked to me for their well-being and their survival. They were eager three-year-olds who had lived their lives permanently on the fringe of death.

We all lived in perpetual springtime there in that beautiful dead country, lying smack dab across the Great Rift Valley where the human element had been the sickness and where all its natural beauty, the rain forests and volcanoes had been the cure. Rwanda was many things much the way New York City was. My native Manhattan was ugly, filthy and beautiful, snobbish, exciting, unworldly, cultural, obscene, brilliant, shallow, radiant, ill-tempered. Rude. And always, deadly. But no matter how deadly, its Republicans did not hack its Democrats to death with machetes.

I talked to Saint Pierre every couple of days and kept him current, then listened to what progress he'd been making. I told him I'd heard that Larry Bayard had moved back to the Republic of Ivory Coast. He had skippered Soling Class in the 1995 Olympics and won a gold medal. He also sailed in the afterguard for *France 3*, as tactician in the last America's Cup. He was originally from the Ivory Coast, but had been raised in Guadeloupe. He had found a place in Abidjan. If we could get him involved this early, we'd have a helmsman. He needed a year's residency. From his photographs, you'd think he was Hutu.

I talked to Aunt Pearl more than I talked to Saint,

I liked calling her. I called and told her the progress of our challenge. She was fascinated with every aspect. It was always morning in New York, and I always woke her.

"How are you, Jib?" She was never surprised.

I felt good I told her.

"Well, dear, that's because you're finally accomplishing something."

"I'm twenty-six. What am I supposed to have accomplished? Uncle Rut flies balloons and sails twelve-meters. He runs in marathons. Everyone else sells bonds."

"Well, that's something."

"Yes, it is. But what?"

"His *Yankee Doodle* syndicate could win back the America's Cup."

"It's a sailboat race, Pearl."

"Yes, it is."

"Of course, it is!"

"Well, I don't know what it is to just win a sailboat race anymore. Or a long distance run, or to jump higher or swim faster than someone else. I don't know what that is anymore. You win and you say what? I jumped higher than you did? What we're doing, here and now, might matter. I hope it does."

"What's wrong, Jibby?"

"Oh, the usual." I told her that Hutu rebels killed nine nuns in Rwetere, and in Burundi next door, one hundred and fifty civilians were dead.

"Tsk, tsk," I could hear her.

"I don't need to be Kierkegaard to see that we live in a world of good and evil, Pearl, but Rwandans live in a world of evil and no good. You and I live in a world of good."

She said, "Isn't it amazing that so many people live in hell, and the others live in America."

Just at the end of our call, she asked me to give Jocelyn a call.

"Why?"

"Just telephone her, Jib. She'd probably like to hear from you."

She was probably pregnant. Anyway, I did call her. She came on the phone unsurprised.

"Jib, dear God. What. A. Surprise." She was already putting periods between her words the way her mother did. "But you sound so ab. Solutely strange."

"I'll bet I do," I said. I wondered why. The debutante emeritus with her long straight hair who looked like an amateur tennis champ, the jaw line of a hood ornament, was not pregnant.

We chatted. I told her things were going well. Why was I even there? I told her about the Cup. She already knew. She told me about the Routledge family fireworks over my defection. She thought it was funny and was worried about me, nothing more.

She had taken a job at a publisher friend of daddy's. "Not too draining." A chic job that left her time for lunches where she could ponder world issues.

"Are you sure you're alright?"

"Yes, fine." But I still wasn't sure why she'd wanted me to call. Then she said, "Do you ever think of me at all, Jib?"

For lack of a better word, I said I did. "Yes," was how I put it.

She said so did she. We'd never really had anything between us, except that my family had a fortune and so did hers. Money is attractive to money.

"Well? Do you ever want to see me again?"

"Sure. I'll be back one day."

"Well, don't sound so dorky about it."

⚑

Elizaphan Bleu

The girl who came to wash and cook for me and to clean my house had begun sleeping over. The first night she stayed, she lay down with me, because I had felt feverish and she took it away. She broke my fever. Afterwards, we lay for a long time without speaking. We knew. She seemed too delicate when she had first come, undernourished. That first morning she changed. She had a man to look after. Now she was radiant. Elizaphan Bleu.

I believed her when she told me she did not know how old she was. In a country where children become heads of households, she was an adult. There were no teenagers there. There was no calendar number that accompanied her. Our rules-numbered society did not apply to her. There were no birthdays attached to her, or to anyone. For the boys, when their little stick got hard, it was time; for the girls, it was blood. In a country where genocide was a philosophy. And there were child *genocidiers*, they aged in dog years, their faces grew old at birth. And what was genocide? Just a philosophy? An idea on how to clear things away? We who assumed life, who got angry at busy telephones, were not qualified to answer. I paid her too much, a dollar a day. She told me I was the opposite of death.

Tall Elizaphan Bleu. She was a perfect mix, her bloodline was half a confusion of Hutu and Tutsi and half Norwegian missionary. Feminine. She lived with a fragment of her brother's family. She brought with her a cow that gave them both blood and milk. Her tangible assets, her nest egg. And she was innately elegant. How can a gap between the front teeth be endearing on an elegant woman? Because it attempts to dismiss her beauty. It is a mar of elegance.

The Men

Each man raised his hand when his name was called.

Ba'ale read the names out every morning before breakfast.

"Mungo. Isaaco. Leopold Cassel. Leopold Zaban. Esperance. Innocent. Caesar. Leon. Moses. Leon Champagne. Leon Bagambiki. Kikongoro. Josue . . ."

The men. At first I had been afraid to touch them. I don't mind saying it. They had come in from the bush some of them, from hiding, frightened, desperate, hungry. They were too bony, dirty, underfed. They seemed infected by parasites, viruses. They had lesions. They were smaller, thinner. There was nothing familiar about them. They were darker, some of them truly black, with clean lean facial features. Their eyes glowed in the dark. These were the terrified ones, the mysterious ones. The ruined ones, the smart ones. I could understand why they'd been terrified. The only thing that had ever terrified me was boredom. They never smiled. They had no reason to smile, haunted by the atrocities; the butchering had been done to them, not by them. It had been done by the others, the Hutus.

The Hutus were not so much black as they were brown, cocoa brown, but one of them, Isaaco Kayijaho, was midnight blue. Their noses, their heads, and their bodies were thicker, and they were short, slow, lazy. The Hutus were arrogant when they first came to our camp. I understood why the Tutsis couldn't smile. Smiles were very important in our lives, but to Tutsis they were signals that they never felt like giving. They felt so little. No emotion except pain. They had come with me only to survive, not to sail, to find something to live for. I understood that.

My men were silent compared to Europeans, Americans, who never stopped chattering. And if there was no one near them they had a telephone in their pocket. But these men were silent. The massacres had left them mute. Their tongues were scarred. There were no jokes.

At first I was afraid to touch them as if they might break. They were fragile from not eating. It turned out in the end, they were as strong as I was.

The Hutus remained arrogant those first weeks when it didn't seem possible that blood enemies could ship together. Then Bujumbura. It was a mystical revelation. Tension slacked. The bishops had everything to do with that, more than I did. Their nightly counseling in the crew's dormitory when they compelled the men to sit on their cots and look at each other across the long room. I would walk in some nights and see that a Tutsi had broken down and was being consoled by a Hutu. I saw with my own eyes a Tutsi hugging a Hutu. So, in time, the men found comfort in our very strange project. Some Tutsis began to smile from a feeling of well-being. And when some of the evil memories began to be replaced, or leave them, and a new life spirit rose in them, their faces shone. They became what they might have once been. Their features became purer. They became handsome.

Early on, after we'd begun training in the Swedish boats, whenever some of them did a good thing out on the lake, I found I wanted to touch them. That was my habit: to touch, to shake hands, to embrace. I'd pat one of them on the back in my horsy American way, but it didn't work out very well. They'd flinch or cower or turn and glare. Back patting was an act of hostility. So, I stopped doing it.

The camp was thriving, morale was good. The *Kinsman* team was ahead of schedule. We sailed every day to practice timing our quickness. It was the most important thing for a crew to learn, the quick tack, the perfect come-about, trimming sheets at high speed, quick sail changes, dousing sails, not to fall overboard. Until the twelve-meters arrived, the actual challenger and the trial horse, we depended on the two K Boats with their fridge-white hulls. Those heavy Swedish keel sloops were the perfect work horses. The Twelves would be touchier, trickier, on every point. They sailed with great pressure built up on oversized sails attached to underweight spars and a hull that was trying to get out of the way of the wind. In the last America's Cup trials and finals, two boats broke and sank, and there were half-a-dozen dismastings.

Time. The weather stayed cool. Four months had passed since Bujumbura was killed. It became our required disaster, our turning point. Things were going well. Everything we had depended on his dying. Bujumbura. Our twelve-meter challenger should be named after him, but I had already agreed to Bishop Jean's name, *Kinsman*. It was a good name, a very good name, too.

⚑

Jocelyn Ortion

Unbelievable. At noon, Jocelyn Ortion showed up at the camp while we were eating. Pristine from her eighteen-hour flight, she was wearing a white linen suit and spectator shoes. What a jolt. The instant I saw her I knew it was wrong. She was leaning beside the U.S. Embassy Jeep that a Marine corporal had very kindly driven her in from the U.S. Embassy. After all, I had said I missed her. I was stunned. I waved without walking toward her.

The men, resting in the shade for the afternoon ahead, watched her as if she were a wingless bird, which I suppose she was. The unwrinkled suit, her very red lips severely scored, her acrobat's legs, tanned arms.

After a minute, I left what I was doing, stood, and walked over to her, amazed. She had pinned back her impossibly long, clean hair into a ball, indicating the sincerity of her visit. We sort of kissed. The men made squealing noises. They liked me. I was fun to watch. I let them kid me.

"How long are you here for?"

"Well, that's not a very friendly question," she said prettily. I didn't know what to say.

"Until you deport me, I guess." Knowing that I would never think of deporting her. I must have nodded.

"Jib, can you please get my bag out of the car so this very nice Corporal Smith can return to the embassy? I'm dying to see your little house." A tennis racket was strapped to her Louis Vuitton *sac polochon*. "I hope we can get in some tennis, to say nothing of sailing." She said it as if she'd flown in for a weekend house party.

Corporal Smith drove the Jeep away, and for the rest of the afternoon Jocelyn sat around in her white linen suit and spectator shoes, dazed from her eighteen-hour flight and watched while I took crews out in A boat and Esperance took them out in B boat. At the end of the day, we came in off the water and stowed the sails, and the men started their exercises again. "They're all so tiny!" she whispered. We left the camp and walked down the narrow sandy beach to my house carrying her shoes. Moses drove her bags down and followed us on the road in the Land Rover.

Still outside, we smelled dinner. Elizaphan opened the door. Corn bread, stew. The women were the same height, but Elizaphan was barefooted. Thinner. She was draped in a *kikoi*, the way I liked her to dress, a single piece of fabric tied. She curtsied to Jocelyn. Jocelyn put on her shoes and asked where the toilet was. She called it the *loo*.

"Out there," I said, pointing to the firewood shack. A vent was cut in the door. I sort of wanted to warn her about the bird-eating spiders that lived among the logs, but I didn't. I heard one single shriek from the shack, but she was trying to act tough. By then, Elizaphan was her immediate concern. When she came back from the *loo,* she frowned at her bringing us tea outside on a tray. Jocelyn knew. Women know; it is silly to think they don't.

"Who is this infant?" she said when Elizaphan set the tray between us on a woven table.

"Don't do that."

"Why?" Jocelyn said.

"It's rude."

"But my cup is filthy."

"Jocelyn, stop. Now," I said.

Elizaphan said, "Bwa?" The truth was, Elizaphan did wash our dirty dishes outside in the laundry bucket with laundry soap.

"Well, then why don't you tell me, Jib, who this infant girl is?"

"She is my wife, Jocelyn." Out it came, which startled me. I suppose I wanted to say it. It immediately solved the Jocelyn problem and the torment of having her sleep in my little house. Ever.

Moses drove her back to the Embassy, and the bureau chief let her sleep in their guest quarters that night. She hadn't been able to get in any tennis or sailing, though she did manage to ease Corporal Smith's tension before she left the embassy the next morning. He told me later she'd been *outstanding,* though maybe a bit *psycho.*

⚐

Saint Pierre

Saint left a message for me at the embassy. I called him back and left him a message. He called me back.

"Can we compete?" he said.

"Yes."

"Can we win?"

I hesitated. Winning. It was an unspoken thing. Nobody ever mentioned it. We talked about racing; winning hadn't occurred to anyone. Much too soon.

"Yes, we can win."

"Well, I can't imagine America being beaten by a country the size of Central Park."

"But it's not as dangerous as Central Park," I said. "And, yes, I can imagine us winning. Think of us as Vietnam."

There was a silence while he assimilated my rudeness.

"Don't take it wrong, Old Jib. I think you're doing a crackerjack job down there, but in all honesty I don't believe we can compete to win. Not against the world of cutting edge technology. Compared to the thirty million buck syndicates, we've got nothing really. You've got no facilities there to test a hull design; no way to float one. No hydrodynamics. Testing apparatus. Keel restraint tests. Models in tanks. Lab tests. Sailmakers."

"Stop," I interrupted. He'd done his homework. "I know all that, okay?"

"So, I guess it's less about sailing than science. What we need to do, I'm afraid. is simply field a great-looking boat and crew, pump that up, get it out there for the world to see. Visibility. Discipline. That's what we want. We'll cause a stir, and that'll be enough for everyone."

"Put on a great show."

"Put on a great show."

I'd suddenly decided we really could win. "I hate to screw everything up, Saint, but I'm planning to win."

"Of course you are, Jib, and so am I. So am I, but we won't. Didn't you say so yourself, 'We don't need to win to win.' Am I quoting you correctly?"

"That meant, in case we lost, we'd still look good."

"And you'll look great. I guarantee you that."

"Lord, I hope so." I was barely hanging on. Why was he trying to take the wind out of my sails?

"By the way, Jib, I meant to tell you, good news. There are plenty of Twelves on the market to choose from," he said. "Plenty of syndicates still in debt from 1995. Everyone's got an old boat for sale cheap. I had some Japanese fellow knock on my door. He'd flown in from Tokyo. One million each, but I didn't like the look of the boats."

It was one of those too-long phone calls that had gotten loose in the Embassy quiet room with me in Rwanda and him in New York, and when I slammed down the phone, I felt like punching out a marine guard then getting drunk.

⚑

The Twelves

After the weekend, Saint called to say that our offer had been officially accepted and that we had now obtained two magnificent boats, the quickest boats in the 1995 Races from Italy, the *Il Moro di Venezia* boats, the red ones. The runners up, but they should have won. Of course, I knew about them. Everyone did. They were the best hulls and had been notoriously well sailed by the Italians and Paul Cayard, but they lost to massive U.S. technology and now the *Il Moro* syndicate was giving them up, and we were taking them. One, as trial horse; the other, as the challenger. Between the two, we'd choose one. He told me our challenger was in excellent condition and was en route from Rigona, Italy, along with its stablemate. The two Twelves should be off-loaded in Abidjan, Ivory Coast, in a month. Saint was exultant. I didn't know another man who knew how to be exultant and negative at the same time. "Just remember, you don't have a chance, Jib."

And Aunt Pearl left a more optimistic message for me at the Embassy with the consul who was known only as "Peter the Spy." She described the call to him as one of dire importance. I could hear her. Because "Peter the Spy" was with the CIA, he sent a corporal with a note down to fetch me. When I reached her, waking her as usual, she said that unbelievably there had been an article in the *Enquirer* about what we were up to "down there." Aunt Pearl and the *Enquirer* were my main connections to the world beyond.

"Who is Len Carter? He's mentioned in the article."

"He's an entrepreneur," I said. "America's guest."

"It calls him a missionary," she said.

I laughed. "Aha! He's with the Hope Church or Faith Chapel or something like that, one of those shiny new religions where everyone smiles when they're pissed off. When I said that Charles Darwin could beat up Saint Paul he told me I'd fry in Hell."

"Well, it quotes this Carter. He says he was down there being a missionary when he saw this ridiculous thing going on. He mentioned you by name."

"I told him to shut up about what we were doing, or else I'd tell someone to kill him with a blunt machete. Obviously, he didn't take me seriously."

A week later, when we were out on the water, the cooks were in the camp looking after our things, and I'd instructed them to throw out any snoopers or thieves. There he was. A reporter named Carter. He was with the press. How did he know how to dress? Why do reporters wear safari jackets with epaulets?

"Hi, Charley, I'm with *Globe International* now."

"We're not open to the public, Carter."

I told him to get out; that we had no need for any press.

"It's a good story, Charley. Little Rwanda taking a run at the America's Cup with a boat crewed by African natives? News is our business. I wouldn't be doing my job if I didn't report it."

"Can't you hold off a bit?"

"We have a moral obligation to our readers."

"Did you know that two hundred and thirty-one Tutsi refugees were killed last weekend near the eastern border?"

"Actually, it was a bit higher. And yes, I did."

"Well? There's your story. No moral obligation to your readers to report that?"

"Not really. It has no impact on our readers."

"Four hundred Algerians were killed the other night?"

"I hadn't heard."

"No. Well, it's in another news district. But now that you do know, what's next? You make the call."

A week later, Len Carter writing in the *Globe International*.

> RWANDA. May 30. As any child will tell you, the America's Cup races have become as interesting as watching Mr. Rogers wash his undershorts in the kitchen sink. And because of its state-of-the-art technology it is considered unwatchable by any rag sailor who loves true sailing. The financial excesses offend even the richest yacht owner. So who's it for? The super rich. Who else? The Cup has attracted the rich who leave in their wakes trails of hundred dollar bills. The money snob versus the money snob. And it has attracted the worst type of fake sportsman.

> Yo. Good news. Down here in Rwanda somebody's decided to change all that. A kid in his twenties named Charley Routledge from New-port, Manhattan and Big Money has taken the blancs des blancs of the money sports and twisted it into an act of charity. No lie. He's doing it for this little downtrodden Central African country. I kid you not. So what was once purely a white bread sport is now twelve grain. And as I said, this is more than a sport. The winning of the Cup

would mean a possible billion bucks seed money to plant a future for this tiny, surprisingly pretty country that has had more than its share of despair in recent years.

Okay, it's an impossible dream, I agree, but it's happening. Routledge's New York backers have underwritten this challenge to the richest, most snobbish, boring, meaningless, whitest sport and tossed it to the poorest, blackest, lowest, smallest, most depleted country on earth. And they're going to go for win, not place or show. If they do win, they'll win big. It'll be more than this country has ever been given.

So we're talking brotherhood of man here. Hollywood will be calling. So stay tuned to this page . . .

A few days later there were a few lines about our *Kinsman* enterprise in the Leisure section of the *Wall Street Journal*:

LITTLE RWANDA ROARS

The America's Cup, also known as the White Bread Trophy, is being challenged by the smallest country in Africa with an all-black crew aboard save one, Newporter Charles Routledge. It's a great story. As to film potential, where is Ron Howard?

A few weeks after Carter's piece, there was an article in *Traveler Magazine* called "Fun Teeny Countries." It listed next year's countries with no GNP for the adventurous traveler: Tanzania, Ethiopia, Sudan, Somalia, Mozambique, Zambia, Uganda, Ghana, Ecuador, Guatemala, Suriname, Tasmania, Madagascar, Rwanda. As if we believed it, the lie would come true. Send me food, not cameramen.

A year earlier, Rwanda had lost its entertainment value. Boring. There was nothing left to say to the world press. The world's interest had moved on. Now they might come back; they had entertainment value again. They were an official blip in the public day's agenda that could be called *news*. And the cycle of attitudes that would form toward Rwanda from ignorance to awareness to sympathy to respect to ridicule to boredom would spin out once again.

We deserved none of it. And they would certainly get it wrong.

It was time to go.

⚑

The Ivory Coast

How many elephants died to be so honored? Died badly. A country named for their tusks. What a tribute.

I hated to close down the compound we'd built, but that had always been the plan. It was June, and we were ready for the second phase. We needed ocean trials in the Twelves that were being delivered to Abidjan, capital of Ivory Coast. On the Atlantic Ocean. We needed to re-locate and find a temporary compound. Would the French cooperate? As Saint Pierre had told me, we were to be given military help directed from Paris, but so far they had withheld it.

Elizaphan and I came to the Ivory Coast a week ahead of the crew. There, through a French Colonel, I heard about six acres of land on a lagoon at Grand Bahou, thirty-five miles west of Abidjan. Abandoned facilities left there by a small sardine canning operation that had closed down, the splintered docks already built, not much work needed to convert the buildings into dormitories, fencing off the area. Perfect. The smell was entirely gone, unless there was an onshore wind. They were asking almost nothing for it. I called Saint Pierre, and he set up the bank account in Abidjan. I was able to ask for a three-month lease.

And from a French construction company came a crane that they weren't using. They even drove it out, rigged it, and installed it. It was big enough to haul a Twelve out of the water. The setup couldn't have been better. Good ocean sailing, constant trade winds, lagoons, dock area. We were in the dry season. Rain forests, sandy beaches. It was pretty remote. We could have peace there. I didn't want our project to raise much curiosity. I brought four extra men, dismembered, so we'd have security around the clock. I made sure we all got injections and pills for a set of the local diseases there. Malaria, tuberculosis, yaws, dysentery, the works.

But for all our luck with the French military and the help they gave us, there was something terribly wrong with them. In Abidjan, just as there was in

Kigali, even though it's three thousand miles west of Rwanda. Of course, the French were imperialists. I got that, but I needed a polygraph to know what they were really thinking. They were well-spoken, such faultless accents, but the lucidity seemed to be a lie. I could never tell how they really felt about this *Kinsman* thing. They all seemed to have impeccable backgrounds, but peccable foregrounds. Illuminating Rwanda to the world was not what they really wanted. No matter how good it would be for its citizens, the despicable state of the country would be seen, and maybe they feared it would eventually come to be seen as their fault. Maybe the truth would come out about their part in the massacres.

It wasn't until months later that I found out their help to us was a politeness, that the French government did not want to be represented by us, that they had begun funding a wealthy French industrialist, Baron Biche, the maker of Biche Sportshoes, who had sailed *France* in the last America's Cup. While they seemed to be helping us, they were underwriting a challenge boat to be sailed by Biche and his crew named *Le Coeur de France,* which was sure to get rid of us in the early stages so that Biche would become the official French entry.

⚑

Larry Bayard & Marcus Cape

I needed a skipper. I had been in touch with Larry Bayard, who now lived in Abidjan and worked as a boat broker. He drove over. I liked him on sight. He told me that Paul Cayard had gotten half-a-million for steering *America3* in the last Cup races. Everyone knew Bill Koch had dropped sixty-nine million on his attempt, so I was sure it probably was true. I said we were spending ten percent of that and I'd be glad to ask Saint Pierre to pay him ten percent of what Cayard got. We shook hands. We were set. Larry Bayard called some friends, experts and technicians. One of them was an old friend of mine from Saint George's School. He'd just gotten out of the navy. Marcus Patrick Cape. We had sailed in the finals of the Star Class Worlds races, and he'd gone on to become navigator on Navy F-111s. I never understood why.

I called him in New York and while we were talking I suddenly realized he just might want to sail aboard *Kinsman* as tactician, the guy who keeps an eye on the other boat and advises the helmsman who's busy watching the wind and the sails and steering. I told him how far we'd come with *Kinsman* and what we had and what our plans were and before I was finished he said, "I'm in." He was through with conventional life for the time being, he said, and this was the perfect answer. Where should he meet us and when? I told him Abidjan. Now. Where's that?

Marcus Cape joined our crew a week later at Grand Bahou. It was great seeing him again. He hadn't changed. The *Il Moro* Twelves were off-loaded from the deck of the tanker at Abidjan and lay dockside without their masts, lipstick red hulls, the sexy bows, red red red. I gasped when I saw them.

"Those boats are very red, but not too red," Larry said. Marcus and I agreed. The hulls were towed without masts to our docks at Grand Bahou, and the three of us oversaw their tuning after the masts were stepped. And when the wind blew, their stays sang.

"They are so beautiful standing there at the dock that I know they're definitely females. I couldn't feel this way about males," Marcus said. Form certainly follows function. The shark is perfect, a beautiful fish, the result of ten million years of evolution. It had arrived. So had these hulls, as if they too were at the end of their evolutionary trail; as if science, wind, weather, speed had dictated the hull's design. They were the most beautiful hulls racing, and *Kinsman's* bow resembled the slippers Aunt Pearl brought back from the Middle East.

"Which one is *Kinsman?*"

"The faster one."

"What's the name of the second boat?"

"*Bujumbura.*"

They were as excited as I've ever seen humans get excited. With them on board, we could begin sea trials. Larry and Marcus would take *Kinsman*, and I'd sail the trialhorse, *Bujumbura*. Both with full crews.

No boat can be known until it sails; neither did we know for sure about these two. The men were nervous. We all were. And during the first weeks of sea trials the crew felt the awesome tension in the rigging between the backstays and the mast. We were not sailing them at speed, only sailing them by the wind and learning the trim, the timing, and the sail changes. Anyone who can stand on a wet slanted fiberglass deck and grind a winch can crew on a twelve- meter sailboat. It is something you can learn. Each boat needs only two or three real sailors to steer and skipper it. I've always known that, and *Kinsman's* crew began proving it that first day. A natural finesse.

Mosquitos swarmed at sunset in Grand Bahou. I usually carried a slight temperature. I was afraid of local fever, malaria, dengue, any fever that could knock me down and so I took quinine pills every day. I drank the strong local tea. We had settled in at Grand Bahou. I did not think about death every few moments the way my crew did, but they were maybe beginning to see that life could be a good thing. Even I'd learned to appreciate it.

It seemed especially sweet those mornings. The Atlantic breeze was constant and cooling, so different from the Rwandan land breeze.

With the two rigged Twelves at our dock, Larry, Marcus and I could train the men in finesse on Twelves, along with attitude attitude attitude and timing timing timing. For discipline, I improved our Lake Kivu routine:

> 5 a.m. rise, wash, shine, exercise
> 6 a.m. food, talk
> 7 .a.m boat work
> 9 a.m. eighteen-mile racing session, weather permitting
> 12 p.m. midday meal on board
> 1 p.m. afternoon racing session, weather permitting
> 6 p.m. exercise ashore
> 6:30 p.m. showers, laundry

7 p.m. food, followed by discussion
8 p.m. talking, dancing, fooling around, banana wine
9 p.m. bed

Elizaphan bought the food and supervised the cooks. Tutsis normally do not eat red meat, but Ba'ale had influenced the other Tutsis to taste it. And having tasted it, they liked it and made it part of their diet. All meals were her responsibility. She made them good. At the tail-end of a wind-burning day, when the men were tired, we danced anyway. And tired as she was, Elizaphan sang. There was no television. Most nights, she led the men in dancing. We danced just about every night. Several men brought ku-kuis, so we had a rhythm section.

She was teaching me to speak Kinyarwandan from a first grade primer, but we talked patois between ourselves. *Bamwe ye ti bo, de ti bo, twa ti bo doo doo. Elizaphan Bleu, I'm falling for yeu.* In our camp at night, I'd look across at her singing, and I could not imagine being there without her. I'd feel my adventure gland puff. Elizaphan Bleu. The title of a romance novel. She had no nickname. She was a wonder. What luck I had in finding her and knowing her.

There are dozens of ways to slice yourself up on these Twelves, and I'd come back from a day with cuts on my fingers from wires and sheets. Like many Rwandans, Elizaphan believed that her body fluids healed. It was a standard belief that her vaginal secretions were medicinal and that her excretions could heal my cuts. The funny thing was, they could. On the other hand, she believed that my semen was pure blood from the brain, and she would do that, too. And so it went.

A phone call from Saint Pierre came as a letdown. New Zealand decreed a new rule. The defender of the Cup had the power to make the rules of its defense. Each country can only be represented by one entry. It was not a bad idea, limiting the challengers. Instead of having about three hundred elimination races in New Zealand, there would be a round robin between the finalists. Each country would be forced to pick their challenger before they went to New Zealand. The French immediately pulled out of any obligation they might have had to our Rwandan team and revealed their plan.

Saint had thought he'd successfully blackmailed them, but no. They would back their own boat. Baron Biche, one of their favorite sportsmen, the godhead of Biche Sportshoes, would try again. In the last America's Cup, his boat broke in two and sank. He was dumped in the Pacific, a humiliating experience for a baron. I asked Saint why they dropped us.

"They don't want their country represented by your crew."

"But Rwanda's their protectorate."

"The government is backing away from you. They don't want the scrutiny of the world on Rwanda. It could show that they had condoned the genocide."

They decided that we would have to race Baron Biche on the French coast in a series of five races.

So. My crew had been aspiring to a world they were unprepared for, a world they had never heard of, a world of winning not only of sailing, but of international competition. The reward was as far over their heads as the sky and that even appealed to them. The news of the French elimination series left them afraid. There was the real possibility of being sent home before the Cup finals even began in New Zealand. Never mind our fifteen months' training and Pearl's money, the two challengers. Rwanda would never be heard from again. A forgotten upstart, a colorful news blip, no matter how precious or human, it had an expiration date. On the other hand, the French boat could break in two and sink again.

A few days later, a courier from the French Embassy came to our camp with a letter. The Cup challenge committee in Paris decreed that the French challenger would be decided in a best-of-five races to be held off La Rochelle, on the Bay of Biscay, known for its rough water, down the coast between Brest and Biarritz. In July.

I called Saint Pierre. He was feeling good, because Pepsico had tendered him an offer to co-sponsor *Kinsman*. I told him to call Aunt Pearl and let her consider it.

"What is there to consider?" he said.

"I'm not sure she wants anything other than the name *Kinsman* on the side of the boat." I was surprised Saint didn't know that. I did.

"What about the sails?"

"It's ugly."

"It pays the bills," he said stiffly.

"Aunt Pearl pays the bills, Saint. I think you should talk to her." I didn't want to argue with him.

When he did, she told him it would be like her walking down Fifth Avenue wearing a sandwich board.

⚑

᠊ᠣ

Aunt Pearl

She should not have come to Abidjan. Another surprise. She just appeared at the compound in Grand Bahou. Amazing woman.

"Where's Jocelyn?" I said.

She smiled wickedly. "She didn't come. I just wanted to see how you were getting along, Jib." Jocelyn had told her about Elizaphan and was I really married to her?

"I'm anxious for you to meet her."

Her driver brought packages for me that included overdue replacement bottles of Irish whiskey and tequila and several pounds of espresso beans and, for some reason, a toothbrush. Pearl had ordered a car and driver and immediately lined up an Episcopalian Church so that she could pray for me. She shouldn't have come. She was not a standard dowager. She could take care of herself, but still there was no Ritz Hotel in el Bahou. What there was, Le Grand Regence, was not. It was a one star hotel that boasted of a mural painted in the style of Carravaggio earnestly copied on the walls of the dining room and below it, metal tables with a menu that listed rack of goat, wine made from corn, iguana eggs.

That evening I introduced Pearl Routledge Hood to Elizaphan Bleu. Pearl approved. I knew she would, even though she couldn't understand a word she was saying. And Elizaphan approved of Pearl, just as I knew she would. After dinner at Le Grand Regence, Pearl told me that in Elizaphan's face she could see true beauty.

"I couldn't agree more," I said, "and she's never been to finishing school."

"She has everything."

"Plus her own cow."

"She's loaded, darling. Snap her up." She gave me her most garish laugh. "She is the world uninterrupted by mankind."

᠊ᠣ

Part Three
La Rochelle

La Rochelle

July 12. We loaded the two twelve-meter sloops on the deck of a tanker bound for Bordeaux, which is just south of La Rochelle.

I had decided that no matter what the consequences, win or lose, I would tell my crew that we must do our best to consider this whole thing *only* a sailboat race. The French were the ones with prestige to lose, not us. We were the sacrificial goats, first timers, laymen sailing out of a landlocked port. It was a miracle that we were there at all. The underdog's underdog, even the title *underdog* was a compliment. Just a sailboat race. And we'd already had a great run. The men could go home proud. They'd earned their share and were rich enough to begin their lives again.

Two weeks later *Kinsman* and *Bujumbura* were berthed in what's called the Vieux Port, where we had no privacy and were gawked at by the curious. No matter how strong the crew had become, they still looked small and emaciated compared to any other known yachting crew. And a lot blacker. They bunked on the top floor of a seaman's hotel, L'Horizon, near the docks.

Le Coeur de France

Le Coeur de France arrived. The French challenger. A dazzling blue. She was as blue as we were red. We watched her from a distance through binoculars as she was being lowered by crane off the deck of a tanker from Marseilles. Terrifying. She had a wing keel, a needle-nose entry, fine sheer, a perfect blue hull marred by words: BANQUE LYONNAISE, BICHE, PERRIER. Aunt Pearl had said it. One creates something as wonderful as a twelve-meter. Why would one cover its skin with billboards? Selling space on a work of art is simply rude.

In the morning, *Kinsman* and *Bujumbura* were towed out through the crowded harbor of La Rochelle into the Atlantic. We began sea trials with both boats in this new water which had less chop than the West African Atlantic, though the swells were higher and it was breezier.

During the first few days of sea trials, Larry, Marcus and I sailed the boats at speed. We drilled damage control. We staged accidents. We dropped sails in the ocean and either cut them loose or recovered them. We practiced the man overboard recovery drill. One mistake could cost us a race.

Le Coeur de France was given the Naval research facilities in a private and remote area away from the harbor, near a beach. The French crew kept to themselves.

We stood on the shore with binoculars trying to determine *Le Coeur de France*'s speed and fine points. If she was a straight line racer, or if she was highly maneuverable. We wanted to know whether to engage her in quick, complicated tacking duels at the start and on the open sea, or whether to sail away from her.

Le Coeur de France was towed out, dropped her line and raised her lightest sails. We couldn't see the cut of her mainsail, because on her big jib was a huge Rolex wristwatch. When she raised her spinnaker, up went a Perrier bottle. When she tacked, we saw a Biche Sportshoe on her mainsail. The ads had stronger outlines than her sails and were far less beautiful. At a distance, all we could see of her was a watch, a shoe, and a bottle sailing rather well. These were part of the cultural gift bestowed to yachting by Dennis Connor, a yachtsman/entrepreneur.

We had no bottles to show, thanks to Aunt Pearl who had, of course, directed Saint to turn down the Pepsico offer. Only one word in black adorned *Kinsman*. On her bows and across her counter: *KINSMAN*. Her hull was alizarin red, and her mast and sails were white. We were very red and very white and very plain.

I was nervous the night before the opening race. Competing against a stranger was always daunting to me. There was always an *anything-can-happen* fear. I expected magic. Until I saw its first weakness (if it had one), and then I knew that it was no different than me. And the *anything-can-happen* happened. Unfortunately, I did not see its first weakness. I had already decided that *Le Coeur de France* had it all.

But when *Le Coeur de France* first unfurled the French flag on her backstay during a trial run, the Tutsis became agitated. The French flag meant death.

Race Day

Race one. After eighteen months. *Jesus, light air.*

We met *Le Coeur de France* near the starting line. At the ten-minute gun, during the starting maneuvers instigated by her, circling exercises trying to out-circle us, circling again and again, finally beating Larry Bayard. The two sloops with their hundred-foot masts were slowly being turned like dancers. She ended up in control of the start and covered us expertly wherever we turned. They were a well-drilled crew. We tacked; she tacked. She was like a giant shade tree; we were her shadow. We swirled in great circles; we sailed together, side-by-side, in tight figure eights. She had proved her point and beat us across the line.

At the starting gun, we set out on a port tack below her, eating her bad air. Still, the first leg was going to be close. We tried everything we knew to stay with them up to and around the first mark as the fluky afternoon wind slowly built to twelve knots. Then, it was clear that both boats would have to change headsails. They were too light and big-bellied, so Larry called for the heavy jib, and the foredeck crew loosened the halyard too soon and down it came and spread out on the water like a white oil slick. It had nearly stopped us. If we kept sailing over it, we could lose the sail. A twenty-five thousand dollar Mylar Genoa.

"Ca-way!" Larry shouted in Kinyarwandan. Leon Mukademezo jumped overboard to keep it from ripping on our keel. Recovering it cost us three minutes and eventually the race.

Race Two

Another light day. The morning paper, *Le Temps de Midi*, carried an interview on *Le Coeur de France*. The crewmen were asked to comment on the Rwandan challenge:

> "What are your thoughts?"
> "That they cannot be serious."
> "So, it is a waste of your time."
> "Not at all. We can practice against a racing horse as well as a racing goat."
> "Who will win?"
> "Imagine."
> "Why do you carry advertisements on *Le Coeur de France,* and there is none on *Kinsman*?"
> "What business would want to be associated with them?"
> "Perhaps *Kinsman* should be decorated with an emblem of crossed machetes painted on their hull."
> "'Bloody machetes,'" another crewman added.

Charles De Gaulle had once said of the French, "We would be nothing without grandeur." I would have preferred "humanity" over "grandeur." Of course, De Gaulle had never visited their colony in Rwanda.

The wind came up a bit by noon. I watched the French crew being towed out to the starting area. The impeccable blue jerseys and white caps. It was hard to believe, looking at them, that we were of the same species, that we lived on the same planet, that we ate the same leaves and defecated.

The start. In a match race, the most important single maneuver is the start; it sometimes determines the race. The start between two great twelve-meter sloops can be breathless. You must get your boat across the starting line *just* as the gun goes off and not a nanosecond before. There are several ways to arrange this. You may circle and circle and flop over the line just ahead of the other boat and then gain speed; or you may sneak over at either end.

But the riskiest start of all is to sail a good distance away from the line, come about, sheet in your sails, then drive your boat at hull speed directly at the line and hope to God that your bow crosses as the puff of smoke rises from the starting gun. This would be like driving a car at fifty toward a red light and hoping it'll turn green as your hood crosses the white line. If it doesn't, you get a ticket. If you sail over the starting line early, you must circle back, re-cross it completely, losing all advantages of a good start while the other boat sails away in clear air, boat lengths ahead of you.

When the five minute flag was hoisted, Larry Bayard had put us a quarter-mile from the committee boat. He was going to charge the line. *Le Coeur de France* had not even come after us, but was tacking back and forth along the line. Some species of insult. They weren't going to match race us.

With less than two minutes on the stopwatch, Larry jibed *Kinsman* down, let the sails out to gather speed on a reach, then rounded up, flattened them and aimed our bow toward the top of the line.

We were on a starboard tack and had the right of way in case *Le Coeur de France* challenged us on port tack. Larry won the start going away. Maybe we weren't doomed after all. I could feel a gasp go up from the silenced French spectator fleet.

The wind was kind to us. We held that lead for the four miles up to the first mark and the four miles to second mark. We were three seconds ahead rounding it, and we managed to stay ahead to the third. We fought well and, after an hour, we were leading to the fifth mark by nearly ten seconds. Half the race was over. Good for a racing goat.

We ran out of air. The wind pooed at the fifth mark. And in the drifting match that followed, the needle-nosed blue boat drifted ahead of us and in slow motion increased her lead at each of the four buoys remaining to round. It was a disaster. The blue boat finished far in the lead, but maybe slightly chastened as to why we were in La Rochelle. Larry had simply outsailed them for the first twelve miles in fairly light conditions.

I didn't see the French weakness that day; only their arrogance. There was laughter aboard *Le Coeur de France* as *Kinsman* crossed the finish line one minute and thirty-five seconds after they had.

We were down zero to two in a best of three-out-of-five series. The next race would be match point. It could be our last one ever. On the way in, we decided to take our lay day and hope for magic winds the day following.

Elizaphan had waved to me from the escort boat, but when I came ashore I couldn't see her anywhere on the dock. I found her in our ten-by-ten room on the top floor of L'Horizon. She was in tears, packing. Bent over.

She sobbed. "If it had been close, but it wasn't close. And the third race tomorrow would be the same. So, why bother? Why not pack? You will go home and leave me forever. I will never never see you again."

She was probably right. I'd never thought about that. She sobbed and sobbed. I couldn't stop her. I had never used the love word; neither had she. We had never mentioned our *longeur*. Of course, I'd go home. What else? Build a cinder-block house in Rwanda? Buy a pig? Do farming? Or maybe take her home with me to Greenwich Village? Drive her up to Newport in my blue Corvette? The family would be amused. I hadn't thought ahead. I guess I'd assumed I'd leave Africa and pick up my life in New York again, mend things with Jocelyn. Suffer Coventry from the Routledge clan. How bad could that be?

But my crew knew exactly where they were going. They'd be returning to their killing grounds, psychotic despair, memories of murder, starvation, and a life that depended on world charity organizations.

In the middle of all this, I was called downstairs. Saint. He had heard. The end was in sight, just as he'd predicted. He was probably just checking to see that the pieces would be picked up. He told me Aunt Pearl was flying in that evening.

"Here?"

"It was to be a surprise, but I decided to warn you."

"Good thinking, Chief."

"Keep the dreams attainable, Jib."

I really needed to hear that. "That's it?"

Before he hung up, he told me to remember that birds don't migrate to the moon. Whatever the hell that meant.

"That's the best you can do? Thanks."

Half an hour later, Aunt Pearl called from the airport just north of Bordeaux. She was here.

"I'm sorry, but there isn't a single *voiture* to be had. Will you be a dear and send someone to pick me up?"

I drove out in one of our rented Renaults. I told her where we stood with the French. I told her we had a lay day tomorrow. I told her about the birds not migrating to the moon.

"What he meant, Jibby, was don't expect a miracle."

"But I do."

Maybe she had guessed. Maybe that was why she was here, to ease the pain of our imminent defeat.

"Naturally, Elizaphan is here," she said. Of course, she was. Good. Pearl had brought gifts.

Our first stop was the dock, most of the men were still there. Of course, they were fond of Pearl, and she was fond of them. She'd brought all of them white caps and red jerseys. For what could be their final race, they would look,

"Stunning, like a real crew." They thanked her one at a time, as one would thank a visiting queen. She had written their names down before she had left Grand Bahou and, one at a time, wished them well the day after next: Mungo Katano. Isaaco Kayijaho. Esperance Mukademezo. Ba'ale Musavene. Leopold Cassel. Leopold Zaban. Moses Mazimpaka. Innocent Hatumaimana. Kikongoro. Josue Valence. Leon Champagne. Leon Mukademezo. Coco Jolicoeur. "The great men of *Kinsman*," she added. She found their names beautiful, and she spoke them beautifully. "Now where is your lady fair?"

We found her in our dreadful room lying on her back with a wet rag over her face. She jumped up when she heard Pearl's voice and hugged her. In a few minutes, the boxes had been opened and their contents spread out on the bed. Two silk dresses, pearl earrings, pretty underwear, a pair of Valentino high-heeled shoes, and fine stockings. Elizaphan cried again. I guess it was the thought that counted.

Maybe my men were nervous that night. Who could tell? I couldn't see it. Marcus and Larry didn't seem too edgy. We danced and clowned until after ten. Pearl and Elizaphan stayed close together. They even danced. Kicked up their heels. No drinking. The Tutsis were great clowns. Actors, jugglers, jesters, mimes, and they were doing it all that night for Aunt Pearl. It was like a carnival. By eight o'clock, we were all dancing, Elizaphan was singing. It went late. Why not? We were pretending not to be scared. We needed to relax.

Race Three

Match point. France, two; Rwanda, nothing. The boat that wins three goes to New Zealand.

The sun rose on a flat Atlantic Ocean. Oh God, spit soup. With the sunrise came moderate east-west swells, a murmur of a breeze; that was all. Summer doldrums. I was terrified. I admit it. Elizaphan was beside herself with worry. Just before I left our room, she pulled me down on the bed and told me that today I would have what I wanted. I half-believed her. I don't know if she did, though. Tears were everywhere. I asked her not to come down to the dock, to please stay at the hotel until we were towed out of sight.

Aunt Pearl was waiting there on the dock. No one could stop her, of course. She saw my fear. When we were about to drop our dock lines and pick up our tow to the starting line, she said, "Squeeze their escargots, Jib." She could always make me laugh even if I felt like vomiting. She looked right at me with her wickedest look and said that logic has never had a place in a quest for the impossible. That something unimaginable needed to shift.

"I know you'll win today." The way she said *I know*. I loved her for that. I half-believed her about as much as I half-believed Elizaphan.

Something was wrong at the pre-start. Larry Bayard gave up trying to out-maneuver them, boat-for-boat. He no longer hoped to win the start by circling and circling. He decided that we should go for time-on-distance start again. The fastest and the riskiest start.

At noon, the ten-minute flag was hoisted on the committee boat: one long and short blast of the fog horn. Marcus and I punched our stop watches. Larry sailed us off alone again, turned, then sailed fast up to the line too soon. We crossed it before the starting gun, so we had to jibe back around and re-cross it while *Le Coeur de France* gave us her transom and sailed on. Larry and Marcus had screwed-up the start, and I let them know it. We'd lost a full minute. The race might be over. I heard faint applause from the watching fleet, and I imagined I heard the distant popping of corks aboard our rival's boat.

It turned out to be a light day, not our weather. We tailed *Le Coeur de France* on a port tack, a dozen boat lengths behind. The mood of our afterguard was down. Even Esperance was glum. Even the crew sensed that the party was over.

Larry called a meeting. He wanted to take a chance and sail close to shore. Crazy. It would take us further away from the mark, but he'd noticed that in the afternoons off the Island of Oleron, a front of warm air always blew off-shore from the mainland. He asked us what we thought.

Marcus told him he felt it was a bad gamble. Esperance and I said, "Why not?" We might scoop *Le Coeur de France*, winner take all. And anyway what else was going on? We needed to take one last desperate chance.

So, Larry made a sudden decision to tack away to play the windshifts along the land and look for a lift. We tacked to starboard toward shore. The blue boat didn't follow.

Baron Biche, Jean Ballon, and their crew had earned the right to feel arrogant. Arrogant people are fun to watch, but not when they're French and not when they're conquering you. Baron Biche and his crew were not only French, they were winning horribly. But there is a strong tradition in match-racing: never separate from your opponent. After all, it doesn't matter how much you win by, just as long as you win. No matter what, you race boat for boat. You stick to each other the way you stick to your man in soccer or basketball. There are only two of you; you're racing against one boat, not a fleet. Only victory matters. You shadow each other until one of you gets the best of the other and breaks away. Not until then do you separate. If Larry drove *Kinsman* down to Bordeaux, *Le Coeur* should follow.

In their arrogance, though, they did not follow us. Biche and his helmsman, Jean Ballon, must have felt they'd earned the right to skip the rules of the game and to ignore us, the clowns. He could have been right.

But Larry was right. He found solid gusts and lifts, and a mile up to wind-ward the blue boat stayed in light air. After twenty minutes, I looked at them through binoculars. Their afterguard seemed to be pouring fluid from a bottle into cups.

In twenty minutes, we'd know.

And in twenty minutes, we did.

Larry's wind and lifts worked. And looking at the blue boat, I saw that she was still standing straight, sails flat, becalmed. I could imagine Baron Biche cursing us in excellent French. We had made the beginnings of a scoop.

Our crew didn't see it, but Larry winked at us, which we both knew was bad luck, but we winked back anyway. He'd been right. And when we crossed Baron Biche again, it was going to be very close.

⚑

The Unimaginable Shift

On the dock just before the race, Aunt Pearl had told me that in order for us to win, something unimaginable needed to shift. While Baron Biche stood pointing toward the mark in dead air, Larry had found us wind. We were crawling upwind toward him, moving over the bottom at between six to eight knots, a hell of a lot faster than the French boat, which wasn't moving at all. We were still way down the coast passing a point of land called *Ile de Re*, nearing the end of our tack. We had about five minutes left until Larry and Marcus figured we could lay the mark. The wind was up to ten knots with rolling east-west swells.

Jolt.

Josue was knocked to the deck, and Moses was knocked overboard. We'd struck a rock. The boat was lifted a foot or two, then settled off and rolled back down. There'd been a thump coming up from the keel. A horrible clanging and a loud wrenching noise. We'd never know for sure what it was, but we struck it deep and hard. It was bad. My first thought was that we might lose the boat. Abandon ship.

Larry cursed and instantly rounded up. We shot upwind, luffed the sails, and stood dead in the water.

"Isaaco! Go below. Check the hull. Esperance, go with him. Bring up the life belts, one for each man."

Kikongoro tossed Moses a line and hauled him on deck.

I was sure we'd sprung a leak. I hit the air horn and signaled our chase boat to catch up with us.

Isaaco stuck his head up. "Skipper. Leak many liters a minute."

"How many."

"Many. Twenty."

"We can handle that. Get the pumps going."

I heard him switch on the power.

Esperance was tossing lifebelts on the deck.

104

"Put those on, men!" Larry shouted. We had never drilled *abandon ship,* and they regarded the lifejackets with horror.

The electric pumps were beginning to shoot water out on both sides. We were still in the race.

The leak was along the keelson and was steady, but the pumps were getting ahead of it and were keeping the bilge dry. But three minutes had passed and we still hadn't gotten under way.

Leopold Zaban was our top diver. Larry told him to dive under the hull and inspect the damage. In he went. When we hauled him back up on deck, he said he couldn't see anything wrong.

Larry bore off the wind, filled away, and reached on toward the mark. Something else was going on.

An odd scraping sound came up from under our feet. The keel. A vibration. A thumping sound.

The wind freshened, and the sound got worse. When we heeled, we heard a continuous thunk-thunk. The keel had definitely been loosened. Bad news. If we lost the keel, we'd lose the boat. The men had not put on their life jackets. A dreadful fashion statement. The men would rather drown, Moses said.

Now Larry ordered them to put them on.

"We don't know how," Caesar called back.

"Marcus, go up and show them." The men slowly put on their lifejackets.

The French boat was still way off to weather and unbelievably still caught in a dead spot. Larry hove to again and told Leopold to take Mungo down again and push hard on the keel and see if they could move it with their hands. When they bobbed up, they said "yes," that maybe the keel was a bit loose and that no matter how the boat rolled, the keel remained up and down, pointing straight at the bottom. I thought it sounded dangerous; Mungo thought it was funny. Leopold said we were not going to lose it, but boat handling might be a problem. The swells had increased to eight feet.

Sailing the rest of the race would be risky if the center of gravity shifted with each swell. If the keel was loose and maybe hanging by a single bolt, and it dropped off, *Kinsman* would capsize flat on its sails and sink in a couple of minutes. Men could get badly injured by spars and rigging. But, on the other hand, DNF: *Did Not Finish* would not be a good motto to remember our final America's Cup challenge by.

I explained the risk to Isaaco, who relayed it to the crew. They were all wearing their lifebelts by now. It was an all-or-nothing choice. We took a quick vote. Four votes from the afterguard, ten from the crew to sail on. Unanimous. That night we could haul her out and check the keel.

The wind picked up. Larry ordered the sails sheeted in. We crossed our fingers, and suddenly we were sailing ten knots. Then eleven. We weren't even trying to, but we were flying. He sailed directly toward the mark. The thumping continued. We had gotten to within half-a-mile from the blue boat. Everything was going well. The sails looked good, the boat was responding beautifully to the seas, and I felt a surge each time we rose over a swell, as if we were being propelled from below. I hadn't felt this on *Kinsman* before, never in Grand Bahou or here. Neither had Larry, nor Marcus. If we could hang onto our keel for the next ten miles, we might just steal the race from the French. We had a chance. I couldn't help grinning.

The men clung to the rail in religious silence. I could see that some of them felt it, too. We were going to reach the sixth mark dead even with the *Coeur de France*. It would be crowded there, and I told Moses to go forward all the way to the bow and yell, "Sea room!" when the boats came within ten meters of each other.

We forced her to give way to us. We slipped inside, between her and the mark, two seconds ahead. I was too busy trimming the sails to notice their facial expressions.

We stayed even on the downwind leg, but we were now sailing as if we had extra sails. It was amazing. We were charged. It was effortless, and I could tell from Larry's bewildered expression that it was unexplainable. He told me to take the wheel for a few minutes. I felt it. Whenever we rose on a swell, we surged forward and the thumping and creaking continued.

We were ahead. For the first time since the series started, we were leading the blue boat in the second half of a race and increasing our lead with every swell.

Two marks to the finish line.

I looked back at her. A ninety-foot-high bottle of Perrier water was looming up behind us. A giant spinnaker. They had been culturally arrested.

Rounding the seventh mark, we had a mishap. Our spinnaker pole was unclipped too soon, dropped in the water, and the sail blew out to hell and was gone. It was a pig's breakfast. *Le Coeur de France* caught up, passed us, and left us behind. They stayed ahead, rounding the final mark a good ten seconds in front of us.

On the downwind run, the wind picked up to eighteen knots. We set the small spinnaker, caught a puff and a swell at the same time, then soared up on the French boat with the kind of speed I associate with catamarans. As we sailed through them, I didn't dare look at Baron Biche or Jean Ballon. No one spoke. We just sailed away from them and drove home.

We crossed the finish line half-a-mile ahead to a stony silence from the spectator fleet. No foghorn blasts for us; no toot-toots from air horns. We dropped our sails beyond the committee boat. Now I saw the stunned expressions of the badly beaten French crew. I didn't notice any wine bottles.

We had won. Something unimaginable had shifted.

B

The Liquid Keel

But none of it made sense. Marcus, Larry, Esperance, and I hardly spoke a word on the tow in after the finish. If it were a magic spell, we didn't want to spoil it. But whatever it was, it had something to do with the keel. We agreed on that.

Back at the dock, Aunt Pearl was ecstatic.

"An ab-solutely ce-lestial victory," she said. She had predicted it, and I told her so.

Elizaphan hugged me 'til my kidneys popped. She called me "darling." I don't think she'd ever said the word before. And she clung to me, afraid to let me out of her sight.

Pearl telephoned Saint Pierre in New York to tell him the news. He used the word *reprieve*.

After supper, Marcus and I met with Larry. He listened to what we had to say. Then in the dark, we dove under the boat with lights to inspect the keel. The hull was clean; the keel was badly scarred, but sound. When we pushed it, we felt slight movement, but our combined weight underwater wasn't enough to do any more than that. Certainly not what tons of rushing water could do to it. The keel was loose. It was dangling, but secure. Marcus said we weren't going to lose it. But because we didn't know for sure what was going on or what we had in *Kinsman*, we decided to exclude Pearl from any knowledge of our discussion. Temporarily, until we figured it out. It wouldn't do any good to have Saint bringing it up in conversation.

We went over the sequence carefully. Marcus made a sketch of *Kinsman* on his laptop computer. It showed her heeled at forty degrees with the keel still vertical at ninety. He tried to analyze the effect of a keel that hung straight down and still moved every time we rolled. It was a pretty good sketch: hull, sail, mast, keel. The sail put pressure and a shifting weight above the waterline. Every time we heeled or rolled through swells, he calculated where our new center of gravity lay.

He said that when the hull was fluctuating normally the keel wasn't. That's what caused it to creak. It was the weight of the bulb at the base of the keel that made it hang limp. Essentially, he said, we were sailing a boat with a keel that would always be in a more favorable position than it normally would be if it were rigid. In heavy weather, the keel would probably divide the wave shock and let us pass through the water with less friction than a normal boat. As far as he could figure, the keel was acting independently, as if it were on a universal hinge, hanging this way and that. Simply obeying gravity, it would always stabilize us at the best angle possible to the wind and offer no drag below. We had created a truly heavy-weather boat.

I looked at the small screen. It showed the keel vertical and the boat in motion heeling at ten degrees, then thirty, then back to ten. He calculated all our new centers of gravity. If the keel were allowed to *float* (as he put it), he figured that the back and forth movement of the keel caused by swells might possibly act in the same way a sculling oar acts on a gondola or the dorsal fin on an orca. It would offer no drag below the hull. In other words, it was a liquid keel. It seemed implausible.

Anyhow, for whatever reason, it wasn't three, zip; now, it was Grandeur two, Poverty one. And there was, indeed, a tomorrow for us. I'm sure the French were bewildered. That night, they announced they would take their lay day.

In the morning, we took *Kinsman* out to sea to test Marcus' findings. It was blowing in gusts of thirty knots and swells of twelve feet. When we came in after three hours of rugged testing, we were grinning. It was confirmed, but he said we needed heavy weather to make it work. Larry said, "I think we got something. Don't mention this to anyone."

"The truth is," Marcus said, "we might have developed a rocket."

⚑

Race Four

Match point. Again number two, another sensitive moment. By evening, I'd know whether every one of us was headed home. All night long Elizaphan had cradled me.

At dawn there were ripples. The wind came up at ten, but not enough to matter. There was a big ground swell. Marcus said we needed over twelve knots blowing to feel the difference, to activate our keel. Start-up money, as Marcus put it. We didn't care what point the wind came from.

By noon, it was blowing in gusts to fifteen, the swells were giants. Our day.

At the ten-minute horn, Larry decided to be careful, maybe sacrifice the start. He circled *Le Coeur de France* and kept us pretty much away from her. We were even, but it didn't really matter. By then, it was blowing twenty, *Kinsman's* best weather. Either we had it, or we didn't. At the gun, Jean Ballon felt he'd beaten us and won the start. He'd gotten the windward position. We had the leeward position, just ahead of their wind.

Riding beautifully as she never had before, *Kinsman* walked right up through her backwind. It didn't take long, maybe five minutes of hard sailing, to catch her. Once we shot out ahead, we stayed ahead. This was our race. I know that Biche and Ballon didn't get it. We had sea room to spare when Larry tacked above the blue boat. On a port tack. It was too good. Larry caught my eye and winked at me. He didn't get it either. None of us understood what was happening.

Marcus had explained that the keel was hanging like a broken wing, but flapping. It wasn't going to drop off either. That was the prayer anyway, but every time we tacked or heeled, the keel creaked. Driving toward the mark, we increased our lead with each gust of wind. *Le Coeur de France* was burying her needle-nose, plunging badly. Driving her hard in this weather was too much for her. I watched her trying to catch us, but she could do nothing. We were the faster boat. We were riding over the swells with absolutely no drag from the keel.

When we rounded the fourth mark halfway through the race, we were flying, two miles ahead of the French. We could even outpoint them a bit, too. We had sailed up at thirty-five degrees into the wind. We were pushing *Kinsman* to the limit, and the keel was knocking with each ride. We were so far ahead that it would have been stupid to lose it at this point. Larry put us into the wind and Leopold Zaban dove over the side to check it out. *Le Coeur de France* was still tacking upwind, and it felt very very good. We'd split the series, two to two. The keel was secure, he said. We were not going to lose it. But Larry decided to ease the sails and finish the race as we were, two miles ahead. We didn't need to gain any more.

We had just rounded the final mark when our starboard side stay parted.

BO-I-NG!

Instantly, Larry rounded us up. To save the mast.

Too sudden for the crew. Moses couldn't release the jib quick enough. The jib split.

We stood there dead in the water, assessing the damage, scrambling. The foredeck crew got the jib down. Mungo stowed it in the sewer and sent another upon deck to await being hoisted. Josue hauled himself aloft in the bosun's chair with a spare cable to set up a jury-rigged stay from the second spreaders. He made off two auxiliary lines that Esperance made off to the grinders. It was a strange-looking rig, but necessary if the mast were to bear the weight of the sails. While he was still up there, *Le Coeur de France* screamed by us, the wind dead aft. The Baron gave us a little salute, and then he seemed to shrug.

Josue came right down, and we finally got the jib up, but the blue boat was gone, at least fifteen boat lengths ahead. And the Perrier bottle was getting smaller and smaller.

Larry took a chance and ordered up our big spinnaker. We had twenty boat lengths to make up; in other words, the race. Now or never. He turned *Kinsman* off the wind. We filled away downwind. And when our sails caught the wind, I could actually feel a thrust. I could feel us accelerating.

The huge spinnaker was set out to starboard away from the main strain of the jury-rigged stay, and the big jib was winged out to port. The mast creaked horribly, the keel thumped, but our bow lifted and we planed on the crests. We flew. Because of the jury-rigged stays, though, we set the course for the low end of the finish line.

We caught *Le Coeur de France* less than a mile above the finish line. Her afterguard had seen our damage and realized we couldn't jibe for fear of losing our mast. So, she tried hard to make us. But no matter what the French boat did, we didn't.

Larry put us high to force them up, as if we wanted to pass her to weather. When she corkscrewed up to block us, he slipped under through her wind and shot by her. It was over for *Le Coeur de France.* By more than two boat lengths, we finished going away

When we crossed the finish line, we dropped our sails right away to save the mast. The French boat crossed the line just after us. Jean Ballon's head was down, and its crew didn't look at us, but Baron Biche gave us another little salute. I shrugged *It's not my fault,* as if I didn't understand what was happening, and I didn't. Neither did he. Up until today, his boat had proved itself to be slightly faster than ours.

In the end, our towline broke, and we had to sail into La Rochelle under our jib. It was early evening, the wind had almost died. And as we ghosted into the old port and dropped our jib a couple of hundred yards before we touched the dock, I could see Aunt Pearl and Elizaphan standing there. They regarded *Kinsman* with reverence.

Saint Pierre called. Was it true? He seemed to disbelieve the result. He congratulated me and the afterguard and crew. I didn't mention that we had accidentally developed a boat that could sail at great speeds in moderate-to-heavy weather. I hadn't decided when to tell them.

"Well, it's not over after all, is it?"

But it was. That night I got called downstairs to the telephone. The series between *Le Coeur de France* and *Kinsman* was officially over. The series would be halted at two to two. I called Larry and Marcus.

"What are they up to now?"

Marcus told me to get a signed, legal confirmation in the morning. Baron Biche had obtained a dispensation from the French Government designating Rwanda as challenger independent of France. We would sail under the Rwandan flag. The news could not have been better.

In the morning, Saint Pierre looked into it and called back. He had come away with a favorable impression. He thought they were legally hedging their bets: lawyers versus sailors. He congratulated me again. "You've won."

"We could have done it the right way."

"Be thankful for what you've got and get the hell out of France before they find out what hit them." Something very important was going on, and he knew it.

The next day, we hauled *Kinsman* out for shipping. We had stumbled upon a device that could put us ahead of any number of challengers when we met them in New Zealand. Or was this just a local joke, good only in the turbulent waters of the Bay of Biscay? We were all still worried that the keel might drop off when it fluctuated wildly in heavy weather. Marcus came up with a simple idea: Why not set each bolt head in a universal ring of ball bearings? Worth a try. We had time. He suggested replacing the existing bolts with twelve stainless steel three-quarter-inch bolts set in universal joints. They'd roll and grind with the weather, but they'd come nowhere near their breaking point.

In the morning, *Les Temps de Le Midi* had an article about our second victory. Should Hollywood consider making the movie, it might well be called *"Chariots of Fire* Meets *Amistad."* The other newspaper simply stated that Baron Biche had been humiliated by a tribe of Africans. That a spear had been thrown through the heart of France. Flowery, but France had (after all) won the World Cup in soccer.

July was ending. In less than four months, we would know what we had. The races would begin at Harauki Gulf off Auckland, the winner to meet New Zealand: The Defender of Record. The great ladies would gather there from America, Australia, England, Switzerland, Japan, Spain, and the official entry from Rwanda. Baron Biche would be on hand, too.

I felt we were ready to face the world. At least a little bit more of it.

Newport

There was nothing more to see out the oval window.

The Air France hostess had brought me six tiny bottles of Cognac and they were gone. Luckily, she hadn't asked me to drive that big gadget across the Atlantic. The air outside must have been fifty degrees below zero. I could have been a little too ecstatic. The trip to Africa had been a success.

I was traveling alone. I stood up and trundled down the aisle back to the pantry to round up more tiny bottles. There were pools of light the length of the cabin: people reading, sleeping, talking. Did any of them know where we are? Above the clouds, blowing fire? That there was no such thing as doing what we were doing? Being hurled through the night sky? It was impossible. I could not imagine it. I was being mailed in an envelope through the stratosphere. In the morning, New York. I stood in the aisle stretching. The cabin was dark, long. I was centered in the plane's night. It had quieted down. It was going to bed. It had closed for the night. But I found some tiny bottles, unfortunately they were Scotch. No matter.

I am oh, so drunk. Why the hell not? We've had a good run. And I need a break. My men are at peace. The boats are safe. Elizaphan is asleep at her brother's house in Rwanda. Sweet dreams. Newport, New York, Saint Pierre. Then, I'll pick you up and take you to New Zealand.

I kiss you goodnight . . . I miss you. How could I miss you so soon?

Do you remember? It was the blackest night ever. I had mosquito fever. In the middle of the universe, for a long time I lay there trembling and didn't know where I was. It didn't matter where, what planet. And with the shakes there was no clock. And anyway, time was nothing, not even place. Without knowing. It was too black to know whether I was alive, or if it was death itself.

I tried to listen for the lake water, but I heard nothing. It was black, without a moon. I was alone. I touched your arm. I jumped, remember? That was the first night you slept in the house by Lake Kivu. I lay shaking in the black beside you, in what I thought was the world. And staying in the black, you rode me the distance. You rode my fever away. You rode it to death. Without me ever knowing if there was time, only that it was black. And in the world again, I was smiling.

The women who came before you, Elizaphan, swept through my fever that night. All of them, through my cotillion school years: debutante girls, sisters of room- mates, pick-ups in Central Park, sleek women in great clothes at gallery openings, dirty girls with dusty muzzles, wounded survivors, friends-of-women-friends, swim- ming through nights at clubs when midnight became 6 am without anyone know- ing it, dancing and grinding, women with huge hair, predator eyes who could do anything except grasp an idea, bald women tattooed, drunks dopers nymphets, nocturnal lady paratroopers falling through the wee hours, nipple-brained bimbolets with splashy hair who did everything, who could suck the chrome off a doorknob, low esteem high esteem, sexual bisexual no sexual, zero to multiple, fast-food slow food gourmet food diner food, interior decorators, receptionists, heiresses, hookers, Israeli militants, smart girls whose sole ambition was to be thin, jammed into clubs slithering to wake-the-dead tempos, skiing through the grand slalom from midnight to six am. And whatever the club, whatever the night, with half-hearted desperation, I needed to harvest just one, to sleep the morning away.

Elizaphan. I want to tell you things I know. I don't know much, but I can tell you about wine, cheese, America, schools. And I can show you islands, streets, large beds, snow. I have had too many choices; you have had none. I want you to choose simple silk dresses in sweet-smelling stores where they play heavy metal music to buy to, fine shoes, lingerie, whatever you want. Room service.

Then, maybe you will talk to me about death, and very slowly tell me about a despair so sweeping that it seems global to you.

It will not be a fair exchange. Your three brothers were killed in massacres. We have skiing accidents. I have had too much of one and none of the other. You've had none of one and too much of the other. Together we will be whole.

Your breasts are not large but are pendulous in the nicest way. I have never asked you about your scar. It runs down you like a shadow. When I see you naked, it defies your beauty and fortifies it. It makes me want to cry out. It is more than a blemish. One day will you tell me?

If I want so many things for you, and if I want to give them to you and give you peace, I suppose then I must love you, Elizaphan Bleu.

I landed in the middle of a bright New York summer morning. In Green- wich Village, the trees were blooming along my block. I was still very much hung over when I got upstairs into my apartment. My cat was waiting for me on the fire escape. It greeted me, as if I'd just gone down the hall. I still didn't know his name. He was hungry. I opened a can of cat food. He didn't go near it. He stared at me until I'd explained myself. Then he ate. All my clothes were worn out. I dropped them off in a laundry bag down the street.

I didn't call Jocelyn. I fell on my bed and passed out for the rest of the day and night. In the morning, I picked up my laundry, had coffee and pastry at my favorite café, got my sky-blue Corvette out the garage and drove up to Newport. Aunt Pearl was waiting for me at Rondelay, and I stayed there.

There was a message waiting for me from Jocelyn Ortion. How had she known I was coming in? She always called me "You!" with an exclamation point. She announced that she was taking the train to Newport to stay at Aunt Pearl's, and the next day she did. I couldn't stop her.

It had been an amazing eighteen months. But, God, I needed a rest. I had parasites that had been living off me like bankers the entire time. The day after I got in, I stayed in bed until evening. I got a formal phone call from Uncle Rut. Would I care to see the *Yankee Doodle* syndicate's training camp? Ledges was only half-a-mile down the road from Rondelay. I walked over the next morning. I saw respect in his look.

"I hardly know what to say to you, Jib. On the one hand, I'm tickled pink that you're being so bodacious, and you've done something remarkable. And on the other hand, you've acted against our family's interests. You're an enemy of the people, buddy. The Cup belongs off that point yonder, and if you think beating France a couple of times means anything, you're crazy. You know very well you're not about to win the Cup for Nambia. On the other hand, what you're doing is simply interfering with our getting it back where it belongs. In other words, you're making it unpleasant for us to do our job. Plus, you'll be missing a good ride.

"Let me tell you what we've got here, and then maybe you can tell me if you're wasting Aunt Pearl's money." Having said that, he showed me around the *Yankee Doodle* compound.

He had set it up in his vast solarium. The crew lived at Ledges. Morning exercises were in progress. Gleaming chrome weights and black machines and their pulleys hung among a dozen large areca palms set in oriental urns. And that chrome was being thrust toward the ceiling by twenty men who looked twice as big as my Rwandans and did not appear to need any more exercise. Small slogans were taped to free-standing mirrors. They said things like, KICK ASS. A slogan that would have been redundant in my training camp, KILL KILL KILL. In fact, I had stopped *Kinsman's* training program until we got to New Zealand. For these five weeks, the men were back at home buying farm tools and working hard.

The dinner at Ledges was chilly. There were fireworks at the long table. Uncle Rut was at one end wearing his BRING BACK THE CUP necktie. Aunt Pearl, at the other, was wearing her best Rwanda kukui beads.

"America versus Nambia. That has a ring to it, Jib." Rut opened with that. I didn't correct him on the geography. "You're standing on your dick if you catch my drift."

I nodded.

"*Yankee Doodle* Syndicate has backing. We've got Pepsi Cola, Marlboro, Cadillac."

"You leased your sails to them?"

"The spinnakers are Pepsi's. Marlboro has the mains. Cadillac has the Genoas."

"Pepsi rots your teeth," I said. "Marlboros kill you, and you go to the cemetery in a Cadillac. Didn't J.P. Morgan say, 'If you need to advertise on your yacht you can't afford to own it.'" He would have wept.

"Then he never met Dennis Connor. Dennis taught us what counts. It's our sails. It's a business venture, Jib, like everything else."

"Well, next year there's going to be a lot of business down there. You'll never know until you send someone. Buy shares now."

"Where?"

"Rwanda."

"What's the bond?"

"The country."

"The country is on the opposite side of anything you'd care to name. If I can't find it on the map, why would I invest in it?"

"Because there's going to be a big market for their products."

"When they win the Cup?"

"Yeah, when they win the Cup. Franchises for hotels, car plants, all computer technology, fast food, coffee, tea. It's an investment like anything else. Better get a head start."

I already knew when I came here yesterday that Uncle Rut would be telling me I was acting like a fool. I knew that he would call me a mutineer. It was why I came. To face it. We were distinctly different breeds.

It was a small discovery to know that by simply changing my attitude I had changed my life. That I believed I was on the right side of something. I felt older. I looked older. Everyone said so. It was the rush of doing something important that I had been assured was impossible.

But it had been tiring being with Uncle Rut.

The talk at dinner had begun quietly enough. Soapy Armstrong was there. The syndicate skipper had been a Princeton halfback. When a journalist called him "Soapy," he had named him for life. Soapy was telling the story of how Beaky Johnstone, an old college pal of Rut's, had died in a burst of glass. Beaky had been a wine connoisseur. He was killed in his wine cellar by an exploding bottle of Champagne. I must have been very tired. The event grabbed me by the throat. The idea of a betrayed wine connoisseur being destroyed by his hobby. I started to laugh and couldn't stop. Poor taste. That did it. Soapy hated me.

Of course, he knew about our two victories over *Le Coeur de France*, and he couldn't figure out how we'd beaten them twice. Once, maybe. But the second time, going away. The French sails and technology far exceeded ours, and yet it seemed for the last two races that we were the better boat. I told him we would have won the fifth race too, if they hadn't chickened out. That by cutting off the series at two to two, Baron Biche had made a smart decision. It was clear statement that he had had enough of us. We would have gone on and won the fifth and the sixth, but nobody wanted to see that happening. He had too much at stake to risk everything on bad luck, gear accident, or fluky winds. I told Soapy we would have beaten him by five minutes if the wind was up. He stared at me as if I'd emptied the gravy boat on my head.

"All you have is primitive technology," he said.

"Like Rwanda," I said. I told him we were using a beautiful recycled hull, the best boat from the last Cup races.

Soapy said I wasn't telling him everything.

Aunt Pearl had been there for the last two races, and she said it was true. "*Kinsman* simply beat *Le Coeur de France* in fair sailing. We all saw it. Everyone."

It all caught up to me. What was the point of convincing them? Anyway, I was really tired. Suddenly I got up and went outside and sat on the wide balustrade just in time to watch the moon rise behind a giant elm that was as old as the estate. It all seemed meaningless to me. In a few minutes, Aunt Pearl joined me. She said there would be fireworks down the hill in Newport.

She asked me about Elizaphan. I told her I might be in love with her. She approved of Elizaphan in my life. A person's nature constantly shows itself in small ways and if you happen to be very rich, as Aunt Pearl was, generosity means nothing and to be snobbish is routine.

But she had always found better ways to be generous and kind. I hadn't been gone long enough for my image of Elizaphan to fade. I had no photograph of her, of course, only her presence in my mind, and that would have to do for the time being.

The fireworks came and went. Suddenly Jocelyn was there, standing on the wide terrace. She was wearing an excellent black dress that shimmered. Her shoulders were bare. She'd been driven over from the station by Aunt Pearl's chauffeur. She had heard that I had had various fevers. She put my touchy behavior down to delirium, mosquito fever. She had invited herself to Rondelay for the weekend to see for herself. Aunt Pearl excused herself with a yawn. I told Jocelyn that I wasn't married to Elizaphan, that I just said it to shock her, and that it was only part of my delirium.

Jocelyn was waiting to be claimed. I couldn't stop her. She had wolf eyes. She wore simple jewelry and always smelled of sensual perfume. She was waiting offstage to go on, to be dreadfully married. A husband was an emblem. It would never matter what he thought as long as he was safe, clean, presentable.

And rich. It wasn't that she worshipped money. She had always had it. It was that she would die without it. Living only for a few minutes, like a beautiful trout on a table.

"You can't imagine what that did to me, You!" Jocelyn said. "Married to that half-breed mulatto. Were you trying to crucify me?"

"If that was what it would take to get you off the African continent."

I told her that I would be going back to Rwanda to bring Elizaphan to New Zealand. She stared at me as if I was a bug. I went to bed.

Monday I met with Saint Pierre in New York and brought him up to date. Tuesday night he flew to New Zealand to lease office space and locate docking on Hauraki Gulf. We couldn't have *Kinsman* and *Bujumbura* arriving there with no place to dock them.

I had told Marcus Cape to stay in La Rochelle and to babysit *Kinsman* and *Bujumbura*. He called late that night. The next day the boats would be loaded on the *Jacob W. Balliet* out of Marseilles bound for Auckland. He would board the ship the following night to see them safely through to Auckland.

Before I had left La Rochelle, I told Larry Bayard to take the crew back down to Rwanda and to keep an eye on them until the end of the month. They had been living on a steady income for eighteen months. Many had bought goats; some, a cow. They lived in cement houses. They had bought land for farming. I'd fly with them to Auckland after we found our facilities there.

Nothing was ever boring now. I was held by the anticipation of what might happen. Four months away. I could feel it, and nothing could touch me. Whatever they said was harmless. I was six years old looking forward to Christmas. Nothing could ever disturb that, and nothing would ever disturb this.

My crew was made up of thirty men who now loved life and who last year had been obsessed with death. That night as I went to sleep, *Kinsman* was being lashed on the deck of the *Jacob W. Balliet*. Red as ever. Its great secret kept hidden, ready to cross the black ocean to New Zealand. I could feel October waiting for me.

⚑

My Crew

My crew. I flew back to Rwanda to pick them up. Elizaphan met me at the airport. We drove to Le Beau Sejour Hotel in Kigali. The morning of the second day I called Larry and the two bishops, and we got the crew down to the old compound with their families for a cookout. Elizaphan and I stayed in our old house. That night, the eerie silence of Rwanda came back to me again. There were no dogs. Elizaphan said that they had all been shot by the UN, because they were eating bodies.

My crew. Their world had been reduced to a single sailboat, and they were thriving on it. Little by little, they had expanded. Eighteen months ago, they entered an imaginary life. And then last summer, we crossed three thousand miles of Africa to the Ivory Coast on the Atlantic Ocean, their first flight. Their gradual emergence from the life that had held them in psychotic quarantine was visible to me. Then came the flight to La Rochelle near Bordeaux, where the world became entirely white for them for the first time; when they became aware of the other world, wider and faster and much richer; where everyone had anything they wanted and almost never killed for it. Then came their first triumph, facing the French, the stand-off with the French boat that brought them merging merging merging into the rest of the world. They had grown cool as metal cools, cooling after the fire.

When it was certain we knew they were going to New Zealand, I took them to a store in Bordeaux, where I bought them suits. To a man, they chose shiny black jackets that looked metallic. Fireproof suits for the carnival in Auckland and then the endless flight to New Zealand to meet the world in their new jackets and trousers. The flight was so long that after the first three hours Ba'ale, then Esperance, came over to look at my face and the expression on it to see if I was frightened.

None of them had watches; not all of them could tell time. Esperance explained to them that it would be another day before we landed.

When Moses asked him, "But where are we?" He looked out the window at thirty-five thousand feet and saw the frosty half-moon. It was an excellent question. Esperance told him it would be best not to think about it. This was their third flight, and the flights were not getting better.

We had the first six rows in coach class. Elizaphan and I slept in the back row. Suddenly, there was a movie in front of them. *Trixie*. The idea that there was a moving picture show at one end of the long room compounded their fears. They watched it stunned. Some sat on the floor in the aisle. As far as I could tell without a headset, *Trixie* was the story of a Mafia hit man who finds a puppy who causes them trouble, including the guy's own timely death. Apparently, this adorable pooch caused the hit man to mend his ways too late, and he is gunned down by another Mafia hit man in the act of performing a good deed. The irony flew by the men. The crew had problems with the storyline, and I refused to explain it. Where they came from, hit men were not funny.

They no longer thought I was trying to kill them, which was nice. But they still regarded me with caution. We never embraced or touched. It was a combination of love and fear. Why not? They'd never put their pasts behind them no matter how many pretty flags fluttered over their heads. No matter how they prospered, they'd always be subjects of their pasts, the way I was the subject of mine. Except that my past was a car crash that smelled of college beer and theirs was watching their mother gang raped, then decapitated by several men with machetes.

Sometimes I prayed. It was a new thing for me. God's available to anyone. I didn't need to choose a club. I never liked the arrogance of clubs like Jews, Catholics, Muslims, Episcopalians. I liked to meet God on the sidewalk outside the office, and I knew he didn't know me from Adam. I was always careful never to ask for any personal favors.

It was times like this that I found it ideal for prayer; times when I felt that I may have walked too far and had become tangled in the thickets walking up an incline where there was nothing ahead of me but sky. I only wanted to tell Him that I believed He might be interested in our syndicate and maybe shed some light on it. I mean, He didn't seem to mind massacres. I said to Him, "Fine, give massacres a chance. Maybe massacres are what we need to kill off the ones you can't get along with. There'd always be plenty of those people, so massacre away. Get it out of their systems." But I reminded God that we could be onto something good here with *Kinsman* and the men who sailed her, the blood rivals.

And so, while I was walking through that thicket up that incline, I prayed. I didn't kneel or bow my head. I didn't think He really cared about that. He knew who He was. I knew who I was. I didn't look up to the clouds. What would He be doing in the clouds? I looked across, around me and I said, "God. These are good men. These are Tutsis and Hutus who have hated each other for so many years that they have almost forgotten why. This is what we're doing here. I can't think of any men on earth who have been through what you've put them through, God. Or any men on earth I'd rather be with. It's true. They never quarrel. They've had enough. They get along with each other, sailing that beautiful red boat Aunt Pearl gave them, in those silly races that can change their lives forever and the life of their country. So, look at us, God. Damn You, look at us, God."

Auckland

When we landed in Auckland, the world became blonder than ever before. Hauraki Gulf was stunning, full of distant islands, brisk winds roaring forties. It was a wild looking place. Great sailing.

"We shall beat the fleet hollow down here," Esperance said looking out over the gulf.

"No problem," Ba'ale said, repeating something he had heard from a flight attendant.

Auckland was too big. It wasn't by American standards, of course. It had less than a million people. It was never set up for the America's Cup. No seafront city was. Why would waterfront real estate be available? Imagine Rio de Janeiro. New York. Auckland was no different. Islands in sight of the city. The huge Hauraki Gulf.

So, the teams and yachts from nine countries had landed and were scrambling for their building quarters and offices, installing cranes big enough to haul out the Twelves, building sheds long enough to repair their hundred-and-five-foot masts, and establishing sail lofts where their sails could be laid flat and altered or repaired.

When Saint Pierre and his contractor had come down the month before, he had bad luck leasing waterfront real estate. He saw that prices had jumped out the window. He even tried to buy land on a buy-back, but could not. And so, he leased a hundred-foot car barge, mounted a crane onto it, and had it towed to Waiheke Island just off Auckland to serve as our dock. We had a hundred-eighty feet of frontage and a long shed for repairs. The crew slept in hammocks in a defunct yacht club, and every time we needed anything in town we took a thirty-minute ferryboat ride. We got a room at a guest house within walking distance of our compound. Mrs. Prosser's Guest House.

There was not a hell of a lot on Waiheke Island (which was good), except a few stores and the Mosquito Café, along with a few hundred sheep. We were a dozen miles from the starting line, farther than any other team who had set up their camps scattered west of Auckland, along the docks past the Westhaven Boat Harbour, living in hotels and guesthouses. But I'm glad we were there away from the city. And for all that had happened up until then, I definitely owed the world, from the seat of my blue-booked butt. And so did everyone on those yachts, except my crew.

My crew! Lord, they had it all. They were not a yachty bunch. I didn't lavish money on them. They were not outgoing. They didn't speak any known language. They reminded people of another world that had nothing to do with the fraternity of yachting. They were simply not part of it.

Most of the crew didn't know where they were, and that was okay. When I'd taken them to the Ivory Coast, there were rumors that their relatives would never see them again, that I was going to sell them as slaves. I told the rumorers that we'd been exercising for eighteen months to get them in shape. The rumorers had answered, "Exactly. Who would want to buy a weak slave?"

The *Kinsman*'s crew was a curious breed, so completely different from the other crews that it was dumb luck they ended up there at all. These men came from a country where the inconceivable occurred to them on a daily basis. Imagine if someone in Middletown had been murdered; not just murdered, but hacked to death the way you hack limbs off a chicken. Then, imagine one million people being hacked to death like chickens. Imagine surviving that during the hot summer months and being maybe the only person in your family who did. My crew was disturbed, and the best place for them was to be among themselves playing their music singing, sailing, eating together. While they regained trust and stability, they still suspected the outside world. The French flag still meant death. They could never forget the past, but they could make the present a better place. And if I could make them understand the rewards of what we were trying to do, they might understand the future.

They were from so far below what we called "the poverty line" that they didn't even know there is one. They could not even grasp the idea of winning a sailboat race, but that was alright. They had true mettle, natural sportsmanship, and perseverance. And on top of that, each man weighed fifty pounds less than a crewman of any other boat. They were as lean as cheetahs with muscles slapped on them out of my Jane Fonda exercise manual. They were proud of their muscles. No one else in Rwanda had cute muscles. The men there were strong without looking it.

We needed to know *Kinsman*'s boatspeed in the Gulf to know for sure if the magic was still with us in those waters. Whether it was really there or not. It was. Every knot of it. We tested *Kinsman* and *Bujumbura* a long way from the harbor. Never to betray our true speed. So, we went down the coast. We asked our follow-boat to check our tachometer readings, and off we sailed on a broad reach. Larry Bayard crammed on the big genoa and tipped her down way off the wind, sails out, and we planed beautifully, sailing over the water, not through it,. So, hull speed hardly meant anything. We hit a solid, sweet eighteen knots, and the follow-boat registered the same. So that's more than enough. We were a true, heavy weather boat. We needed this weather. We couldn't do it on calm days. But when the wind was up (and it was usually on Harauki Gulf), we were in the awkward position of having to sail badly. When it was blowing and we were among the other boats, we towed a sea anchor.

The Odds

The press corps had pretty much shied away from us. The blood had dried. Once we'd been their favorite sports phenomenon, a human interest story, but no longer. For a while, we'd been a Cinderella story. Poor old Cinderella. She'd taken on a few too many identities. She'd been boxers, football players, hockey teams, and now we were the strangest Cinderella of all: a tall sloop with a red hull, sailed by small, black men from the central jungles and highlands of Africa and the Nile Valley. It didn't get any better than that. A black Cinderella.

But it must have caught up to us. Not pretty enough for a Cinderella, nor a white hope, and not even a dark horse. The press had made a special niche for us and forgotten where it was. Aside for some colorful rags-to-riches-back-to-rags stories, there just wasn't anything more they felt like saying about us. Which was good. But we still had by far the blackest crew, the oldest boat, the smallest team, and we remained the poorest. Curious, maybe, but we were not going to win anything. End of story.

The other teams were less heartwarming. They were run by directors, officers, surrounded by designers, technical experts, physical trainers, legal departments, technologists, financial experts, fund-raisers, and catering crews.

We did have Saint Pierre, who set up an office in Auckland for himself and Aunt Pearl, along with a staff of four who looked after spending and acquiring and financing repairs. They also looked after disease control, medical checkups. I looked after team morale.

An Australian reporter named Ryan Somebody came over on the ferry to Waiheke Island and met me at the Mosquito Café to ask a few questions about *Kinsman*. He ordered coffee and quince pie.

"Why do you call your boat *Kinsman*?"

"Because we're kin."

"Meaning?"

"Blood relation."

"But you're white."

I didn't bother.

"It's incredible for me to believe that you're takin' yourself so seriously to say anything," he said. "You know you don't have a tinker's chance." He told me that it was common knowledge that our challenge was perceived as little more than a PR coup by Rwanda to force itself onto the map of the world.

If Ryan ever found out about our floppy keel and what we could do in weather, that we may have developed a rocket, I'd be forced to kill him before he could snap open his cell phone to call in the story. It would be one of those unfortunate drownings that are so frequent in the treacherous waters off our docks. He would have been swimming with me below *Kinsman*'s hull on an inspection tour of our boat. One thinks of everything when one lies down to go to sleep. And any syndicate could copy our keel in twenty-four hours.

Only three knew our secret. Marcus, Larry, and me. The crew sort of knew something was going on. I had hinted to Saint Pierre and Aunt Pearl that we had made some small breakthrough. But I thought it would be best to save it as a surprise.

Ryan went on, "Aren't you taking yourself a little bit too seriously, mate?"

"Yes, I am, mate." I told him that in my homeland the press doesn't allow creative people to be seen taking themselves seriously, that you must be amused by yourself. The press loves you for that, even though it's a lie. But, then, the press is mostly made up of junkyard dogs. Ryan winced.

"Do you happen to know what your going odds are at the betting shops in Las Vegas?" Ryan said.

I told him no, but I did.

"Ten thousand to one," he smiled. To his credit, he didn't poke me in the ribs. "They don't have confidence."

"I do. You ought to put a hundred on us, Ryan. That's a million payback right there, minus your booking fee," I said. "We're going all the way."

"All the way back to Africa." He stuck me with the check. International press etiquette.

I hadn't mentioned it to him, but every day I'd been laying a few dollars on *Kinsman* under various names of the crewmen. I didn't have to put a hell of a lot down to set each one of my men up for life as millionaires.

Ryan wrote a mean, little piece for some Australian fishwrapper, *The Gazette*, calling me Lawrence of Rwanda. "He resembles the noble white man who brought the warring Arab tribes together." Luckily, no one read the article, except Marcus who addressed me as Lawrence of Rwanda until I pushed him off the dock.

The surprise came at the Royal Auckland Yacht Squadron's formal gathering to announce the pairings for the opening race. In the first series, every country would meet every country:

Sweden versus France

Australia versus Japan
Great Britain bye
Spain versus Switzerland
USA versus Rwanda

USA versus Rwanda? Uncle Rut's *Yankee Doodle* versus Jib Routledge's *Kinsman*. It didn't look good. USA was the favorite, and we couldn't be seen beating the favorite in the opening race. We discussed it, Marcus, Larry and I. And we decided we had to give it to them. Throw the race. Make it seem easy for them. Hide our power for as long as we could. No rumors. Save our best for last. Weather permitting, we could take any challenger in the fleet. So, we bet on the weather and decided on a risky plan. Instead of going ahead four-zip, we'd lose the opener, then squeak through the preliminary races and be around for the finals. This would keep the odds as high as possible against us.

What lay ahead of us was a ten-week-long challenger series of races. The quarter-finals would narrow the fleet to four boats; the semi-finals would leave two boats; the final, the best-of-seven-races that would decide which boat would win the Vuitton Cup and go on to meet the New Zealand defender, *Black Lion*. No one knew anything about *Black Lion* except that she was entirely black and very fast.

"Wind's up tomorrow," Larry said.

"The meteorologist says twenty plus."

"We'll have to tow a bucket."

So, the night before the first race we needed to devise a way we could drop a few seconds every mile to avoid the powerful surge that *Kinsman* developed every time she came off a ten-foot sea in a strong wind. What we devised that night was so simple that it was funny. We'd rig a line leading aft towing a sea anchor. A heavy-duty, Dacron sea anchor that opened like an umbrella and could nullify our boatspeed. It would trail us on a long line and stay deep. But we needed to test it before we met *Yankee Doodle*. It could be a disaster. It could stop us dead or do nothing.

So, the day of the race we got towed out early to the mouth of the gulf. The sea anchor worked. You couldn't see it, and it nullified our hullspeed on all points. It took a couple of knots off and, with poor trimming or a bad choice of sail, we'd be able to foot with *Yankee Doodle* and make it look close, that we were never quite able to grab the lead from her. Able to stay with her, not overtake her, but always on the verge of pulling ahead. We could round eight marks this way, nipping at *Yankee Doodle*'s heels like a terrier on a long chain and making her look very, very good. We came in to our dock around ten, ready to race. I wasn't going to lay any money on us this time out.

⚐

Yankee Doodle

What a day. This was it. *Yankee Doodle* dropped her towline, got her sails up, and bore off the wind. She looked phenomenal. Very white and very fast. She had it all. Technology out the wazoo. Masthead to boom video cameras, fluid dynamic computers, radical sails, twin rudders, airfoil stern. We might not need to throw this one.

There was no turning back now. There never was. A dream doesn't work that way. A dream goes on until you feel yourself falling. Then you wake up. The world owed me nothing. I owed the world. I never realized just how much until that first morning when Moses tossed a tugboat bowline around our bollard, and I felt the towline stiffen and yank, hauling *Kinsman* out to the starting line of the twenty-four-mile course for the first elimination race. You couldn't disturb my dream. It was a safe place to be. Nothing could go wrong during my anticipation. It was never boring. I carried it with me everywhere I went. Dreams. What can I tell you? The most protected species of mood on earth. I could not fail during one. I could not be rejected. I slept chained to that dream, and the excitement I felt could not be improved upon. But also there was fear in it. What if it ended too soon? Our secret was waiting to be revealed.

That first morning, the wind was up, and eight boats were being towed out through a harbor full of spectator boats. These elegant ladies dressed in their sails. You couldn't cross an ocean in one. They depended on the fine tuning of a violin, or they'd snap in two under pressure.

As we were being towed, hundreds of lesser boats caught up. Knockabouts, powerboats, stinkpots, fishing boats, yawls, sloops. All churning the waters around us, jockeying for a better glimpse of us. Bright red boat, plain topsides, small black crew. All the fleet's mainsails were raised and luffing. Waiting for various starts on various courses. The graceful yellow Spanish boat *El Matador*, the immaculate white Swiss boat *Saint Yves*, the slim-hipped Australian boat with its rainbow-colored hull, Uncle Routledge's white *Yankee Doodle* with its sharp clipper bow, the pale blue Swedish boat with its clean spoon bow, and our own *Kinsman* with her alizarin red hull, the fairest of the fair.

I felt a whoosh of pride that I knew would come back to me years later, and always would at the strangest times, and it would never feel bad. No matter what came next, it would never feel bad. And that vision I had then of the flamboyant beauty of raised sails surrounding us, raised to the sky, would always be there close to me. Just as to my crew the vision of screaming red-wet massacres would always be there close to them.

The wind was up and steady, our weather. It was up to twenty-five knots and blowing the tops off the waves. Our weather. Rough, full of brief rain squalls. Still, if it didn't let up, the committee boat would call the races off.

We needed to get the sea anchor over the side. We were now on view from the spectator fleet of small boats. Larry sailed us toward the mouth of the Gulf and slowly tacked, turning the length of our topsides away from the crowd. Esperance slipped it over the side. The Dacron submerged slowly; we watched it open slightly.

The race started on time at ten minutes to twelve with a quick horn and a red sock raised on the mast spreader of *Lady Anne*, the committee boat. The ten-minute gun. The pre-start ritual quickly developed into a complex frenzy of circling maneuvers to jockey for position. Soapy Armstrong must have heard from the French that our crew was not as quick on tacking and jibing, and so that's what he gave us for the pre-start. I could feel the sea anchor slowing us.

At the gun, *Yankee Doodle* had already given us a pounding. She crossed well ahead of us. We were already looking bad.

It was wet on the upwind leg and, as if we were trying our hardest, we clung to them with the bucket under tow giving them a lead. When we converged at the first mark, they were a solid ten seconds ahead

Winning was easy. Once we started to do it, losing was hard. And in this weather, losing had become a problem. It was tough to sail on the losing boat. If we hadn't been towing that bucket, we would have knocked out *Yankee Doodle* right down to her gudgeons and trunnions.

The wind was up to twenty-five knots with a rolling sea.

Larry was over-steering to slow us down, but you never move faster on a Twelve than you do with all sails set, running before the wind, spinnaker rising, lifting your bow, surfing, the seas bouncing us around. We couldn't help making up lost time on the downwind legs. We were straining our bucket. The line was taut as the top string on a violin, and I could sense its pull churning deep under our wake; its towline rigid, running under the hull. I could feel our keel switching back and forth in the under-swell, moving through the turbulence like a shark's fin, still trying to propel us. We were in our best weather and, even towing a sea anchor and with our small spinnaker set, we'd crept up and were threatening *Yankee Doodle*'s lead again.

Now, *Kinsman* was nearly even with them. We were catching them from behind on the final leg, knocking the wind out of their five thousand-foot spinnaker. Both of us were on port tack, and it was a crucial time for them. Then *Yankee Doodle* caught her wind back, and her spinnaker bellied out. They had us, passing us close. Finally. Regardless of the weather, crewmen whisper at close quarters. She was about to take the lead, fair and square.

As she pulled ahead, I could feel the smugness blowing upwind. I lay staring at her Pepsi Cola bottle marring the horizon and wanted to pull ahead of her, if only to get rid of that vision. And maybe, to disrupt the gentlemanly smugness of her crew, put the ad campaign behind us, and get back to true sailing.

I lay flat, feeling our suppressed power. Moses and Mungo shifted our spinnaker pole that extended thirty-five feet from the mast and held the spinnaker guy out over the water. The running backstays were taut and humming. We were now two boat lengths behind *Yankee Doodle*. It had looked close.

We were riding in her wake safely behind when I felt a minor jolt. Larry and I noticed it at the same moment. Was it the keel? Had we struck something? Esperance crawled forward to check the bow. Suddenly, we were surging ahead, leaping forward like an impala. In a moment of snappy contemplation, I figured out what had happened. The trailing line was slack.

"We lost the fucking bucket," I yelled to Larry. Maybe the line had parted, or maybe the sea anchor had split. Whatever it was, we were walking right up to *Yankee Doodle* and in a few seconds we'd blow past her going away. And there was the committee boat two miles ahead, the bright orange buoy at the pin end of the finish line, and the entire spectator fleet. We were in full view. With this rattling burst of speed, we'd finish a dozen boat lengths ahead of *Yankee Doodle* and even a moron would see that there was something weird about it, that we couldn't suddenly flat out whip the American boat's ass after eighteen miles of tense boat-for-boat racing. And, of course, the experts would try to explain our sudden reserve rocket of speed; it was supernatural. They'd get to the bottom of it.

There'd be no stopping us now. Larry couldn't slow us down. He ordered our spinnaker jibed, a maneuver that would put us on starboard tack. It took me ten thoughtful seconds to come up with a plan. I whispered "man overboard" to Larry and crawled toward the lee rail. And as I rolled off, just before I plunged into a trough between a pair of breaking seas, I detonated my life belt. The boat was flying away from me. I felt very much alone.

"Man overboard!" Larry yelled. He rounded *Kinsman* up into the wind. "Douse the spinnaker!"

Leopold and a couple of sheetmen pointed wildly at my bobbing head lost from sight between the crests of breaking waves and by the time Larry could call a jibe, he was downwind of me and the men had hauled in the pole and lowered it and flattened the main. *Yankee Doodle* was long gone, and we had effectively lost the race. Which is, of course, what we wanted. I heard the gun and a cheer for *Yankee Doodle*. We lost by fifty-five seconds.

After the race, we were told to come to the Royal Auckland Yacht Club. It was out of our way, because our dock was on Harauki Island. But it was the custom for all the skippers of the yachts to sit at a long table with bottles of water and face a bank of lights and field reporters' questions.

All the wire services were there, along with newspapers and magazines from each country represented by a challenger. This was the first time we were exposed internationally. The questions to Larry Bayard were not demanding; there was sympathy in them. He'd tried; he'd been thrashed. Our days were limited in Auckland. There were rivalries between America and almost any country you could name, but there was no known rivalry between the United States and Rwanda. Not many people knew it then, but the United States had overlooked the genocide in Rwanda. Our State Department had redefined the word. Soapy Armstrong looked like a mail-order catalogue yachtsman; Larry was born on the Ivory Coast and a Hutu. He looked like the sort of person you did not want to anger. So, when he was asked about *Kinsman*'s two victories over *Le Coeur de France* in La Rochelle, "How can you explain this miracle?" the reporter from France was expecting the sort of humility from Larry that media people so admire and expect from tamed blacks who have entered a white world.

Larry shrugged, "Why not? We'll beat them again here."

Jean Ballon, the French skipper turned and raked Larry with a French glare. But it was the look of a clown, because Ballon still had zinc ointment on his lips and nose.

Such ego, *mon dieu*, the French reporter did not expect it. He pressed Larry as to why *Le Coeur de France* broke off the series in La Rochelle. Larry said "quit" was a better word than "broke off." He glanced at Baron Biche, who was staring straight ahead, nose high.

Ballon leaned into his microphone. "It would make no sense to decide an elimination race in La Rochelle where conditions were radically different from conditions in New Zealand." Meaning that to lose in light air and smooth seas suggested that you might better be able to win in strong wind and heavy seas. True. But the French had clearly seen the end and had been afraid of losing the pivotal race to Rwanda.

The focus was still on Larry Bayard, not Jean Ballon.

"Mr. Bayard, then you must feel that your boat and crew are better than the French?" *The New York Times.*

"Of course," Larry nodded. "We're the better boat." It was too daring, but Larry was tired and getting angry.

131

"Are you better than the American boat, too?" a drooling Australian reporter asked Larry. He was goading him.

"I think we are," Larry said simply. "But not today."

It was a loaded answer. He was saying, "You can expect more from the Rwandan boat before the series is over. But *Kinsman* was meant to lose. Everyone knew it. Why couldn't they just lose quietly and go away?" After a pause and when it seemed like there were no more questions to ask Larry (after all, this had been a predictable race between top dog and underdog), a reporter who had just entered the room raised his hand.

"Monsieur Bayard, if you please?" A French accent, a smoker's husky rasp.

"Yes?"

"Monsieur Bayard. On the final downwind leg when we all thought you had been beaten, suddenly your boat jumped forward and you caught up with the American. But at the instant you were about to pass them, your alternate helmsman jumped overboard, no? I must ask why."

"He did not jump overboard, sir."

"I contend that he did. I have just seen a videotape taken from a press helicopter. The gentleman made definitely a leap into the water. Perhaps you could explain."

Larry Bayard made a croaking sound, something like a laugh, but I wasn't convinced.

"Whoever you are, you have a weird sense of humor."

"Claude la Luc, *Paris Match*. I firmly disagree."

"If he did as you say, a moronic thing, and jumped overboard, he cost us the race."

"Exactly."

"Why would he do that?"

"Perhaps because he is related to Laurence Routledge? The owner of the *Yankee Doodle* syndicate? They are both named Routledge you see. Perhaps it was because your Mister Routledge did not want to embarrass his uncle?"

Larry Bayard put his head down on the table. When he brought it up, he scanned the reporters for another question. But there was none, and so he returned to Claude la Luc from *Paris Match*. He pushed his chair back from the table. He was still wearing his red jersey with the lone word KINSMAN in bold black letters. He stared through the light's haze to where the reporter was sitting.

"Do I remember you from La Rochelle?"

He could not clearly see Claude La Luc, a smallish personage in a dark blazer and black hair combed flat. It was a woman, but Larry couldn't see that.

"Weren't you the reporter who called us African bushmen?"

La Luc stared straight ahead.

"Whose only talent was to kill?" Larry Bayard half rose. His dark face and arms had been further darkened by the sun's weather. He was stiff with salt. "Yes or no?"

La Luc nodded "yes."

"Get out."

"It is not your right to tell me so."

Larry got up and walked out of the room. He had made a few friends as an underdog black with attitude. A few reporters had their lead sentence.

On the darker side, for the next day the meteorologist predicted a fluky warm front, light airs. Not our first choice. We were down one race. In race two, we'd be facing the yellow boat from Spain, *El Matador*. If we lost to them, the pressure would be on us. We'd need to win both the next races against France and Sweden to advance to the semi-finals. Or be eliminated. We might have done something really dumb that first day.

Spain

Race two. A rare calm day. I knew in bed before I got up. The wind was staying away. A racing death for us. It would be a drifting match. Would it be called off for lack of wind? No. The yellow boat with the red stripe took us for all we had. We were left standing in dead air in a millpond somewhere east of Kansas. And by the time we finally strayed over the finish line, *El Matador* was tied off to her dock, hosed down, sails stowed, lines made up. We were down mentally. Another flat day and we'd lose our challenge.

The day following our loss to *El Matador,* we took our lay day, because we were waiting for a cold front to come in with true wind and good seas: *Kinsman's* weather.

We had to face *Saint Yves* the next day. The Swiss boat was also known as the *White Feather,* because it only took a breath of air to move her over the bottom. She had been built for the light airs of Lake Geneva or somewhere, underestimating the New Zealand winds. Our confidence in the governing winds called the "roaring forties" had backfired. The Swiss turned out to be right, at least for that week. A warm front had come in and sat down, and the sea was like Lake Placid, New York. *Kinsman's* advance to the quarter finals was meant to look mysterious to outsiders, but this was getting too mysterious. And now we'd probably face the Swiss boat in light air, and that would be it. We wouldn't advance to the quarter finals. We had to get by the Swiss boat.

Dumber than a box of rocks. We felt like complete idiots. We'd thrown a race knowing that we could beat the next challengers, *El Matador* and *Saint Yves*; however, a notoriously slow boat beat us, because the weather was so calm that even the oldest locals didn't remember a day without a breath of air in the Hauraki Gulf. But we'd remember it, wouldn't we?

Once again we were on familiar ground: down zero to two. Facing extinction. We knew – Larry, Marcus, and I – that if the warm front didn't dissolve and give us back the trade winds, we'd be going home.

I hadn't entirely given up on prayer. I took another shot at it. I hated to make a fool of myself. I mean, after a while it sounds like begging, especially since the Almighty did come through in La Rochelle when he put that big rock in front of our keel, and we sailed the French to a draw. So I was waiting for another miracle. Or, as Aunt Pearl had put it so well, I was waiting for something unimaginable to shift.

I didn't like the odds. The weather wasn't supposed to change back to normal until Wednesday, and it was only Monday. So, it looked like we'd have to race the *White Feather* in a zephyr. The earliest long range forecast I could get from the meteorologist was that it would be sunny, cool and that the wind might get up to ten knots by Wednesday. I smelled elimination. *Kinsman* was not designed for drifting matches.

We'd already burnt our lay day waiting for this imaginary cold front to settle in and the weather to change, but maybe we were just postponing the moment of defeat. The Swiss crew was probably washing everything in sight, practicing starts, tuning stays, repairing, but we just took the day off. Elizaphan and I slept late and ate well.

⚑

Ace Gordon

That afternoon Ace Gordon suddenly materialized at our camp. I had never met him. The New Zealand skipper of *Black Lion* was a local legend with an Olympic gold in Dragon Class, and as far as I could make out, a truly upstanding fellow with no axe. He'd taken the thirty-minute ferryboat ride alone over to our Waiheke Island camp and called me from the Mosquito Café and walked over. He's my height, but handsome, square-headed, square-shouldered, square-jawed, a shock of white blond hair and, of course, he talked funny like the rest of them do down there.

When we shook hands, he told me he wasn't worried about our chances. Of course he wasn't worried. How could he be worried? He knew we wouldn't be guests in his country after this week. He said he simply wanted to meet the boys and see what we were made of. Not one of my cousins from *Yankee Doodle* had been able to break away. The crews kept isolated from each other, and the island made us even more isolated, but Gordon had taken the trouble to come over on his own as an act of good will to say that his country welcomed us and to congratulate us on getting as far as we had. "Staggering as far as we had," I corrected him. He liked our style. I think he realized what a huge effort it must have been for us to get to Auckland. Some people were still calling our crew "bushmen" or "Pygmies," he said.

In reality, Ace Gordon had come to say goodbye to us. So, the crew took a break and shook his hand. He greeted the men one at a time, saying "Well done!" to each of them, royally, much the same as Aunt Pearl had done. When he got to Moses, one of our two crew chiefs and captain of the foredeck, who spoke fair English, Moses looked up at his face and said to him, "It is of great pleasure to meet you Mister Ace Gordon. I really, really look forward to meeting you again in the finals."

Which, of course, was absurd. Gordon had not come here to wish us good luck in the finals. He had come to bid us farewell. But still holding his hand, he smiled a champion smile and said as sincerely as he could, "I'm sure we will meet each other in the finals, Moses."

"And at that meeting, Mister Ace Gordon, we will best your ass."

Gordon was dismasted. He burst out laughing. "I expect you will try, Moses," he said. "And it's 'beat my ass,' not 'best my ass.'" He looked over at me, and I could see that he was truly impressed with our spirit. "That's real gameness," he said to me.

He couldn't get over it. It was Moses, after all, who had renamed the *Black Lion*, the *Black Goat*, but he didn't tell Ace Gordon that when he looked down upon the Hutu warrior and put his arm around his shoulder and squeezed. He couldn't have known this was a forceful act of hostility in Rwanda. Ace Gordon would recall this pleasant exchange many times, especially at night during the finals when he was trying to fall asleep.

Downtown Auckland

That evening I was walking in circles. There was nothing left for me to do except worry, or possibly vomit from nerves. So Elizaphan told me that we should take the ferryboat to the mainland for supper at one of the cafés. We invited the crew, but only Asoferwa, Esperance, the two Leopolds, and Moses wanted to tag along with us.

We stopped at a McDonalds. But when the men got outside and saw what it was they were holding in their hands, they dropped them in the gutter and spit out the rest. I tried to explain that these special sauces were very popular in America.

Then we stopped in the Mainsail Café on Queen Street.

Almost no one knew who we were. We weren't wearing our *Kinsman* reds. Baron Biche was there. He didn't recognize me from La Rochelle, but he eyed Elizaphan, who was wearing an Aunt Pearl outfit, a plain halter dress and espadrilles. She looked like society. I wanted to remind Biche that these were the "bushmen" who had beaten him in two races. Perhaps another time. I'd catch up with him before he left for the airport and the flight back to France. I knew we would beat him when the wind came back. I felt a twinge. I was ashamed of our power. Was it guilt?

I recognized Kruppmann, head of the Swiss syndicate. He was in conversation with Biche and Raleigh Smite and several other men I didn't recognize. It was their money talk. There was an unmistakable air of money. Capitalism under sail on a port tack, more business than yachting. So, here was Felix Kruppmann, a brand new, world-class yachtsman, a man who'd bought up faltering companies, leveraged them into solvency, sold them, and now collected yachts and wines. He had so far put thirty-four million dollars into the Swiss challenge, and he dressed like a crewman. In the privilege of yachting, they all dressed the same as their crewmen, these yachting impresarios. Dacron twill trousers and twill shirt, same labels, big watches. It must confuse the hell out of sycophants who can't tell the difference between a mainsheetman and the chairman of the syndicate. And how much more the rich talk about it than the poor.

One carbon crystal mainsail, fifty thousand dollars; one carbon fiber mast, five hundred thousand dollars. So, if you need to question what it costs, it is not a sport for you. The days of yachting went up in smoke years ago. America's Cup yachtsmen are now little more than corporate CEOs.

At the table was Bill Koch, in Auckland as an observer. Koch had managed to drop sixty-nine million on his loss in 1995, and a couple million of that had gone into surveillance and espionage on the rival boats.

Kruppmann seemed unruffled, fresh from *Saint Yves'* win over Sweden in light air. His feather boat had won. And if the calm held for another day, he would win against Rwanda. Tomorrow and tomorrow and tomorrow, the latest forecast looked dim.

Yachtsmen from the eight challenging countries assembled at the Mainsail, and whenever they were spotted at cafés, they bore a cockiness that had more to do with fear than confidence. Each as much scientist, engineer, naval architect, sailmaker, businessman as yachtsman. To sail what each believed to be his swiftest, most advanced designs.

We couldn't stay at the Mainsail. Elizaphan had found a place that served garlic leg of lamb, Plusone. That and the sweet potatoes made the men feel close to Rwanda. Drinking the New Zealand wine was a test of loyalty that I barely passed, but I ordered a local merlot.

It wasn't too difficult, but a local reporter sitting with his wife at dinner figured out who we must have been and came over. Ace Gordon had told him the Moses Mazimpaka anecdote, so he congratulated Moses again on his gameness. "Rashness," he told me. For a while longer, he would hug us warmly. He couldn't imagine a better underdog. We had it all. We were black, we were poor, we were rookies, we were gnarly, we were noble, we were uneducated, unimportant, rash, from a tiny landlocked country without a zip code no one had ever heard of, dead center on the other side of the globe no matter where you stood. And he said, "You boys are from Mars." I told him we were, but from a good neighborhood on Mars. Still, he said he didn't think we had the fighting edge that the other teams had. We had an attitude, but even that didn't seem entirely serious. I guess he'd seen our loss to *Yankee Doodle*. I told him we were very serious, but somehow our crew avoided showing it. It wasn't their nature to be seen caring about sailboat racing. They took it lightly because they had survived so much.

⚑

The Alternate

At sunrise in the stillness, Elizaphan and I walked hand-in-hand from our guest house to our camp. There she stood, moored to the dock inside *Bujumbura*, her soaring white mast with its five sets of spreaders, her hull lean and very red in the first light. *Kinsman* was held to the dock by six lines, and every winch on her deck sparkled with dew.

Ba-ale, our watchman, stepped forward. I said good morning to him. He answered me in English. He had no right hand. We had four one-handed men on our team, survivors of the massacres. Two were cooks; two were security. Technically, Ba'ale considered himself two-handed, but one of them was wood. Out of teak, he had carved himself a startling right hand that was extended in a permanent handshake. He'd put a ring on each wood finger, and now he pointed them toward *Kinsman's* bow. There on the foredeck stood Isaaco, leaning out over the water, clinging to the headstay in one hand and gripping a wine bottle in the other. The sound of the lapping ripples was magnified by the lightness of the hull. It was a shell. There was nothing inside, an empty land crab. The sunrise was so still I could hear Isaaco draining his kidneys into the gulf. Rational behavior. But it was the wine bottle that caught my eye. We had no room for drunkenness on our team, especially on race days. Today was crucial. Our game had gotten out of hand. If the wind didn't pick up by the starting gun, it would be fatal.

When Isaaco had finished draining himself, he walked forward and, as I watched, he uncorked the bottle and poured its contents over the clean white deck and down our red bows.

"Isaaco!" I yelled.

He ignored me. Ba-ale stepped forward and stood in my way. The top of his head came to my chin, average height for a Tutsi. I looked down at him. "Ba'ale? Ke-we?" I said. *What the hell is he thinking?*

Ba'ale answered, "Blood."

"I know it's blood."

But why was he pouring blood on our boat from a wine bottle? Blood was not a good sign. I preferred the wine idea. I was in no hurry to find out whose blood it was. It could have been anyone's. Even French. I watched Isaaco, the sun behind him through the rigging of both boats, pouring. It was a remarkable sight. I waited until he'd emptied the bottle on our bows and corked it. He stepped off the boat onto the dock.

"Oh, good morning, Boss."

"Good morning, Isaaco." I sucked in some air. "Whose blood was that?"

"I obtained it from cow."

Whew.

"A cow who is still alive?"

"Oh, yes, yes, yes. Cow doing very well."

I felt a lift. Ritual bleeding.

Later in the morning, Aunt Pearl came over on the ferry to wish us God-speed, as she put it. She brought an armful of daisies wrapped in silk that she presented to Elizaphan. Aunt Pearl always acknowledged her presence one way or another; always sincerely. She adored Elizaphan; she had never done anything like that with Jocelyn.

A man came running down the hill toward our fence. A dark man, one of our crew, he clawed his way over the fence and dropped down. Moses.

"*He-we! He-we!* Boss Routledge!" he yelled. "Boss!"

I followed him back to a guest house. It was Larry Bayard. He hadn't gotten up. Mrs. Prosser had gone to his room after breakfast. She'd thought he was dead, because he'd been unable to move. He was a shade of yellow I'd never seen, and his eyes glistened chrome yellow. It wasn't his malaria. He was too sick to tell us if it was something he had eaten. Mrs. Prosser was uncertain, but she said that Larry had probably eaten fish the night before. The doctor she brought over said he should be hospitalized, and so he was taken over to Auckland on Aunt Pearl's boat. He was off *Kinsman*.

Officially, I was listed as alternate helmsman. That didn't mean that I was ever supposed to sail, or felt prepared. My job had been as sailing master, getting the right jib up while the wrong one was coming down, dousing the spinnaker, jibing it. As far as I was concerned, Larry Bayard had to be on *Kinsman*'s helm today. Period. I was standby. How could I handle the helm and the sails?

But when I thought about it after the lightning-struck moments, I saw that I could. Esperance would become sailing master for today. Marcus and I would watch him. The weather looked light. There isn't a hell of a lot I don't know about match racing. It's wind, current, tide, water, choice of sails, strategy, and sailing, which I do very well. When I was ten, match racing sixteen-foot Cape Cod sloops, we'd go boat-for-boat changing leads for miles. I sailed so much that I could close my eyes and sail by feel. I could tell when I was too far up or when I had fallen off too far. I could tell when the boat was sailing at its best point by the hit of the waves, the heel, the tension. So I knew a boat's best speed. Once as a kid I was neck-and-neck with Paul Stanton heading for the finish line full blast when I blindfolded myself and crossed ahead of him. When he looked over and saw me, he let out a yell.

Later when we were all fourteen years old, long before we had cars, we sailed boats and developed the precision of surgeons. The harbor was crowded and getting to open water was a series of tacks between moored boats and their mooring lines. Briggs Cunningham had a fleet of sailboats painted the deepest green: a Lightning, a Star, an Atlantic class and a seventy-foot schooner called the *Brilliant*. They would have grown-up cocktail parties aboard the *Brilliant* that I was not invited to, and guests would sit along the rail. And I was so confident, so sure, so skilled, so comfortable within my boat that it was my own skin, and I could sail full-out on a reach, aiming my Cape Cod directly at the *Brilliant* and her guests. I would never bear off, or never seem to notice the perfect, dark green schooner looming up ahead of me. And when I screamed past her uninvited, you couldn't slide a playing card between our topsides. Scraping the *Brilliant* would have been a major setback in my career. I would have been banished from the yacht club and lose my Cape Cod sailing privileges. But that made it more fun.

It wasn't until I won my first junior national championship at sixteen that I felt the amazing reality that I was a winner. The long, slow rush I felt pulling away from the other boat was my doing; from bettering the other skipper who was trying to win just as hard as I was trying. The frozen stares on the rival boat, pretending not to notice that you were inching ahead of them, the whispers and smiles among your crew and you staring straight ahead as if you had expected it. And, all the while, moving mysteriously ahead of the other boat.

Yes, I could do it today. I could skipper *Kinsman* against the *Saint Yves* that afternoon in the twenty-second challenge for the America's Cup. *No problemo.*

Saint Yves

Airless. Dead calm. When we dropped the towline from our chase boat, I let us shoot forward from the weight of our keel, moving us a quarter mile. Not a ripple. Eventually, I ordered a light headsail raised, our big jennaker. The legal minimum was three knots. Less than that, the boats wouldn't be allowed to start. My hope was that the race would be called off for lack of wind.

I was stiff with tension. The wind had failed to show up, and all morning long I had felt the responsibility of losing. This was the key race. Win or fade. But Marcus was sitting in the cockpit making small talk and Esperance was chattering away excitedly. We hadn't seen the Swiss boat yet. I was waiting for her to be towed out before I got the main up. The spectator fleet and press boats were kept back a hundred yards off the line for fear their wakes would empty our sails. But I could see Elizaphan and Aunt Pearl waving gaily at us from a chartered power boat. They didn't know. The shark fin keel would not help us today. On another power boat I spotted somebody with long blonde hair and a white-brimmed hat who resembled Jocelyn Ortion. More bad luck?

At noon, we were standing still at the starting line in the flat water with our jennaker raised to steady us. *Saint Yves* came out in tow, sails up, carrying a slight luff. Everything about her was white. Appliance white. Ads everywhere. Her lightness was evident. She rode higher in the water than we did. She bobbed. Her mast seemed taller than ours and was raked back giving her an extra hundred feet of sail area and amidships, along her white topsides, was a red shield with a white cross in the center, the symbol of Switzerland.

Anytime I face a new boat, I still feel that stab of anxiety close to fear, and it still stayed with me until I saw no reason for it and dismissed it when I saw that I had a chance to win. And it stayed with me. At the ten-minute horn, I told Esperance to order the mainsail up. A kitten's breath crossed the water rippling it. Both boats were ghosting along out to the starting line. Both our sails hung limp, and the anxiety had not left me. I'd chosen our lightest sails. There was still a slight hope for a postponement.

At the five-minute horn, the breeze shot up to five knots, over the legal minimum, but still nothing more than cat's paws on the surface, just enough to qualify the race, and enough to move the Swiss boat, that white feather, the lightest of all the challengers.

Just before the start, the wind pooed out again, and we were stuck at the pin end of the line. The gun. We were even at the start and moved slowly across the line, but the feather could move faster than us. And after we crossed the line, I was lucky to keep *Kinsman*'s bow up and to hold her sailing above *Saint Yves,* and catch a mild lift that put us ahead. Unbelievably, we stayed ahead until the first mark.

When *Saint Yves* passed us on the downwind leg, she took the race away from us. By the time they rounded the fifth mark, we were trailing her by a full minute. We were still sailing downwind, spinnaker up, when they crossed us tacking to the sixth mark. *Saint Yves* was a quarter-mile away when we heard a shot, like the top string on a violin cello snapping. *Saint Yves* had stopped dead. Her backstay runner had parted. We all heard it, a beautiful sound, but an ugly consequence. *Saint Yves'* mast's main support was gone. The mast was coming down. It lurched forward. The height of a ten-story building hung a moment midway; another stay let go, then it fell rattling and stopped with a crash along the foredeck and far ahead of her bow into the calm sea. We heard a ripping sound. As it fell, it tore her steps loose from her chainplates. The hull jerked backwards as if it felt the pain of dismemberment.

We'd come within a hundred yards of her, and I rounded *Kinsman* up into the breeze. Marcus scanned her with binoculars. He said no one aboard *Saint Yves* had been hurt. Their crew was paralyzed. They stood in their places, bewildered. Some men held dead lines in their hands; others gripped winch handles. Their chase boat had moved in close and was standing by. The hull was filling; she was settling in the water. Only her skipper seemed to realize that they were going to sink.

Because the hull was eggshell thin, it had cracked like one on its way to an omelet. The startling white topsides were disappearing under the blue-green sea. There was no other sound, except the awful scraping and creaking of expensive laminates being shredded. My crew stood in a stupor. Marcus said their skipper had thrown his cap in the water in disgust. Now, he stood on the wide afterdeck counter behind the cockpit. "*Sauvez vous. Sauvez vous.*" I could hear him saying to his crew, again and again in a kindly voice, not loudly, but loud enough for them to hear him. There was no response from them. There was an embarrassed calm. The spectator fleet off in the near distance had gone silent. In the silence I could hear radios tuned to the same station. A New Zealand announcer was describing with exclamation points what we were actually witnessing, the sinking of a stricken boat as if it were the sinking of *Titanic.* But this was not the *Titanic*; this was going to be rather quick sinking.

Our chase boat had gone over to them and was standing by ready to pick up survivors. Aboard *Kinsman,* we stood in shocked silence. Nothing to do. After a few moments and when I saw that *Saint Yves* was settling for her final time before going to the bottom, I waved.

Their skipper had stayed surprisingly calm. *"Mes amis, alors, Sauvez vous. Je vous en pris. Sauvez vous."* He became annoyed, his men had not moved to save themselves. This was not anything that they had drilled for. Now he shouted. *"Pour le bon Dieu, abandonez le bateau, abandonez le bateau!"*

And it was then that the first crewman took the plunge off the bow; then another, until there were ten heads bobbing in the water. The *Saint Yves* was not going down by the bow or by the stern, but by her beam. She had cracked amidships. Her prow rose a few feet, and her counter rose fore and aft as she started to slip below the surface in a giant V. If it hadn't been such an expensive boat, it would have been funny. These things happen when a vessel is underbuilt and overstressed. But it is an awful thing to see. The million-dollar boat simply becomes a huge toy.

In the deep hush that followed her sinking, after the men had been picked up and all the bubbles had risen and popped on the surface from certain pockets in its sail locker, in its computers, in its lazareets, and in its video cameras, across the flat water I heard the New Zealand announcer who had been narrating the sinking say very distinctly, "She simply folded up and sank like a Swiss Army boat."

We had only to round six, seven and eight, the remaining marks, then cross the finish line to be declared the winner of the race. There was nothing we could do to help her. We saluted the crew standing in the chase boat and sailed away.

Following our victory and after we'd made *Kinsman* off to our dock, Aunt Pearl took Elizaphan and found a church, Episcopal or Anglican, and fell to her knees. And when she'd prayed her thanks to God, they came back on her chartered boat to our compound.

It was still daylight when we saw them again stepping onto our dock at Waiheke Island. A man carrying a box followed Aunt Pearl off the boat. Pearl's driver. The box was full of Champagne bottles in ice. Champagne wasn't what I felt like or that the crew should have. We hadn't won; *Saint Yves* had lost horribly. But what the hell, we'd survived another certain loss guided only by Aunt Pearl's philosophy that, in a quest for the impossible, something unimaginable needed to shift. And, once again, it had. I was beginning to believe that a force other than dumb luck had intended us to stay on in New Zealand a while longer.

We stood around while we drank Aunt Pearl's Champagne. She was delighted that we'd managed to register a win, honest or not. And, yes, it really had been Jocelyn I'd seen on that spectator boat. She had hung back prettily at the finish line, but then just after dark she stepped off a power boat onto our dock. She had the astounding ability to turn up. A necessary quality for a post debutante with a plan. Nothing could stop her. She embraced a startled Aunt Pearl, ignored Elizaphan, and walked over to me.

"Does your mother know you're out, Jocelyn?" I said.

"Oh, Jib, real-ly. Don't be silly."

"Why did you come?

"I just couldn't miss it. Congratulations, Skipper." She leaned in and kissed me on the cheek. Elizaphan was watching

"Have you seen Elizaphan?" I said.

"I haven't seen her for ages." She was bulletproof. "Oh, don't look so glum, Jib. You're entitled to your life, whatever that may be. I just came to cheer you on. Aren't you glad?" She loved a party.

Elizaphan came over. She knew. She whispered. "If you want her to stay, she must stay, Charles. She has come a long distance." Her type of assurance wouldn't work in Manhattan.

"Oh, hello, Elizaphan. You look fabulous. I love your dress." Perfect Jocelyn.

Of course, she loved it. It was from Aunt Pearl who'd gotten her size. It was one of a half dozen summer frocks she had ordered from J.Crew.

"Thank you, Jocelyn." She pronounced it *Joss-line.*

Then, to my amazement, Jocelyn reached into her military purse and brought out a small box sharply wrapped in crimson paper, Cartier, and handed it to Elizaphan. Probably a gold pen and pencil set.

"A token to try to make up for my utter rudeness to you in Rwanda."

It was a square wristwatch with a small sapphire on the stem and a black leather strap. There she was in action, the debutante emeritus.

Elizaphan was stunned. A pretty watch. "O-oh, thank you Joss-line." She wanted to kiss her, but didn't.

Suddenly, I was in the water. Several crew members had pushed me off the dock. I was the skipper *pro tem,* and they'd seen pictures of skippers being thrown off docks by their crews after victories. So, in I went. It was refreshing, though I didn't want to tell them that an accidental win was not the best time to celebrate, only the final victory when it's all over and everyone can afford to mellow out and douche the skipper. Moses and Esperance hauled me out, laughing as hard as I'd ever seen them laugh. And for that, it was worth it.

Then, Elizaphan pushed Jocelyn off the dock. I'm not sure why. There is no tradition between defeated girlfriends. But that's exactly what happened. As usual, Jocelyn was wearing white: white-linen skirt, white sleeveless blouse, wide hat and, as she went off the dock, she didn't plunge into the water. She seemed to stand on the surface for an instant before deciding to continue. It wasn't a bad moment. It could have been horrible, but it wasn't at all. She welcomed the attention. Jocelyn made it work. She smiled up at us, still holding her glass of Champagne, the other hand on her hat, her blonde hair swirling wide around her. She stayed in the water as long as she could. She knew she looked well, and she wasn't drowning. She was an athlete: swimming, diving, field hockey, tennis. When she climbed up the ladder, water clinging, all bra lines and panty lines, everyone took notice. She hugged Elizaphan. She would not change clothes or dry off, but just stood around looking wonderful until the party moved on, holding her glass and laughing. She had won whatever there was to win.

Aunt Pearl was standing with Elizaphan, who seemed okay about her upstaging. "There's something funny about everything, Elizaphan. You only have to find it."

"I have found it, thanks."

We went on and celebrated around the tables at the Mosquito Café, out in the stone garden out back, and ate nothing but salted crawfish from the South Island, Stewart Island oysters in beer sauce, grilled John Dory and potatoes boiled in broth. Pearl's Champagne stood in plastic garden buckets chilled by jagged fragments of ice floating in water. Some said Switzerland had withdrawn from the Cup. I had assumed she'd continue with her second boat. We raised our glasses to her.

The next day was a bye for us. Our wind was due back Thursday, the day we were to face the British boat, *Princess Di.*

The Cup

It was time for my crew to see the America's Cup. Following our victory over Switzerland and before our fourth race. I had held off showing it to them until we had settled in with a victory, and they knew we had a fighting chance to bring it back home. I hadn't seen it since I'd been taken to the New York Yacht Club when I was six.

I phoned the Royal Auckland Yacht Club to make sure that I could bring *Kinsman's* crew over. On the way, we stopped at the hospital, and the men saw Larry, who seemed weak and very uncomfortable with my having brought our crew. He'd been diagnosed with fish poisoning. He would not be available for *Princess Di* even though he was feeling better; he wasn't well enough to leave his bed. It looked like he wouldn't be able to sail *Kinsman* until the Japanese race on Friday. The lay day had not helped, and I was to be helmsman again.

We walked in full force down to the Royal Yacht Club several blocks away behind Princess Wharf. Pedestrians turned to stare at the clan of black yachtsmen wearing red golf shirts with black lettering. At the yacht club, we were shown into a modern building. The rooms were full of yacht models in glass cases; the walls of hulls in relief. We were led into a room where the Cup stood in its huge bell jar in the center. The room was a cube, fifteen-by-fifteen and had been built to accommodate it. The Cup stood on a low plinth covered by maroon velvet that hid the bolts holding it to the floor. As we entered the room, a light went on overhead and sent the Cup spinning with reflections from its silver curlicues and faggoting.

It had not changed, nor had I. It was not like anything else I had ever seen. It was an urn attempting to pass as a pitcher. But though it is legally defined as a pitcher, it wouldn't hold more than two pints of beer, and it would take a muscular Victorian nymph to empty it. I've won dozens of bowls and cups, but never anything as excessive as this item. Nothing close. You could not have it in your home. It is wondrously absurd. It might have been designed by a cartoonist. It bespoke snobbism in art and it glorified possessions.

148

"This will be in Rwanda," I told the men.

The men fell silent. They were appalled.

"Even if we lose?" Moses asked. The men clucked.

But they accepted this idea with little enthusiasm. Bringing them had been a mistake. They had expected more than a parody of white taste.

"We will build a little house for it on the shore of Lake Kivu."

"Why?" Kikongoro asked.

"Why?" I answered, "Because it is here and it should be there."

I tried to explain that it was a symbol of genius and bravery. Without my noticing, a reporter had tagged along and Moses was quoted, "Even if we lose?" in the *Auckland Star* and picked up by others. It takes so little to fill a newspaper.

Leaving the Royal Yacht Club, I realized that the men did not want to bring the America's Cup back with them. They wanted to bring something real. What they really wanted more of was what they had already gotten, an extended vacation and start-up money for their new farms. They were considering every aspect of bringing this silver into their country. It would clearly be an embarrassment for them to have worked two years to win it and then to have it displayed for the next generation to see as an example of their fathers' genius and bravery.

England

I was awed, but less awed. Just looking at *Princess Di*, I knew that we could smoke her in gale force winds. She had beaten Japan, but she had lost to America and France. She faced elimination. She needed this race as much as we needed it. This was my second race, and I knew *Kinsman* could smoke the fleet in a gale and overcome one or two rookie mistakes, maybe a cracked spinnaker pole.

We watched the *Princess Di*, blue hull with red slashes across her topsides interrupted by the row of product logotypes. She was being slowly towed out to the mark. *Princess Di*, as she was known, was said to be a quick boat in moderate chop, but she was a barge in heavier seas and tended to plow. The wind looked like it might settle in at fifteen to twenty knots. Good for us, better than yesterday, not as good as tomorrow. Boat speed is everything. You can have a rookie crew and a lame skipper. But if you have a quick hull, you have the race. Having a fast boat was more important than having the best crew and all the strategy and maneuvering in the world. Samurai versus gunslinger. There may have been other fast boats out there among the challengers, but that day we were the boat to beat.

Naturally, the most important man on board is the skipper, and I wish he hadn't been me again. I did not want the glory. I only wanted to get us into the quarter finals and to turn the helm back over to Larry Bayard.

I knew that when we faced *Princess Di* we'd need to be just as careful as before. She had not been as fast as *Yankee Doodle*, but she had kept their race tight until the final beat before the downwind leg, when the wind kicked up and she buried her nose, plunging like a hobby horse, pushing the water away like a pug-nosed tugboat. Until then, in the lighter air, she had a clean entry and was yare.

At the gun, *Princess Di* beat me across the starting line by ten big seconds. I managed to hang onto a safe leeward position and stayed below her and out of her used wind. She stayed a couple of boat lengths ahead at the first mark, exactly where I wanted her to be. Safely ahead. I could keep an eye on her without turning around all the time. I had plenty of time. I needed searoom for *Kinsman*. I'd wait my time, then let her out. I'd wait until the seventh mark and make it look natural. If the wind blew up before then, I'd have to hold her back, but I had no doubt we could take the British. I wanted to try to push them into making a mistake.

At the third mark, the wind was howling, the swells were breaking over each other, jarring the boat; the racket was deafening. Twelves are wet boats and *Kinsman* was the wettest, maybe because of our upcurved gondola prow with the tip of a Turkish slipper atop her keelson. Instead of dashing the breaking waves away from her, sometimes she flicked them high and free and let the wind carry the spume all the way aft to the cockpit. There, with each cloud I saw flying toward me, I lowered my head and let my visor drain the water off.

I was holding her back. We were splitting tacks now with the British, making it look close. Heading for the seventh mark, *Kinsman* was set down by a puff, and I headed her up, then down off the wind to gain speed again. And this is what must have triggered what happened next.

We had evened up the race. We might have been ahead of them, but I wouldn't know for sure until our paths crossed. We were on starboard tack, hull down, plunging nicely, sails flat as blades. *Princess Di* was on port tack, heading toward an invisible meeting place with us somewhere on the unmarked parade of waves between us. She was still a long way off, but I could see her crew, navy blue lined militarily on their windward rail.

The weather had gotten downright ugly, but not for us. We'd always been a weather boat, but ugly in a racing sense. Rigging was in danger, sails; visibility was way down, calculations were off. It's one thing to sail in rough weather, but it's another to race in rough weather flying as much laundry as you can from your masthead. Normally, sailing through a black gale, you'd call for a sail change and get your smallest jib up and your heaviest mainsail. Or without that much time, take in a couple of reefs, cutting the area of your mainsail in half. The runners (that is, the stays that support the towering mast) were crucial at these times. Maintaining their tension, loosening them slightly, easing certain sheets was crucial to having your boat survive. It is, after all, an instrument. A fabulous instrument, and it is tuned as a violin is tuned, but with a ton of wind pressure against the sails, and that pressure that changes with each jolt as your bow rises and plunges. The survival of your rig while racing depends upon your stays.

The British boat was planning to cross our bow. She was rising higher and falling further than we were. Now she was a tenth-of-a-mile away and heading toward that invisible meeting point somewhere. When two racing sailboats meet at right angles, point to point, one on port tack must bear off and give way if it decides it cannot cross in front of the other boat. The boat that does not have the right of way, the British boat, turns quickly off the wind and passes under the boat that does have the right of way, us.

Now the wind was blowing up in gusts of thirty knots, and then falling back down to twenty. I was surprised the race hadn't been called off because of dangerous conditions. I was hoping that it wouldn't be, that we could finish it. But the gale had built and both boats were in danger of having their sails shredded or even being dismasted.

She was coming toward us alright. Navy blue hull with great gashes of red swept across her, knifing and wallowing during her recovery from each wave. I sensed that *Princess Di* felt it was crucial to maintain her lead and round the seventh mark ahead of us before it headed for the final mark and the downwind run to the finish line.

But it didn't look like she was going to make it. I wasn't going to give way. I would hold my starboard tack. In such a duel, whatever I did was right. This went back to the sixteen-foot Cape Cods: *Get the hell out of my way!* They had three choices left. One was to come as close to us as they felt safe, then tack, hoping to get out from under our wind shadow. Of course, they'd lose their position, but in this weather it wasn't that crucial. Another was to come up to us, point to point, and then at the last second, when they were still maybe as close as thirty feet, go hard right rudder and swoop down below us. They would gain speed, but they would still have lost the mark to us. Third, I could ram her.

We were at three hundred yards and closing fast. It was too fluky to judge whether she could cross our bow or not. With one leap, it seemed improbable; with another, easy.

I was talking sail trim to Esperance and cursing to Marcus. No one heard me. No one could hear anything. The hull was banging and rattling, the wind was hissing, and I kept yelling, "She's going to try it! She's going to try it! She's going to try it!" This was going to be her big mistake. I eased the helm as much as I could to sail her up to speed, then pointed her as high as I could. The men lay in a safe line, flat as slugs, their lifelines clipped from their waists to a stainless steel vang that ran from the mast.

We had no bowman. No one was capable of clinging for long to the headstay on our steep plunging bow without losing it. Even clipped off to a lifeline. It would do no good.

"Kikongoro!" I yelled forward. "Kikongoro!" The rattling, banging noise was deafening. When I caught his eye, I waved him aft. He unclipped himself and slid toward me, keeping one hand for himself, one for the boat. Kikongoro was the only Pygmy on our crew. Not pure Pygmy, he was well over five feet, but Pygmy enough and he was our best climber. When he got close to my face with a wide expectant expression, I told him to get forward right away and clip on to the headstay and hang on. And when *Princess Di* had closed to within a hundred yards of our bow to yell "starboard!" at her, loud as he could in their direction. "Starboard! Starboard! Starboard!" And keep yelling it. We were on starboard tack, but it needed to be mentioned. Yachting is, after all, a gentlemen's sport, and you wouldn't want to disqualify your opponent in such an important race without first warning him of your intentions. Just as in chess you say "check" rather quietly, you do not yell it, but it is the same thing. A polite warning.

More than any of the others, Kikongoro is one I could trust to not fall overboard. He had the agility of a rhesus monkey. A year ago, when he first came on board, he told me he was neither Hutu, nor Tutsi, but that his race had settled Rwanda in the centuries before the Hutu came east from the Congo and long before the Tutsis came south up the Nile.

Hand over hand, Kikongoro danced forward. Half awash, he moved forward only when our bow rose, then huddled flat when the wave hit. "Man overboard!" in this weather would not be taken as lightly as it might in calmer weather. Today, it could easily be fatal. Jibing the boat quickly around to find your approximate position where your man went in would be a tactical nightmare, and we might not be good enough, easing and sheeting all the way around in gale force winds.

When I could, I glanced at him. He got there and clipped his brass snap hook to the headstay, wrapped a leg around it, and stood securely as he could on the steep fiberglass incline in the wash that came in knee high with each wave.

"Starboard!" he yelled into the wind again and again. "Starboard!"

Princess Di kept coming.

"She's not going to make it," I yelled. No one heard me. We rode quickly down on her as she knifed forward, now aimed at the point where we'd cross. Should I give way? Her bow would cross ours, but we'd ram her amidships.

If we did, we'd sink her and possibly sink ourselves, so we would lose two boats in a messed-up sea. We would be the only one capable now of bearing off, and if we were forced off our course, then I'd raise a protest flag and disqualify the British boat. But in this weather, bearing off might not be visible to the committee boat, and so our protest would be ruled out.

Princess Di did not change course, but came on. She desperately needed to round the final mark ahead of us and kick off on the downwind run. And her last choice was to bull her way through, betting her hull and her race on getting up enough speed to cross unscathed upwind of *Kinsman*. If she lost this one, she'd be eliminated, just like us.

She shouldn't try that against us; not in this weather, not in any weather. It is the boldest step in match racing. It puts all your confidence in the shoot of your boat and all that you know about time and distance and wind to work. And in the few instants of immense danger, you somehow try to eke your boat your crew and all your fine rigging up up up ahead of the boat on the starboard tack. Today, it would be an irrational act.

Princess Di was a hundred feet away. I was sure her crew could hear Kikongoro's yells. She was huge. The steeple mast bore down on us. I could hear the din of her hull racketing coming closer as well as our own din. She was going to try to cross our bow at full speed.

Seventy-five feet. Way forward on the point of our bow, Kikongoro, the black Pygmy in the wet, red shirt yelling "Starboard!" at them as they crashed heaving toward us.

I wish Larry Bayard had been on board. I had no one but myself and Marcus, who wasn't talking. That was okay. I didn't have anyone when I was sailing the Cape Cods. But I did want to discuss this with someone beside Marcus. I was talking to myself. I can disqualify *Princess Di*. I can ram her or miss her. Where's the rules boat?

Fifty feet. At that instant, I glimpsed a dozen soaked, white faces staring wide-eyed at *Kinsman*'s bow. I had them, and we all knew it. It didn't help at all that I was being blinded for a couple of seconds each time a wave crossed our foredeck.

No one can see us. No witnesses. If I veer off, it'll be my word against theirs, an alternate skipper and his all-tribesman crew against the word of the seasoned British syndicate. If I veer off, they'll squirm out of my protest. I want them disqualified. I won't need to show them our amazing stuff on the final downwind leg, not in this weather. I don't want to get into how we win.

Now I could hear someone in their afterguard yell, "Sea room, sea room!" whatever the hell that meant. Not on this sea, pal. *Princess Di* had absolutely no right to that claim.

Her skipper made no decision. Or else, he made a bad one.

If he maintained his speed and I maintained ours, I would ram *Princess Di* amidships. He knew I could ram his boat, but he doubted I would. He'd made a grave mistake trying to read my mind, and he knew it. Now he could no longer get away. He had put his boat directly in front of me, and he could no longer swoop under our stern. Ramming them was unthinkable.

"Come back! Kikongoro! Come back!" I yelled, but all he could hear was the wind in his ears, and he stayed on as bowman. If we hit, he could be crushed between the hulls.

I had one split moment to decide. The choice was mine. If I held my course, I'd ram her amidships. Or I could veer downwind and clip off her stern. Did I want to knock off a piece of their boat? It could be bad. I could come down hard and take a chunk off hers, as well as my beautiful gondola bow. Either way, I was going to rattle her gudgeons.

I had them, and we all knew it. They saw I was holding my course, about to ram them hard. Yes. In the last unimaginable second, with *Princess Di* still trying to skim by us at full speed, I spun the wheel to port, fell off the wind, and ran our bow down her length, then struck her hard across her counter.

We struck *Princess Di*, our bow up and her stern down, with a hollow crack, then an ugly crash that knocked her counter hard and flung the last piece of her stern into the sea. Her chainplate broke free, and her backstay shot up out of sight with a *whoosh*.

I felt a slight jolt and heard the scream of fiberglass ripping, and I felt that we'd lost a piece of our own bow, but I couldn't tell how much from where I stood. Kikongoro was pointing down, so I spun the wheel back up and hove *Kinsman* to and called Esperance back and told him to keep her bow into the wind until I could inspect our damage.

As I ran forward, I glanced at the British boat. She stood stiffly in irons, her sails luffing, glaring, cursing as if she'd been insulted. And she had. Her afterguard was inspecting their damage, which was slight. I had clipped part of her counter; no gear lost, one stay parted, a stern cleat gone, maybe a fairleader lost. It had to be done. If I hadn't touched her, any sea lawyer ashore could have argued Britain's way out of it. But now it was obvious. Anyone could see it. Their starboard rail had been struck. Port tack versus starboard tack.

I'd taken an ugly bite out of our own bow. It looked like a surprised mouth. It might not be repairable before the race against Japan's *Samurai* the next day.

I couldn't find our protest flag in the lazareet, so I took off my red shirt and clipped it onto the backstay, then took the helm and bore off. We sailed home flying a protest tee shirt. We had won.

We sailed past *Princess Di*. She was still standing in irons. Her crew was moving slowly. Their skipper gave me a mild salute, and I saluted him back. He knew. This America's Cup was over for him. I was in no hurry now. I gave Esperance the helm. Water was spilling in at our bow each time we plunged. The electric pumps were getting it out faster than it was coming in. In no hurry now, I changed my headsail and tacked *Kinsman* back around the disputed mark, rounded it, and eased her downwind with our smallest jib and mainsail.

The gun sounded good as we crossed the line. We had done it again. Victory over the British boat eliminated them and kept us in. Now only the Nippon Challenge's *Samurai* stood between us and the semi-finals, and they seemed to have the entire Japanese empire behind it.

The damage to our bow was visible to the committee boat and everyone else. There were boos from the spectator fleet, but also a smattering of applause, the kind a comedian gets when he's died onstage. They were getting to like us, but the boat that does the ramming always appears to be guilty.

We were towed back slowly to our dock. The sea water had stopped coming in at our bow. We were no longer sailing into chop. She stood calm, moored at our dock with a gouge missing from her bow, but she rode tall, red and white.

Now it was my turn. The resentment against me was clear at the post-race press conference. It poured out. I took my place behind a microphone, but my body was still pitching from the twenty-four-mile race. There's an uneasy alliance between Britain and New Zealand, and so my unpopularity quickly went international. From the start, *Kinsman* had made enemies easily and its few friends the hard way.

Claude la Luc, the *Paris Match* reporter, was the most scathing. She called it a typical *attaque sauvage*. So unnecessary. None of the other questions mentioned our victory, only my ramming of the British boat. One television personage asked, "What in God's name were you trying to prove?"

"I wanted to win."

"But you struck her!"

"I did indeed," I said. "They made a major error, and none of you would have believed they had." And I had.

Before I took the ferry back to our camp on Waiheke Island, I visited Larry Bayard as I had every day since he'd been hospitalized. He had been moved to a smaller clinic, and he looked pretty bad. Gray blue. His illness had not gotten better. What might have been fish poisoning was now being treated as a mild form of salmonella. There was talk of flying him to one of Saint's specialists in New York. He seemed very tired. I explained the conditions of how I came to ram the British boat. He listened and then nodded, "I woulda rammed 'er." But he was feverish.

Still, sick as he was, I did need him on board. I wanted him bundled in a blanket and stuffed in the cockpit. There were too many decisions for one man to make. All the other boats had three or four in their afterguard: helmsman, skipper, tactician, navigator. It was absurd that we'd come this far with Larry, and now (when it mattered the most) I was alone on board as substitute skipper.

⚑

Aunt Pearl

"Give us a bucket of oysters and a keg of beer," Aunt Pearl said, which meant that she was going to be hostess for dinner served for us all at the Mosquito Café. I asked her if she expected Jocelyn to come, or if she was still in Auckland, or if she had flown home.

"Sissy? Why she's going to the French party at Mainsail with a nice-looking young man she introduced me to named Leonard Gordon."

"Good God. Leonard Gordon?"

"Oh, he's not *that* bad, Jib. And they look adorable together; both outdoorsy, both blond."

"She's landed on her feet. That's Ace Gordon."

"I didn't know. Is it?"

"It would have to be, if I know my Jocelyn Ortion. Ace Gordon's the New Zealand skipper."

She never expected less. To Jocelyn Ortion, it was all a board game, played with painted tokens. She had moved her spectator shoe to New Zealand with dreams as long as her hair. To her, caviar was peanut butter. She could even look wonderful at airports, coming and going, which was impossible.

The evening was perfect, and all I know is that the best way to eat oysters is in a light rainfall, sitting outside behind the Mosquito Café with my crew, with Aunt Pearl, and with Marcus and holding a very cold pint of local beer.

"Now Raleigh Smite has his gimlet eye on me, for God's sake," she told me. "He wants to come over and join us." This was Sir Raleigh Smite, the chairman of the British challenge that I'd just knocked out of the cup races.

"What did you tell him?"

"I told him I'd be delighted, but that there'd be no fooling around on our first date."

Sir Raleigh Smite was a novelty. He'd earned his knighthood by housing the poor, an Evelyn Waugh Englishman with a Monte Python smirk. He kept Pearl in stitches throughout supper, telling her stories, guzzling beer, and eating oysters. Widow and widower, they knew their way around life's disorders, but still it was surprising for a man whose syndicate had just lost the America's Cup challenge to her syndicate to be dining with it that night.

I loved my Aunt Pearl. She certainly wasn't used up the way so many women her age are. She was the center of levity at whatever group she joined. She told jokes better than most men, she had a vaudevillian's laugh, and she let you know immediately if you were boring people. She liked to drink, but I never saw her drunk, only gay (in the best sense of the word). Never off-guard.

Age had tussled with her face. But her face had won. Her nose was somewhat larger now than in photographs I'd seen, but still fabulous, still elegant. Her eyes gleamed over it with a look of malicious humor and kindness. The lines at the corners of her mouth might easily have been removed by office surgery. Everyone else in New York had done it, but that was not her way. She seemed to belittle the aging process; she did not avoid it. Aging was what happened to you. Age, age, Pearl Routledge!

Throughout her lifetime, her achievements in charity had won her awards, a presidential medal. She had said that fame was an inconvenience and, of course, it was. For her. At one ceremony, she was praised for her work in charity. "It has never been work," she replied kindly.

Her natural air of composure always gave me confidence. She had great clarity. She was a woman one followed. Anyone would follow her. To a man, the crew adored her. Even the Pygmy Kikongoro, who adored no one, adored Aunt Pearl.

She had married clever, handsome men who had made their own way; men who had invented devices before they became obvious. But now they'd gone away, and she was gloriously alone. In one of those marriages, she had lost a son. It was before I was born, a little boy who had died of a brain tumor at the age of four.

"He was too young," was all she ever told me about him. Not even his name. When she buried him, she tucked his favorite book beside him in his coffin. *Winnie the Pooh.*

For all her money, she befriended anyone. It was her right and her pleasure. She knew she was a target, that people thrust themselves at her because of her reputation and her wealth. But she chose friends simply. Her conditions were: "If we can be friends, we can; if not, we cannot." She meant that the friendship needed to come from both, and for good reasons.

She had been through the most difficult thing of all so she understood about Rwanda, the mindless hatred, the extreme sadness lurking in these men, my crewmen. She understood their psychoses from the massacres. She would look to them with caring, which was better than love. She had become their temple.

⚑

The Sinking

Ba'ale woke us with his ebony hand knocking on our door. It was before sunrise, barely gray. When I opened it and saw Ba'ale's face, I knew it was bad. He had seen something terrible. It took him a few moments. *Kinsman* had sunk.

I ran down the three flights, waking Mrs. Prosser's Guest House for the day, and kept ahead of him down to our dock. From the road in the darkness, I could make out the white mast with its five spreaders still standing perfectly straight, but six feet lower than it was yesterday. When we got to the dock, there she was, sunk, her keel firmly on the bottom, her hull still lashed to the dock. With his flashlight I could see her bright chrome winches and grinders, the twin helms and cleats, the clear white deck plan six feet underwater. She always looked beautiful, and still did. All was perfect, except it was slightly tinted green, under the rippling water. Two spring lines remained taut and two breast lines. She hung balanced, straining at two spring lines; the other lines had parted and two of those had ripped cleats up off of her deck.

But if a wind came up and there was surge, they would part and she would sink fully, lying on her side. Looking at her, I knew that she could not have sunk by herself. Someone had sunk her. The question was: who?

I needed to float her. I called the Coast Guard. They recommended a shipyard. When it was getting light, a boat came over and pumped her out. When she'd been floated and was almost dry, I dove down and searched her hull for tell-tale signs of espionage, but I discovered that she'd been sunk by a slow leak, a fine fracture no one had noticed that ran from the point of impact with *Princess Di* along the keelson. What we thought had been a minor wound to her bow, was a gash that could not be repaired before the race against Japan that day. I called the race committee and asked for a postponement. They called back in an hour. No. Since the incident with the British boat, *Kinsman's* popularity had slipped to a new ebb.

I went back over to the guest house and woke up Marcus. He was overwhelmed. He knew what it meant, that we would need to transfer all our sails over to *Bujumbura*, and take her out early for a shakedown run. And all the sails needed to be hosed down, rinsed and dried, but there was no time for it. And *Bujumbura* had a fixed keel, and we both knew that sailing our trial horse without the floppy keel we had no chance to beat the *Samurai*. She was not notoriously fast, but she was well-skippered, and her highly-disciplined crew made up for her shortcomings.

That morning *Kinsman* was hauled out for repairs to her hull. She would be out of the water a day-and-a-half. Ready for the finals. If we won against Nippon Challenge that afternoon. Then, at midmorning the Race Committee called and said that Nippon Challenge had agreed to grant us an emergency lay day. We had twenty-four hours to get *Kinsman* in sailing order.

Japan

Race day. Winds of five to ten knots were predicted, so we put on our lightest main and jib and were towed out to the starting line at noon. We watched the Japanese boat following us out. She had an ominous-looking hull with a red sun rising from the waterline that spread stem to stern across her hull. She'd been good in light weather and had beaten Spain, Switzerland and Sweden, but had lost to America and France, putting her right with us in the middle of the pack.

I was worried. Why not? We were on a shake-down cruise with an unraced boat. I was hoping to beat *Samurai* on tactics and with Marcus aboard we had a fighting chance. And I was especially nervous. I'd never really sailed *Bujumbura* before, and although she was similar to *Kinsman*, she was not the same. She had smaller rudders and responded sluggishly. I could not hope to outmaneuver *Samurai*. In the pre-start, I was very edgy and kept turning back to Marcus.

He really helped. He had a stopwatch in his palm, awaiting the moment to say, "Ready . . . tack." Then, I'd call out the command. It gave me freedom to concentrate on the sailing.

The air was light, and Marcus had me take her a long way behind the pin end of the line, so far I thought the breeze would never bring us back in time. *Samurai* did not follow us. And finally, when we had three minutes to start, Marcus said, "Ready . . . tack."

I was on the edge of my butt. But he put us on the line at the gun, and we beat the Nippon Challenge by a couple of boat lengths, and we held onto the lead up and around the first mark. I was amazed. Esperance kept the sails trimmed while I kept her nose up to the wind.

We rounded the mark ahead by three seconds. It would be a close reach out to the wing mark.

Marcus noticed the horizon. Something was building up that looked like a black squall. In ten minutes, we knew. I sheeted the sails flat, hoping to sail through it standing up, hoping it would pass over us and move on when all of a sudden it was on us. And before I knew it, both our sails had been blown out. We stood high in the water with our sails crackling out behind us in strips like pennants and with us facing into the wind like a weathervane. The crackling noise of the ripped sails was deafening. And as they blew, they lost pieces that were being blown away. It's over, I thought. This is it; we're dead.

Then I saw *Samurai*. She'd blown out, too. She'd rigged her lightest sails, too, and they'd been blown away like ours. And so there we stood, vertical, both boats a quarter mile apart, standing on their bare poles, what was left of their sails blowing like flags of surrender. An amazing sight.

Marcus was yelling above the crackling noise. "Move move move. Go for it, Jib. Go now!"

We had to re-rig our sails ahead of *Samurai*. Whichever did would win. I couldn't remember for the moment who was in the sewer, so I yelled, "Sewerman!" Then, I remembered it was Kikonburo. "Kikonburo, blue main number three! Now!"

Up it came. Moses began hauling it up on deck.

"Help there, Moses, Mungo."

"Rig it! Rig it! Now! Jennaker! Jennaker! Up, up to the mark!" Then, "Get the number two jib out! Sail change at the mark!"

The jennaker was our biggest reaching jib, and we could handle it for this tack, which was a broad reach. I glanced at *Samurai*. Something was wrong.

"Marcus, what the hell are they doing?"

He took the binoculars.

"They're not getting their main down."

"What's left of it."

He looked a bit longer, then put the glasses down and turned to me. "They got trouble. They can't get it down, Jib."

It had fouled. They'd rigged the halyard in a travel car and were ripping the mainsail down to the deck. Was he smiling?

"Well, we can."

Ours didn't want to come down either, but it did. I yelled forward, "Innocent, Isaaco, Josue, haul her down! Haul her down!"

"How are they doing?"

"They're not."

Now, ours was down, and we were reeving the number three mainsail. And in a minute, we'd be under way. I could see the confusion on *Samurai*'s deck. They seemed to be hauling a man aloft in a bosun's chair on the spinnaker halyard to free I couldn't see what.

"Their main's fouled on their top spreader," Marcus said. Somehow a strip of their mainsail had tied itself in a knot at their top spreader near the masthead, and the sail could not be hauled down from the deck so a crewman was being sent up to cut it free.

The gale had passed over us, and now the wind turned fluky. But it was blowing fifteen knots in spurts.

The number three mainsail was rolling up the mast. A glorious sight. We got her rigged, and *Samurai* was still out of the race, struggling when we rounded the mark a mile ahead of her. But when she got going, she pursued us like a cheetah. She was taking all risks. Marcus figured she was gaining five seconds a mile. At the final mark, when we broke out our spinnaker, we were ahead of her by thirty-three seconds according to Marcus.

They were sailing beautifully.

"Don't look back at her," Marcus said. "I'll keep you posted."

Samurai was gaining. She had hoisted a spinnaker half again the size of ours with the word SONY spread across it. She was gaining on us with every surge and had gotten it close enough to collapse half our spinnaker.

Down *Samurai* came behind us, closer and closer. I could hear them coming. I could hear their bow wave. I could hear the commands. She'd blanketed us and was about to pass us to windward.

"Head up, head up," Marcus whispered. It was a desperate maneuver to drive her off our back upwind while we still could. He did not yet have an overlap on us. Even though their bowman was yelling, "Overlap overlap" at us, I turned the wheel to port and forced *Kinsman* up high enough to collapse *Samurai*'s spinnaker completely, then I spun the wheel to starboard, and we drove down for the finish line and got the gun two seconds ahead of *Samurai*'s horn, the closest finish so far in this series.

We were in the finals.

Aunt Pearl joined us for a very quiet celebration at the Mosquito Café. Sir Raleigh Smite was otherwise engaged, thank you very much. She'd come from church. She said we had won yet another race by the hand of God. I reminded her of the crew and the skipper. "That, too," she said, "but you couldn't have done it without his hand on *Samurai*'s masthead."

She had expected what everyone had expected: *Bujumbura* to lose respectfully to *Samurai*. Maybe I did, too, but somehow we'd won.

We were pretty sure to be facing *Yankee Doodle* in three days, but we wouldn't know until she'd raced *Le Coeur de France* and either eliminated her, or been eliminated by her. So, it was either America or France in the challenger finals. We'd be in good company. We toasted both. After eating garlic leg of lamb, we escorted Aunt Pearl down to our dock and saw her off on her chartered boat headed back across to Auckland. Elizaphan and I walked home to our guest house arm-in-arm. We had the next two days off. We were magic.

౿

France Versus America

Now, only *Le Coeur de France* stood between *Yankee Doodle* meeting us in the finals. I'd rather have faced *Le Coeur de France*. We'd already beaten her, though I felt pretty good about beating both of them.

Larry stayed at the clinic. Marcus and I went out with the spectator fleet to watch the race-off aboard Aunt Pearl's boat. She had looked in at the *Yankee Doodle* party and had seen Jocelyn Ortion.

And there she was, on a New Zealand power cruiser heading out to watch the race. Our boats were heading out at the same speed a hundred feet apart. She stood on deck forward. In the wind, her blonde hair back, she carried herself like a firm young queen waiting to be franked. I hardly recognized her, but I did recognize the man who came up behind her and put his arms around her waist. Ace Gordon. They were both lean, blond, square-featured, a handsome couple, and as similar a couple as a pair of molded models. I pointed her out to Aunt Pearl.

"But doesn't she look beautiful." Then I saw it. The debutante emeritus had made her New Zealand debut, followed by a conquest. She had harpooned Ace Gordon, whom she called Leonard. After all, that was his given name. I waved to them; she hailed me as if I were a taxi.

The race wasn't as close as it should have been. The wind was fluky, and the tides were strong. *Le Coeur de France* had a sweet hull for lighter weather, and she picked up light air up early where she could find it in pockets, but it wasn't enough. *Yankee Doodle's* skipper, Soapy Armstrong, was a bit of a sorcerer, a naval navigator, able to find the currents, and he kept *Yankee Doodle* moving over the bottom, even though she sometimes looked like she was standing still. When the wind finally picked up, it picked up for *Yankee Doodle* and not for *Le Coeur de France*. The American boat was well out in front of her, and the American boat crossed the finish line nearly two minutes ahead of the French boat. France was out.

After the gun, when they'd picked up their towline, *Yankee Doodle's* tender, the *Dodo*, came alongside and delivered cold bottles of Champagne. It was time for them to party. They wouldn't meet us until the weekend for a seven-race series.

So, it was going to be USA versus Rwanda for the privilege to meet New Zealand in the America's Cup finals. If we won the series against USA, the finals would be the weirdest match-up there had ever been in the one-hundred-and-forty-eight-year history of the old Cup.

The Diver

The next day, *Kinsman* was launched and towed to our dock looking fit again, her bow sealed, ready to sail in the finals against *Yankee Doodle* in two days.

That night I couldn't sleep. I asked Elizaphan if she wanted to go for a walk. She said no, but by the time I'd gotten downstairs, she'd caught up with me, and we tiptoed out across Mrs. Prosser's front porch and walked out into the night, hand-in-hand toward our camp.

The winner would face the boat we'd all been waiting to see: *Black Lion*, the New Zealand Cup defender, waiting in his den, the great *Black Lion*. That had yet to be seen in action. Based on rumors, the lion's stature had grown to mythical size. She was rumored to be faster than anyone, never mind America and France (and, of course, us), but no one knew. There were only the rumors of its great speed. She was absolutely top of the line. The Kiwis would do anything to retain the Cup and defend it every few years and so on, forever; just as we had done for a hundred and forty-eight years. And they might just do that. They were good at sailing in their own waters. They knew the vagaries. And it only took one vagary to turn a race around.

There was no moon, but I could see the outline of *Kinsman* lying in her berth alongside the dock. I never got tired of looking at her. In the dark, I sensed her white mast soaring ten stories above us. She was ready to race.

The gouge in her bow had been patched, the long hairline crack had been repaired with Kevlar, and she was ready for *Yankee Doodle*.

I gave Elizaphan my hand and tugged her on board, and we dropped onto the sails in the sewer and lay down on a nylon jib called the wobbler. The hull was rocking slightly on the surge, and by the time we'd gotten comfortable one thing led to another and pretty soon I was too sleepy to get up on deck. So we lay there naked, talking from time to time until pretty soon I was asleep.

It was very late when she woke me whispering in my ear. "Charles something kuku going on."

"Where?" I whispered.

She pointed down, under me, under the sail, through the hull, underwater. She pressed her finger to my lips and tugged me up. Barefooted, we carefully climbed the aluminum companionway and from the deck looked down onto the surface, and there it was. A phosphorous light. Then, a tell-tale bubble. The light was moving. Then, it was black. More bubbles. Then, it was on again and moving. A large form in scuba gear was swimming under our hull. I slithered across the deck and slid over the side and into the water without making a splash, took in a lungfull and swam down. The light went on. Without a mask, I could see a man. He was wearing black diving gear facing the other way. The light went off. I went to the surface for air and swam away from the boat. I dove. The light went on again. Under the light was a camera. What I needed to do was simple.

I rose to the surface for air and came down again behind him. And when the light went on again, I reached around him and grabbed the light and camera. It was quick. I grabbed the air hose out of his mouth and dragged him along toward the dock. I cut off his air and forced him up, then towed him in. It was easy. He was struggling. When we broke the surface, Elizaphan was waiting on the deck. The diver was gasping for air and before he could speak, she cracked him on the head with a boat hook. We hauled him up on the dock. He lay on his back.

"Who are you?"

He didn't answer me.

He seemed quite reticent about his identity. He struggled to his feet, but stood duck footed, helplessly in place by his huge work fins, his double air bottles. He wasn't going anywhere. Elizaphan had bound his ankles with the end of a spring line. I kept the flashlight shining in his face not sure what to do next. We'd definitely caught a big fish. I gave him a shove. He lost his balance. He fell on his air bottles and lay on the dock like a bug. I dropped down with a knee on his chest.

"What were you doing down there?"

"Searching for bags," he said, "*bugs*, that is, lobsters." He seemed Australian.

"Were you taking their pictures?"

He didn't want to play.

Ba'ale our one-handed night watchman had become interested in our catch and had wandered over to watch. He had brought his old machete with him all the way from Rwanda to help out in his security duties. He kept it achingly sharp, sharp enough to dice fruit in mid-air. Ba'ale was proud of his machete. It had a history, he said, but I hadn't asked what.

I don't know what the Australian thought of Ba'ale, when he threw his machete into the dock beside him, splintering the dry wood. The diver became chatty. He said he was a New Zealander, not an Australian. He had been ethnically insulted.

"What were you photographing?"

He had been photographing whatever it was we had under our boat. There had been rumors.

"What kind rumors?"

"About what makes it go fast."

"We make it go fast."

"I was to look for something else."

"You must have been curious."

"Not me."

"Who was curious?"

He didn't answer.

"What did you expect to see?" Like the stainless steel bolt swivels on the wobbly keel. "Get any good snapshots?"

"Nah."

"Well, just in case you did, for my own peace of mind, why don't I give you your camera back in the morning. How does that sound?"

"You can give it back to me now."

"Right after I hand you over to the police for spying."

"You are hiding something. They were right."

"What's your name?"

"Derek."

We stood there in the dark while my flashlight made moons along the stringy wood dock. Of the four of us, one spy and three captors, Derek was the calmest. I stayed loyal to my pessimism.

"Where'd you come from?"

"Off."

"Just swam over?"

"'At's right."

"From the mainland?"

"'At's right."

Derek had the liar's whine. I knew he hadn't swum over from the mainland. Then I saw it. Nothing more than a green wink a hundred yards off shore on the black water. A boat. Now we had something. I pulled him to his feet.

"Signal him to come in."

"Like hell I will."

I nodded to Ba'ale. It was then that he showed Derek his beautiful teak hand with the rings on every finger. With his machete under his arm, Ba'ale twisted his hand backwards for him to see its mobility. Then he glanced at Derek's left hand, as if there was some connection between his twisted hand and Derek's healthy hand. Derek was trembling. It could have been the night chill or it might have been from the sight of this thin person with a bejeweled teak right hand holding a machete in his left hand. I don't know what Derek thought

Ba'ale might do to him. You could never tell by looking at Ba'ale's face what he might do. He was fine-featured; his face was navy blue-black, uneven and calm, devoid of expression. His ancestors had come from the mouth of the Nile, from Egypt Sudan Ethiopia.

He pulled his machete out of the dock, raised it, and in a move too quick to follow, brought it down freely in one downward *swish* that severed the strap from the goggles Derek had been holding in his right hand. The goggles clattered onto the dock; the strap dangled in his hand. It was good. Derek was breathless.

"Who sent you?" I said again.

"The American boat."

I sucked in air. That would be my Uncle Rut. This was a family affair.

"Just tell 'em ya caught me spyin' will ya? I'll sign a paper. You can keep the camera and off I go."

"Signal your boat."

"I don't think I can."

Ba'ale held his machete under the newcomer's chin, this time actually dimpling his throat.

In a few minutes, the boat was standing alongside our dock.

There it was: the *Dodo*, less than twenty-feet long and loaded. I had heard rumors. Uncle Rut had bought a powerboat already named *Dodo*, probably because it was tubby like the bird, and installed computerized electronic spying systems, as well as an underwater scanning device, a periscope pointing straight down so that he could scan the rudders and keels of his rivals. The *Dodo* had cost a million to convert. Our *entire* challenge cost less than three-point-five million.

Uncle Rut's philosophy, if you could call it philosophy, included spying. He was quoted in the press as saying: "It is my job to find out everything I can about my opposition. I would be remiss in my duty to my investors. They would be not be served unless I did that. I am in the business of winning, and I will continue to instruct my people to do whatever, repeat, *whatever* it takes to increase our knowledge of what my opponents have in store for us."

According to Derek, his subjects had been the quickest boats. He had done night studies on all of them: *Nippon Challenge*, equal to them in light air, the Swedish boat (they called it the *Häagen-Dazs*), and *Le Coeur de France*. The blue boat had seemed almost impermeable, sometimes faster than *Yankee Doodle*.

But Uncle Routledge's syndicate had suspected from the beginning that something strange was going on with *Kinsman*. To any keen observer, it was obvious. We were making all the blunders. Yet, in the end we were still there, prime contenders, finalists. Just as much as they were. What was it? It couldn't be beginner's luck. Or could it? We'd made mistakes, and we'd still won. In our race against *Yankee Doodle*, we'd lost our sea anchor. They'd seen our speed. Before I could slow us down, their navigator, Anton Schwartz, had timed one of our bursts that had lasted a couple of miles between windward and leeward marks. He had used an electronic timer, and our speed came out to an incredible eighteen knots, much faster than any challenger. They had been stunned by our ability and unable to explain it.

Anton Schwartz and Soapy Armstrong were the brains of *Yankee Doodle's* afterguard. Schwartz had won the Star Class World Championship in Bermuda, and now he was sailing as their tactician, and the crew called him Bermuda Schwartz. *Kinsman* didn't even have a tactician.

Naturally, we had shipped *Kinsman* just as she was with her floppy keel. We had no reason to disguise it. It looked like a mistake. Still, only seven living people knew about it. Of these, two were in a French shipyard and didn't speak English. Only myself, Marcus Cape, and Larry Bayard knew. Saint Pierre, Aunt Pearl. And certainly not Uncle Rut.

Elizaphan overheard Kikongoro talking with a kitchen employee at the Mosquito Café saying that we'd broken our keel off La Rochelle during the elimination against the French boat. When he was questioned, he said that in any good wind the keel wobbles, and he is frightened that it will fall off, but the boat rides smoother in heavy seas than it did before.

"Why don't they fix it?" the cook asked.

"They don't want to fix it," he said. "They like the keel to wobble."

"It has been fixed, Kikongoro," Elizaphan said. "It almost fell off, and the men were very afraid, but it is good again now."

More curiosity. Exposing our keel was our very real fear. Between the semifinals and the finals, the syndicates can alter any rig. They can move their masts, drop five tons from their keel, add five tons, put their rudder on the bow, do everything but add a motor. Or change boats. Any syndicate could copy it in a day. Figuring it out, to Uncle Rut, included spying.

The next day, I saw Derek's pictures. He was good. I wanted to keep one. They were sharp and clearly showed our rudder and our keel from all sides and our underside from all angles. Nothing.

Now there was a leak, of sorts. Ba'ale told some locals at the café about the man with the camera that we'd fished out of Hauraki Gulf. We not only had caught the *Dodo* monitoring us, he said, but also we had their photographs. One of the listeners knew the cook.

So, two days after their loss to *Yankee Doodle* and their elimination from the challenge, Baron Biche sent his emissary, Christian (I didn't get his last name) to see me. We disliked each other on sight, of course. So, here he was. What was I going to do about it?

"Clearly, the Americans should be eliminated. It is *us* who should advance to the finals against you, *not* the Americans. We understand that you have the evidence to legally eliminate the USA syndicate. It is your duty, and you should carry it out without further consideration." And so on. "There is little question that the American syndicate has been caught cheating. It is clearly stated. Rule 75, no? It has been violated."

Yes, I had the photographs Derek had taken of our keel. I had their camera, too. I had their statement. I did have *Yankee Doodle* cooked. And we'd already beaten the French boat. We could eliminate America and beat France again in the challenger finals and advance to the finals against New Zealand. It was tempting.

But this had become a family feud. Blood is thicker than sea water, thicker than *vin rouge*, but not as thick as oatmeal, whatever that means. And I would never be able to feel as good about beating France as I would about beating Uncle Routledge and his *Yankee Doodle* syndicate boat-for-boat on the twenty-four-mile America's Cup course. Four-out-of-seven races would be unforgettable, especially for him.

And anyway, ever since La Rochelle there had been bad blood between the French and us. Even last week, Claude la Luc had quoted one of their crewman in a French paper, saying that *Kinsman* resembled *UN boll de Glee farmhouse avec des raisins*, a bowl of raspberry Jell-O with raisins. And Moses Mazimpaka had been quoted in the *Auckland Star*, "Rats are French. Listen to their accent when they talk."

I told Christian that I had lost the damning evidence. Some idiot had accidentally flushed the pictures down a toilet, and one of my men had sold the camera to a tourist. And the diver, Derek (I never learned his last name), had gone to Tuscany for the winter months.

He called me a liar in the name of good sportsmanship. I called him a liar in the name of a million dead Rwandans. I tried not to hit him, but I did push him off the dock.

So, everything stood fast. It would be a classic match and now maybe the United States would pay attention to Rwanda.

᠅

The Conditions of Winning

We had done it. The challenger finals. The best four-out-of-seven races. If the forecast was right, in three days we'd have gale force winds. And with our heavy duty speed, I felt we'd smoke America four straight. We might even give them another race, not two, just to keep it honest, but I wasn't sure about that.

God knows what New Zealand had waiting for us, the *Black Lion*. There'd been rumors; no one knew for sure. She'd been spotted sailing on the back side of the North Island, and even Uncle Rut with his espionage arm hadn't been able to get the story on her speed or capture her on film. It was said that she had a bow sharp enough to slice prosciutto, a mast that changed shape according to the force of the wind, translucent sails, a pair of winged razor blades for keels, along with rudders fore and aft, and a hull as lacquered as a Steinway grand. The Kiwis could always be counted on to invent ways to win, and they had a fierce attacking style. The Cup belonged to them now, and they wanted to keep it forever. Just as America had.

We had a cookout Friday night, and Aunt Pearl called me Saturday morning. She wanted me to ask the crew to church on Sunday. The word "ask" was a joke. *Kinsman's* sole backer was telling us all to report to church.

"What kind of church?" I asked.

"It doesn't matter, Jib. We all know how to pray. I'm only providing the hall."

"Good. We can ask the Almighty to slow down the *Doodle*."

"Jib. It's a prayer of thanks. I want us to pray thanks for what we've done so far. It's got nothing to do with beating anyone."

I made it compulsory. I told each man to wear his white shirt and that we were going to pray thanks to almighty God in a church, and then we'd all go and eat boiled lobster and fried chicken and drink ale at Fisherman's Wharf. I told them not to wear the French suits I'd bought them after winning at La Rochelle, the black shiny ones. Walking together, they might frighten the pedestrians. And, neatly dressed in white shirts, Elizaphan wearing a dress with flowers, we all trooped over on the ten o'clock ferry Sunday morning to Auckland, where Aunt Pearl had met us at the dock. The church turned out to be Anglican.

"Look around you," she said. It had no vertical walls. It looked temporary. Its glass apex was aimed at the heart of the sky, as if the church itself were a climax, rather than the people in it or their prayers or God. The architecture, senior-student-project, was so modern it had set the church in motion. Pearl was angry about it. "No, this isn't a good church to pray from. Just try to thank God for being here at all."

The place was flooded with sun. The men were on their knees, bowed toward a lazy sliver of gold modeled into a cross on a great slice of yellow marble. The men were deeply involved, as if they needed to be there. Aunt Pearl had been right, of course. She was hemispherical. It had been a good idea. It made good sense to stop and pray. She had known that the men and even Larry, Marcus, and I needed this pause to reflect before going into the finals.

At first, when I'd recruited the men as soccer players in a non-yachting country and I'd begun training them, I had thought of them as children. And then, during the long time it took me to move from my butt into my head, I'd learned that they were smarter than I was about so many things I would never know about. About the line. The line that separates us from the dead. I looked at them. They were my men. They had changed me, and I liked the change so I prayed thanks to them for it. And I had turned them into what they would never have been able to become under the rules of starvation. Now they had nutrition, training, exercise and hope; they were superb natural athletes. I had had an outrageous dream, and Aunt Pearl had put wheels under it and wings on it. And then later, Larry and Marcus and these great men had propelled us to the place we were standing at right now. It seemed to be too solemn an occasion for the amount of excitement I was feeling. I could not have been happier that Sunday morning.

After church, as Pearl had promised, we all went to lunch at Fisherman's Wharf and ate fried chicken and lobster, and all the ale we could drink. Then we straggled back on the ferry to Waiheke Island and went to the Mosquito Café and sat around the tables out back smoking cigars. Aunt Pearl wanted to listen to the men. She needed to hear what they were feeling. She'd noticed something in church. The men had sat like old men. Anyway, we sat around outside, and she listened.

Leopold and Moses, Kikongoro and Isaaco had gotten pretty drunk on the local ale and had been talking freely. And while one of them talked, Esperance translated for her. "Yes, it was good to be here. It was nice to be in good health to send money back home," to win at *le lotterie* (as they called my betting system) that would save money for them to buy farms. The men stood to gain. Aunt Pearl had been right. As I looked around at them, they didn't seem as happy as they should have been. They had proved they could survive, but they were existing without joy. We were only dancing once or twice a week at the end of the days. Leopold said it was that (in spite of our victories) the men felt that this was a very good job, but without a future, and that it would be over soon. They had been kept in isolation without their families on this island off of Auckland, where they knew nobody but themselves. It was now five months that they'd been away from home, except for the two weeks in October. How could they be happy?

Aunt Pearl said, "But that seems ridiculous."

"I agree with you Aunt Pearl," Leopold said. "It is not that which we fear. You want us to be happier than we are."

"Yes, of course, I do. I think you should be extremely grateful for all that has happened."

"What do you see when you close your eyes before you go to sleep Aunt Pearl?"

"I see many things, Leopold. Beautiful things. I see what has happened during the day, or I can see what I will do tomorrow, or I think about someone I love who is no longer here. It is never the same."

"Of course, it isn't."

"What do you see Leopold?"

"It is always the same."

No one spoke. She knew. She broke the silence.

"But is there nothing that can ever change that?"

"I don't think so, Aunt Pearl. I don't think so."

Our dreams were dreams of winning, dreams of luxuries, of pleasures and inconveniences. They were *our* dreams, not theirs. White dreams.

Leopold's dreams came any time. All day long, glimpses of atrocities whenever there was silence. And it was worse at night, because the night was one long stretch of silence for atrocities to enter. And if he slept in the morning, he woke to the ringing of a machete striking his father's skull and the exact memory of his father's head being divided six feet in front of him.

So, even if we pulled it off and beat the American boat, won big, and maybe beat New Zealand, it was possible. But it would never be enough for Leopold. It would never be enough to remove the atrocity from his consciousness, because once you have atrocity, you can have nothing better. Victory, however grand, would never change him. He said he no longer looked under his bed or behind doors, but he slept badly and sometimes woke Moses or Esperance to talk through the night until it got light and better. An atrocity is an atrocity. There is no statute of limitations, no exact definition; an atrocity ages well and stays fresh throughout your lifetime. Leopold said that a crocodile may kill your baby that has fallen into the river. And that is very, very bad, and it is a horrible mistake, but it is not an atrocity. An atrocity is not a mistake; it has been done to you on purpose. It cannot be done by animals, but by your neighbors, men you know who look you in the eye, thinking men. It is not enough to say that an act of cruelty is extremely wicked, atrocious, brutal. Those are words to furnish newspaper sentences. Ink on paper. No one knows, or can tell you what the world has forgiven on its soil. Leopold survived atrocities, but it is like your operation; you cannot expect anyone to care unless he has had his own atrocity. And no one except these men, certainly not Aunt Pearl, has had his own atrocity. Leopold said to her very quietly, "Have you ever seen your baby daughter thrown into a bonfire?"

"No, Leopold," she answered just as quietly. "I have not."

But that is what Leopold had seen. Elizaphan covered her mouth.

So, even though *Kinsman* was no longer a mere boat to me or Pearl, but a dream, it remained to the men a series of nightmares. It was a white man's boat and, regardless of our glorious hopes, the men were not able to see beyond it to its salvation, or to its power to heal their wounds. Or the wounds of a country beset. It was a colorful distraction that could never stop a nightmare. And the men had never stopped having nightmares.

Of course, they wanted to go home. I did too, somewhat. The thought of certain things like Reggio's espresso, drinks at Chumley's, meatball sandwiches at Julius' made me think of the Village, but not enough to want to go back there.

Until that night, I had not let myself envision the moment of winning during the eighteen months of training. I had only thought of competing, winning here and there, one boat at a time. But now, winning the Cup had been all I had thought about these past few weeks. I had seen the way luck was turning our way. And with our liquid keel and phenomenal speed, I saw it as a reality, and the thought of it gave me a rush. But I saw that to the men winning was something they were beginning to fear. That the closer they got to the Cup, the more they feared the possibility of winning it. When Pearl asked Leopold why, he said that there may be dangers in winning, that winning carried punishment with it.

"What do you want, Leopold?"

"What I want is a wife, and we will have a farm, two cows, goats, and a generator for a refrigerator and a light. We would like nothing else. Oh. A radio. We will be first class citizens." Moses nodded. Kikongoro had gone home.

"Well, you will have that," I said.

I tried to explain the good of winning. Of being better than all the others. All the good things winning would carry with it. The new buildings that would be built, all the people that would come, the new roads and cars and airports all of the industry it would inspire, the rich people who would come, the hotels and new streets that would be built. All that it would do for their country. And it all sounded ridiculous. By the time I was through, I was tired of my own voice. As Esperance had methodically translated each wonderful improvement, I could see by their faces that the men wanted none of it.

Isaaco who had gotten quite drunk and sad, said, "But you see if we do win and when you come and build my country the way you would like it to be, then I will disappear under it."

Moses said, "The buildings that you imagine have nothing to do with me, and I will disappear, and I will be a second class citizen again."

Ba'ale said, "And I will be ashamed."

Eventually the party, if that's what it was, wound down, and we broke up. I suppose it had been a success, finding out what was inside the men, but Aunt Pearl was disappointed, and she was left with depressed feelings. "After all I've done," she said. Finding out that there were two sets of dreams: theirs and ours. She wasn't prepared for that.

"Pearl, you can't expect them to see what we see. They're partly right. If it happens that we win, Rwanda will step from one horrible to another horrible without stopping at Go."

"What do you mean by Go?"

"Just good; nice normal good. I don't know. Something between what they've got and industrialized imperialism."

Pearl went back to Auckland on her chartered boat. I told Elizaphan I wanted to stop by the compound. She went on back to our guest house.

When I got to the compound it was dark. Ba'ale's security lights were off. He was our watchman, and he was nowhere to be seen. I tried the door to our shed. Locked.

I called Ba'ale. I heard loud, hollow noises coming from the direction of the dock: a clank-clank-clank, clacking; sometimes, a metallic ringing. It sounded like a bad drum beat. The noise was coming from *Kinsman*. From below decks. I called Ba'ale. The banging stopped. I went aboard her. I turned on her spreader lights. They shone down on her deck. Nothing looked wrong. I stepped onto the dock. I saw dozens of cut marks along her hull and on her bow and topsides. I jumped on board and looked down the after companionway.

"Ba'ale. You down there?"

Kikongoro burst onto the deck from the forward hatch, swinging a machete wide. He struck the mast the stays, staggering, swinging at anything in his way, winches and grinders, the deck. He was attacking the boat. He was very drunk.

"Kikongoro! Stop!"

He saw me. He dropped the machete on the deck and fell backward into the gulf. Then I heard Ba'ale. He was in the water clinging to the stern line with his good hand. He looked terrified. Kikongoro must have disarmed him and shoved him in. As far as I knew, Ba'ale owned the only machete in our camp. I reached a boat-hook down and hauled Ba'ale on deck. He picked up his machete and inspected it. He stood there dripping, looking down at Kikongoro warily, with mixed feelings. Kikongoro stayed in the water hanging onto the bow line for my interview. The water had done nothing to sober him up. I stood there amazed.

"What were you thinking, Effie?"

"This boat is not good."

"Who is to say that?"

"I am to say it." He hit *Kinsman*'s topsides with the flat of his hand making an echoing cello sound. "It is an instrument of your tyranny." Which, of course, was partly true if you thought about it for more than a second. "I will not become a second class citizen again in my own country."

"And Leopold?"

"Yes, Leopold, too. Moses and Isaaco."

"This is not what they meant."

"They are Tutsi and Hutu, but I am neither. I am Pygmy." He announced this with pride. I had heard this many times. "Rwanda is a land that was ours five hundred years before any Hutu or the Tutsi ever set foot to it. It is not for you to decide whose it is."

"We must talk about it tomorrow with Leopold and Isaaco and Moses. Now, are you finished trying to kill *Kinsman*?"

"Yes."

I hauled him up on deck. Kikongoro was very ashamed. His eyes were pink, and I realized his cheeks were widely spent with tears, not sea water. Kikongoro was very sad.

So was I.

"Don't be sad, Kikongoro. You are right. We are both right. We must try to find out how we can make that possible."

That night I knew I wasn't going to sleep, and I knew Aunt Pearl wouldn't be able to, either. Too much had been said. That my men would become second class citizens. That the ruling class would remain the ruling class. That *Kinsman* was an instrument of our tyranny. I'd been blind to their true needs, and that blindness left me wondering what I was going tell Kikongoro and the rest of them about our future together.

There had been difficult lessons for me to learn this past year. One of them was not to condescend. Being a casual aristocrat from the spires of Newport, it had always been my nature to feel that anyone who was not from my neighborhood was at a disadvantage in life. To be a Pygmy, well, that was an easy one. I was beginning to imagine that one could draw great pride in himself in a world of elms when one was a weed. I had a lot to learn.

⚑

The Mutiny

Two days.

Yankee Doodle had it all. Beautifully sailed by Soapy Armstrong, electronically navigated by Uncle Rut, and having Bermuda Schwartz as her tactician, she also had tons of money in her war chest, along with every cutting edge digital computerized satellite powered electronic gimcrack thus far devised by sailing experts. But she did not have what we had: the sheer power of our liquid keel. We'd sail *Kinsman* full out against her, hull down, with our keel pushing us. There'd be no more mystery about our speed, only some discretion. I'd do my best to humiliate *Yankee Doodle*.

Larry Bayard might be well enough to sail. But if he wasn't, I'd install his hospital bed in the cockpit beside me. He'd been having a lousy time, his face had turned from lemon yellow to French blue. His doctor couldn't seem to put his finger on it, but he was using the word *botulism*. He couldn't get his blood count up.

It was my birthday. Happy birthday. I was twenty-eight. All this Cup business had started when I was twenty-six. I'd swapped two key years for it. Aunt Pearl had forgotten, Elizaphan had never known, and I didn't want to bring it up. It was simply my birthday. So what? But I had to mention it, or it wouldn't exist. So, just about midnight back in our room, I told Elizaphan while she was undressing for bed. "It is my birthday today." She stood there nude, her arms at her sides.

She said, "Happy Birthday, Charles," quietly. The room was chilly. She didn't ask how old I was. She didn't move to kiss me. She simply stood there; she could do that. She could stand without posing arms at her sides, undisguised by makeup, unprotected by clothing, ecru. She was the color of unbleached linen, a pale sepia. Her breasts were soft-colored, mother-of-pearl, poignant, unused, free, stiff.

"What is it?" I said. It could have been anything.

She tossed her cotton nightgown over her head and let it fall over her shoulders, down her body, her breasts stiff against the fabric.

178

"When is yours?" I said, "and please don't tell me your birth-sign."

It was too late. I had forgotten; there was no birthday. She had none. It had been lost. She was not on the calendar. Her father, the Norwegian missionary, had vanished; her mother, the schoolteacher, had been raped and killed. She'd been too young to know and so never did. I picked her up and laid her across the bed.

"Don't be sad, Charles. I am not," she said. "I never wanted one. Now I do, so I will make one up. I will take yours. Today will be my birthday, too, from now on and forever."

Later, when she was asleep and the moon was singing loudly through my pillow, the faces of my men drove me from the bed. I put on clothes and went downstairs as quietly as I could. I walked to the dock. It is always slightly downhill toward sea level. There was something vivid in the air. Something intense. Unsure. I was confused. I passed Ba'ale, who sat with Moses in the doorway of the long boat shed. He was not surprised. Moses was Bahutu; Ba'ale was Batutsi. It had been raining earlier in the evening, and they had sheltered. I had interrupted their conversation. They stopped talking when they saw me.

"Good evening, Skipper," they said more or less in unison. It was good that they had stopped calling me boss, but now skipper was a problem, because Larry was the true skipper. I was just the fill-in skipper. Ba'ale was more alert than usual. As far as I knew, he never slept.

"Hello Ba'ale. Hello, Moses. May I sit?"

They nodded. I sat on a box.

"Rain," Ba'ale said. For a few moments, we sat contemplating rain. From my shirt pocket, I brought out the alligator skin cigar case Jocelyn had given me. In it were four small Monte Cristos, and I found myself giving them each a cigar. You give to a Rwandan, you don't offer.

Moses was smiling. He said Ba'ale was telling him about Louis Veeton. He asked me was it true.

"Is he really a maker of valises that are the most expensive in the world?"

"Probably," I said.

"Do you pay five thousand dollars for a *sac de nuit*?"

I told him yes.

"And we will win valises. Is it true?"

"Probably, if we beat the Americans. See, it goes to the best of the challengers. You know, England, France, Spain, Japan, America."

"Us."

"And us, yes."

"Why is he the name of the race?"

"Maybe because yacht people are able to buy overpriced bags."

Luis Vuitton. Perfect. My dream sponsor. Is five grand too steep for an overnight bag? Well, darling, you shouldn't complain. Your mainsail cost ninety grand.

I'd seen the Luis Vuitton Cup. It was unpardonable. A silver slash of art deco. As tasteless in its way as the Cup was in its way. It made me want to cough up my introduction to yacht racing.

I needed to be alone. Sitting and smoking with them was the last thing I wanted to do. But I was drawn to them, whether they wanted me with them or not, and I found myself lighting our cigars and not wanting to be alone that night after all.

Ba'ale and Moses smoked their cigars through their nostrils rather than their mouths. The mouth was for eating. The mouth was not to be soiled by smoke; smoke was for the head. It was a head trip, after all. When I was with them, I always took a few puffs through my nostrils, and I did that night. The three of us sat without speaking. I had a problem to solve that night and no desire to work it out. I wanted it magically solved.

I noticed Kikongoro standing off in the shadows. He had been watching us. Ominously. He had probably gone to take a piss. He had forgotten to zip up his pants. I gave him a cigar. He reached his hand out, took it. He didn't say anything. He seemed angry.

I had promised to talk to him, but I knew nothing more than I did the night before. He sat down on a box.

"You promised to talk to me."

"Kikongoro. I will talk to you tomorrow."

"You know, Patron, what Kikongoro say?" Ba'ale said.

"Yes, of course."

I understood the problem. I didn't have the answer. I needed more time. Still, part of me was annoyed at them for making it hard to concentrate on the finals with America.

"I heard." I said, "Winning the Cup will not be such a big thing after all."

"That's right."

"I understand that he's upset that hotels, business, tall buildings will be built, and that tourists will come."

"No," Moses said. "He says you still do not understand. It will be men of influence who will come to change Rwanda, like the French and the Belgians. We are always looking up to people of influence. The power to say "kill" and some of us obey. These were the big men behind this genocide. We are poor ignorant people. We look up to everyone. We always say "yes" to them. That is how the trouble started. I am Bahutu. They gave us hand grenades, the Kalashnikov gun; we bring our own machetes, our masus."

Ba'ale and Kikongoro were nodding, half-understanding what Moses was saying. "I am alive by accident," he said in French. "I am meant to be dead with my family. I still do not understand why I am alive."

"You were a lucky one."

"I was. But I am meant to have a family and where are they? I was supposed to die like them."

"How did you live?"

"I had given up any doubt I would be killed, of course, by machete. I was hiding, but I had given up the will. The only fear left was the machete; it is much better to die by a bullet. Three soldiers found me. I had one goat, so I arranged not to die by machete. That I would be shot in my own house. It was late in the afternoon. They cut my heel tendon so I couldn't run away and went away to find a gun. I waited for them all night long. They showed up in the morning still drunk. They were laughing. There was no gun, so one of them cut my right hand off. They took my goat. It is a miracle my tendons healed."

"You were very lucky, Ba'ale."

"Was I not? Sometimes I cannot be sure of that." He sniffed up a long nostril full of smoke and blew it away in a cloud. "But this is a very good cigar."

Kikongoro had been making clicking sounds with his tongue and hissing from time to time.

"I live in a country of great fear. I detest that fear," he said. In the dark, I could feel his eyes watching my face.

"I am still afraid," Ba'ale said in French. "All my life I am afraid. It is with me now. It will always wake me too early. I try to forget, but of course it is impossible."

Kikongoro hissed. "I don't want that again!" he said in a fierce whisper. I saw his eyes flash white in the dark. He resembled an angry dog, too smart to bare his teeth, but I knew he was angry and that he would lunge if I came too close within his chain. He truly did not want the spoils of victory. And I saw that now on the brink of realizing my dreamed-of success, there could easily be a mutiny. During one of the races something could go wrong. Kikongoro was the starboard tailer, which meant that he also handled a running backstay, a crucial position, the stress on the mast calculated in tonnage. Conceivably, he could cause a bad accident. Or man overboard. One man overboard in each race. The men knew how. I had taught them.

I told them that by placing bets on *Kinsman* now Moses, Kikongoro, and Ba'ale, Isaaco, the two Leopolds, Josue, all of the crew, had made a pile. We were being discovered. We had done well. The odds against us were falling. On the Las Vegas tote board, they were down, thirty to one. Each man knew he had made enough money so far to be secure. But nothing was going to be enough to get rid of their fear of a repetition or of their psychoses.

"I will talk to you soon about it. That is my promise. Now I must go."

I said goodnight and went on board *Kinsman* and sat in the cockpit. This was going to be another long night for me. They had all gotten long, but this

181

would be the longest, longer than my first flight home from Rwanda after I'd seen the massacres.

It was pleasant on a calm night to listen to *Kinsman* speaking. No matter how calm the sea, it was never calm enough for her. She could not be silent. A ripple echoed up from her hull hollowness; there was nothing below decks to baffle the sound. I saw faces as I lay there. I would be dozing off, but then I would see Kikongoro's face, his anger. The ancient debasement of humanity was a not a thing you could forget. And each time I saw his face tired from anger, I woke up again. Finally, lying curled between winches, I slept on deck.

I was surprised by the morning. I woke up in the cockpit wet with dew. It had come to me. I might have the answer. And it was Ba'ale and Moses who had helped me. Without going back to Mrs. Prosser's, I walked down to the ferry dock and took the early boat to Auckland. It was still early when I knocked on Aunt Pearl's door.

She opened it wearing a dressing gown. I noticed the door to her bedroom was closed.

"Are you alone?"

"Jibby." Her eyes were marvelously wicked.

She was having breakfast on her balcony. She asked me to join her and called room service and ordered me breakfast, coffee, toast, and eggs. I noticed a second cup and saucer on the table, but I didn't mention it.

I told her how Kikongoro had attacked *Kinsman*. She was dumbfounded.

"Last night?"

"With Ba'ale's machete."

"I can't understand that."

I told her I could.

"I'm white, Aunt Pearl. Listen to me. You know I'm white, but please believe me when I tell you I was black before I was white. So were you. It's weird, isn't it, when you realize that? I felt that last night. You understand? I'm not being melodramatic."

"Oh, yes you are my darling, very. But I see your point although I never feel black myself." She looked worried.

"Kikongoro's not alone. He may have acted alone, and he may have been drunk, but I can tell others feel the way he does. We could have a mutiny on our hands, believe it or not."

"I choose not to believe it."

I began. I repeated some of what she already knew. That if we won the Cup all the men would come home to Rwanda national heroes, and all hell would break loose. There'd be a parade for them. President Bizimungu would give them medals. So far, so good. The men would like that, but it would lead to more. What they were saying, was that there would be big outside forces sweeping in that could repeat what had happened before.

"Of course, that's if we have victory," Pearl said.

"It'll all depend on that," I said. "If we don't have victory, it won't be a problem. *Kinsman* won't exist and we'll be like that Jamaican bobsled team, a dumb joke without a punchline. But if we do win, Pearl, what's in it for them?"

"Aren't they being a bit ungrateful? Everything, of course."

"That's what they're afraid of and, believe me, last night so was I. They were talking."

"Do you have a plan?"

I nodded. "I might."

"Keep the dreams attainable, old boy." As Saint told me a year ago.

"So far, I have." I took a sip of coffee. "If we win, why couldn't President Bizimungu do something for them, not just medals but create a committee made up of them and *only* them to oversee the building of rehab centers through-out Rwanda. It could even be named after them, the Kinsmen, plural."

"Why, it's a brilliant idea, Jib. You keep surpassing yourself, to say nothing of surprising me."

"Now all we have to do is win."

"What's the next step?"

"I'd like to have something to tell the men before the first race."

"That's forty-eight hours. I'll call Saint. It's still last night in New York. I'll wake him."

"Tell him that Bizimungu must be urged to sign a paper creating a delegation. Think Saint can persuade him to do it?"

"If anyone can. Of course, he was in diplomatique for ages. He'll fly right to Rwanda and discuss this with their president –"

"Pasteur Bizimungu."

I took the ferryboat back to Waiheke Island. Sky-high. Aunt Pearl had telephoned Saint Pierre while I was there and told him the plan, and he had agreed to call the Rwandan Embassy in Washington, and he loved the idea. He agreed to make an appointment with Bizimungu, then fly to Rwanda.

When I arrived at our camp, our work crew was just about finished patching the machete cuts on *Kinsman's* wounded topsides from Kikongoro's attack. The caulking in the scars was white and would stay white until we could get our special shade of red paint, a special shade of alizarin red that needed to be flown in from Italy. The caulking gave the topsides a crazed look.

I spotted Kikongoro patching the bow on the outside of the hull where he couldn't be seen. I asked Esperance to gather the men. When they'd come into the shed and squatted, I told them that Saint was going to meet with their president and ask him to form a committee made up of the boat's crew. I told them its responsibilities. None of them would be made to join it, but no one else could, only *Kinsman's* crewmen could become members. It would be called the Kinsmen, and it would be exclusively theirs. I talked to the men.

They were not shaky. They seemed strong about winning, as far as I could sense. Kikongoro had been subdued, but not forever. He was ashamed that he had attacked *Kinsman*. But he could do anything and say what he felt and some men would always listen to him; Moses was one, and Ba'ale was another.

"So, you see, victory can only bring you good," I said

"Has it happened?"

"No, not yet."

"We will wait," Moses said.

"Yes, why don't we wait." I answered. Fair enough. "But while we are waiting, will you sail the ass off *Kinsman* against the American boat?"

No one said anything. Kikongoro smiled.

The Bet

The next morning I picked up the film from Derek's underwater camera. The quality of the pictures was remarkable, but the photographs revealed no secrets. I called Aunt Pearl and asked her to deliver a package with the film and the camera in it to Uncle Rut. Our camp and Team *Yankee Doodle*'s were distantly separated not only by our island, but by my betrayal. But then I decided to face him.

We met at the TYD offices at the Marina. Uncle Rut looked fit. So did I. Sailing will do that. We shook hands firmly. His accountant was there; Reid, a dull shaft of a man whose polite manners embalmed our meeting. I shut the door and sat down. They remained standing. Rut looked confident. So did I. He didn't appear to loathe me; on the other hand, he congratulated me. Of course, he was sure I was going to lose to him.

"The French want you out of the finals, Uncle Rut. They know what you've been doing."

"And what the hell do you suppose that is?" He showed no surprise. He'd never thought too highly of me; that opinion had just dropped.

"Baron Biche says you violated the Rules of Challenge by spying on other boats. He says he can disqualify you. He sent a man named Christian Somebody who begged me to turn my evidence over to the Race Committee and invoke Rule 75.

"Fair Sailing Rule, Laurence," The accountant said.

"I know the Fair Sailing Rule, God damn it!" He snapped.

"We admit nothing," the accountant said to me, as if he were a defense attorney on retainer.

"Reid, for Christ's sake."

"What did you tell this person?" Reid asked me.

"I told him I'd lost the film and the camera."

"We've done absolutely nothing wrong," Uncle Rut said.

I opened my bag and dumped its contents onto the table. Out fell the un-

185

derwater camera, a dozen photographs of our keel, and what was left of Derek's face mask. "And here it is."

"What the hell is this stuff?" Under his sunburn, his face reddened. He was insulted, not embarrassed. It was an embarrassment for me. Rich, successful men fibbing. I told him "goodbye."

"Where are you going?"

I had to catch the ten a.m. ferry, I said. "It's okay, Uncle Rut. I understand."

"You understand?" Now he was outraged. Nothing strikes quite so hard as massed guilt.

"Disqualification is the only way you could possibly beat us, kid."

I really didn't care, and that was the truth. I told him it was alright either way. His espionage may have been a failure, but I certainly wasn't about to turn him into the French. What kind of nephew would do that? I wanted to save him for the finals and beat him with my Negro yachtsmen. I didn't say that. Instead, I went to the door. I wanted to hang onto my temper. What I did tell him was that our boat, not his, was going to go on to meet New Zealand.

He said, "Bull. Shit."

"Okay, bullshit, but we will," I told him. I added blindly, "Watch."

"With your crew of mongrels?"

"Yes, with my crew of mongrels. You're the mongrel, by the way. All us Routledges, we're a mixed breed: English, French, German, Irish, and Welsh; a family tree of apples and potatoes? Ba'ale Musavene, Innocent Hatumaimana, Moses Mazimpaka, any Batutsi or Bahutu on my crew, is purer than you are. Not diluted by French, German, English, or Welsh Irish blood, they are so pure they can trace their family lineage back thousands of years, maybe a million. That's why they kill them, because they're pure. So you'd better call my crew thoroughbreds, Uncle Rut, because they haven't interbred the way the Routledges have." I had outpointed him. I opened the door. "And they're going to beat you, four straight."

"You're going to beat us four straight?"

I was too pissed off to hang around.

"I just told you that."

"You want to put down a bet?"

"Bet?" A new thought.

"*Kinsman* against *Yankee Doodle*."

"Sure, why not?"

"Name the stakes. Yours to name, Jib," he said quickly.

"Is a thousand too high?"

He grabbed the moment by the neck and ran with it.

"Is a million too high?" There is no fury like the fury of an uncle from

Newport, Rhode Island who has just been insulted by his ne'er-do-well nephew.

"Dollars?" I said stupidly.

"Yes, dollars." He allowed himself a chuckle.

"Okay, a million dollars." My head was turning into Styrofoam. "Okay, let's bet one million dollars."

He spoke carefully. "You bet that your boat, *Kinsman*, the Rwanda challenger with its crew of Negroes, will eliminate our boat, *Yankee Doodle*, the American challenger, from the America's Cup Finals."

"Yup." I'd need to discuss this move with my exchequer, Aunt Pearl.

"Better write that down, Reid. I don't want to hear any whining later on."

Nor do I, I thought.

We stood looking at various gray appliances standing on the desks around the room until Reid had been able to jot the sentence down, date it, make a photocopy of it, and notarize both copies. It was a gentlemen's bet. But just to be sure, we three signed the original and the copy in silence. I folded mine and put it in my back pocket. We shook hands even more firmly than before. I knew I could beat him; all I needed was a gale. Force Ten.

"Good luck tomorrow, Uncle Rut."

"Good luck to you, kid." We shook hands firmly again.

Actually, too firmly. Yacht racing was a gentleman's sport after all.

Being a member of the Routledge family felt as if I were locked in a subway with random passengers for life.

I didn't catch the ten o'clock ferryboat. I went straight over to Aunt Pearl's hotel. It was her money I'd bet. After all, I didn't have any million dollars, and I wasn't sure how she was going to take it.

She answered the door wordlessly and let me in. I had obviously awakened her. She ordered breakfast and disappeared into her bedroom and wouldn't reappear until it had been wheeled out onto the balcony. She sat in her dressing gown, her grey hair piled high, sipping tea overlooking the gulf.

"Now, tell me, darling, why am I having my early morning tea with you two days in a row? Is this about your mutiny?"

I told her it seemed to be off for the moment.

"I thought it might be."

"What about Saint?"

"I just spoke to him. It's five in New York; I adore waking him. He has an appointment with President Bizimungu the day after tomorrow, and I asked him to call me immediately from there when he got out of their meeting."

I told her I'd had an unforeseen business expense.

"Oh?" she said.

When I told her what had happened between her brother and me, how he'd sort of made me trap myself, she flushed, her face expanded wonderfully, she laughed, she raised her royal nose. "I really and truly adore a good wager, don't you know, Jibby?" Of course, she approved; she was proud of me. A good wager was money well-invested, she said, and making her brother Laurence hand over his personal check for one million dollars would be celestial. It would go beyond simply beating him under sail. It was perfect, and just one more treat that made this whole Cup thing intoxicating. If Aunt Pearl were a man, I would have called her a perfect gentleman.

Prelude

It was blowing the morning of the race. When I walked down to the compound early, no one was around and whoever was around wasn't doing anything. No one was getting the boat ready. The sails were still hanging in the shed. The boat was dirty. A halyard dangled. I got to the bottom of it pretty quickly. Ba'ale told me that the men were refusing to sail that day. Race day. I knew who started the mutiny, but I didn't want to find out who was for it or against it. I didn't want to divide the crew again. There was no way I could have the race postponed five hours before the start. We'd be zero to one by forfeit. I phoned Aunt Pearl from the shed.

"Has Saint left for Rwanda yet?"

"He's on his way to the airport as we speak."

"Did he speak to President Bizimungu?"

"Yes, they had a wonderful chat."

"You'd better get over here and tell that to the men. We have a mutiny."

"No."

"Yes. They refuse to race without knowing something definite." My word wasn't good enough.

Pearl's boat came alongside forty-five minutes later and docked at around nine-thirty. She came into the shed. The men had grown agitated, but they fell silent when they saw her. There was great affection between them. Though she had never said so, the men sensed that she loved them. Esperance asked her if she wanted coffee and buttered bread leftover from breakfast. She said yes she did. He brought them to her on a tray. The men sensed that Pearl had something important to tell them and fell silent and squatted, facing her respectfully. She opened the pages of her small, blue leather notebook with the gold-edged, blue pages. She read to them slowly from her notes. She read well, and Esperance translated.

"Our ambassador, Saint Pierre Forrester," as she preferred to call Saint, "has spoken to your President, Pasteur Bizimungu. He has asked him that should you bring the America's Cup home to Rwanda, you be declared national heroes."

Leopold Cassel interrupted. Esperance translated his question: "Is he going to give us medals?"

"I think he will give you medals, of course, Leopold, but Saint Pierre told him that you should be given more than medals. You should be given the right to form a council." Esperance translated, carefully making sure every man understood. "Your council will oversee the construction of hospitals and rehabilitation centers in all of the nine prefectures in Rwanda. These centers will be for all of the dismembered and blinded survivors of the massacres. They will each have a place. For all the mentally unbalanced survivors of the genocide, those with severest mental problems, they will have a place to be made better."

Mungo Kayjaho asked a question.

"Who will pay for this?" Esperance translated.

"You should be rewarded by your government," Aunt Pearl said.

Kikongoro reflected the doubt that most Rwandans felt for their government.

"It will be money your government will take from the investments that outside businesses will make in Rwanda."

"Why should we believe this?" It was Josue Valence.

Aunt Pearl took a moment to look offended. "Why, you have no reason to doubt it, Josue, because I am the one telling you. Don't you see that if you win the America's Cup, money will come from the world into your country? You have no idea how rich the outer world is."

"You say, then, let us wait and see if we win."

"Of course, Josue. What President Bizimungu said to Saint Pierre is that *if* you do win the Cup *and* Rwanda becomes the host country for the defense, whatever outside money comes into the country to build hotels or to establish businesses, instead of the usual graft, a small percentage will be skimmed off the top for your council to set up its rehabilitation centers. Your president says that. Your ambassador will come here tomorrow. You must accept my word."

The men made clucking sounds, their version of applause. The mutiny was over for today. It was just one more amazing moment in a year of amazing moments.

"Can we go sailing now?" I said.

⚑

America Versus Rwanda

Out on the course, the wind was howling, gusting dangerously to twenty-five. The seas were falling in deep troughs between peaks fifty feet across. It was rough out there. If it got any worse, the committee would call the race. But we could ride those swells beautifully, perfect for our shark's fin keel. I'd gotten Larry Bayard's doctor to loan him to me for the day, to pronounce him well enough to sail; that is, well enough to sit in the cockpit and give me advice. Aunt Pearl would carry him out on her chartered boat, and he'd join us before the start near the line.

On our dock at Waiheke Island before we caught the towline, the men listened to me like boxers between rounds, nodding. I was trying to give them a pep talk, to instill in them the idea of winning. It didn't matter what I said, I didn't speak Kinyarwandan well enough. So, I left the translation up to the crew chiefs, Isaaco and Esperance. I told them that this was more than a mere sailboat race and to be strong and not to fall overboard. I had gotten their bets down. I bet each crewman's winnings. The odds were still kind to us. It was risky, but they could make a bundle. They'd have much more than their farms.

During the pre-start maneuvers, *Yankee Doodle* was caught in the heavy chop, and she was riding the waves like a hobby horse. We crested and drove. And each time we dipped, we made a fine corkscrew turn and came over the next wave and crested again. We were flying. It was our weather. I knew we could beat America.

Larry sat propped-up in the cockpit looking like a Sioux papoose, and very miserable. I felt sorry for him. The doctor had allowed him aboard *Kinsman*, but nothing more, on condition that there be no work, mental or physical. I wondered why he thought I wanted him on board; an afternoon of sailing?

Larry was in charge of the start and the course. Marcus was on the stopwatch and the wind. I was on the helm. Esperance was on the sails. At the ten-minute gun, he separated *Kinsman* from *Yankee Doodle*. And in the pre-start, he all but ignored her. Larry's starting tactic seemed frivolous at the time. But nine minutes and fifty seconds later, when Marcus said, "Ten seconds!" we were charging *Yankee Doodle* at the line on starboard tack; Moses on the bow yelling, "Right of way!" I could see what Larry had done. He had bluffed *Yankee Doodle* and forced her across the starting line early at the windward end of the mark. We hit the line at the gun. The American boat was left standing in our bad air, and when she finally did get across the line again, she stayed behind us for the beat up to the first mark. We clung to our lead as planned. We looked good. Very smart, very normal.

When we converged at the wing mark, we were a very solid twelve seconds ahead. *Yankee Doodle*'s crew was clearly surprised. We were not supposed to be doing this. And when *Yankee Doodle* swung around the mark after us and heeled to her beams end, we could all see her radical carbon fiber keel, which seemed as small as a dagger for a rig as tall as she had.

Whenever we crossed her bow, her crew looked straight ahead like the perfect gentlemen they were, while our crew couldn't take their eyes off of them, smiling away. Soapy Armstrong held his chin high, the way we all taught ourselves to do as kids when we were match racing close to another boat. The pose. The alternative would have been for us to burst out laughing when we passed them close, which is what some of the men did.

Esperance had gotten Mungo and Kikongoro to winch the mainsail in flat, and at the third mark we had kept the windward edge and kept our lead, but it was too close. The race was closer than I expected it to be, especially for this weather. Anything could happen. We needed to post a win. The men needed to know we could win. And, anyway, I had a good deal of their money bet on it.

This time out I didn't give a damn who knew just what about our speed. Rounding the eighth mark, we showed them our heels. The weather blew up and gave us phenomenal speed that afternoon. We rode each wave down beautifully. The keel was liquid, and I could feel it shifting under my feet.

We crossed the finish line flying through a rain squall, surfing each wave down, with our biggest pure white spinnaker set, all lines taut, the stays humming. A mile behind us, *Yankee Doodle* was charging down on us, churning her bow wave off to either side, her great Pepsi Cola spinnaker clearly readable in case we wanted to buy any that afternoon. I'm a Coke man myself.

The foredeck crew doused the spinnaker as we flashed across the line at about fifteen knots, the rest of the crew waving their white caps at the race committee aboard *Lady Anne*, who did not wave back.

"Get the main down," I said. "We're going in on the jib."

Aunt Pearl's chartered boat picked up Larry Bayard, who seemed to be asleep on medication. I glanced back at the American boat when I heard the toot from *Lady Anne* as she finished. Something red was flying from their after stay. I asked Marcus to put the binoculars on it.

"What is it?"

I knew what it was before he got the binoculars on it. It was a protest flag on the jumper stay.

"Protest," he said.

"We didn't go near them," I said. The protest remained a mystery until we got back to our dock. A man wearing a suit and black shoes was waiting for me when we tied up.

He asked how I was and gave me a letter from a law firm that I needed to sign for. After the man had left, Marcus read the letter. He handed it back to me and pushed a big sigh. In a Cockney accent, he said, "Oy bin nabbed!"

The letter was on TYD stationery and quoted the Rule of Residency. It stated that Marcus Patrick Cape was sailing as tactician illegally aboard *Kinsman*. Team *Yankee Doodle* demanded our disqualification from race one. If we'd lost the race, I'm sure TYP would have postponed delivery until we had won one. The letter stated that the Race Committee had been notified.

This was the end of Marcus Cape, as we knew him. I had no choice. He was lost to us; I had to put him ashore. He had resided in Rwanda and Ivory Coast the required year, but he had taken off for a month. How could Uncle Rut have found that out? Espionage? The Embassy? Passports? Maybe Leonard Carter had volunteered the information. I still had what there was of Larry Bayard. But we were without a sailing technician, as well as a navigator, and likely to remain so. And no computer. We were down one race. That didn't bother me much. What did bother me was the loss of Marcus Cape.

ϸ

Race Two

Rain. It woke up raining, bad luck, and throughout the morning the rain built; flat heavy rain, but the race was not called off. After the crew and the men had eaten breakfast, we stayed a long time in the long shed waiting for the rain to let up. The world was suspended. Some of the men were playing games, wari, cards.

Through the window, *Kinsman* looked good, her hull caulked, glassed, ready to go. The scars from Kikongoro's machete stood out white against her red topsides. But she was sound. I watched her swing listlessly, a thoroughbred on race day.

I saw some of the men forming around Moses and Kikongoro. What now? I wanted to tell them that Saint Pierre had flown to Rwanda and had met with their president, but it ought to come from Aunt Pearl. And if there was any sign of another mutiny, it would come from her. The men respected me, but they knew I was driving them to win. Aunt Pearl was someone else; she held a mythological status.

Before noon, the rain had let up, and as we were being towed out to the starting line, the skies cleared, but the wind never came up. We needed this race.

No Marcus. I'd forced poor Larry to come on board again. Even stoked-up on Nembutal, he was being very brave. We took him off Aunt Pearl's boat near the starting line. Marcus looked down on the transaction in silence. When he was comfortably seated in a his half-inflated cocoon beside me, he gave them a sad wave. Aunt Pearl blew a kiss. Elizaphan smiled and rolled her eyes sensuously. We drifted away to get our sails up. When we'd gotten the main up and were beginning to move, Marcus waved his arms and shouted something to me, but I couldn't hear what it was. It sounded urgent.

After the ten-minute gun, I sailed within a couple of hundred yards of Pearl's boat and Marcus yelled again, but I still couldn't make it out. I asked Larry if he had been able to hear it. He nodded, "Fourteenth man."

That left me with a puzzle that I was too busy to solve. I forgot about it. The wind hadn't come up. Light to moderate breeze, six to eight knots, not *Kinsman* weather. We'd have to fight for everything we got today. I tried to get away from *Yankee Doodle* in the pre-start, but she shadowed me. Pushing me. Larry was calling the start bundled in his cocoon.

At the five-minute gun, we were still together. *Yankee Doodle* wasn't going to let me get away. "You got to, Jib. Soapy doesn't want to race you. He's trying to trip you up. He wants to close you down again. He wants to win this thing on a foul before the gun." He was right.

"Lookout, Jib, here he comes. Tack, tack, now!" Esperance tapped the deck twice with a winch handle.

Trying to get away, I tacked around the committee boat, but they stayed on me like a Westhampton hostess. The moment I got underway, they forced me to tack again. Soapy Armstrong was spinning their helm; Bermuda Schwartz was calling the sails; van Riper Smith was in the cockpit as alternate tactician something or other; Uncle Routledge was there calling the time.

Every time she blanketed us, she gave us dirty air. The action was severe.

If Larry whispered, "Jibe! Jibe!" I'd tap the deck with a winch handle three times quick, the signal to the foredeck to walk the jib around. *Yankee Doodle* stalked us perfectly.

"False tack," Larry said, and I'd call it so loud their afterguard could hear me across the water, "Ready and . . . Now!" I'd spin the helm alee and round up smart as I could, then drop away, hoping to ease *Yankee Doodle* around on the other tack.

But we were clumsy at the game, and they read me like a black headline. I'd jibe away; they'd jibe away and meet me coming up. I was being pushed into making a mistake. And with one minute left, it happened. Just as Larry said it would. There she was, *Lady Anne*. With half-a-minute to the start, Soapy Armstrong cornered me. He'd set a trap and driven me in a circle too close to *Lady Anne*.

"Sea room!" someone yelled from *Yankee Doodle*'s foredeck.

Too late.

Our boom whacked *Lady Anne*'s anchor buoy. Everyone had seen it. You could have seen it from a weather satellite. There was no defense; we had touched the committee boat's buoy. Not severely. But in these races, a touch was enough, and up went their red protest flag for the second time in two days.

I ran a white rag up my runner stay and sailed home. I explained to Esperance why we were going in early, and he transferred the news to the crew, who were a bit bewildered at the brevity of the race.

If the first race had been a bad joke, what would you call this one?

Another bad joke.

Maybe, instead of a third race, Uncle Rut ought to send his lawyer again. Take a meeting. He had us down two to nothing, and we'd hardly gotten our hull wet.

⚑

Race Three

When I'd seen Marcus after the race, I'd asked him what he'd been yelling at me. "Fourteenth man," he said. The fourteenth man on a racing Twelve sat behind the helm in a seat that was traditionally reserved for board members, backers, sponsors. Any non-sailing guest who sat in that place was known as the fourteenth man. It was a great honor to be invited. Marcus was applying for that invitation. It was an intriguing idea. We both knew he would not be allowed to give me advice, that he could only talk about the race in general terms. I accepted.

On the way out, the wind piped-up.

Larry Bayard. I couldn't imagine sailing without him either. Aunt Pearl picked him up at the clinic and brought him out in her boat. It came alongside just before the ten-minute gun. We took him on board and bundled him into the cockpit. Poor Larry, he was feeling pretty sick. He couldn't even touch the helm, but he had volunteered to call the sails for me, and maybe some tacks. He didn't want to be out there, but he knew how badly I needed him. He was on medication, taking a drug so powerful that I told him *Kinsman* could probably sail on it to win. Marcus was on board waiting for me to invite him.

"Fourteenth man," I called out. He leapt aboard and took his place between the helm and the after rail.

"No talking," I said.

He smiled, "Whispering okay?"

He sat behind me in the syndicate chair, secretly punching his stopwatch and whispering the minutes and seconds; Larry telling me when to tack, giving me advice. Fair start. Somehow, Soapy Armstrong beat me over the line for the second time this time by a boat length.

Windy. Brutal chop.

On the beat to the first mark, *Yankee Doodle* forced me into a tacking duel, and we tacked a couple of dozen times. Our crew was being pushed to their

197

limits, tacking and jibing. *Yankee Doodle* did everything I did, except they did it better. She was attacking us, testing our jibing expertise. I knew my men. They had unlimited endurance. But given the amount of tacks and jibes, the sheer technicalities involved, and the timing, I knew endurance was not going to be enough. Something was going to go. Moses went over, but he clung to a line and was hauled back on the deck. A small setback, but I was braced for anything.

On the windward beat to the third mark, things went well. I stayed below them in the safe leeward position and kept the hell away from them. We held our position and were a couple of seconds behind rounding the mark. Sailing to the wing mark on an open reach, we pulled ahead. I sailed *Kinsman* full and by, just the way she liked it, her keel waving below us, straining at her stainless pins. Widening our lead to the fifth mark. We were ahead by about twenty-five seconds.

There were two helms: a pair of stainless steel wheels four feet in diameter, windward and leeward. We had left the setup just as it was when we bought the boat from Italy, from the time when *Kinsman* was the *Il Moro*, the pride of the Italian syndicate that almost dethroned *America3*. I was able to reach the runner winches on both sides. Marcus was everywhere. Larry did what he could. I was training Esperance as my alternate helmsman. But I was doing too much.

I needed two more hands. That's when I got in trouble, helping out Kikongoro. Coming about, we stood in irons too long. A wave flogged us and sent the boom back directly at my head. I went down quickly and came up into the runner block that had just been released and was swinging like a drunk in a pub. Down I went again. I must have slipped unconscious for a few seconds. When I came up, we were still in irons, but I didn't notice because I didn't even know why I'd gone sailing that afternoon. Marcus took the wheel.

No one knew what to do except Larry, who came out of his cocoon long enough to tell Moses to come aft and help Esperance. For the next half hour, while my head pounded from here to Palookaville, I could hear Larry saying, "Down down. Hold it there. You hold it hold it. Lookout, down quick! That's good, hold it there. Okay, come up up up. That's good. Pinch her. Flatten the jib, Kikongoro, grind her in. Come on, grind her in. Moses, more more, way nuff." And on and on.

Marcus took her around the mark and got the spinnaker up. The crew was actually sailing the boat. But good as they were, the white boat had taken advantage and had opened a lead, I didn't know how many boat lengths. Maybe two dozen and they were heading for the horizon when I took the helm.

On the final beat to the final mark, I felt the hull in my hands, I drove her down for speed, then came up raging. I pinched her higher and higher above my lay line. I hadn't realized I'd gained three minutes so that when we rounded the last mark and set the spinnaker for the downwind run, we were two minutes behind. The seas were rolling us just right. I felt the keel winging and set my sight on the huge bottle of Absolut Vodka flying on the spinnaker above the white boat. Vodka made an improved statement, less sugar.

Two minutes is a lot to make up on one leg against a masterpiece of technology and design, even if we did have the better boat under these conditions. Now the wind was up. The valleys of the swells had widened between the wave tops, perfect for our keel. I knew we could take the white boat. I kept driving *Kinsman* down hard, hoping that nothing would bust.

She increased her boatspeed to fifteen knots. The swells had gotten up to eight feet. We were surfing. We began to disturb *Yankee Doodle*'s wind a mile from the finish line. When we got up to her, she wouldn't let through. We were close behind her just about touching her counter. That was when Uncle Rut spotted Marcus. Luckily, he wasn't talking to me; he was just staring at them.

Rut must have commented, because Bermuda turned to look, then the others. It threw them for an instant. Instead of going to weather and taking *Yankee Doodle*'s wind, we swept by under her and stole the race with two hundred yards to go.

We won by a solid ten seconds. After *Lady Anne* gave us the gun, she signaled us and officially asked me if *Kinsman* wanted a lay day. And I said "No, we were ready to roll." So, the fourth race was set for the next day.

That night I prayed for a hurricane. We were still down, but down two to one. After the finish, I had expected to see Uncle Rut hoist a protest flag, but he didn't. There was, however, a polite message waiting for me from the Race Committee reminding me that the same fourteenth man cannot be carried in two consecutive races. Marcus would be lost to us until the fifth race.

⚑

Race Four

A shiftless wind. All we got were gusts of maybe twelve knots. Otherwise, it stayed uselessly low. By midday, things hadn't improved.

This race would be skippered by Esperance. Moses would be sailing master and call the sails. Josue was captain of the foredeck, as usual. Isaaco was crew chief. I was going to sit behind Larry and Esperance and sail as fourteenth man. I'd call out advice. All I told Esperance was not to get close to *Yankee Doodle*.

Aunt Pearl's boat followed us out to the starting line, carrying Larry. It came alongside, and we took him on board just before the ten-minute gun. Aunt Pearl was startled to see Esperance at the helm with Josue beside him. Kikongoro and Mungo settled Larry into the cockpit. He was very weak. All he said was, "Kick ass, Esperance."

"What kind of start, Larry?" Esperance said.

"Keep away from them." He nodded his head away from the starting line. "Give them a Marcus Cape." He'd be watching from Aunt Pearl's boat a quarter mile away.

So he did. He called for a false tack in a loud voice. It was a bluff, but it brought *Yankee Doodle* up in irons. Then he drove down on a port reach and got the hell away from the starting line. But he couldn't shake them. Soapy was onto him and covered him like a wet army blanket, so we crossed the starting line at flank speed so close that the two boats could have been a catamaran. But *Yankee Doodle* was the windward hull.

That didn't bother me. Neither boat held the advantage. We tacked only six times up to the first mark and around. The choppy seas were not that bad, so we were equal. I could tell it was going to go like this all the way to the final mark. And it did.

For the last twenty miles, we swapped leads. We punched at each other, trying to knock the other out of the race. At each mark, we'd be a few seconds ahead or a few seconds behind, and we were getting punched out.

200

Each time we tacked at close quarters, I held my breath hoping we'd make it, that we wouldn't fall down. And each time, my crew timed the tack perfectly, all at once releasing the weather stay and winching in the leeward stay just as we rounded up into the wind, sails crackling, releasing the jib sheet and hauling it in on the leeward grinder, not too soon not too late, filling away on the new tack. Never more than four seconds around.

Larry was cautious, afraid that we'd eventually have an accident trying to keep up with them, lose someone overboard, the men had a problem staying on deck. But no one fell overboard, and I was amazed at the doggedness of my men. Isaaco and his crew were brilliant. Esperance, Moses, all of them.

Then, going upwind for the last leg before the run to the finish, Soapy Armstrong and Bermuda Schwartz, their think tank, started a tacking duel. I relieved Esperance at the helm, and they threw forty tacks at us trying to break our backs one last time, trying to force us into making an error.

They'd force us to tack. And then, a few seconds later, we'd go through the same routine again. Then again. We were bound to slip up somewhere. I didn't think my men would hold up. We were slightly slower; the white boat was better drilled in tacking duels. She gradually pulled ahead. The wind had lightened up, and that hurt us, too. And so, I saw the sight I hated the most: the words *Yankee Doodle* spread in golden script across her transom.

A rain squall was catching up to us. We kept punching. Four miles left after the final mark. And there we were. We were catching them. When we rounded the final mark leaving it to port, I punched the stopwatch and told Esperance that the white boat had gained fifteen seconds on us. There was little more to do downwind but turn *Kinsman* loose. *Yankee Doodle* had a twenty-two second lead, and a safe weather position, but we were the better runner, and both boats were now running, full out at their fastest point. The downwind leg would be won by whomever happened to be ahead at the finish line. Musical chairs with hundred foot masts. It was going to be anybody's race, and it would be up to the wind to decide. I'd given the helm back to Esperance for the final leg. With the squall behind us, I knew it was our race.

"It's in the bag," I told him. He held the course nicely.

"Easy," he said. He was too excited to stay seated. He stood behind the helm, gripping the chrome wheel wide on either side. He was glowing. He made a direct line not for the finish line, but for the Pepsi bottle, and we came right down on them in pursuit. The finish was going to be close.

After two miles, halfway to the line, the squall caught up to us and Esperance caught up to *Yankee Doodle*. We'd made up twenty-two seconds in two miles on a flying run, and we passed them rain smashing down on us. We showed them our transom; if they cared to read it, *Kinsman*. Read *that*, suckers.

A minute later, they caught us. It was only a matter of sliding up behind us, stealing our wind, and passing us. Sometimes it works like that. I looked over at *Yankee Doodle* and scanned the crew. All fourteen heads faced forward. Now the duel to finish was on. Each boat changed leads a dozen times.

As we neared the line still a mile away, the wind pooed out. Both boats were ghosting toward the finish line, left with their great sails draped like laundry on the line. The finish line was still half-a-mile away when the wind died. Both boats stood dead in the water. "We're dead even," I whispered to Larry.

Match racing is the only race in the world, car racing, horse racing, running the mile, where you can stop and stare at your opponent in silence at the end of the race. I thought their afterguard must have noticed who was skippering *Kinsman*, but now one of them discovered Esperance. Then another. Heads turned. Soapy, Rut, Bermuda, each crew member had to see for himself who might beat them. I glanced at Rut from my seat behind Esperance. I had been sailing as fourteenth man. He looked as if he were going to vomit.

Somehow *Yankee Doodle* was slipping ahead of us. It was the time for whispering. Esperance looked back at me, as if I could tell him what to do. I told him that there was nothing left for us to do but whistle for the wind. I asked Esperance to send someone, Isaaco, forward to touch the mast and whistle. "That usually worked," I said.

"There's nothing else to do, so now," I told him. "You can only will your boat." He spoke to Isaaco, who skipped forward barefoot, touched the mast, and whistled; then whispered to Moses on the foredeck.

I heard a chant very low, spontaneously coming aft from the half-dozen men on our foredeck: Mungo, Joseph, Moses, Leopold, Innocent, Kikongoro, Josue. It was a Kinyarwandan chant that I had never heard before. A beautiful soft sound. Esperance told me it was a simple shepherd's song. The deck was flat, because we were on a run. The men barely moved back and forth, shyly moving. One at a time, each member of the *Yankee Doodle* crew glanced over at us. That look. They'd probably never heard a boat sing, not during a race anyway. I hadn't either, but I was glad it was us. It was a good thing to do.

"What's that music?" Larry opened his eyes. He was finished with this race. With a thousand yards to go, we'd stayed alongside *Yankee Doodle*, hull for hull, spitting distance. And I wanted to.

None of their crew had looked at us. Then, one of them did. And then, one by one, they all did. A Tutsi warrior was standing at our helm sailing *Kinsman* past them. As far as Moses could tell, though, both masts were even.

Then with a hundred yards left, we both got a puff, and the boats glided forward. They stayed even, mast to mast, until we were about to cross the line. Suddenly, *Yankee Doodle* released her spinnaker sheet and guy, both lines. Out it shot, high in the wind, flying full out ahead of their bow and ours. It was a disastrous move. For us.

Her spinnaker crossed the finish line ahead of ours. I'd never seen anything like it, never heard of that done. The gun for first and the horn for second went off simultaneously. The closest finish in the history of challenger finals, less than a second. They had won. Their afterguard lost it completely, jumped up and down and hugged each other, Soapy and Bermuda, van Riper, Rut.

Was it legal? Larry said I should protest. It was my turn to, and I flew my red *Kinsman*'s t-shirt from our runner stay and rounded up to *Lady Anne* for a ruling. The race committee denied it on the spot. They said the American boat's sail was clearly ahead of ours. It had broken the plane of the finish line first. We had lost.

We were beaten and exhausted. I had expected to tie the series two to two. We were down one to three. This was getting too near to the end of the story. I'd never admit we were doomed, but it was starting to look conceivable. All we had to do was to win the next three races; *Yankee Doodle* needed one more win, her final.

I requested and was granted a lay day.

Aboard *Kinsman*, we didn't speak. We picked up our tow boat first. And as we passed the white boat with our tow line taut, I saw her crew, not noticing us pass. They were singing very quietly, ". . . we are poor little lambs who have gone astray, *ba-ah, ba-ah, ba-ah . . .*"

"Fuck you," I said just loud enough for it to cross the water between me and their afterguard. Horrible sportsmanship. Aunt Pearl's boat came by for Larry. Elizaphan was so mad she was in tears. Aunt Pearl could hardly speak.

The men were quiet that evening at our cookout. I think they sensed the end, the extinction of *Kinsman*. We would be disbanded forever; at the camp, their sadness overwhelmed me. Now when I looked at the men, it was as if we had never been meant to win. It seemed so obvious. Even I could see the end. The men packing, stopping by the Mosquito Café for the final beer. Saying goodbye to me, to Aunt Pearl. Flying home. Without the America's Cup, there would be no Kinsmen Council. It would never go any further than the paper stage. No world money would pour into Rwanda. Once again, there would be Hutu and Tutsi living across the road from each other and no guarantee, none at all, that they would stay good neighbors and that the coals of hatred would not flare up into fires at the first neighborly dispute.

ᚏ

Race Five

Teetering. This was serious. Match Point.

There are only two styles of match racing. Well, three, but I'm not talking about dismastings and sinkings. Just two. The first is when your boat wins the start and stays ahead, and widens its lead with each mark, and ends ahead at the finish line, and the boats are so far apart that it's a one-sided race. The other style is like the duel that developed between *Kinsman* and *Yankee Doodle* in the fourth race and that changed leads so many times with neither one of us more than a couple of boat lengths apart.

I knew we had the better sea boat. I knew it. But if the wind kept diddling around, lightening up cat's paws, then we were dead, and the series would go by. We'd be out of the finals, having proved our strength only in bursts. It could happen. The meteorologist had promised trades. Where were they?

The men were quiet, joyless. While we were being towed out to the starting line, I couldn't get the men to speak. Great sadness on board. It was over, or so they thought. Everyone knew the numbers. "This is very bad," Esperance said to me gravely on the way. During the tow in or out, I'd let various crewmen take the helm to get the feel of it. But today, when I asked Josue, he turned me down. Where was Moses and Kikongoro? Send in the clowns. Esperance shrugged. So did Isaaco, which surprised me. Leopold shook his head "no." Finally, Mungo came aft and took the helm.

There was a light chop and a brisk wind from the north. The starting line had been moved from east to west. We had twenty minutes to kill before the ten-minute gun. We dropped our towline, and Aunt Pearl's boat overtook us Her captain maneuvered her boat alongside, and a crewman dropped chafing gear between our hulls. We lifted Larry Bayard on board. Marcus jumped down on deck and took his place as fourteenth man, "You got 'em where you want 'em, Jib."

Aunt Pearl asked me to bring the crew to aft and get Esperance to translate. She needed to say to them something that she had heard from Saint. So I got

Moses to put up the steadying jib, the little spitfire, and *Kinsman* stood facing the wind like a weathervane. When the twelve men had gathered, she smiled at them all.

"Please do not look so worried," she said. "You will win this race." Whether they believed in her power to cause victory or if they didn't, they were still very fond of her, and they knew she liked and admired them.

She unfolded a single sheet of paper. "This is a telefax from your president. Your president has agreed," she said slowly, waiting to be translated by Esperance. "When you go home, you will be first class citizens. You will be on a special council. There will be no more Hutu or Tutsi. You will be friends and neighbors at home, just as you are here."

I was amazed at what Saint Pierre had accomplished, and his timing was weak.

She repeated its purpose: the building of rehab centers for all the dismembered survivors of the genocide, all those whose arms and legs have been chopped off, all those who had been blinded; there would be psychiatric staffs for those with brain damage, the ones who could not speak, who could not understand why they were alive, who were left without families, who had nothing to live for, whose only memory was that of people being executed before them.

"Yes, but it is *only* if we win the Cup," someone standing at the mast said, not to her. It might have been Josue.

Aunt Pearl looked toward him. "No, Josue," she said. "You do *not* need to win the Cup. You *already* are honored citizens. It has begun."

When the translation reached his ears, he lit up.

We would win that day. I could feel it that morning. No secrets anymore. We'd sail full out. Embarrass them. They wouldn't have a clue why they're losing to us.

By noon, the wind had shifted to the east and was howling. The trade winds had come. So far, so good. I'd take the helm. It looked like we'd be able to get off to a fast start and avoid a risky dogfight. Get ahead and stay ahead: no match racing, no dueling, just good and hard sailing. We were the better boat that day. All I needed to do was point *Kinsman* at the marks, then keep the stays taut and the men from falling overboard.

When the ten-minute gun sounded, Marcus secretly punched his stopwatch and called out, "Ten."

I turned *Kinsman* away from the starting line just as he'd told me to do. I was sailing full out on a broad reach with *Yankee Doodle* on my tail. She couldn't keep up. And when I tacked back toward the line at the five minute gun, she was stuck somewhere below me. We'd already scooped her.

Then, I pulled off one of Larry's heart stopping, all-or-nothing starts and crossed the line at the gun, sailing hull down at thirteen knots and caught

Yankee Doodle luffing. By the time she fell away and gained headway, we were gone. The wind freshened, and the sea got choppy, and we led from the start. We scorched them at every turn. The men were impeccable. The white boat never once led, not for a moment in the twenty-four miles. We showed them what we had. It was a one-sided victory. A blowout. And it felt good. Everything went right. It was simple sailing.

By now, our crew was made up of many confident sailors: as good as most, better than some, but they were also clowns. Moses and Kikongoro were the headline clowns, and every time we passed *Yankee Doodle* there was much laughing and pointing of fingers. I drew the line at yelling "Loser!" at them.

But in spite of the fuss, Soapy Armstrong, Bermuda Schwartz, van Riper Smith, and Laurence Routledge were composed and not at all amused. Sack Smith and Nick Routledge, lying forward of the mast on the weather rail and wet as seals, would look over at me with sad smiles. But when we were on our final downwind run to the finish line and *Yankee Doodle* was still pushing herself into heavy chop upwind toward the eighth mark, she crossed us. And our foredeck crew, who had nothing to do, calmly pantomimed a tea party. It was in extremely bad taste, of course, but it was my kind of bad taste. I managed not to laugh.

We were down three-two. We were catching them. We would catch them. I could feel it. The trades had been promised through the sixth race. *Yankee Doodle* took a lay day. It was they who had blinked, not us.

⚑

Race Six

But every race has its own personality. And this one was over before the starting gun was fired.

With a minute-and-a-half to start, *Yankee Doodle's* main halyard parted. She never recovered. It was a perfect day for a sail. Light to moderate winds, two-foot seas. So, we took *Kinsman* around the twenty-four-mile course. Esperance skippered, Isaaco called the tacks, Moses called the sails. Leopold, Josue, and even Kikongoro and Mungo all took their trick at the helm. Esperance and I played dominoes on the afterdeck.

Officially we finished four minutes and forty-five seconds ahead of *Yankee Doodle,* but it would been a lot more if we'd raised our spinnaker on the four downwind legs.

Three to three.

The Eve of Race Seven

Every race watcher from every country had assumed, expected, well, *known*, that America would be the eventual winner. Certainly, they *should* be the ones to challenge New Zealand. The challenger finals were expected to be a formality. A tune-up session for America. It no longer was true.

Maybe America was the favorite, but that didn't mean the race watchers wanted America to be there. They just assumed that they would be. It was never been meant to be us, but suddenly it was to be. And that had changed everything, including the odds which had climbed to a respectable two-to-one. And now, we were for everyone: the boat of the people. And the media loved us. We were the new darlings, the comers, the contenders. We might accidentally go all the way to the finals. Now, they needed us. They had turned their backs on us, and now they turned their fronts. All was forgiven.

I didn't care, one way or another. The media meant nothing to me. We had always been good material, but a back page story; nothing front page. *Kinsman* hadn't been for everyone. We'd been a quaint story, homely and doomed, for those readers who like their cornbread drizzled with sugar and sopped in maple syrup. Anything could happen, and some of it already had. After our second victory over the American syndicate, when it looked like we might go all the way, I told Aunt Pearl that we needed to order a chain link fence built around our compound, and I hired a local kid as a second watchman to help Ba'ale on security.

I sat rocking on the porch, long after midnight, waiting for the sunrise. Clouds were scudding across the moon. I wished that the race could be held then, with the wind just right.

Waiting waiting waiting. I had to sleep.

Eventually, I walked to the camp and rattled the new gate. Ba'ale let me in. I had to get to the boat. I could sleep there on her sailbags, feel her bridle against her lines in the night's rising breeze.

I lay there in the sail sewer, my mind turned and turned. My nerves were fierce. For the first time in this whole series, from France to here, I was really scared of losing. I couldn't get rid of the fear, so I decided that it was okay to be scared.

When I got used to being scared, I found that there was something else keeping me awake; something I had been feeling, but never let myself know it. It was that maybe I wasn't supposed to win. I was trying to knock my own country off. But hadn't I been trying to do that for the last six races? Yes, but maybe until tonight, I never truly believed we could. It was a little late for this soul searching. America was my country; after all, it was where I was raised. I loved it as much as anyone can love soil and ideas. It had allowed me to have everything I'd ever wanted, including this moment. I am not Rwandan. I do not speak much Kinyarwandan. My crew did not ask to live in Rwanda, just as I didn't ask to live in America. I am as white as possible, but it's weird: being with these men has made me feel that I was black before I was white.

Aunt Pearl was appalled when I told her that. But it was true. Believe me when I tell you that. Eons ago. The migrations over millions of years, the ones across to China where they became Mongolian, the ones up to northern Europe who became Nordic, the ones who stayed in Africa, and the ones who moved to Newport.

I decided that it wasn't America I was trying to knock off; it was my family. It was my Uncle Routledge, maybe for having said, "Negroes I have enjoyed talking with while yachting," when we were playing clever games in Newport. It was all of them: Nick Routledge, Soapy Armstrong, van Riper Smith, Sack Smith. It was their boat, too, that I was trying to knock off. It was their thousands of square feet of advertising space: the Pepsi Challenge. It was the ten times more that their syndicate had spent than had ours. It was their spying, their putting Marcus Cape ashore. Of course, Aunt Pearl was paying Larry Bayard and Marcus Cape, and she bought two great boats cheap from the Italians, and set up camps at Lake Kivu, Grand Bahou and Waiheke Island, and we've been eating and we've been traveling.

Of course, we were never part of the social side of yachting. How could we be? We'd never gotten past being *uitlanders*, outsiders, as the men called themselves. We'd hear chatter and joking among the other crews, or aloof silence or simply quiet seriousness. Walking down Queen Street in Auckland, we were ignored.

The writer of a *Vanity Fair* story on the Cup had a few lines on us. He quoted a group of leftovers drinking at Sails. The rumor that Rwanda must not advance. The permanent harm to the Cup. Africans, voodoo. "If Rwanda did, by any chance, win it," he quoted, "none of the syndicates would want to go to Lake Tanganyika or Lake Kivu to retrieve it." It would never survive the trip. Well, they're not going to win it, are they? Why are they even involved? They're not yachtsmen, so what's their point? Hello. Their point is money. Well, then let's give them money. Seriously, what if they *do* win? Bite your tongue. I'd boycott the races. Everyone would go along with me. Hello. They'd keep the Cup forever. Bite your tongue again.

Oddly enough, the night before the race I never doubted we'd win. From midnight or one a.m., when I watched the moon come out. Its soft golden ring before the clouds hid it, and I remembered a childhood poem by Longfellow:

> *Last night the moon had a golden ring,*
> *Tonight no moon we see.*
> *The skipper blew a whiff from his pipe,*
> *And a scornful laugh laughed he . . .*
> *It was going to blow like hell.*

The Race

The wind woke me, a good sign. I was aboard *Kinsman,* sleeping on deck, shivering with cold. When the dawn came, it came gray. I could see across the gulf, clear and sharp. It would be a wet day on a wet boat. Our day. Match point number three.

A few minutes after sunrise, I watched Isaaco walk through the compound carrying a wine bottle and step from the dock onto *Kinsman's* bow, the sun behind him.

"Good morning, Skipper."

"Good morning, Isaaco."

He stood by the fore-stay, and once again I watched him pour the contents of a bottle, blood, over our bow and down our already red topsides. The blood clung to the bow's overhang before it flowed into the water, darkening it.

He held the bottle upside down until it was empty, then dropped it into the water and watched it sink. It was a remarkable sight. He stepped off the deck back onto the dock.

"Whose blood was that, Isaaco?"

"I obtained it from a goat."

"And how is the goat doing?"

"Well. Very well, Skipper."

"Good. Let's eat breakfast."

I didn't say another word. It had worked for us the last time. We were ready to sail and win. As always, it would be a grudge match.

The race that day was going to be electrifying. It had it all; family betrayal, unsavory sportsmanship, bad blood, possible humiliation, a million-dollar side bet. The money would mean nothing to Uncle Rut compared to the humiliation of having America edged out of the Cup finals by us. If there ever was an important race in his yachting lifetime, *this* was it. He must have been terrified that morning.

On the way out to the starting line, I turned the helm over to Esperance.

There was a bad chop to the water, caused by a sharp wind that hit the current at right angles, but he was a natural helmsman, and he kept our bow directly lined up with the towboat's wake.

In every race so far, we've flown a small Rwandan flag off our stern, committee rules. But that morning on the way out to the starting line, I unfurled a flag I'd been saving: a huge flag, three chunks of color (green, red and yellow), like the Italian flag but with a big black R dead center. Disruptive. I ran it up a runner stay on the spinnaker halyard, fifty feet in the air, so everyone could see it. I'd strike it before we used our spinnaker, but I wanted to show them our colors: the Rwandan colors. And when the crew saw it, they made all sorts of bird calls and cheering noises. I knew they were ready. *Yankee Doodle,* with her New York Yacht Club burgee flapping correctly behind them, saw it. Everyone else saw it, too, on the spectator fleet. They could see it clearly a quarter mile away, and a cheer went up from them. I'd assumed that they were always rooting for the other boat, any boat other than ours.

But when we were towed out with our flag flying halfway up the mast, I heard our own cheers. For the first time, they were cheering for us. They were cheering on the bull, not the matador. We had officially become the dangerous portion of the America's Cup Challenge, the gut shot. At first, I thought these new fans were America haters, but our government hadn't done anything outrageous to New Zealand. As far as I knew, they still kind of admired America, so I could only figure that it was a general fear of any Big Casino and they wanted them out of the regatta instead of us, Little Casino, so that New Zealand would be better off facing the red boat with the barefoot blacks than the satellite controlled United States of America boat with all its computerized magic. God knows how we'd gotten there. No one had figured that one out, but New Zealand was supposed to win in the end, and they sure as hell wanted to keep the Cup. In the meantime, I'd decided that we should definitely be the ones to challenge them and that America should lose to us in the finals.

When Aunt Pearl's boat came alongside to drop off Larry Bayard, Saint Pierre surprised me by being on board. He hailed us like a new president from the small wheelhouse.

"I thought you were in Rwanda."

"I was, but now I'm here," he said with a laugh, one arm around Aunt Pearl, who was smiling just as much. "It's a short hop if you come by way of the Indian Ocean." He gave us all a hearty thumbs up. And I gave him one right back for what he'd accomplished in Rwanda for the crew and for the last two races.

Elizaphan jumped on board, and she propped Larry up in the cockpit. He nodded, "Thanks."

"This is your day," he said. "Don't fuck it up."

I could see right away that his condition had improved a bit. He'd be up for this race. I hoped he'd be able to give me tidbits, calling the start and the tacks. Marcus jumped aboard once again as my special guest and repeated his mantra, "You got 'em right where you want 'em, Jibber." My name was always easily distorted.

I called out to Saint, "You got the wine?"

"I do indeed." He opened the aft lazareet and hauled out a case of twelve with ice chips dropping from it.

"Will this do?"

"What is it?"

"Taittinger."

"I'm thirsty," I said.

"Don't be long."

"Don't worry about it, Saint."

Marcus told me that we'd gotten quite a compliment from the bettors in Las Vegas; the odds had come down and that America was listed last night on the tote board as two-to-one favorites.

We were tied alongside too close, and the chop and wind kept banging us together, so I cut the visit short. Elizaphan and I were wrapped around each other. She wanted to stay, but I told her that she would be a big distraction. She already was. Our hulls parted, and Aunt Pearl's boat pulled away. I blew the two women kisses, and gave Saint another thumbs up.

The tension had built to a numbing climax during the last six races. I could see it in my hands on the wheel. They were gripping the chrome too tightly. I could see it in the faces of *Yankee Doodle*'s crew when she passed us being towed to the starting line. Grim as chess champions. I was terrified. I could easily imagine what they were feeling. They had let this all go much further than anyone of them had ever imagined that it would go, and here they were facing the mongrel underdog's underdog for the right to exist, a right that should have been theirs by fate.

I watched them rig their jib. They did not seem happy. It was not possible, after three years of preparation, planning their manifesto, the tens of millions of dollars spent on design research, high technology, sail fiber development, hull construction, spar engineering, and their shore team of chairmen, presidents, directors, technicians, public relations experts, espionage agents, legal teams, software programmers, computer repairmen, quality controllers, intelligence people, electronics people, meteorology scientists, naval advisors, lodging, chartering boats, leasing cars, purchasing, catering, all their geniuses in the afterguard, the strategists, navigator, tactician, meteorologist, skipper, Soapy Armstrong, Bermuda Schwartz, all of them; they were on the verge of being humiliated and sent home by a boatload of skinny, barefooted, black bodies from a landlocked, nameless non-place where the life expectancy of a man was lower than a stray dog's.

It was all teetering, about to come crashing down, and it just wasn't fair.

I ordered our heaviest mainsail up and a medium jib hoisted a few minutes before the ten-minute gun. I began lazy, weaving, circling maneuvers. At the ten-minute gun, Esperance punched the stopwatch. "Ten minutes," he said. Marcus gave us our speed and our trim; Larry called our first tack. We were set.

I felt sick to my gut, but in charge of the race. We were the boat to beat. We had the momentum. It might have felt that way aboard *Yankee Doodle*, but I was going to sail them under. Some of them feared it; maybe some of them knew it. Looking across at her, writhing to keep up with us, they looked fierce but frantic.

I wanted to break them. The ones to beat are the ones that matter, the great ones. And they had a great crew, and a great afterguard with Soapy and Bermuda. She was a computerized boat as complete as the first console at NASA, but she also had a great human crew: disciplined, sharp. They knew each other well. They weren't just names; they were old shipmates, and when things broke down, they got together. And there they were, running us down. And it would give me great pleasure to beat their asses off.

"Five minutes," Esperance said quietly.

"Ready to jibe," Larry said.

At that instant, I felt it again. The rush. I knew we were going to win that day.

"Jibe," Larry said.

We dove away, and I drove down as far as I could, sails flat as blades and jibed and jibed again. I went wherever I wanted and, for once, we were on top all the way through the pre-start. Larry and Marcus and I were the better strategists today. We had the jump. We outmaneuvered them with ease, faking them into false tacks and once making Soapy throw the wheel hard over to avoid grazing us and risking his race on a protest.

"Thirty seconds," Esperance said.

"Count twenty, call it, and jibe," Larry said.

Just before the starting gun, we jockeyed a final spinning jibe that landed us underway, hull down, just below the committee boat, and we crossed the line close enough to sail through and smell the smoke from her starting cannon. A perfect start. We left *Yankee Doodle* standing on its dick with its thumbs poked into many orifices.

I pushed *Kinsman* hard on the windward beat to the first mark. I wanted to stack up as big a lead as I could early. In case something went wrong. Or they got lucky. I recognized their power to come back.

The wind freshened. I could feel the hull's surge through the water. The chop was ours. We got around the first mark well ahead, leading by a dozen boat lengths, and drove to the second mark.

We were off and running. I felt the rare harmony that happens once in a while between the elements: the shape of your hull, your entry, your wetted surface, the angle of the waves banging you like a kettle drum, and the wind. Sometimes it can be all perfect, and it was going to be for us that day.

Sailing well, but far behind, *Yankee Doodle* had gone way up on a starboard tack and gotten a lift. She might threaten us at the second mark. I wouldn't know until we tacked. She had done something smart. I should have covered her. She was to windward, and the wind was fluky. But it favored her, not me.

Marcus said she was coming up on us. She might have taken over the lead, but it was too soon to tell. It was going to be close at the second mark. And when we got there, it was. But it was still our lead by six boat lengths. She rounded the mark on our heels and rode with us to the third mark. I covered her. She kept it pretty, even though she never headed us.

The wind had lightened. I changed jibs as we rounded the third still ahead. We easily outfooted her to the wing mark; our best point so far that day. When we rounded the wing mark, she was ten boat lengths behind. *Yankee Doodle* could no longer stay with us. She'd never catch us now. *Kinsman* was a long, slim-hulled boat, but she skipped when I put her head down and drove her. She never dug in. She kicked-up nicely and rose through the wave each time. And the racket! It as like a body shop at noon. I never got used to the racket that her giant, empty shell made under way. The Twelves were not like the great Stevens, Alden, Herreshoff boats that I was raised on in Narragansett Bay: the heavy S-Boats. No, these boats were made by a branch of Mattel Toys to serve one purpose: match racing. They were not broad-swords; they were fencing foils. Sea foils.

Up through my bare foot, I could feel our shark's fin keel waving below us, sculling us on. Like my crew, I never wore deck shoes. I never had as boy growing up; I'd always sailed barefooted, and I liked to feel my toes gripping the deck.

At the halfway mark, the fifth, we had them by twenty boat lengths. With less than a dozen miles to go, something high above my head went *CRACK!* I feared the worst.

"Heads!" I yelled without looking up, the command to save yourself. "Heads up!"

A snarling *s-c-r-a-a-a-p-e*, then *BOOING!*

A stay had parted. A man lay flat on the deck near the mast, swept to leeward, one leg overboard. There was blood.

"Get him in!"

"He tied off," someone yelled aft.

I looked aloft.

Our first and second spreaders had been carried away from the mast. The main side-stay had parted from her chain plate and was flying free. It had turned into a whip, a heavyweight stainless steel whip, capable of killing.

"Leopold, make that stay off. Now. Watch yourself."

"Yes, Skipper."

"Who's down?"

"Moses." Kikongoro called back.

The mastman. Now there was blood everywhere. The sea wash was making the deck red.

"Get him in!"

"He okay, Skipper."

In what way? The deck was slippery from his blood. These are tough men. Blood is blood; they'd seen it before. The color of blood was as familiar to them as the color of Cognac is in Newport.

"Where's he hurt?"

"Haid."

Then I saw it; a steel spreader block had broken loose and clobbered him.

"Get him below!"

"He tied off."

I saw his lifeline clipped to the mast by the big chrome snap-hook.

"Unclip him."

Good for Moses. If he hadn't been clipped off, he'd be overboard. And overboard and unconscious in this weather meant drowned, maybe deep. I found myself figuring out that the rules stated that you had to finish with the same complement you started with, fourteen in our case. In other words, by drowning deep, Moses would have cost us the race and sent us home losers. But he'd clipped himself off. I had a hell of a crew.

"Get him in the sewer. Now!"

"The sails, Skipper."

Joseph meant bloody the sails.

"The sewer. Kikongoro, Mungo. Now!"

"Yes, Skipper."

No one wanted to soil the white sails. I'd hoist a bloody jib if I had to; it might frighten the boys from Newport.

"Cut those lines, Leopold! Fling that steel block!"

Leopold pulled out his case knife, cut the lines, and dropped the broken block into the sea to leeward. He was skating on the blood.

"Innocent, soojee the deck," I yelled. Over the side went a canvas bucket and came up full of saltwater, and he scrubbed the slickness off the deck with a coil of line.

The parted stay was more than a slow-down; it meant that the mast was crippled. Its weakness would last for the rest of the race. There were tons of wind stress on it. On port tack, it would now be supported only by a single runner stay made off beside me. If that stay parted, the mast would crash forward into the sea ahead of us. It might destroy the hull.

When the deck was clear, I eased off the wind and filled away. Esperance said it had taken us four minutes to get back under way. The best thing to do, of course, would be to shorten sail, to try one of the new small sails we'd bought from the Swiss boat. But I couldn't let up; I'd have to sail her down. I'd rather sink us by trying than lose by being prudent.

I glanced back at *Yankee Doodle*. She was much closer, sailing full out, while I was carrying a slight luff in my main. Marcus guessed that she was now a quarter-mile behind us, but she was walking up to us, he said. We hung on to the lead to the sixth mark, and when we rounded it, she was maybe only a dozen boat lengths behind us. The wind had blown up to twenty, and I had no choice but to carry a slight luff to take the strain off the mast. She was gaining. They were sailing her too hard, Marcus said.

By the seventh mark, the American boat had the lead for the first time. We were ten seconds behind, rounding it. My best bet for regaining the lead now was on the final downwind leg. I'd need to keep *Kinsman* on starboard tack all the way to the finish, but I'd need a clear lead for that.

I had to change jibs again. With two miles to go to the eighth mark, Marcus had the binoculars on *Yankee Doodle*'s sheetmen, who were grinding in their mainsail when it suddenly blew out.

"Her main's gone." I heard the Mylar crack. I turned to see *Yankee Doodle* broaching downwind, slopping on the waves. She rounded up. Bobbing sluggishly. She was stalled dead in the water. I could hear the noise of the Mylar pennants snapping in the wind. What was left of her mainsail, crackling loose, sounded like gun shots.

We were ahead. Still, I wanted to break her.

Larry opened his eyes and squinted through the binoculars. "You've got 'em, Jib."

As we sailed closer to them, I could see their deck was an array of men and lines. The crew was trying to haul the Mylar streamers and rags down the mast.

We sailed up to *Yankee Doodle* and passed her within fifty feet. Everyone on her deck was busy working, Soapy, Bermuda, van Riper. No one looked up. Only Uncle Rut glanced over at us. He looked like the portrait of Dorian Gray.

As we passed them, their crew was hauling their heavyweight mainsail up out of the sewer, rigging the halyard, and beginning to bend the new sail on the mast and boom. Marcus said if they had no more snags, it looked like they'd be able to bear off in two minutes. He said they had chosen too light a sail. When the wind had suddenly blown up, so had their main. "I told you so," he said.

It couldn't have happened to us. We were using our heaviest main, tough as stainless steel, and I'd been playing it in and out.

After a minute or so, I glanced back at *Yankee Doodle*, and I didn't like the look of things. They'd gotten her main up. In another thirty seconds, it was full and drawing and here they came, surfing down after us.

A header had caused us to drop down. We could no longer lay the eighth mark, and she looked like she could; she'd tacked and stayed above us. We were on starboard tack a quarter-mile away from the mark, and the last thing I wanted to do was go over on a port tack.

"*Trim, trim!*" I yelled to Josue and Kikongoro, the main sheetmen. No matter how I pinched her, we were still too low to make it without another tack. Then we got headed again. Jesus, we were below the mark by a mile, the American boat was on a perfect layline for it, and instead of being ten boat lengths behind us, I guessed she was now about even with us.

Yankee Doodle's troubles weren't over. Larry kept the glasses on them. They had a man overboard, dragging him behind the boat, trailing them on a single sheet. They'd been trying to winch him in, but he hadn't been able to hang on. So he'd let go, and they had to jibe around and haul him in.

"Your voodoo's improving," Larry said to Esperance and closed his eyes again. "Keep it up." He was feeling better, very weak.

"Fuck it," I said. "I'm not saving any more chances." I had a good chance to catch them, so I called for a crippling port tack. And when I'd gotten to windward of them, luffing all the way, I spun the wheel hard and brought us down over them on starboard. When we caught them, our mast was actually bending. Luckily, it had no steel in it.

They tacked, and I called a quick tack, spun the wheel to windward and rounded up too soon. Stopped dead in slop, we couldn't make headway. It cost us time, and they pulled ahead. But I knew then that I could take them. After twenty miles, we had one more mark to round, then the downwind run, our best point. It was blowing like hell, rough and tumble, rock and roll. I felt the helm in my hands; the boat in my helm. And rough as it was, I held her with my fingertips, power steering. And for the first time, the helm was mine; not Larry Bayard's, with me filling in as alternate helmsman, but mine. And each time we bucked, up from my bare feet, we gained a yard on *Yankee Doodle*, as if my body were *Kinsman*'s hull.

I hardened the sheets and pinched her high enough to lay the eighth mark. A quarter-mile from it, *Yankee Doodle* converged on us. I could see we wouldn't make it. It was going to be their mark, or it was going to be too close. It looked like I'd made another mistake.

But we got a gift. The wind gave us a slight lift. I pointed her high and laid the mark, cutting inside the American boat, Kikongoro forward yelling, "Sea room! Sea room!"

Their red flag shot up on their after stick in protest, but it didn't have a prayer this time. We had established an overlap, and there were plenty of witnesses from a news helicopter that was being swatted around by the wind, risking its life to film this final mark.

We broke out our small spinnaker a full five seconds ahead of her and leapt out away toward the finish line, nicely ahead, out from under their wind shadow, cresting nicely, our liquid keel sculling us in perfect rhythm. The finish line was less than a mile away. It was all being decided here, right now, at each slight turn of our helm.

I don't remember much of the last five minutes, just that the American boat hoisted the biggest, ugliest sail I'd ever seen since the last time I saw it. Five thousand square feet of soda pop, red, white and sordid looking, too big for this wind. It should have blown out, but she was trying anything, and her crew was playing it beautifully and kept a big belly full of wind. And down they came. They were looming. I felt I was being chased by Ringling Brothers.

"Heads up, Jibber. Here she comes," Marcus said, staring back at her. They weren't letting up.

Larry had come around. "Don't let 'em get you into a tacking duel," he said.

That's what they wanted. And before I knew it, I was in their wind shadow. Turning away, but not getting away. In the next two minutes, it would be all over.

"Jibe and reach," Larry said quietly. *"Now."*

Esperance tapped the deck with the winch handle three times quick, sending the signal, "Jibe," echoing forward. And then when Isaaco looked aft and caught my eye and nodded, without a word I spun the wheel hard to weather, jibing us. I made a quick jibe. The mast was making ugly noises, as if it were in pain. I took her to port, which I did not want to do, and headed for the pin end of the line. I had to get away from the circus tent. They covered us with it, killed our spinnaker, and slipped up to our weather side. They had a slight edge.

"Jibe up over them and reach," Larry said.

Esperance tapped the deck three times. It all came down to this. Perfectly at once, Isaaco, Leopold and Innocent unclipped the spinnaker pole and hauled it in one last time. Josue released the vang on the main boom. Mungo and Kikongoro hauled in the mainsheet on the lee grinder and paid it out fast when the boom swung across our heads. The mainsail filled with a thunderclap; the mast screeched and squealed; and using the spinnaker as a jenny on a broad reach without losing hullspeed, our sails were filling out to port and now aiming at the committee boat end of the line. We rode up gathering speed to weather of the white boat and came down hard over it, deadening their wind.

To a ballet dancer, it would be a *grand jete*; to a gunslinger, it would be fanning six; to a tennis player, it would be an ace. All in six seconds.

Now I was sailing her down, rail under, and Esperance, whose eye was on the tachometer, quietly said, "Twenty."

Twenty.

Yankee Doodle rolled through breaking seas, Soapy Armstrong sailing her full, big-bellied, trying like hell to catch us, but he could do no such thing. The race was over. In that one surge, *Kinsman* had done her in. It had been the lethal blow. *Yankee Doodle* was finished; the race was ours. We rose on crests, and I played the helm hard and soft and surfed. She tried to get out from under us, to run straight for the line. But now the angle was too steep, and the angle was ours. It was simple geometry. I was aiming *Kinsman* to clip the near end of the line, back to the pin end, a hundred yards from the committee boat.

Try as I may, I don't remember anything else about the final thousand yards. It stays blank. A pleasant blank. I was just staring at our bow's playing each wave, getting off one and getting up on another. I wasn't sure how close the white boat was, but I knew we were doing it better than they were.

I heard the cannon in the distance, saw the smoke; we had crossed the line at the far end. I ordered the spinnaker doused to slow us down and save the mast any further stress. Horns shrieked and blasted from the spectator fleet. One of them was the horn for *Yankee Doodle* when she crossed the line.

Esperance said, "Nine seconds."

I hugged him. I hugged Marcus. I patted Larry on the head. Larry was pretty much out of it again, bent forward. I stood and stretched. I couldn't straighten my body. I had cramps from my calves to my fingers. I was shivering. I turned the helm over to Esperance and went forward and gently touched the men. Body toasts. I noticed my hands were shaking.

"Fabulous, fabulous, fabulous!" Aunt Pearl's boat was suddenly there. I hadn't seen it come up. I told Josue to flatten the main, to slow us as much as possible, so that they could tie up alongside us and drop off Elizaphan.

Saint Pierre, standing with his arm around Aunt Pearl, called from above. "I'm proud of you, men. Well done, every one of you. Congratulations."

"It's absolutely impossible," Pearl was holding a glass of Champagne and waving a *Kinsman* t-shirt on a stick. She kept saying, "Absolutely impossible." Saint Pierre kissed her and stepped down aboard *Kinsman*.

Elizaphan had already jumped aboard and come forward to where I was with the men. She had climbed up on me, staggering me backwards, nearly knocking us both over the side.

"It's great, what you've done, Charles. It's simply, impossibly great." She was actually sobbing.

The case of Champagne was now in the cockpit. It had been split open, bottles were being opened, corks fired off, shot out over the water, plastic tumblers foaming. Larry had already been transferred back to Aunt Pearl's boat. Marcus kept filling plastic cups of Champagne for everyone. When I got my cup filled, my first toast was to Larry Bayard. Someone said he was lying down below deck, but that he'd heard my toast. If possible, I wanted to avoid the custom of getting thrown overboard by my crew. And of turning Champagne bottles into fire extinguishers and squirting excellent Champagne on each other. Luckily, my men weren't yachtsmen. They were sailors and had never heard of these rituals.

I toasted *Kinsman*. In those moments, I knew what it felt like to love a boat. There were many toasts to Aunt Pearl, to the crew, man-by-man, to each other, and on and on. The Champagne was chilled, as if Aunt Pearl and Saint had expected all this.

We cast off. That evening I did not want to be towed in. I wanted to drive *Kinsman* to our dock under sail. I was doing my best to remember that it wasn't over for us. That we had a ways to go.

⚑

Defeat

Yankee Doodle was slow to douse her spinnaker. I glanced over at her, and she looked bereft. Her crew wasn't busy. Most of them sat, exhausted, maybe bewildered, heads down the way that athletes sit when they have lost the Big Game. It was very private, even though each one of them felt the same thing. They'd been broken. All their arrogance had fallen overboard. The afterguard, van Riper, Bermuda, Rut, sat motionless; Soapy's left hand dangled from the losing helm. Two or three of the crewmen were up, heads down, making the deck ship-shape, keeping busy, unable to stop moving, coiling lines, hauling, bagging the jib, stowing the spinnaker. It was the opposite of a celebration. There was nothing left for them in Auckland. It was a very bad moment, one that these crewmen would never forget. Their own American atrocity.

I felt exhilarated, of course. We had done "the impossible," as Aunt Pearl kept describing it, but I felt a great letdown, too; that it was over and that I couldn't take just one more whack at them. They were champions, and I had loved beating them. I felt a pang of sadness. I was glad we'd won, but sorry it was them we'd beaten and sorry that they'd lost at all. They were a superb crew.

I asked the men if they would mind, as a great kindness to me, to sing a song to the fine boat that we had defeated, to salute their brave crew. They nodded "yes." They would be very very happy to sing to them. Holding their wine, they gathered forward, ahead of the mast. Our headsails were down and stowed so they had the foredeck to themselves. They sang very quietly; I could barely hear them. They moved their feet back and forth, and the song grew louder.

Elizaphan said it was "Baya, Bayumba," a Rwandan song that Bishop Demaseine had taught them. "It means, 'We are all together. We are the one tribe here on earth.'"

As we idled up to *Yankee Doodle,* one of their crewman was on his knees forward, making off their bowline to the towboat. My men were singing softly to them in Kinyarwandan, moving back and forth. As we glided past them under our mainsail, spontaneously, they raised their cups filled with wine to *Yankee Doodle.*

Someone spoke sharply on their afterguard. A brief word or two. No one looked over at *Kinsman.* Not one of them even glanced at my crew. It was impossible.

We moved away from *Yankee Doodle* and left her astern. When we'd gone a quarter-mile, the men stopped singing and got busy on the deck. Elizaphan and I were aft in the cockpit with Marcus. Then, out of the silence of the spectator fleet we had left, behind came an odd sound. It was a cheer.

For *us?*

Could it be?

I turned around. It *was* them, the *Yankee* crew. To my eternal shock and joy, they were giving us a cheer.

"Hip hip hooray! Hip hip hooray! Hip hip hooray!"

This was pretty good stuff, for a sport whose integrity had turned into a mush of product management. Mush that defied its beauty, the reason that sailing was; that defiled the things they sailed and had dropped them all swirling down the dollar toilet. It wasn't too late. I could hear remnants of grace and sportsmanship, pure yachting, echoing in my ears.

Hip hip hooray!

Three ragged cheers. They died in our wake. But they stayed with me until I slept.

Nacre

We had won. That night at the camp between the dock and the shed, we cooked out, lamb African; everyone ate meat now. Elizaphan sang and Kikongoro plinked his inkadiddy. Ba'ale scraped his kukui. There was much eating, smoking cigars, and drinking. We all danced as usual. Saint Pierre spent the evening within arm's length of Aunt Pearl. He danced with her in the dust, holding her tightly to him. It was beginning to look like the real thing.

"One might well ask where Sir Raleigh Smite is celebrating our victory this evening," I said to her.

"Alone, alas, alone on British Airways." She kicked up a heel behind her. "He was just filling in, Jib. I thought you could tell."

First, it had been the Champagne; then, the whiskey that Saint Pierre had found in Auckland. A sipping whiskey that he and I drank whole. The bartender at the Mosquito Café had fermented a cauldron of bananas and made wine for the men. It was no good, they said, but they drank it anyway. In spite of the Champagne, the banana wine, the ale and the hams, lamb, cassava roots, sweet potatoes, beans, in spite of the music, there was an etch of loneliness that I could see in the men. I felt sorry that they were alone at this moment of triumph. We had a long way to go, but not the next day or the day after.

I hadn't been that bombed since the night I'd flown out of Rwanda the first time when I'd found myself comparing Elizaphan to all the girls I'd ever known and made the discovery that (of all things) I might actually love her. And that, by the time I'd landed in New York, I realized she might be the woman I wanted to spend time with and not anyone else. That she was funnier, smarter, prettier, younger, deeper, stronger than my betrothed. That there was suspense, even danger in knowing her. That she made me feel better. That she offered me freedom from what I had always feared, that she had offered me her being, complete as she was, her mind as well as her history.

224

With her help, I backed away from the party. I felt like an opera singer able to sustain any note. Walking had become a problem. Luckily, I wasn't driving. Elizaphan guided me home, even though she said she was as dizzy as me.

"You're my backstay don't let go, don't let go," I kept telling her. When we climbed the stairs she led the way, turning at each landing and whispering, "Shhhh."

"I didn't say anything!"

There was something importantly different between us that night. Whatever she felt, I felt. And it shot back and forth. I felt we had come to a plateau, and I felt like lying down on it. She felt that I was a man who had done the impossible. I was of mythological size to have done what I had done. That was important to her. But it scared her.

She had taken off my shoes in the hallway downstairs. She had unbuttoned my shirt as I lay on the bed. I had fallen on and off the bed. I'd been riding on that final broad reach and all I saw was spinnakers spinnakers spinnakers spinnakers. I sat up and rolled forward. She had undressed me so many nights when I'd been too tired to move, and she undressed me again tonight.

Elizaphan had never believed in our ultimate victory. That victory had become a mantra that she'd heard me repeat a hundred times before sleep, or rather, before I'd passed out on the bed. So many nights she had undressed me. Cramps in my sleep. Noisy dreams that woke her. The tension even on lay days. No one knew, but her. She had not believed in our ultimate victory. And no one had even seen the *Black Lion*, not even a photograph. Aunt Pearl had told her a secret that she said she should never repeat to me, but that night she broke the trust and told me that Aunt Pearl had expected me to do well, but that we were not going to win. She was fond of Elizaphan and wanted to prepare her for the ending. Woman to woman. She hadn't said so, but, of course, abandonment was to be part of that ending.

I think we were both undressed, except that I was on the bed and she was on the floor. Since we'd been in New Zealand, we had not forgotten about sex, but almost. Sex had been a casualty of stress. She sat on the floor naked with her knees up under her chin and her arms wrapped around her legs. A beautiful package; tonight I wanted to open her.

"Tell me everything," I said. I stared at her. I was so drunk. I wanted to hear about them that night. "About the others," I said. She stared at me and somehow understood what I meant.

"Before?"

"Yes."

"I will tell you anything, Charles, but there is so little."

"Tell me anyway."

"Of course, I will, but why?"

"It's an American thing."

Sex to her had been a red-eyed white man with a belt who had come to her.

"What was his name?"

"Marc."

"No last name?"

"Marc, that's all."

She had been far too young. At first, she thought him to be English, but then she had understood without asking that he was French, maybe Belgian. Not a businessman; there were none of those left in Rwanda. She never saw him in uniform, but he was a soldier. What else would he have been? What they called "Peacekeepers," which was silly, because they never did. They could have stopped everything bad that was going on there, she said, but they were all on the side of the Hutus. He had found her at the market while she was walking with the baby brother of an uncle. He had followed her on foot down the road, and when they were alone he had spoken to her. He commented on her unusual color.

"He used the word *paleur*. He called me Nacre."

"What does it mean, *nacre*?"

She shrugged. "Just that I didn't look like anybody else."

"You still don't, Elizaphan."

The man took her through a field to an abandoned house. It was a house like all the others. It was off by itself. There was a dirt floor so hard that it could have been cement. There were the remains of a sofa that could hardly bear his weight. There was a wooden chair without a back on it, and that was all. That first night he took off his belt and used it on her.

"Where?"

"Down there." She patted her bottom.

"Did he make you bleed?"

"Of course, he was the first."

"No, I didn't mean that," I was embarrassed. "I meant did the belt hurt?"

"A bit, why not?"

"Did the belt make you bleed?"

"Oh no! It wasn't like that. It wasn't bad, the belt. He was very quick; he would smack me once or twice. Then it would be over."

"Why did he do it?"

"I think he needed to."

"Did he do it often?"

"Every time we met at that house. I got to expect it."

"Why did you go back?"

"I fell asleep on the sofa that first night, and when I woke up I found money."

He had slid folded Rwandan francs between the cheeks of her buttocks. It became another custom whenever he would take her to that house.

"But later. After the belt. Tell me."

"It was a great relief, of course."

"Yes, but did it feel good?"

"Yes."

"Thank God."

He always told her to wash. He would bring strong-smelling soap and tell her to wash *en bas*. Down there. One night he brought her a pretty box. In it was a very special soap, a nice soap that smelled of flowers. He never brought the other soap again. They would always meet at that abandoned house where the people had either fled or been killed. No one ever knew which. Absent.

"Tell me."

"One night he brought a bottle of French wine and lit his candles and put them on the dirt floor. He was celebrating something. He put a big flat box on the dirt floor beside the candles where I could see it. On it said, 'Pour Nacre.' In it was a dress and underwear. The dress was very thin and beautiful. It was my first real dress; it closed all the way down the front with buttons. There were nineteen buttons. For the nineteen verses of the *Koran*. The underwear was like nothing I had ever seen before. He told me to put it on. The dress was too big. He yanked his belt out of his pants."

The belt he smacked her with. Without being told, she got on her knees, on all fours, but he only picked her up and buckled the belt around her to make the dress fit her. It went around her waist twice. In another box was a pair of new shoes. The shoes were too tight and made her taller than he was. It didn't matter. "They were beautiful," she said.

Then he sat down on the sofa and left her standing alone in the middle of the room. He just sat and stared at her. Every time she moved, he told her not to, just to stand still. He asked her to turn her back to him. She didn't want to see what he was doing. Then he asked her to dance and took her right hand in his and put his arm around her waist. It was all new to her. There was no music in the abandoned house, so they hummed the only song they both new which was the *Marseillaise,* and they danced that.

Then he sat down again and told her to undress, and she did. She dropped her dress at her feet. He was outraged at that, because she had dropped her clothes the way you do when you are tired. And he told her to put her dress back on and to take it off very nicely. All this in a room with two candles on the compacted dirt floor.

"Was he married?"

"I always thought he was. I never asked. He never said so. Once he showed me a photograph of a car. There was a woman inside it, but she was on the other side. I couldn't see her face, so it was a photograph of the car that he was showing me."

"What kind of car was it?"

"Of course, I don't know the make. It was red and shiny. A very pretty car."

"He was proud of the car."

"He seemed to be, yes."

"He wanted to show you he was important."

"No. He didn't care about me."

"But he cared about himself."

Later on, she thought that the man had begun to regard sex as a near-death experience. As if he were trying to kill her with his very own mutton sword. During their sex, when she saw his face, it was the mask of death. And the belt had begun to hurt her."

"Do you think he ever loved you?"

"Maybe the way you love a child."

"Why did he spank you?"

"I tried to understand that. I think it was something he needed to do to me."

She said that he was a soldier alone in a strange country where he did not want to be surrounded by death, and he was trying to find a way to blame her. Their sex was coming closer to her death. It was dangerous. She needed to be away from him. And that was when she hid.

That night we made love, really, for the first time since we'd gotten to Waiheke Island.

The next day I called Aunt Pearl and asked her what *nacre* meant

"Mother-of-pearl," she said.

Winning

Winning meant money, among other things. That morning I was surprised again. The man in the black shoes came back to our compound at nine with an envelope addressed to me and marked with the *Yankee Doodle* syndicate logo. I signed a receipt. In it, I found Laurence Routledge's personal check drawn on the Chase Manhattan Bank and made out to me, Charles Routledge, for one million dollars. No note, but on the bottom left hand corner of the check on the blank line he had written, "For winning." A gentlemen's bet. I folded it in my pocket when I went over to Auckland later that morning and gave it to Aunt Pearl, who refused to accept it, and she opened a bank account at Chase Manhattan in my name. A bump. Start-up money for my next life, a life I had hardly imagined.

Winning meant a two-week layoff. At mid-morning, we hauled *Kinsman* up on the crane and set her in a cradle on the dock. We turned her so that the scaffolding covered her private parts: where the severed keel had parted ways from the keelson and the hull. What a hull. What a lady. She had brought us all this way. Looking up, we walked around her. I think we all felt the same thrill. Unbelievably, her dark green bottom paint had grown a fine film on it, even though we scrubbed her before every race. Her alizarin red paint had arrived from Italy. Now we could spray the topsides and cover Kikongoro's machete cuts. Her bow looked solid, doubly reinforced following that brush with the British boat. The second day was calm, the wind let up, the sun came out, a good painting day, and Joseph, Moses and Esperance sprayed the hull red.

But Marcus was worried about the keel, the twenty-four stainless steel bolts holding the twelve-ton keel bulb, that he had installed after the accident in France. The bolts were eroded from the constant pounding of rough water, and somehow we'd lost some ball bearings. They needed to be replaced. He put them on a rush order to an American company, PittSteel in Pennsylvania. The ball bearings arrived a week later. I got a call from a Customs Inspector in Auckland to come get them. The case marked "*Kinsman* Group" had been pried open, inspected, and passed.

He asked me on the phone, "So why would a yacht without a motor need ball bearings?"

That was a good question. I couldn't answer it, because of the sudden drilling noise in the shed, so I sent Isaaco (who didn't know what ball bearings were) to pick up the crate. I told him not to even to attempt speaking English.

Winning meant adoration. By the media. Their excitement had built. Out they trooped to *Kinsman*'s camp from America, Germany, Australia. They took the ferry and looked ridiculous; all epaulets and pockets, agendas, minicams, shotgun mikes, peering at us through glass eyes on tubes poked through the chain link fence. Ba'ale, with his sense of order and his well-honed machete and his ornamented teak right hand, had no trouble keeping them behind that fence. He was fun to watch. They said they only wanted to give their public a glimpse of us.

They photographed Ba'ale through the fence, and they photographed us at a distance doing whatever we did all day long: morning calisthenics, buffing and painting *Kinsman*'s hull, eating lunch *al fresco*, sleeping in the shade, taking the grinders apart, lubricating the winches, all through the day to our evening cookout where we ate at tables by the dock unless it was raining.

They wanted to make us look interesting, which of course they couldn't. We were dull, we were tired, we were busy. Could we do something authentic? Could the boys dance an African rain ceremony? Could the boys throw spears? A California photographer for *Sports Illustrated* wanted to do a swimsuit layout with Elizaphan. No. Still, he managed to get a few telephoto shots of her swimming off the dock, eating lunch, hugging me. He tried to guess her race, age, family background and occupation. No one from our camp ever saw the article, and I never showed it to her.

And each evening, after the last ferryboat had taken the last photographer away home to bed, we cooked and danced and drank the local ale.

Winning meant endorsements. Aunt Pearl called and said she'd been approached by several big name clothing companies to sponsor *Kinsman*. She had said "no" to all of them, except one.

"Except one?" I said. "I thought we agreed: There shall be no endorsements."

"It'll be fun. Aren't we supposed to be having fun?"

"I hadn't thought of it that way."

"Well, we are."

"Who'd you pick?"

"Listen, I'll tell you who I did not pick. Some little company named, Colors of the World. Dreadful." No one said "dreadful" better.

"What if Rwanda had a company called, White Folks of the World."

"Okay."

"I also did not pick Banana Republic. What if Guatemala, which is a marvelous country, called us a Mega-Power Pig?"

"Okay, okay, so who'd you pick?" I liked the way she beefed-up her stories.

"I fell for Ralph Lauren."

"Why?" I said.

"He's adorable! He believes that poor people aspire to polo. He takes out ads in magazines with only a photograph of himself in them. Don't you think that's wonderful? No one does that. He's a delight! I must meet him."

"But why else?"

"Don't be such a sourpuss. He'll have your crew clad in . . ."

I could hear paper sounds.

"In his very own slacks, shorts, trunks, shirts, jerseys, underpants, caps, every one of them with a teeny polo player stitched somewhere on it. Your men will be using his cologne, shaving cream, purses, pens, stationery, watches. Come on, Jib, smile. It's . . ."

I could see her eyes sparkling.

"It's absolutely celestial. Some of them even bear his family's royal crest. His family name is Lipshitz. It's delicious."

"I can't wait for the fun to start." It seemed like a joke on the men. "Polo Black," I said. I sounded sour.

"Oh, come on. It will be fun."

She did have a keen nose for the absurd. Hutus and Tutsis, the great men of *Kinsman*, dressed in blazers with royal crests on their breast pockets? Yachting and polo: the one and two priciest, snob sports together at last?

"Why doesn't he just send them food."

"Oh, he will." That was in the letter of agreement they signed.

Winning meant headlines. It meant meeting our TV public. They had awakened, come to life, and there they were standing behind our chain link fence. There was no one left to look at, so they came to look at us. They're like that. They would have preferred looking at us on their TV screens, but we just weren't on them.

They seemed to have just gotten out of bed; they were still wearing their bedding. After all, for the last three generations, they'd been drinking cathode rays like pure helium and had grown into hybrid mutations of the man-in-the-street and the family-on-the sofa, and they could no longer radiate more than half-a-watt of heat from their brain cells, not enough to power a spider's reading light. And so they needed something special, these sleepy folk whose swollen fingers never strayed far from the off-button on learning. They knew nothing. But even better, they wanted to know nothing and preferred that it not ask them hard questions.

But the America's Cup was not exciting enough for them. Humanoid wads of lunchmeat able to watch television sports and little else, able to sit for hours, dimly aware that they were alive, waiting for a man in an odd suit to strike a ball. They studied rich men bent over golf balls. When they sat facing their screens, they stirred when hockey players stuffed like teddy bears bloodied each other's faces. They tilted their heads when cars spun out of control. So, to them (this fickle breed to whom all sponsorship is dedicated), we were not interesting. Deep down inside them (if there were such a place), they had not wanted us to win. Not really. Rwanda versus New Zealand was not good television. Neither did Nike, Pepsi, Sony, Timex, Bic, nor Smirnoff think so. The heavyweight championship fight should be fought between Billy and Bobby. Now they had to watch the "Who cares, folks?" fight it out. Oh, God. Not ideal television. Send for a map. Where was it again? Now they needed a cartographer.

But never mind the bleary-eyed family perched on their sofa. Or sponsors. What about yachting? Yacht racing had never been created to been seen by *those* people. These duels were meant to be played out near yacht clubs, between warriors with zinc ointment painted on their noses, with drinks in hand, while spinnaker size was discussed on the verandah between the elders and the young, who looked identical.

It was bad enough that Rwanda had beaten America. If Rwanda beat New Zealand, there would simply be no more America's Cup. It would all peter out. No yachtsman in his right mind would ever consider traveling to Central Africa to win it back. If Rwanda actually beat America (shudder, and they might just; they had come this far, after all), yes, the entire yachting world would have to choke on, well, outsiders, total strangers, who had never even heard of zinc ointment. It would be the same as nibbling Camembert rolled in Spam. Rwanda didn't even have a yacht club, for God's sake. Where did they plan to house this Holy Grail, if they *did* win it? In the market square, *if* they even had one?

No, they were pushing it, these wiry little black people who had never laid eyes on a yacht until twenty months ago when Charley Routledge, our very own Jib, had introduced yachting to a country that feasted on every single part of the goat. And, when they were lucky, rice provided by international hunger agencies. A country where a kid growing up did not have the life expectancy of a running dog. There should never be that sort of democracy in yachting. America's Cup yachting will always believe that society comes first, stillborn money barons and dilettantes. No. This Rwanda thing was not yachting. This was humanitarian aid.

But it is exactly the punishment that can visit a grand sport when it loses the run of itself. What next? Rodeo riders from Montana riding polo ponies in Monaco? Please. It has no more to do with yachting or seamanship than health care has to do with health care or the humane society has to do with humanity. In spite of everything, we were probably ready.

Winning meant stock options.

"Jib, Saint called. He's done this marvelous thing. He's devised a scheme for Rwanda to sell stock."

"What's the bond?"

"The country, darling, Rwandan bonds. Businessmen can invest in shares in Rwanda."

"Do you think they will?"

"They already have."

"What a mind. You ought to snap him up."

"Maybe I should." Winning meant glory. The Luis Vuitton Cup.

But Elizaphan was embarrassed by outsiders' constant scrutiny of her. She didn't know what to make of the attention. Who was she supposed to be in their eyes? It made her uncomfortable. More and more she'd begun staying alone in our room at Mrs. Prosser's Guest House. It was the upstairs room. I thought it was the best one, because of the privacy, as well as the view of trees and the gulf.

She was afraid of sailing. She never came out with me on *Kinsman*. She had filled our room with flowers and growing things. The flowers grew in tin cans, and she kept cut flowers in jars. The room always smelled fresh as outdoors. Ba'ale had always been protective of her and when he saw how she was being and had nothing much to do, he encouraged her to make pictures, to draw. He bought her crayons and white paper. In the room, she began drawing constantly, as if she were a child who has just discovered that she can actually make images. She drew our room. This is what she drew, except when I wandered in, and she drew me.

ಠ

Miniature Bocce

The hull paint set nicely, and two days later we all buffed her topsides until they gleamed like nail polish on a gala night.

Because *Kinsman* had landed in the curiosity box, we were being observed. More people than necessary became aware of this ball bearing shipment. *Kinsman* watchers were baffled. As the inspector had queried: "Why would a sailboat need ball bearings?"

I got a call from a reporter named Iggy or Itzy, Italian. The first question he asked was about the shipment. Luckily, I was in the shed I told him the ball bearings were for a game. "Yeah, that's it; a game," I laughed vivaciously, "a game we played during the boring off hours when we had to stay in camp with nothing to do."

"Oh, me, I like games," he said. "Tell me, please, what game?"

It was noisy in the shed. I spoke before I'd finished thinking.

"Sort of a miniature bocce-ball game," I said. The word *bocce* was out before I could stop it. I was barely able to reach for a high-speed drill without interrupting him.

"I love bocce," he said.

Of course. And pasta. Why couldn't I have said marbles? Wari? Pachinko?

"And we all love bocce over here."

I turned the drill on.

"I can't hear you!" he yelled, which was true. The drill made a screaming noise. I hung up. When he called back, Ba'ale answered the phone. As night watchman, he had needed to learn several key phrases. Among them: "Go away, thank you." "Please who are you?" "Get out!" And "Freeze!" was probably his favorite.

Ever since the winged keel was invented (Australia's greatest yacht racing resource, the secret weapon that won them the America's Cup), the top Cup racers have been subjects of scrutiny, even suspicion. Our shipment of ball bearings was the stuff rumors are made of. In the event that someone could accept the fact that we were actually qualified to be there, one might still not fathom why we were. A secret weapon was the obvious answer. And if New Zealand wanted to copy it, now would be the time. And if they did, I wasn't so sure that we could beat them, boat-for-boat, skipper-for-skipper.

Later that morning, Ba'ale came looking for me and said the Italian reporter, Iggy, was on his way over.

Damn. How could I have used the word *bocce* to an Italian? The word alone had heated his blood; maybe he was lonely.

When he arrived, Ba'ale sent the kid running to tell me. We could see Iggy waving at us from behind the fence. I told Ba'ale to open the gate. Four of us had quickly set up a tiny bocce game, Moses and Esperance versus Elizaphan and I. We were on our knees in the dust. We were tossing half-inch ball bearings at a raw pea. We were taking our turn rolling ball bearings at the pea along the dusty ground. Iggy watched us for a while with a puzzled look, like a sea gull. I wasn't sure he wanted to play with us anymore. We concentrated on the game, ignoring him. Finally, when I said we could, we all stood. Iggy handed me his card.

IGNACIO BRAGGI
Cronista Speciale
IL SPORTIVO

"*Il maggiore famoso sport periodico entro Italia*," Iggy explained and left me to figure it out. Moses collected the ball bearings and put them in his pocket. There were eight of them.

"Nice-a game," Iggy said, but he didn't mean it. He wanted to know if miniature bocce was an African game.

Good, he was brain-dead.

"It certainly is!" I explained to him that, "Yes, it was, a sort of African thing that had evolved from children tossing dried animal droppings."

"What kind animal?"

"Usually impala."

He thanked me. It was a good story for *Il Sportivo*, he said. He needed a picture. Okay. We got on our knees again. He lowered his voice to a whisper. "Please-a, no girl." He told me politely that women were never allowed to play bocce in Italy. I lowered my voice and told him that if she was deprived of miniature bocce she would kick me out of her bed. That was *migliori*. He loved it. He kissed his fingernails.

The secret weapon rumor died that afternoon, although anyone thinking about it for a moment would have to ask himself, "Why did these people send to Pennsylvania for ball bearings when sheep droppings (so similar in size and weight to impala droppings) were common to New Zealand?"

Marcus, Kikongoro, Innocent, Esperance and I had to work that night and for the next three nights installing the ball bearings tightly into each well where the fat one-inch bolts came up from the keel. It was not easy.

It was a blessing that our camp was on Waiheke Island and that the photographers took their inquiring eyes home on the ferryboat every evening. Except for one, a kid learning his trade. He wouldn't give me his name. He was probably ten years younger than me. He stayed one evening after dark and stood back from the fence and got some pictures of us eating and dancing. And later, some pictures of bright lights under a tent, the crew working above and below deck, pictures of us working inside the boat. He came back the next day and showed them to me.

"Curious-looking pictures," he said.

He had heard tapping metal. "What was that?" Tightening the keel.

So that wasn't suspicious and nothing odd showed up on film and there wasn't enough to even start up the rumor again. So it stayed dead.

The kid's name was Sammy Winslow, and I was very sorry to find out he was from the *Auckland Star*. He came back the next day; he wanted more. He asked me about the ball bearings. I told him about miniature bocce. The African game. He couldn't stop laughing. I told him to shut up. He asked me please to say the part again about how impala droppings were different from just about anything else. He told me he had three questions for me and that, with or without my help, he was going to get three satisfactory answers. The questions were: Why was *Kinsman* capable of such outrageous bursts of high speed? Why did *Kinsman* need ball bearings? What I was hiding?

I didn't say anything. I lie better that way.

"I'll find out," he said and laughed again. "Miniature bocce," he repeated, just because he liked to say it aloud. He looked healthy, the sort of kid who could easily scramble over a chain link fence in the dark. I doubled the watch that night.

⚑

Prelude

In the two weeks before the Cup finals, whenever I went into Auckland to talk to Aunt Pearl, *Black Lion* was everywhere. Banners, posters, boat models. They even brought out a *Black Lion* Ale. It was so young that it was green, but that didn't bother anyone. *Black Lion* t-shirts were on everyone walking around the streets: the lion rampant was on the front; the words GIANT KILLER, written across the back. New Zealand had been given the giant killer tag last time around when they creamed the United States five to nothing. New Zealand is a smaller country than Montana.

I didn't see one bright red t-shirt with *Kinsman* written on it. Rwanda was a giant killer, too. And you could stuff thirty Rwandas into one New Zealand. If you wanted to. How *small* are we? On the map of the world, if New Zealand were a strip of bacon, then Rwanda'd be the fly upon it. So, when we beat New Zealand, and I intended to, we'd be entitled to wear GIANT KILLER'S GIANT KILLER t-shirts. If we wanted to.

Of course, I'd never seen the *Black Lion*. No one of us had. No one knew. The rumors of her magic speed and of her breakthrough sail fabric had grown every week. Her legendary skipper, Ace Gordon. She had been shipped by freighter into Auckland at night, up from the south end of the island, Wellington. I was asleep. I heard about it in the morning from Aunt Pearl, who'd been coming home with Saint Pierre after dinner. They'd seen bright lights down at marine harbor. Apparently *Black Lion* had been off-loaded in slings and lowered onto her dock without touching the water. She and her running mate, *Black Magic*, were to be housed next to the recently abandoned French headquarters. I knew she needed sea trials in Harauki Gulf. I needed to see her. They'd all seen us. Ace Gordon had been spotted by Marcus during our series with the American boat. Gordon had been out in the spectator fleet watching us through binoculars.

That afternoon, I got an excited call from Pearl who had heard that *Black Lion* was going out for shake-down runs and while we were on the phone she spotted her. Pearl was standing at her window and could actually see it. "There she is," she said. *Black Magic* was being towed from her dock. I told her to get right on her boat and pick us up.

An hour later in the distance, I got my first glimpse I had of her. She was dead in the water, sails down, barely under tow. From the first glance, I felt a cool rush of fear. There was a mist blowing low across the water, but I could see a crewman aloft in a bosun's chair doing repairs, reeving a line or something at the masthead. Even with her sails down she was impressive. When the mist blew away, I saw her hull clearly. Low to the water, she had a cutter bow, a sharp vertical line. She was entirely black, even her mast was carbon black. Black black black. The glint of gold, there was a touch of it forward, maybe the outline a lion on her bows. Not a library lion, but the angry lion with both forepaws extended that I'd seen on the t-shirts. Outlined in gold. When the hull turned away, though, I saw it. She carried a bowsprit, a sword stuck straight out ahead of her: a jibboom, to crowd on another five hundred feet of sail in light weather just like the sandbagger sloops had in the 1800s.

It wasn't blowing. When the crewman hauled himself down off her mast, she dropped her towline and raised a translucent mainsail, almost clear. I'd never seen one before. This was the breakthrough fabric we'd heard about. They raised a mid-sized jib, and she fell away on a starboard tack gaining speed. The sea was calm; the wind maybe blowing eight. It was a beautiful sight. I still couldn't judge anything about her performance. Neither could Larry or Marcus. But the rumors about her looked safe. She resembled a revenue runner from Hell. How could anything that looked like she did ever lose a race? We were about to find out, weren't we? But from all appearances the rumors were firmly confirmed.

Ace Gordon drove her beautifully. As if she were something he had dreamed up and then taken out for a day sail with friends. Gordon ran his crew hard and well. They practiced sail changes and eventually they must have raised and dropped all her sails twice. They never stopped and never made a mistake. It was a continuous flow. The advertising on her hull and sails was low and modest compared to America and France, but they were still there marring her lines. Ale, shoes, computers, banks.

We kept our distance and watched her through binoculars. The sea was calm, her hull long and low. And the rampant lion circumscribed in gold forward on her topsides stayed dry, just above the bow wave. I couldn't gauge her speed; there were no measured buoys. She was fast. How fast? I couldn't tell. In these light conditions, she seemed faster than us. But these had never been our conditions. And when Gordon had her main, her Genoa and her spinnaker up, I could hardly see the hull. She rode so low that she looked like a cloud that had been underlined.

From hard-a-lee to rounding up to filling away, *Black Lion*'s tacks took four seconds. The sheets were on and off the grinders. The crew stood like naval cadets waiting for orders. I was amazed by their drill. *Yankee Doodle* had a great crew, but these guys were better. At least they were in this light weather. After an hour watching sail changes, watching her streak back and forth up and down, there were fifty spectator boats bobbing with their beers at a very respectful distance. No New Zealander dared intrude. He heeled close by us and showed us the deep green bottom paint of her underside, her gleaming silver-winged keel, her very blackness. Then, as if he knew that Marcus, Larry, Esperance, and I, the entire brain trust of *Kinsman*, were on board, he tacked sharply twenty yards above us and filled away on starboard, giving us a look at everything but his middle finger. He was showing us her crew, her equipment, her deckplan. The crew wore black. There was Ace with two men seated facing him. Where was the helm? He didn't have his hand on a wheel; there was no wheel. There was a tiller. Gordon sat low, like a fox hunting at twilight, with his chin on the deck and his right hand holding a long, bowed length of dark wood (maybe aluminum), that ran from his hand through the afterdeck to the rudder post. I'd never seen a seventy-five-foot yacht steered by a tiller before, but there it was. His control was immediate; that's how he could steer the *Lion* like a Thistle or a Star: the two classes he had won his Olympic gold medals in. But still, I couldn't help wondering how the kick of the weather helm would be diffused. How could he hold the rein on that much boat for twenty-four miles on a sloppy day?

Today was calm compared to other days I'd seen in the gulf, but he knew what he was doing. I was impressed. He dominated the boat; it quailed under him. I could see it. He was handling its rig as if it were a Starboat. How could we beat *Black Magic*? And Ace Gordon? Jesus.

"Are we awed?" I said.

"Don't be absurd," Aunt Pearl said.

Esperance nodded.

"Most certainly not," Marcus added. He had always maintained the eastern seaboard syntax that I had succeeded in dismissing in myself. But he had stayed on within it. He still wore the clothes he'd worn as a little boy at the Choate School. Oxford blue shirts, raglan jerseys.

But I was most definitely impressed with the *Lion*. Streaking back and forth, upwind, downwind, trying on a huge spinnaker, then another, a golliwobbler the size of Monaco. Gordon was unafraid, of course, showing us everything. What could anyone possibly do about it? Prepare? He had no secrets.

But even though she was at home in Harauki Gulf, *Black Lion* was the new girl in town. It seemed hard to believe, but in getting to where we stood today, we'd had thirty-nine races behind us, plus the four at La Rochelle. *Black*

Lion had none. She had never raced anyone, but her trial horse, *Black Magic*. We were battle-weary after three months of hard-nosed racing, most of them crucial. And with *Kinsman* up and in her cradle, all we were doing was replacing sails, bolts, rigging and, in general, honing the red blade. I'd gotten used to feeling coolly uneasy, nagged by my gut. But *Black Lion* worried me.

We hadn't peaked. I didn't feel we had. I'd gotten used to living up to my expectations. I'd been doing that for twelve weeks. I was used to pointing to a direction and driving there. It was the finest feeling to come out of all this. We needed a rest. We were tired, but good and sure. We knew our boat in all weather.

No one in New Zealand was pulling for us to win, of course, and that didn't matter. We were doing the pulling. Some people had maybe wanted us to win a race; maybe two, to make it interesting. But the prospect of losing to Rwanda and going there for the next America's Cup and eating boiled roots, cassava soup, as well as trinkets of goat on corn grits, just wasn't on. The oldest trophy in all of sport. Open to all nations, a phrase the organizers may learn to regret one day.

The night before the first race, the moon was much too bright. Again. Sleep was way out of the question. I was downstairs, as usual, on the porch and walking to the camp to be with *Kinsman*. I had so much to thank her for. The final twist she had made that eked us across the line ahead of *Yankee Doodle*. It could only have come from some force not available to any naval architect's learning. As always, the race would depend on the wind, and the wind wasn't telling us. I couldn't afford myself the luxury of fear, but there I was: as nervous as I was on the eve my first Labor Day race when I was twelve.

⚑

Part Four

The America's Cup

The America's Cup XXX

Hauraki Gulf. The morning came fair. Patchy sky, breezy. The weather would be pretty much ours, if it held. I couldn't calm my nerves. Luckily, I had Marcus in the cockpit and a very sick Larry to hold my hand, as well as Esperance, who was indispensable.

At the ten-minute gun, Ace Gordon raised his invisible mainsail. I could see right through it. I was close to it today, and I still didn't know what it was they had. I'd never seen fabric like theirs. I hadn't believed it even existed. We had Mylar and we felt that was the best, but theirs had a life of its own and seemed to be breathing with the wind.

Black Lion shot past us, the black-masted spear without freeboard. Ace Gordon gave me a small salute. I couldn't get my hand up in time to answer him. He did not disappoint his fans. He sailed circles around us during the prestart. His style was very much like that of the French skipper, Ballon, and he left me standing still, sucking air with not a lot of trouble, at the start. Larry was feeling too sick to help out, but Esperance and a few of the crewmen who'd gotten sharp at starts looked hurt.

But the weather was ours again. I didn't care how we did it. I didn't care who knew. *Black Lion* leapt off to a huge lead, at least ten boat lengths, and *Kinsman* set off after her, baying like a staghound hunting a blood spoor. I took a wild port tack straight into a bruising chop that kept flicking our keel back and forth. Every time we struck a sharp wave, it blew back blasts of spray the length of the boat, blinding me at the helm. We were gaining.

The *Black Lion* drove through the chop without flinching. She must have been carrying more weight in her keel than we were in ours, maybe twenty-one tons. She skewered, cut, and sliced with her bowsprit diving. But she didn't rise or fall the way we did, roiling, rolling, careening. She was plowing. We gained a couple of yards with each thrust.

We caught her at the first mark, but I let her take it, set the spinnaker, and shot off tacking downwind, sailing like hell. We drove past her and down she went. There was nothing Ace Gordon could do about it. We rounded the final mark, sailed well ahead downwind, and won.

The New Zealand spectator fleet watched in silent horror; the alizarin red boat slid across the finish line at high speed a mile ahead of their black boat. The silence was eerie. Out of fifteen hundred spectator boats, one was flying a Rwandan flag. The only sound was the *BOOM* of the cannon as we crossed the line and, much later, the *SQUEEE* of the horn for *Black Lion*.

We had taken her decisively. It was a brilliant victory. We had won the first race clean, and we would win the second. It hadn't been a mistake. We had become a logical threat to the national security of the Cup. All New Zealand was stunned. So was I.

⚐

The Race

The black-bordered headline read:

RWANDA 1, KIWI 0.

I was no longer nervous.

The New Year's winds had come to stay. Under the rules, Marcus would have to skip this race, so I invited Elizaphan to be fourteenth man. She was afraid of water and had never wanted to do any sailing and wasn't crazy about the idea, but finally she couldn't resist the idea of seeing a race from the boat itself. So, we held off until midday to see what the seas would be like. The wind was up at the pre-start, but the seas were smooth. So she came along and sat behind Esperance, Larry and me in the fourteenth seat. She didn't like it one bit.

After five minutes of being circled and tricked by *Black Lion*, Larry told me to break it off and cut the hell away from her and the line on a port reach, then leave Ace Gordon to out-maneuver himself. The move was so fast that *Black Lion* was caught facing the wrong way. We won the start.

When we went into the first gut-busting, uphill beat to the first mark, Elizaphan got seasick, and there was nothing I could do about it. I felt so sorry for her, wet from sheets of fine spray, seeing her vomitus washed over the transom.

Our lead didn't last. *Black Lion* crept up on us. Sailing well on a steep heel, her spike bow cutting nicely, she passed above us close, stole our wind and left us in disturbed air. The first mark was hers and close once again. It looked like more of a race than I had expected. On the reach to the wing mark, it all came together for us. We had the race won after we rounded the third mark with five left to go. Our dorsal fin keel was responding beautifully; our sail choices and changes were perfect. We'd done it again. We sailed home the clear winner.

This time Esperance had taken the wheel, sailing half the race, four downwind legs including the finish. I had taken the start and the beats. And poor Elizaphan had stayed sick for the entire twenty-four miles, plunge by plunge, dying a little more with each sickening plunge until we crossed the finish line, dropped the sails, and slowed down. She no longer cared about living. I told her we'd won, but she either didn't hear me, or she didn't give a damn.

Aunt Pearl and Saint Pierre came alongside all smiles. The miracle was the norm. Marcus and I helped Elizaphan off our deck and onto Aunt Pearl's boat, but by then it was calm and the power boat was rolling more than we. *Kinsman* was the steadier boat. Ace Gordon had sailed an excellent race. Nothing had gone wrong, no mistakes. Everything had worked out well. We had simply sailed over him; that was the puzzle. Perhaps with the shock of seeing a Central African native skipper a Twelve across the line ahead of him, he asked for (and he got) a layday.

When I got back to the compound, I found a nearly square envelope waiting for me, postmarked New York and addressed in fine script. An envelope brittle as glass. My fingers were still cramped from the race, but I got it open. Good Lord:

> *Mr and Mrs Longstreet Ortion*
> *of West Palm Beach and New York City*
> *are pleased to announce the engagement of their daughter*
> *Miss Maynard Jocelyn Ortion*
> *to Mr Alec Lester Gordon, Junior,*
> *son of Mr and Mrs Alec Lester Gordon*
> *of Auckland, New Zealand.*

That was quick. Alec Lester Gordon? Jocelyn, you've scored yourself the Wizard of Wellington, heir to Gordon Wells, a bankrupt well-drilling outfit on the South Island and, hey, Ace, what could you have been thinking? You've taken a Manhattan heiress for a bride. I thought you were the shy type. Shy a few million bucks, probably.

I noticed that the ceremony was set for June, well after the Cup races had been resolved. I sent a note to Jocelyn through Aunt Pearl offering to give her away. I'd lost my own family. Over on *Yankee Doodle,* I had two cousins, Nick and Sack. I never heard from them. Okay, okay, I'd gone out on a limb of the family tree. Sure, I'd challenged them. Did I betray them? No. I'd competed against Uncle Routledge's syndicate. It was a wild idea. I'd had a vision, a dream, an idea as impossible as turning a cobweb into gold. But somehow it had started to turn, and there I was standing on a golden cobweb. Rwanda versus New Zealand. What a ring that had. I never could have dreamed it. Well, yes, actually I could have.

℞

Race Three

The gears had shifted. Aunt Pearl called with the morning headlines. *The Auckland Star:*

RWANDA TO NEW ZEALAND: BUG OFF MATE
African Boat Humiliates Kiwis In Twin Openers

Too true, as any local who had witnessed *Kinsman* whipping their national treasure would tell you. Worry. Outside of the Team New Zealand headquarters, an idea was beginning to form in average New Zealanders' minds. They could actually feel their Cup being sucked away from them. They could foresee the dawn when movers would come to crate it up. It. *L'objet d'art* that had started it all, fagotted with silver rococo, the nadir of ostentatious taste. New Zealand, normally at the bottom of any desk-top globe, had been for the moment at the center of the yachting world. They did not want that to go away. Two losses was two too many.

For me, two was not enough; it would have to be five before we'd really whipped *Black Lion*. But it was a phone call that helped me decide to throw the third race.

It was also the climate. Beating New Zealand twice badly on their home turf was not a friendly gesture and, of course, I sensed hatred from the spectator fleet as we sailed in after the second race. Some of it was prejudice, of course. I'd heard the usual jingoisms, but it was the phrase *slave ship* that caught my ear. That was ugly. It was naked hatred. Once again, that night I sequestered my men. I didn't want them tumbling into an Auckland pub brawl or getting killed in a street fight. I honestly didn't think that they were even aware of what was happening, of what an amazing thing they'd done, or of the reaction that was causing. They didn't seem to feel the wave of resentment or sense the potential danger in it. I had still wanted five straight; that was how New Zealand had won last time around. But then, Ba'ale called me to the phone in the shed.

246

"Mister Rotledged?" A man's voice. Rot-ledged?

"Yes? Who's this?"

"Doctor Katz. Lose the race today or die."

It was too quick. I wasn't sure I'd heard him right.

"Capisce?"

"I'm not quite sure." It was awfully early for this.

"What part didn't you understand?"

"Both parts."

"Let me help you those parts, Mister Rotledged. I do not want to have to deal with any confusion later on." He spoke slowly. "New Zealand wins the sailboat race today. Or you die." This time I heard him very clearly.

"What are you thoughts?" he said after a silence.

I couldn't think of any thoughts other than "Why wasn't this call being monitored for my protection?"

"You had your coffee yet, Mister Rotledged?" He said it *CAW-fee.*

"This is a death threat." It was my first.

"Correct. This is a death threat, okay?"

"Okay." I didn't mean "okay," I just meant "okay."

"We win or you lose."

"Who's we?"

"We is *not* you."

He hung up. It was a fatherly voice, someone I could trust to keep his promise. It took me a moment to register what I had been told not to do. He had spoken in slow syllables and in only one tone, not a local voice, New Zealand or Australia. There was a trace of New York in it. It could have been a long distance call, God knows from where. But later on, I'd heard the odds had shot up in Las Vegas. After a minute, the phone rang again. I was still standing beside it. No hello.

"You win, you're a dead man. That's easy to remember isn't it?" Before I could agree, he'd hung up.

What he was saying was, "Throw the race. Or die." Either/or. Finding the motive to kill me that morning in New Zealand would have been a snap. Finding the person who did it might pose a problem. The police probably wouldn't even bother to sort through the three million rap sheets of the suspects who wanted me dead. So, they'd probably decide to leave the file open and wait for a confession. And what would I care then?

Doctor Katz called back a third time. I told him, "We take a dive. I don't see the problem." I had Robert deNiro in mind. Make it look interesting, throw a race, calm the locals, I always say. This time, I personally dove down and made off a new sea anchor to the bulb of the keel. Deep.

℞

Race Four

The night before, once again, a Rwandan moon had risen too bright, horrible above the mainland hills. We had sailed home the clear winner in races one and two, and then been edged out in number three. A slight mishap not far from the finish line had ruined our chances and put us behind *Black Lion* by two boat lengths. We had their number, but my idea of our going five to nothing now seemed ghoulish, especially in the light of Doctor Katz's philosophy. Certainly, two to one sounded better. But two to two did not. Still, just to make sure, I wasn't taking any calls that morning.

I wanted twenty knots. And I got it. Larry told me to tack away from the line, and when it seemed we'd gone a mile too far, he said, "Tack." And we drove back, crossing the line dead even at flank speed, kicking up a wake. Side by side, we drove across like a pair of race horses at a country fair. We beat them at the start, thanks to Larry, and once again we kicked up a wake. *Black Lion* stayed close, but we simply outsailed them. The waves were five feet. She kept digging her needle-nose into the seas, and we were flying over them. Our dorsal fin was superb; the interior refraction of each wave shoved us over them. Over the twenty-four-mile Cup course, all we needed was to be quicker by one second a mile, and we'd have a lop-sided win. And we did.

Once again, to the horror of the spectator fleet, that's just what happened. We beat them that afternoon sailing home so far ahead of them that they looked like a child's sailboat on a pond in a park. It was simple; we had the keel, and they didn't. It was probably too late for them. They would have to wait three years with the rest of the yachting world to battle it out for the right to meet us on Lake Kivu, Rwanda. Or maybe, Lake Tanganyika next door. Either way: Central Africa.

That evening at the press conference, Ace Gordon requested a lay day. He had smiled at me. Why? As I was leaving, Jocelyn waved to me. She was smiling, too. It was not a good smile. It was a New York I-know-too-much smile. They were down three to one. Why were they smiling at me?

Even though it was subdued, our celebration that night was (because of the lay day) "subdued" until one in the morning. We had them down three to one; we needed two more. Everyone was getting scared or excited; either one, depending on what your address was. Me? Both. It could really happen. The handwriting was on the wall, and the chalk was in my hand.

No one was prepared. God knows what was being said at the New York Yacht Club. And what about Newport? To have fallen this far, to have allowed the Cup to fall into enemy hands and vanish into darkest Africa. At some Nilotic Congolese yacht club without a Midsummer Dance? Or even a burgee? Yikes! It might have worked in basketball, but this was *yachting*, for goodness sake. It was *their* Cup. The Holy Grail. How could you be sure those people weren't going to pawn it? How could you trust them not to melt it down? Was this some hideous wisecrack invented by Common Cause?

I was in the shed early the next morning when the phone rang. Aunt Pearl.

"Darling, I'm glad I caught you. Something unusual's happened. The Race Committee jolted me out of bed just now. This man Lyle or Kyle, the upshot is that they've gone and granted New Zealand a postponement."

"They just got a lay day."

"On top of it. They've taken a week."

"It's not legal."

"Oh, yes, it is. We invented the rule."

There is a law in the charter invented by us, naturally, that says the defender can jolly well take a chunk of time off whenever he deems it necessary to his defense of the Cup.

"What do you think it means?" I asked.

"It means I can go back to bed."

It seemed like a long time just to recover from three losses. They were in danger, but we had a way to go. We had three. We needed two. Five was the magic number. It didn't look like the series could go to nine.

At midday, Aunt Pearl called. She'd gotten the *'Granny' Herald*. There was a nice piece about the postponement. "Listen," she said. "I'm reading: 'Prime Minister Edward Stone has responded favorably to many complaints of hazardous flotsam that have floated into Hauraki Gulf, submerged logs and so forth, and it will take a week to clear them away.'"

We'd become a natural disaster.

"The lion is licking his wounded paw," she said. "Would you agree?"

"That's a lot of paw licking," I said.

"That's a stack of shit," said Marcus when I told him. We all agreed it was, but they'd done it. And it was very strange, it didn't sound right to any one of us at the camp.

⚑

Black Thursday

At eight o'clock the next morning I knew.

"Did you see the paper, dear?" Aunt Pearl.

"We're on an island, remember? They don't deliver 'til ten."

Silence. I could tell right away that she wasn't smiling.

"Bad news?"

"Very," she said. "Let me read you what it says." There was a great rustling of newspapers. "They're onto you."

Jesus, I knew it. My gut liquefied and poured into my feet. I didn't say a word. The keel. I'd been waiting.

"Page one, if you please, in the *Star* has the headline, 'Dark Horse Wins With Wobbly Leg,' and then below that it calls us a 'Rocking Horse Winner.' Well," she added, "this *is* horse country."

Neither of us was amused. Our secret was out.

"Well, there's a scoop for you. Who's name is on it?"

"The byline is," there was a pause, "Sammy Winslow."

The laughing boy. He had done it. I pitched my can of kiwi soda into an oil drum; it burst, on contact, in a flare of spray. It was that kid who'd enjoyed my miniature bocce story so much.

"Damn." How had he found out?

"He says your keel acts like a dorsal and that it's the only reason you've been winning."

The word *dorsal*. It stopped me. My word. A coincidence?

"No one's ever used that word *dorsal* but me. I never heard Marcus or Larry use it. It's not all Sammy Winslow."

"It could be just a little too late for all of this, darling," Pearl said.

"Okay. They know." Now we had a problem.

It had been too good too long. Anyone who'd been watching us handle *Kinsman* in heavy weather against *Yankee Doodle*, anyone who'd seen us surge against *Black Lion* in the first three races could have seen something. But even though they could see our thrusts, there was no way anyone could measure their speed. We were not consistently faster sailing, boat for boat. It was our sudden surges in good seas, our simulated surfing, our leaps from a sculling power that no other boat possessed. It had been all we needed; just enough surges buried into those distances, mile-for-mile, to have given us the winning edge.

"We have a leak over here, Pearl." I said it grimly. I was confused. Disloyalty among my crew had never occurred to me until then. The men rarely went over to the main island, rarely spoke to outsiders. I had even worried about their isolation. Blacks were not as highly regarded in New Zealand as they were in our own country. I kept my crewmen pretty isolated.

"He's going to be interviewed on television tonight."

"Don't try to cheer me up."

"You're on the verge of winning the Cup, Jib. What can they do?"

"Isn't it obvious?" I told her that Ace Gordon had taken his week, more than enough time to install *Black Lion* with her very own dorsal fin keel just like ours. Throwing the fourth race might have been a mistake.

That evening, when Sammy Winslow was interviewed on Auckland's number one television talk show "Evenin' Folks!", Aunt Pearl told me he was positively kittenish. His discovery was going down as derring-do espionage. Clandestine stuff. But what a story. We had not only beaten their perfect dream boat three times, we had done it with our dirty little secret. Of course we had, they went on. How else could a twenty-something, back-up skipper like Jib Routledge have beaten the ordained Lord of Sail, Ace Gordon? Sammy Winslow was asked if he was going to write a book. He would consider it.

The press was clearly embarrassed. Flabbergasted. No one had ever kept an America's Cup secret from them this long. Because no one with a breakthrough design had ever dared to risk losing as much as we had to disguise our secret. Anyway, it was out.

The next day, as the scandal ripened, a local paper's headline read "Keel Scam Uncovered." Another cried, "Foul!" An Australian daily chose the mindless "Keelgate." There seemed to be a faint stink of scandal surrounding us on top of everything else. But not for long. They stopped short of calling it "an unfair advantage." Our keel was as legitimate as Australia's renowned wing keel had been when it won the Cup in 1983.

The press was flabbergasted for another reason. Ego, the great watermelon. It wasn't our right to do what we had done to them. They had not served their public well. It took *Paris Match*'s Claude La Luc to go over our win-loss statistics, to note weather conditions, and to discover that whenever *Kinsman* lost, I had not placed a bet on the race. *J'accuse!* She was alleging that I had fixed certain races, that I had intentionally risked all we had gained. The gall. Of our nine losses in forty-one starts, five had been tanked. *Pourquoi?* To disguise our secret. We could have sued her, of course, but one cannot sue the French press. They are allowed to say what they please. Anyway, it was true.

From her hotel suite windows, the best seat in the house, Aunt Pearl watched their compound at the Yacht Harbour. Their work lights came on in the evenings and burned all night while our crew slept. For the next five nights, Team New Zealand worked to devise a way to alter *Black Lion* to conform to *Kinsman*, to dangle their keel like a killer whale's dorsal fin. It wasn't patented.

But I needed to know. Did one of my men sell our secret to Sammy Winslow? I had no idea why any man in our camp would do it. Even if he was paid to sell us out, losing the Cup would send him home empty-handed and cost him much more in the end.

I had less than a week. If one of my men had betrayed us, I wanted him off the boat, put ashore, and sent back to Rwanda. Preferably, on ice. I decided to take a long shot and look up an old acquaintance.

Six weeks earlier, when it didn't matter who I or *Kinsman* was, I'd bumped into McKinlay Fogge at a coffee shop. McKinlay was on the foredeck crew of *Black Lion,* and back then I had not been a serious contender. And as far as he could imagine, I would never be. *Kinsman* was then considered to be at the bottom of the challenger heap: a curiosity, a loser. The tote board on the wall of the Corner Café explained why. The odds that had been written in chalk numbers, said it all: ten thousand to one. Against us.

He had just wanted to talk, to hear about my life in America. And it had been safe for McKinlay to talk to me; I wouldn't be around too long. We had left the café and, on the way out walking down the alley, he had stopped and turned. Did I want a smoke? No. Not really, thanks. But he did, and he brought out a roach and straightened it with his fingertips; then, he lit it. It was partly a show. Was I impressed? I was caught off-guard.

He was a kid. He told me he was the youngest member of the New Zealand crew. But I was an American, a back-up skipper. Maybe he needed to measure up to some fake international notion of nonchalance. No one had ever seen *Black Lion* then. But I knew that Team New Zealand was trained to perfection and that being on the team was a great honor. There was no room for smoking grass; the liquor and narcotics laws were clearly posted. The excruciating exercises and rigid discipline left no doubt as to the military discipline required to race for New Zealand. It was not a community project or anyone's hobby; it was a national enterprise.

During that first month, I had seen McKinlay Fogge, on and off. He liked me. I was from another world. He'd invited me to his parents house for dinner, but I hadn't been able to go. I don't remember why. I knew that he lived at home and walked to the Team New Zealand compound whenever they needed him. Morning exercises had been on. With *Black Lion* still in Wellington for outfitting, there was no call for him between exercises. The crew only had to show up for meals at the compound, where they ate well on a scientifically balanced diet. They kept fit in the weight rooms and watched their diet. But McKinlay went out in the afternoons and hung around this coffee shop, where he listened to music that sounded like a blend of three CDs, which it was. And he smoked grass at certain times each day. Big local taboo.

I was surprised. There he was at the same café, and it seemed to be good enough for me to use his recreational smoking as a conversation starter on who had sold our secret to the press. He might know. He remained friendly, but was surprised to see me. He was tight-lipped. Something was going on, and it was unfair of me to ask. I told him I was hesitant to share his smoking habits with my good friend, Ace Gordon.

Sammy Winslow had not bought the story from one of my crewmen. Sammy had swum to our dock to avoid being seen by the guards, then crawled and crept into *Kinsman's* hull late at night. There he studied our keel fasteners and photographed them, then passed his information on to Ace Gordon. They were, after all, countrymen. There had been no treason. I was elated.

⚑

Race Five

We were out early, on the course at midday. The wind was blowing out of Hell. *Kinsman*'s weather. And maybe, now *Black Lion*'s. No one would know until the starting gun.

She was late. We met her for the pre-start. At the ten-minute gun, the rain came on the wind. We hadn't seen the black boat for a week, and she seemed to be holding it in, trying not to show us what she had, just turning and wheeling as usual, deft as ever, waiting for the starting gun.

Ace Gordon gave me his drag racer's salute. He was ready. With thirty seconds to go, we both tacked, heeled way down, then headed up toward the line, setting our sails for the first beat as we crossed it. I had taken the windward position; Ace had the safe leeward, an even start. In those first minutes, I was sure. I knew. *Black Lion* had what we had. Every bit of it.

Ace had done it. He had suspended her keel on universal joints just as ours was. Her keel hung as free as ours. She footed with us. And when we set the pace, she matched us. We weren't going to gain two seconds a mile; we weren't going to gain *anything* a mile. She was sailing us down. I called for a trim. This was going to be our first true test against New Zealand. I stuck close, afraid to separate to the first mark; our crew sailed beautifully. No layoff rust. We hung on to them. But after the second, we'd fallen four boat lengths behind her.

With the rain, now came mist; nothing much at first. And then fog blew in with all the mysteries of full-out blind sailing. And the visibility dropped and dropped. One minute, I could see the mark a quarter-mile away; the next, I couldn't see the rise in our own prow. The visibility varied between a hundred yards and our foredeck. *Black Lion* vanished. Just as we had vanished to her. If the black boat suddenly appeared on our bow, I could have done nothing about it. So, I put two men ahead of the jib clipped onto the headstay. If they saw *Black Lion*, there two words to yell aft to me: *"Tack!"* and *"Jibe!"* There'd be no time for me to think, just time to spin the wheel.

254

I sensed that we were close to the black boat at the fourth mark. I heard sounds to windward. I listened. Voices. Water slapping a bow. A hull slicing quietly compared to our rattling hull. I couldn't see her. But I knew. She was just above us to port. There were other noises: cranking winches and grinders squeezing out sheets, an occasional voice yelling "*Clear!*" or "*Out!*" or other short words.

It was the moment for me to do something really interesting.

"What do you think?" I said.

Larry answered, "Tack."

Marcus nodded, "And make a lot of noise doing it."

I ordered a tack. I brought her into the wind yelling, "*Hard alee!*" It was as dangerous as an ocean liner steaming at flank speed into a flock of icebergs on a black night.

Now we were on port tack. The moment we made headway, I heard a distinct Kiwi voice say, "Helm's alee!" Maybe Ace Gordon's. The tinny, rattling racket and zinging of sails in irons, then the thwack as they filled away, and *Black Lion* passed our bow unseen to windward. We had been close enough to hear them talking, but we hadn't seen her. We were only a boat length behind. It was eerie not knowing where she was, but having her that close. It could have been night.

Larry and Marcus agreed on a bluff. I was ready. I did my best Naval Academy command, *"Hard alee!"*

We'd gone back over to starboard. Now we had an insurance policy, whatever happened. I could no longer see the mark or even know if we could lay it. I didn't care. I was after *Black Lion,* not the mark. Not a good situation, but we were on starboard tack sailing fast through the fog.

Just as we filled away, the fog blew open, the curtain rose. There it was: the fourth mark, the inflated fluorescent orange pyramid, just ahead. And there *she* was! *Black Lion.* Sailing out of the fog on port tack, two hundred yards away. The spike on the tip of the black cutter bow was low, sharp, and fast; her crew were low as gunners, heading across us; and it looked like she'd get by and beat us to the mark. Driving hard, driving out in front of us, trying to cross, trying to pull it off. What a maneuver. We all knew *Kinsman* had right of way. If *Lion* didn't tack onto our course soon, we might have to alter our own to avoid ramming her. And if we did alter our course, *Lion* would be out. I smelled disqualification.

She didn't tack. She was gunning for that mark. It was crazy. Ace Gordon was willing to let it happen. He was sure of her new speed. He was right. But just when he looked free and clear, I caught a lift and sailed up on it. Our positions changed. I was now a bit higher to the wind; *Black Lion* was a bit lower. She was still charging. She still looked good, but she wasn't going to make it across *Kinsman.* She was ours. I saw her crew lining the weather rail, all faces staring at our bow closing on them. I held my course. One of us had to change course.

"*Starboard!*" Moses was hanging onto the headstay on our prow out over the water, swept by seas to his knees, yelling, "*Starboard!*"

Ace Gordon knew he could make it, and he could have. He was moving fast enough, but the lift I had gotten still held. If he didn't tack in the next twenty seconds, *Kinsman* would ram *Black Lion* directly amidships. If we struck her there, we'd sink her quick. I turned to stone. Well, pudding. My fingers froze. It was happening fast now. Time was almost up.

"Bear off, bear off, bear off," Marcus was saying, "For Christ's sake, Jib, just bear off. Let 'em by."

"No witnesses," I said. It was true. It would be their word against ours. No protest. The committee boat was lost.

Larry seemed to be aware of everything. He was nodding. He seemed to approve. Or he was not objecting. I was not aware of Esperance.

Ten seconds. Marcus shouted, "*Bear off, bear off, Jib! Don't do it!*" He grabbed the leeward wheel and tried to turn it toward him.

"*Hands off!*" I was shouting, too. "*Get 'em off it, now!*"

He dropped his hands, fell back down and braced himself. "Jesus Christ, Jib. You lost your mind?"

This is what was flashing through my lost mind: I saw in those hot instants our whole two years of preparation and that, if I let *Lion* get away with this cross, I'd lose. Maybe *everything*. That we'd never bring the Cup to Rwanda. Maybe I was wrong in those final ten seconds. If I let her off the hook the way I did with *Princess Diana*, no one would know. *Black Lion* might win this race, tie us up two to two, then go on to win the series. She had the speed. I believed that. She had it all: a light-and-heavy-weather hull now, a top crew, Ace Gordon. Our bow had been reinforced since our collision, doubly strong and sharp; my speed was high, thirteen knots.

All this passed through my lost mind, at dreamspeed, with five seconds left. That's when I decided not to bear off, but to sink her. *Black Lion* was hull down; her lee rail, awash, steep; her crew, safe to weather; her white deck, the lion's pale belly, open to us. I was standing on my feet, legs wide, gripping the weather helm. Everyone aboard both boats saw it coming.

"*Starboard!*" I hollered from the cockpit in the last second, just before I rammed her, dead center, just ahead of the mast. What a racket!

Kinsman's bow came crashing down on *Black Lion*'s deck just before the main chain plates, the bolts that fasten the side stays. Our bow cut between the stays. They all went. Ripping, screaming, steel screeching. A horrendous crack. We had penetrated her hull, broke her open a good six feet.

There were shouts. I heard a howl. Their afterguard was safe. Their crew clung to the windward rail; one or two were knocked overboard. Oddly enough, both boats were still sailing. We were stuck into her, joined at right angles forming a giant T. We had to get away. Her mast could go.

We stayed with her maybe two minutes until the wind managed to pull us free. *Black Lion* was going to sink. She maintained her forward motion. Every other word I heard coming from her deck was "Fuck!" A lot of yelling. Orders for everything. "Slack off! Slack off!" Her sails had blown out over the water and were hanging free, unsheeted, taking the tons of strain off her mast that was getting ready to topple.

One of her crewmen was hauled up on our foredeck. Her crewmen on deck were running fore and aft. There was nothing left for them to do. *Lion* gradually pulled away from us, scraping, turning us back down onto a starboard reach. Her chase boat appeared and stood off. The crewman who'd been hauled aboard *Kinsman*, jumped. We were sailing free, sails out. *Black Lion* had lost all forward motion and was settling in the water, resigned to her death. The gouge in her topsides was fatal: a vertical gash, a yard wide. She was sinking, filling amidships, filling fast, with no buoyancy. None. A giant toy boat being pulled straight to the bottom by its twenty-ton keel.

Amazingly, her mast remained vertical; her beautifully-cut, translucent mainsail still full of wind; she was sailing and sinking.

It must have been Ace Gordon who first yelled, *"Abandon ship!"* Others picked it up. For a sailor, even a for yachtsman, abandoning ship is not a natural act. When I heard it yelled across the water, it cut me. One crewman jumped. Then another. Then they all went in. Their chase boat circled. The golden silhouette of the lion rampant painted on *Black Lion*'s topsides rose above the water once just before her hull settled and disappeared for good. She went quickly. She went in straight; her black mast and sails perpendicular. She made one sound. Then her masthead vanished. It was the sound of an extended searing shush, a cool, beautiful sound. I can never forget it.

She left nothing behind her on the surface. The swimmers were being hauled up. We had moved a couple of hundred feet away.

"Moses. Damage!" I yelled forward.

Moses, who'd come in from the forestay just before we struck, now stepped out over our bow. Looking down, he waved and shook his head "Okay."

"No damage, Skipper!" he yelled aft. He meant our bow.

The collision had appeared to be avoidable. I knew differently and, of course, so did Ace. I might have ducked under their stern in the last fifteen seconds. Or maybe not. We'd never know. We had sunk *Black Lion*. And it was their fault. Ace Gordon had miscalculated his speed. But even worse, he had miscalculated ours. He had believed up until the end that he had made *Black Lion* faster than she really was.

⚑

The Sinking

McKinlay Fogge, mastman of the *Black Lion*, stared dumbly across the water at the departing *Kinsman*. She looked as if she were fleeing the scene of a crime. She was. She sailed away undamaged, still heading for the fourth mark and unchallenged victory. To be made official, all the marks needed to be rounded; the finish line needed to be crossed.

He told me later that he was in shock along with the rest of his crewmates, standing on the deck and dripping from the sea water they had just hauled him out of. He had been knocked overboard. In the water around him, McKinlay could see a wide circle of objects popping to the surface, sparsely floating debris. Piece by piece, they burst up from below. A life vest broke the surface beside him, escaped from the hull settling on the bottom; a sailbag worked its way free from the sewer and rose, bubbling; a cork-handled knife leaped up, lunging. So little to mark the existence of his beloved *Black Lion*, except the blinking buoy that Ace Gordon had released to mark the position of her mast.

The mist closed in and *Kinsman* was gone. *Black Lion*'s crew were left standing on their chase boat, alone with bobbing artifacts that were never meant to float by themselves. The entire crew had come through unhurt. They were athletes, swimmers. Now they stood silently appraising their nemesis, *Kinsman*, as she faded into the mist, sailing quickly away from them toward her fourth victory in five starts. *Kinsman*'s last victory over the *Black Lion*. The crew stood in silence. They were through cursing, beyond words, not able to begin mourning the sudden death of their great hero. A hero that had not calculated *Kinsman*'s speed. Or her own.

It made no sense to McKinlay. One minute, they'd been screaming along, hull down, fighting *Kinsman* for the lead in a daring duel, just the kind of duel he had trained for all his life. And the next moment, his boat was gone, dropping quickly to the bottom. He could hear organ music rising up from the depths, in lament. The kind of church music played at funerals in movies. In his imagination, he knew just what his boat looked like down there, standing on the ocean floor. She had hit bottom with a bump led by her twenty-ton keel, and now stood vertically, as if supported on all sides as she had been in dry dock. The model of a twelve-meter at his parents' house. Her keel would hold her there displayed for years. His shoulders shook, and he began to cry. He hadn't meant to cry, but there he was sobbing out of control as if he were having a fit. At seventeen, McKinlay was the youngest crewman. His job was to stay by the mast and control the halyards.

Bucky Ryder, main sheetman, standing wet on the chase boat, put his arm around McKinlay. When he was able to stop crying, he began to shiver. He was soaked through, but he wasn't shivering from the cold; he was shivering from fear. Loss. A wrenching pain in his stomach. His dream had been for stardom, the kind of permanent stardom people in smallish countries enjoy and that dream was now officially dead. There would be no grinning photograph of MacKinlay hung in the café; not one. Or, if one was, it would be shrouded in black.

"Come on, Mac," Bucky said. "There you go."

"Whatever the hell that means," McKinlay said. He was angry now. Bucky had been a weight lifter, brought on board for his brawn. He'd been a fisherman and had never sailed before in the Cup races, but he had trained with the crew and lasted out the year and had learned how to release and to haul in the main sheet at high speed, again and again: a brutal, uncomplicated assignment. Beside the two stood Dick Smallet, the other mainsheetman who was openly crying. Smallet was the stronger of the two. They were all strong, but Smallet was the one who would swing himself out over the water like a chimpanzee to repair damage and dangle there until the job was done. One time it had taken him half a race, twelve miles, almost two hours. None of the three had cried since grammar school, as far as they could later recall.

"This is my fault, Tommy." It was Ace Gordon, taller and leaner. "I want you to know that." He said it to his tactician Tommy Tarlington, who was able to smile nod and quietly say, "I already do."

Piece by piece, the horror (there was no other word) of it was accumulating in Ace Gordon's mind. The syndicate's backers, of course; the team; the sponsors; hell, the whole country would be down on him for losing their beloved *Black Lion*. Wouldn't they? He still couldn't see it clearly or quite imagine how it had happened. He'd been absolutely certain he could make it. In all his years of racing, he had never had a boat shot out from under him. And for all those years, all he had done, the sum of his legend, nothing close to this had ever happened to him. There had been blemishes; he had been foolish, but nothing of this magnitude. What had happened to him today was impossible. He had effectively eliminated his country in one reckless gamble. What had happened?

He knew his own boatspeed had been ten knots, but he'd underestimated *Kinsman*'s. If he had called a quick tack to the mark at ten knots, he would have made it across her bow. But something had happened. *Kinsman* had surged. She seemed to leap forward in the crucial last seconds. Impossible. He'd seen her bow point, as if it were reaching up, trying to attack his hull. He should have known better than to fight that hard for a mark early in the race. He shouldn't have been there. He knew how to cross a bow; he'd done it more times than he'd had hot dinners. The maneuver was a simple one: you cross just above the other boat's bow, tack immediately, covering it close as a good overcoat, stealing all the other boat's wind and leaving it adrift, standing in its own dead air. The Americans called this a "slam dunk," but Ace didn't play basketball. He simply called it a "quick fuck." And he'd once told Tarlington that, when he pulled it off right, it was even *better* than sex.

New Zealand was down three races and were without a boat. We needed one more race to pick up all the marbles. It couldn't get any worse than that for them. But didn't Ace Gordon have *Kinsman*'s secret? And didn't he have just as good a hull in *Black Magic*? Now there'd be two old boats. Before she became *Kinsman*, hadn't she once been *Il Moro* in a previous life? In the last Cup races versus *Black Magic*? And hadn't *Black Magic* won it all back then? How bad could that be?

Ace would only ask for a week, that's all he would need. He'd get a diver down to *Black Lion* for its computer boxes, sail lockers, maybe even the mast. Why wouldn't they be able to unstep her mast? Was it too deep where she went down? Eventually, they'd get her hull up, but not in time for this series, not with the amount of repair work involved. His mind was racing. From today on, this was going to be the time when champions came through, he thought. One of the only times, really, when the odds were steep.

"Come on gentlemen, let 'er go," Ace said. "She's sunk."

It was very offensive to McKinlay. The organ dirge that had been crowding his ears was silenced. He felt a surge of rage. He remembered turning, raising his fist and holding it. "Jesus, Skipper. What the fuck are you talking about?"

"Wipe your face, kiddy."

"You sunk her!" McKinlay clenched his fists and squeezed his eyes shut, forcing the last tears out. "You lost us everything." They stood ready to fight.

"Yes, I did," Gordon said. "It's not all over." He smiled at McKinlay; he liked the kid's rage. He clapped him on the shoulder. "Back off, Fogge, you've got a race coming up next week." They stood on the deck of the chase boat in a light rain now.

"What race, Skipper?" Bucky said.

"*Black Magic*."

He hadn't thought ahead. It was silly, but none of them had. *Black Magic*. Of course, why not? Maybe she could be rigged.

Now MacKinlay started thinking, "Wasn't *Black Magic* the boat that beat *America3* five straight in San Diego? She was still a damned good hull, every bit as fine as *Black Lion*. A good stable-mate, too; sometimes too good, beating the *Lion* in a couple of trial races, even though the *Lion* had all the breakthrough equipment, sails, mast, computer. Yeah, *Black Magic*. Why not? Ace had sailed her then, and he could sail her now." McKinlay felt a quick surge of hope shoot up through his anus. The surge that meant everything. Maybe the grinning picture of him would hang on the wall of the café after all. In it, he would be wet with victory Champagne. Girls would introduce themselves to him in the café, and others would recognize him and say "hello" in the street.

The mist was still down, hung, low visibility. A news helicopter appeared too late; then another. They throbbed by in maddening clusters of noise, too low and too loud. One would throb out of sight. Then, another would come searching for pictures. But there was nothing: only bags, life preservers, food lockers, and the blinking buoy marking her grave.

The memorial was brief. She lay in twenty fathoms.

"Okay, take her in," Ace said to the skipper of the chase boat. Just then, he heard a voice call out.

"Ace!"

Jocelyn. A spectator boat had cut through the fog. She had heard the news and was sending him all sorts of therapeutic facial signals, rolling her eyes, commiserating, grimacing, mouthing words he didn't want to hear just then. And he didn't want her on the tender, playing out her role as supportive wife-to-be. She came aboard anyway and hugged him. "Oh Lester, darling, I hate him so. Typical typical typical. He did it to *Princess Di*. He's a madman." Ace didn't say anything. He knew.

In the distance, out of sight through the mist, a muted boom echoed across the water, the small cannon on the housing of the *Lady Anne*. *Kinsman* had crossed the finish line alone. There were no air horns; there was no jubilation.

"Ready guys?" The crew had been generally silent, some squatting, looking away. Time to face the world. The throttle was put in gear, and the tender began a slow turn toward shore. Time to get started.

⚑

Aboard *Kinsman*

Sailing away, I felt more disorientated than I had in my entire life. My mind was howling. My stomach was in full flight. I went back and forth. I was dead wrong. I had done the right thing. I killed a great boat. I saved us. It could go either way. I was terrified by what I had done. I stood by and kept *Kinsman* in irons watching *Black Lion*'s crew swim to safety, ready to assist, waiting until they'd all been picked up by their tender. Ace and Tarlington stood on the deck until the last man jumped; it was nearly too late when they dove in off the transom to avoid the speeding rigging. The swimming crewmen glared up at us from the water. We were a privateer; this was piracy. When I saw that they'd all been picked up by their chase boat, I fell off and filled away for the mark we'd been fighting for before the collision. After a quarter-mile, the tender was at last lost behind me in the fog, but I could still feel their eyes drilling me through the mist.

What the hell had I done? Over the years, I'd clipped a couple of boats. I'd dismasted a Starboat once, when it wouldn't give way, by tearing away its chainplate. I was sixteen. Now I had certainly destroyed New Zealand's chances. Not by outsailing them. I had had the right of way. I had the right to ram them, anyone could see it. But because of the fog, there were no outside witnesses. Did I need to do it? It might not even have been necessary. Maybe I should have clipped them. In those final boiling seconds when the choice was mine. When it counted, when I could have spun the wheel, she might have gotten off with a nick on her transom and nothing more. My mind had shut down. I had kept driving. There were moments when Ace must have thought he could squeak by me; instants when it was all still possible without the thinness of a sail between our skins, but we had leapt forward on a lift and closed that gap, unbelievably sprung somehow on a surging wave. Sure, Ace Gordon had been wrong. He'd been trying to steal the mark. Sure, he was wrong, and I was wrong too. He had crossed my bow. He had taken the chance. I hadn't.

We had to round the remaining marks: four, five, six, seven, eight. I turned the helm over to Esperance. Thinking back over it, as we rounded the final mark and headed for the finish line on the downwind leg sailing only under mainsail and jib, I knew I could have ducked away and slipped behind *Lion*. I knew it. Maybe it didn't look that way to anyone else, but I knew it. Ace Gordon knew it, too. I had not needed to sink the *Black Lion*.

Now he'd have to get *Black Magic* out of mothballs and do his damnedest to figure something out. I'd give him all the time he wanted when he asked for it. He'd need a week to haul her out and rig her and suspend his keel just like ours. We'd have our hands full when he launched *Black Magic*. But it was one to four against him. He'd have to take four straight from me. He might take one or two, but he'd never take four.

I jerked when the cannon went off. I hadn't realized we were over the line. We passed the *Lady Anne* in silence; the silence was one of contempt. We had sailed the final leg without a spinnaker, not trying to flaunt our speed. We had sailed back into enemy country now, into a country of scorn far far worse than ever. I saw Aunt Pearl's boat. It was slow to come alongside to pick up Larry. The Rwandan flag was down.

Elizaphan gave me a small wave and a sad smile.

From about twenty feet away, Aunt Pearl said very quietly, "How dare you?" She looked away and wouldn't meet my look. I had never known her to be angry or to lose faith in me, but she had.

Elizaphan shrugged helplessly. That was closer to what I was feeling.

When we docked, it was evident that word had spread. I felt the deep anger. I'd keep my crew sequestered in the compound tonight, no walking in downtown Auckland. I could get killed accidentally. A log could roll off a truck. It was a small country, but I had made a couple of million blood enemies, and it would only take one.

⚑

The Handshake

Walking into the press conference, I faced a wall of international disdain. My new enemies. Standing room only. I was a hit. I took my seat at the long table. Larry Bayard had been too sick to come along in his weakened condition, and I let Marcus off the hook. He probably wouldn't have come anyway. I said I could handle it, so I was there alone and more unwelcome than ever. Even though there was a chill out on the water in the wind, it was sweaty under the lights. The table was slightly raised, a white cloth over it, two microphones, two pitchers of ice water, one for each skipper, mine probably poisoned. As protocol, the press was not allowed to speak until both skippers had been seated and made what remarks they cared to make about the day's race. After all, we were the warriors, fatigued, and these races even on the calmest of days were grueling. I still wore white grease on my face even though the day had been grey and overcast. Someone tossed me a paper napkin, and I began to wipe it off.

A minute passed. No Ace Gordon.

The international press was drooling. What fun. A conflict story. The dreadful Claude La Luc sat in the front row, a boat hook's length away. After France had lost its bid, she had stayed to report on the finals. She had never forgiven us for embarrassing Baron Biche in La Rochelle. This evening she was relaxing, a radiant smile on her face. Was she slavering? Her photographer waited until I had the paper napkin on my face before he would shoot a picture. I wiped; he clicked.

No one seemed certain whether or not Ace Gordon would show. And if he did, what would he say to me? Or do? That was the story. Would he point at me and call me names. "Reckless bastard?" Would he say I needed to put a few more years' experience behind me?

The reporters began to chat. Tired of waiting, Claude la Luc broke protocol. She had a man's haircut, and spoke in precise broken English with austere sarcasm. From the first row she began speaking in her ashtray voice without addressing the chairman of the Race Committee, without raising her hand, without calling me by my name; she looked at me and said, "Aren't you ashamed of what you did?"

The megawatt camera lights turned on me. I was already sweating. I kept wiping the grease off my face. Trying to steady the table. Where the hell was Ace?

"Sir? Sir. I ask you a question?"

A local reporter from the 'Granny' Herald with an Etonian accent said, "For Heaven sake, Mr. Routledge, can you speak up please?"

La Luc said, "Do you feel remorse?"

A friendly-sounding American voice from the middle of the room said, "You didn't need to destroy his boat, Jib."

He couldn't have known that. With the amount of mist blowing when we collided, there were no witnesses other than our own.

Back to La Luc. "Would you mind responding to my query?"

Ace wasn't going to show.

"You couldn't possibly know what I had to do," I said. I felt very young. "I had no choice."

"We'll be anxious to hear what Mr. Gordon will say to that," someone said. "My guess is that he will vehemently contradict you."

The friendly American reporter said, "Jib. What the hell were you thinking?"

"You weren't there."

"Maybe I should have been. It's a lousy way to win." Some Americans hadn't recovered from their seventh-race loss to us.

They were all baying for my blood. It would flow from my body into their veins, through their electronic bones, and coagulate into lead sentences.

They were in storyland heaven, and Ace Gordon hadn't even shown up yet. He had, but no one had seen him. He had slipped in from an exit door and had been standing out of the lights in the back of the room. None of them realized it until they saw him coming through the room, his back to them.

When he reached the long, white cloth-covered table that had been serving as my life-raft and stepped up onto the riser, he stood and looked at me. He poured himself a glass of ice water. I expected him to dash it in my face, but he drank it whole.

Ace Gordon. Lean, taller than me, ten or fifteen years older.

I was waiting for the blow to come, when he shook my hand. His fingers were surprisingly dry; his hand felt sanded; his grip was light, yet I felt handcuffed to him. If the table hadn't been between us, he would have hugged me. He looked into my eyes directly, the pale, furious eyes. He wasn't finished with me yet, but he was for today. I was waiting.

A couple of seconds passed.

He could go either way.

I spotted Jocelyn, who must have come in just after him. She was standing against the wall in the back, still wearing her summer hat. Her face was a blank.

Ace Gordon spoke low, for my ears only. He called me by my nickname. He looked weather-beaten, exhausted.

"Jib," he said so low that the first few rows couldn't hear him, gripping my hand, "what happened out there today was my doing, and mine alone. If there was something you could have done, I don't know what it would have been. You've got guts. I wouldn't expect you to turn away from a challenge. Today was today."

And still gently handcuffed to me, he turned to the international press corps, who were now grinning like Radio City Music Hall Rockettes, poised, waiting for their high kick, waiting for Ace Gordon to skewer me and spurt my blood into their newsprint.

"Ladies and gentlemen, I made a decision out there today. I ran my country at risk and put us under direct danger of *Kinsman's* bow. Jib Routledge is a fine sailor, and there was nothing he could have done. My mistake cost me and my many friends a great boat."

Stunned silence.

No, no! Stop!

"I will beg the members of Team New Zealand to forgive me and to decide whether they will allow me to continue as their skipper." The humility of the man. "We have a grand champion of a boat in *Black Magic*. Remember her?

"If my team decides to keep me on, tomorrow we shall begin rigging my old *Black Magic,* and in a week we shall face *Kinsman* once again, and we shall beat her soundly and save the Cup." He was good. It was a Winston Churchill moment. The story might have shaped up into something serviceable. Everyone there knew about *Black Magic*. But the words of great sportsmen have never made great headlines.

They wanted him to deliver my head to them. But a couple of reporters managed to applaud. After all, Ace Gordon was an amazing master of ceremony. I expected cue cards.

"If my brave rival here, Jib Routledge, will allow us one more week, I promise you we will have her ready to win." The way he said "ready to win" sounded like he actually expected to win. Don't ever close the door on New Zealand. The brave rival nodded dumbly, my hand still being lightly held in his in what had become the longest handshake in history. Next I expected him to close the ceremony with a few verses of John Donne's "No Man Is An Island."

Then I saw it. Alec Lester Ace Gordon, Junior, national-treasure-in-waiting, was not just going for the Holy Grail next week. He was going for more.

266

Down four match points and sailing a backup boat, he planned to beat us four straight. And when he pulled that off, he knew that they'd give him New Zealand. I turned to him and spoke so low no one else could hear me.

"Pull it off and they'll make you Prime Minister," I whispered.

"D'you think?" He smiled innocently. "Not such an evil ambition. Is it?"

Victory?

We had won. In dubious victory, we did not celebrate.

That night at the compound, we cooked out as usual. Saint told me he was secretly delighted. When Ace Gordon's testimonial was repeated to Aunt Pearl she was still appalled, but it tempered her opinion of me.

"He wasn't just saying that, was he?"

"With all New Zealand watching?"

"I know you, Jibby. You've always been a scalawag."

"It happened very fast, Pearl. He gave me no choice."

She relented. She gave me her guarded blessing.

The Rwandan Ambassador-at-Large to the South Pacific and Australia had flown in that afternoon and forced a celebration that we didn't feel like having by arranging to buy the crew a sheep and have it slaughtered. A goat had not been immediately available. The men roasted the sheep end-to-end on a spit hung on chains above an oakwood fire blazing in half a steel drum. Dinner was excellent, far better than it looked, always the case with our cooking. Some of the men drank from a new batch of banana wine and some drank the local ale and, as usual, nothing stronger. No whiskey, gin, tequila, rum. Marcus and I drank Saint's Irish whiskey. Elizaphan abstained.

After we'd eaten, Pierre Kagame, the ambassador, had something to say. He spoke eloquently in Kinyarwandan, and Elizaphan translated to Aunt Pearl, Saint, Marcus and me. He told the men that the Rwandan government was officially sending praise to *Kinsman*'s crew for its great accomplishment. In the event that they actually brought the Cup home with them, the government was bracing itself for our homecoming. The men chuckled like poultry. He reminded them that their Council of Kinsmen would be implemented to oversee construction of rehabilitation centers, but Kagame said nothing else that was of any interest to them. As I understood it from Elizaphan's sometimes halting translation, he was saying that theirs was a new land in an old world, albeit the country itself was beautiful, the circumstances lying ahead of Rwanda were not. There would be difficulties. But there would be time to prepare. The first order of business, he told the men would be that the government needed right away to secure international financing to bring Rwanda up to and into the twenty-first century before the world descended on them for the Cup races on Lake Kivu in three years time.

The men fidgeted and whispered. I could see that this financial news was of no immediate interest to men who dreamt of cattle. A goat, a cow, a field, new farming tools. After Kagame had spoken, the men clucked, then again stood and thanked him for the sheep. Elizaphan sang and Kikongoro plinked his inkadiddy, Ba'ale scraped his kukui with a spoon, and we all danced the usual five miles in slow circles until very late.

Aunt Pearl had left by then with an "I'll see you tomorrow, goodnight." She was not through with this sinking business, I could tell. She had realized that Ace Gordon was a sportsman and had taken very good care to exonerate me. He could have easily destroyed us and hurt the Cup by turning opinion against us. A famous scandal. But he hadn't.

None of the crew could go to Auckland; it was out of bounds, no longer ours. Even our Mosquito Café was borderline. And we needed to be careful at our own compound. All through that evening, I changed watches and kept a man in a dinghy floating near Kinsman's hull. A fanatic might swim in and stick a charge in Kinsman's rudder well to even things up. I'd had a torn mainsail draped around the hull and weighted it so that it hung below the keel line and that night I asked a crewman to stand watch on the deck and another to sleep on deck. I didn't want any surprises. I decided to have Kinsman hauled out in the morning for a complete going over and to protect her from reprisals.

In spite of the sinking and because of it, Elizaphan and I had something to be thankful for that night. Whatever had happened brought us close together again. We fell asleep making love and didn't stir until long after sunrise and until the coffee, toasted bread and bacon fumes had risen up through the guest house to the top floor into our bedroom.

₽

The Day After

Another layoff.

The breakfast gong had gonged "last call," but Mrs. Prosser made us a special breakfast anyway. The phone had rung all morning; she told me the first call came in at seven. The sinking. Reporters from the local *Star*, the *Herald* and the *Sydney Herald* asked me questions about it.

By midday, I had to get out.

Elizaphan and I walked away from the guest house in the opposite direction of the compound. We met Aunt Pearl's boat at a fishing dock and snuck into Auckland and saw an old black-and-white movie. Unbelievably, we had never gone to the movies together.

It was mid-afternoon when we got back to Waiheke Island. We decided to avoid the guest house and go for a walk. We walked across the width of the island, right through the middle of it. We stuck to paths. It was good to be away from everything. We walked. It was surprisingly green. When we came down a slope on the other side, we glimpsed the Pacific Ocean to the north and felt the sea wind.

I had to sit down. My calves were permanently cramped from tension; my fingers made fists when I didn't want them to. I had a continuous headache. Walking had become difficult. We took a path up a hill away from the houses and found a spot still in sight of the ocean.

Boys were playing soccer way down the hill, and the sea breeze streamed up across the soft grass. It was probably five by then; I'd forgotten to wear a watch. A quick rain caught up with us with the sun still blazing. We hid from it under a huge tree. I sat; she stood under the tree sheltering after the rain had stopped. She was still wearing the pale blue dress she'd worn to the movies. It buttoned down the front top to bottom.

She had been confused about the sinking, she said, and wanted to know about it. I told her I was confused, too, but that it was the only thing I had wanted to do. She thought that was strange thing to say. I told her that winning involved doing strange things and that I'd been willing to do them because otherwise I felt we would have been beaten.

"But wasn't it unfair?"

"It was, but I was thinking of my men."

We didn't talk much after that.

The grass was rich. I was sitting. I reached up and drew her down beside me. Her pale blue dress had gotten sprinkled with rain; there were dark dots and spots here and there.

The sun stayed out, still shining bright when the rain came back. It was nothing to the boys down the hill. They continued their soccer game. We stayed under the tree in the soft grass. I lay; she sat. We didn't talk. I touched her neck and shoulder.

We weren't going to make love. I knew that. We couldn't. From the beginning, from the first night Elizaphan had stayed over at my house on Lake Kivu, she could never make love unless we were completely hidden. To her, it was something we should not be doing. It was naughty, wrong. She would say, "No no no," sometimes while she was coming. Hiding was part of it. So, we had never done it anywhere but in our dark room always with the shades drawn, never in the daylight, never under a lightbulb, never in front of an open window. At night at Lake Kivu, she would blow the lantern out. Darkness was everything to her.

I pulled her down anyway, and we lay side-by-side in the rich grass looking up through the massed leaves to the fragments of blue sky. She touched me on the cheek.

"I understand, I think."

I didn't know what she meant by that.

"The sinking," she said.

"Oh, that. Well, you want to understand." That was the important thing.

She ran her fingers over my hand. Three buttons were undone on her dress. I unbuttoned a fourth; there were many more. I didn't know what I was doing. I ran my fingers inside her blouse. She wore a brassiere. It meant nothing, of course; her breasts stood alone. She wore it because it was pretty. It was, too. It was white. She had bought it when we were in La Rochelle.

Her breathing became exaggerated. I saw what might be happening. Were we going to make love? We were outside in the wind under the blazing sun.

She took my hand away from her breasts and held it. She asked me about movie stars. She was a girl from a small country. Did I know Ingrid Bergman?

I told her no.

"Do I remind you of a film star?"

I told her no, that she was different; she was better than any film star or supermodel, because she hadn't struggled for what she had.

"What is a supermodel?"

I explained what a supermodel was. A hard-working, tall girl with legs covering fifty percent of her body, no bottom, and small steady breasts.

"Can I become a supermodel?"

"Why would you want to?"

While she was asking me about movie stars, we had begun rubbing, pressing each other in the grass. We were going to make love by daylight outdoors. Her dress was nearly gone. Her pretty brassiere was clipped around her waist. She gave me the small secret landscape of her body set against the larger landscape of the Southern Ocean.

"You have to make love to me here, Charles," she said.

"I know."

"You have to fuck me, please."

Her shyness had always excited me; now her openness did, her crudeness. She wanted to be dirty. Her wetness excited me. When I sank into her under the sun with the leaves blowing overhead, it was as if she knew much more than I did. Her loudness excited me on the hillside under the tree where she could cry out with the birds, overlooking the Pacific Ocean. The clouds with their rain folded inside them.

Marc had taught her nothing, but to wait for it and to take it. Marc had been the first one; I was the other one. I had not been a good lover. I had taught her little. And there had been no one between. That was all she knew. She was inexperienced and yet suddenly unvirginal. We had made love for the first time. I was glad neither of us knew her age; no numbers, please. Without numbers, she could be anybody; she could exceed herself beyond reality, beyond fiction.

When I withdrew from her, we were surrounded by nature. This was where good babies came from, I thought. I began laughing, and she joined me and we both lay there laughing out of astounded happiness. God, love-sex was so much more fun than anything else. How much more fun it was than eating or sleeping or drinking. People who couldn't have it, or didn't know what it was had invented distractions; they did other things instead. They collected wine, bought fine cigars, cars, jets; they match raced, wrote stories.

We had replenished each other. We had had time to be. I felt nourished. I had come down from where I had been.

That evening, I watched the men swim straps around *Kinsman*'s hull and then the crane lift her dripping up in her sling across the dock and into her cradle. The great red Turkish slipper. After she'd been secured in her cradle, we scoured her for flaws.

These layoffs were beginning to work on me too. We'd been given one more, one too many; this one too long. We didn't need a layoff; we needed a Cup. It would be six days before we'd launch *Kinsman* for what I hoped would be our final meeting with Ace Gordon.

Of course, he wanted victory every bit as much as I did, but what kept nagging me about him was that he felt he had a chance of beating us. I was damned if I could figure out why. *Black Magic* was a good boat. She'd once been a great boat, but something was missing. Designs change. Gordon's last look at me at the press conference was strangely confident. He had not actually winked, but his pale eyes and chilly smile indicated that I had gotten in over my head and had been in there for quite a while.

Lion in Repose

The locals newspapers were not vicious, thanks to Ace Gordon. The next morning's headline in the *Herald* read:

THE *LION* IS DEAD
LONG LIVE THE *MAGIC*
LET'S GO NEW ZEALAND

It was hardly a pleasant piece, but it was not malicious. The *Star* didn't say much, just that the country now, more than ever, stood locked behind their flawed hero, the man who had erred and had promised to rally and give them a stirring comeback. Even if he failed, a noble attempt would do very nicely.

Because the water was calm that morning, *Black Lion* was an easy dive. The Team New Zealand divers went to work right away. The water was clean; everything was clear. She had dropped straight down and stood vertically just as McKinlay imagined she had. She stood in twenty-two fathoms. That put her masthead just twenty or so feet below the surface. Everything about her was intact, except her hull. The fatal gash. Her sails hung well and even looked good. Because the depth was not much more than a hundred and thirty feet, the Auckland paper sent its own diver down to photograph her and that afternoon an eerie photo appeared on its front page. Their beautiful *Black Lion*. A yacht sailing in a dreamworld at rest on the ocean floor, all sails set, her translucent mainsail barely alive.

The caption-head read, LION AT REST.

It was another *Titanic*. The underwater photo zipped around the world on wire services and television networks, the soft-news circuit. The vast society of soiled-fingered TV viewers rustling on their sofas needed only to tilt their heads slightly to glimpse and dismiss the picture of a beautiful ghost ship sailing underwater.

By evening, *Black Lion*'s masthead had been secured to an inflated submarine rescue doughnut. Divers had been unable to lower her mainsail by winch

274

and so had been forced to cut it away with no hope for saving it, this break-through sail. Then, with an acetylene torch, a diver cut through the chainplates that held her mainstays on the port side; her starboard stays had been severed. And working with two boats and rotating a crew of divers, they unstepped her mast at the keel and raised it to the surface, pulled by another set of floats, and it was only then that its twelve-story height could be supported, every dozen or so feet, by the floats securing her. Quite a large audience of spectator boats witnessed the mast-raising operation and the long tow into Team New Zealand's dock. The cannibalizing had begun. Her bones were being floated up. When *Black Lion*'s tiller was detached and brought to the surface it resembled a dinosaur rib.

Black Magic

When I first saw *Black Magic* in the 1995 Cup races. I knew she was a great bottom. When she beat America and went on to victory, she did not do it by mistake. It was her skipper and crew, her sails, her hull that had carried her there. And she bore a certain mystery with her, too.

Now I was looking at her again. Same hull. Same skipper. Same mystery. I stood on the Team New Zealand dock admiring her. Ace Gordon and I, after lunch. He had done a curious thing and invited me over to his camp to look her over. When he called me, I thought it was a crank caller. But when he mentioned Jocelyn Ortion, I knew it was him. I'd gotten it from the start that he liked our *Kinsman* enterprise. He'd been the only skipper who had taken the ferryboat over to meet us when we'd first come to Auckland and set up our camp. That was nearly a month-and-a-half ago.

I had first seen him on Waiheke Island at the Mosquito Café. I liked him immediately. He spoke frankly. He said that he'd been worried about our chances, and he'd wanted to meet my African crew before they disappeared for good. He had heard our story, but he hadn't fully believed it. Blacks were rare in New Zealand. I saw one that first month, a medical student. So, here was an entire boatload of them: sailors, cooks, and watchmen. And Ace Gordon met each one of them with pleasure. He asked me not to be offended, but that we both knew *Kinsman* wouldn't be around here very long. And so, he'd come over on his own to say, "Well done," and to say that his country welcomed us, whether it did or not.

I thanked him and Esperance and told him that we'd see him in the finals and to be sure that his bow was on the starting line when the gun went off or he might never catch us. Gordon had smiled sympathetically. He probably felt he could do "Hello" and "Goodbye" at the same time. He was the skipper of *Black Lion*, after all, the Sultan of Sail, dripping with legend.

That was just six weeks ago. How could he have possibly imagined that we would actually be racing against him in the finals, that we had recorded four victories, that he stood on the brink of elimination? That, in one split second of bad judgment or indecision, I had rammed and sunk his beloved *Black Lion*? And that I was now standing beside him on a sunny afternoon?

"No hard feelings," he said when he had telephoned. Why would I harbor any hard feelings? He asked me if I wanted to come over to his camp and have a look at *Black Magic*. I had assumed he'd wavered after the sinking, but apparently he was still fascinated by us.

"Sure," I said. Why not? It was unheard of for rival skippers to inspect each other's boats before a race. We'd eat lunch on the dock at his camp, he said. Was crab, spuds, and ale okay?

"Yeah, sure."

Did I want to bring anyone along?

"Thanks." I told him who.

This was how it was done. Medieval knights dining before jousts. Enemy World War I pilots having lunch after a duel. Great adversaries love one another, I guess. I must have graduated. I didn't suspect him of anything, of course. Maybe I should have, thinking back, but why would he need schemes? He wanted to see what I was made of. I never intended to lose to him, I showed him that, and I wasn't expecting to. But if I had to lose to anyone, I'd rather lose to Ace Gordon than to Soapy Armstrong or Jacques Ballon.

Now, at his invitation, Elizaphan, Esperance, and I stood on the Team New Zealand dock with him inspecting *Black Magic*. His crewmen were tuning the stays right in front of us, listening to their pitch as if she were a cello. Occasionally glancing over at us. I wasn't wearing my red *Kinsman* sweatshirt, of course. I could have been anyone. No one could tell who I was, but they sure as hell could tell a black man from a white. And Esperance was black enough, though they couldn't possibly know that he was Nilotic, from the lower Nile, a Tutsi who had learned English from an Irish tutor. They could only see that he was not brown, but black, and that he spoke with brogue. They could also see the beauty of Elizaphan, lean and straight, wearing a baby blue blowing dress, her skin the color of desert sand.

Ace Gordon. Some of his men probably understood him; some probably never would. Some would say he was a class act; others would say, eccentric, even crazy. But they could all admire him. I called him a man in the traditional sense. You did not have to understand him. He was giving me my first close look at *Black Magic* since 1995. She had more hull than *Black Lion* had, she rode higher, and with her twin rudders she could turn like an eel.

What makes a boat important? It is her hull. It must float kindly. It must enter the water nicely, meet every wave, but not push through them; it must slice them. A hull must always meet the sea nicely, finely, treat each wave as a guest, not an enemy; that is what a racing hull is for. It must be seaworthy in heavy weather and be kind in flat seas. Any hull. An America's Cup sloop, a double-ended Tahiti ketch, a Norwegian lugger. The hull of an Irish hooker. It is the hull. But a Cup racer does not haul fish, or any cargo. It is a blank sloop. There is nothing below its decks. Its sole purpose is to engage the sea's surface and to pass through it as quickly as possible, to sail keenly. It is a beautiful sight. That is its cargo.

A Cup racer's hull must be keen as a needle, but with enough cheek to rise and get it out of the water. It must not spend itself sucking waves along with it. It must knife through choppy seas upwind. It mustn't buck and wobble. Its bow may slap, but not slap too much. It must be able to squirt away, to sail fast, heeled steep on its side, shipping water. Its keelson must be slightly-rounded, making the hull free to plane, even to surf the seas downwind. It must be yare; an exotic word, *yare*, a word as old as fore-and-after rigging, that means "quick, agile, lively, nimble to the helm." It is what one hopes for at sea. And there is nothing like the sea.

A hull must have low windage along the length of its topsides, especially a racing hull. And below its waterline, little interruption to cause turmoil in the water rushing by. Or in light air, when its sails hang limp as shirts on a clothesline, it must be able to move over the bottom below it, the way a bird's neck feather glides across the surface. A hull must be able to ghost.

Ace had done a masterful job with *Black Magic* in just four days' time. Aunt Pearl had seen the lights in the yacht harbor from her hotel room. *Black Magic* had been hidden in Team New Zealand's shed, of course. She had not been in sailing condition, but Gordon had brought her up to here and now. Her new black mast seemed slightly taller on her and slightly raked, the way it had looked on *Black Lion*. I saw *Black Lion's* tiller, but there was doubt that it could be rigged. It seemed that her keel had been lightened by a few thousand pounds. I saw more topsides than I had remembered. And, of course, Ace Gordon had had her keel re-hung.

Boatyard workers came and went, passing tools in front of us, tightening the martingales on *Black Lion's* jibboom, the small bowsprit that shot out ahead of the bow over the water and gave *Black Magic* another few hundred square feet of sail.

I recognized the sails laid out on the dock as those that divers had salvaged and hung up to dry in their shed. Now *Black Magic* would have all the right sails, the right rig, the right hull, the right crew, and, primarily, the right keel. She was every bit a winner, yet different from us in essential ways.

I got that unmistakable impression that Ace didn't give a damn what I saw; it was as if he knew he could win. It was possible that he could win the next four races. We both knew it. He wasn't being cocky; he had no fear.

"Hey, Ace," he turned around. I recognized Tommy Tarlington, dark haired, underweight, serious as a country priest. Ace's age, thirty-five, maybe forty, he sailed for New Zealand as their top tactician in their nearly invisible afterguard.

He was standing with Cornelius Bone, captain of their foredeck, who looked fit enough to jump out of a plane without a parachute.

"You really ought to check that headstay before we get the big jenny on her," Bone said. "It's getting old."

"Tommy, Corny, I'd like you to meet Jib Routledge, Elizaphan Bleu, Esperance Mukademezo."

Neither Tommy Tarlington, nor Cornelius Bone registered any surprise. They knew me by name, not by face. Tarlington took my hand as if he were shopping for gloves; Bone wrung it like a pump handle.

"You're the Yank that sank us last week," Tarlington said and made a small smile, and his eyelight lightened. I reddened. It is a weakness. I wish I didn't do that; they both saw it.

"Nobody over here's pissed off at you, Jib," Bone said. "We all love a good scrap."

Unbelievably, there was no bad feeling. But among the few crew I saw milling around, I had imagined either a powerful vengeful force, or else a need for blood reprisals.

Jocelyn Ortion appeared. She looked fine, the face of a young queen franked on a Nordic coin. When we were once meant to be (she, a post-debutante; me, a crewman on the *Yankee* in the 1995 America's Cup), Jocelyn seemed to be everything I was supposed to aspire to want in a woman. The only deb I'd ever known who was truly athletic; now less than thirty, her only sport was herself. She took Ace's hand, then hugged him. She was very happy, and he seemed to be, too. Destined always to be debutante emeritus. She had a way of hurling herself at a man and, at the same time, ignoring his needs. She was an heiress, after all; Ace was a hero. They both were lucky.

She said, "Hel-lo, Jib," with a sad finality; Poor Jib, as if I had just lost the last race. What did she know? She reached out and gave Esperance a one pump Blue Book handshake. She nodded slightly toward Elizaphan. She scanned my neck for the van Cleef and Arpels chain she had given to me as a goodbye present when I had left for Africa to organize my crew. And when she saw it hanging down Elizaphan's neck, she ignored her the way a cat does, just enough to make it interesting.

Maybe she had been the cause for this invitation. Could Ace possibly be feeling guilt over having taken her away from me? Was he thanking me for the gift of her? He shouldn't. He might have felt that I had brought her to him. I hadn't, of course. She'd only followed me to his country. But we were still cousins, Ace and I, in the Parisian sense. Men became "cousins" in France when they have had an affair of some kind with the same woman, and maybe Ace considered me a relative, part of his extended family.

⚑

The Eve of Destiny

We'd come all that way. Forty-one races. One more win and it would be over.

Kinsman would be balanced, boat-for-boat, with *Black Magic*, an even match-up, except that Ace Gordon was the greatest living yacht racer, and I was not. He was a better sailor than I was. I was always the first to admit that. Why not? I had other skills. I wasn't burnt out by my own legend. By my own appointment I had been made *Kinsman's* back-up skipper. But on a good day, weather up, hull down, sails set, I was as good as any skipper; as good as my crew, my sails and my hull; as good as the weather. Ace Gordon's trophy room ashore must have been overwhelming, but it didn't float. And on the water, I felt I had every good chance to beat him. I wasn't afraid of him. And that's what I kept telling myself. *Kinsman* winning the America's Cup had, from the beginning, been an impossibility. This whole long time, these eighteen months. The idea had been sketchy when I first brought it up to Aunt Pearl in her private chapel that Sunday morning as we sat under her Matisse rosette window. And now, there we stood with only one final detail to clean up, and it was oh, so *very* possible. We'd be facing a boat the same as ours, one that had everything we had, nothing more. A brilliant design. The best other boat in the last Cup races.

We launched that afternoon on the eve of the race and tuned *Kinsman's* stays like a huge Martin guitar. I had done everything I could. We were set. One to go. But I knew I had no more advantage. I had nothing more to rely on, but myself and my crew. It would be hull for hull, pure sailing down to the line. Regardless of what our edge had once been, Ace Gordon could now pull off four straight victories just as easily as he could pull off a dozen straight. *Kinsman* no longer had the mystical X advantage.

Match Point

I woke to an echoing grey overcast sky. The low pressure was so low I could hear my own blood in my veins. It was a low that precedes famous hurricanes. It would either be a hurricane, or Central Park Lake, and I'd rather have a hurricane than a lake. By mid-morning the wind was up, and it looked as if it could even get chancy. Maybe even be canceled. I called our tow boat in early. When we got out, *Black Magic* was already out there. She'd just dropped her towline.

When I looked again, her sails were up, and there she was, making her turns, shakedown drills, and practice runs. Turning and wheeling, deft but not great, her movements were a bit clumsy. She'd dip way down and rise slowly, as if she weren't balanced. She was sailing heeled, just as we were doing, but she seemed to be carrying too much sail. Or maybe she wasn't sailing full out, trying not to show us what she had, waiting for the starting gun.

"Put the glasses on her Marcus, what do you see?"

"I see a bowsprit."

"That's what's pulling her down."

"I see a tiller."

"He must be happy with that." His control over *Magic.*

There'd been doubt, but he'd been able to do it. He must have actually ripped the pulleys and wheels out of *Black Lion* and installed her long tiller in *Magic*. Her mast was stepped way back over her keel, ten feet further aft than ours. The mast must have been over a hundred and ten feet, taller than ours. Her displacement was lighter at eighteen tons. She had a cutter bow, a narrower hull, so she could accelerate faster. With her twin rudders, she could make a U-turn on her boat length. And she had a jibboom, a spike leading her by six feet. It looked like *Black Lion*'s. *Kinsman* and *Black Magic* were so different.

I watched her crew, not with binoculars, looking for clues. They had definitely cannibalized *Black Lion*'s equipment, and the gossip was they had installed all of her sophisticated tracking gear, air speed, bottom speed, sail monitors, direction finders, wind gauges, a computerized data base on everything. And her mast, of course. *Black Magic* was followed by a fleet of her sycophants, cheerleaders, adoring fans, their boats draped in Southern Cross flags flying everywhere in sight, horns going *toot toot wah wa-ah beep beep*, and only one *peep* for *Kinsman*. I picked out Aunt Pearl's chartered boat with its small, rather scrappy-looking Rwandan flag on the masthead.

We still looked as if we were meant to be. But for the first time since the series started, I didn't want to be out there. I wasn't nervous; I was off. I wanted to be ashore in bed with Elizaphan looking at the ceiling. Where was Larry Bayard? He was supposed to be the skipper. Yesterday he'd had a setback, temporary paralysis similar to a temporary stroke. He was very upset about not being able to sail. Marcus was off the boat for the race. And Esperance was good, but no help. I'd taught him; he hadn't taught me.

At the ten-minute gun, *Black Magic* let us have a glimpse. What a calendar of great yachting poses. Every one a photograph. She'd changed jibs, shortened sail, and looked great, every bit as yare as *Lion*. She was ready. I felt more challenged than I wanted to feel. Passing close, I could see her crew looked pissed off. And in those first moments, I knew. I could lose.

We were both sailing in steep chop, and it would worsen. Anyone could tell. We were in for a day of real sailing, not yachting. When we tacked and set the pace, she matched us. Nothing more. I didn't think we'd gain a foot a mile on her. Maybe an inch. She was sailing in grand style. She maneuvered with us, pointed with us, and the race hadn't even started.

"Twenty seconds," Esperance said.

I tacked, she tacked, and together we heeled on port tacks toward the starting line with our sails set for the beat to windward. Just as he had before, Ace had gotten the safe leeward position and put me to windward ahead of him. It was going to be a pretty fair start. Then, in one of the memorable maneuvers of my brief history in yachting, Ace Gordon pinched *Black Magic* up and forced me to the line with one second to go, and *Kinsman*'s bow was over before the gun. But, at the gun, *Black Magic*'s bow crossed the line. In the next stupefying moments, I spun the wheel to leeward and yelled, *"Jibe Jibe!"* And we fell off in a horrendous jibe that caught everyone off-guard, including my own crew that was asleep. And why not? We'd never drilled sudden starting line jibes. The jibe might have toppled our mast. No backstay was set in time to catch the weight of the sail when the boom swung, so I had to release the mainsail and run it out over the water to shake the air out of it. And we stood there, holding our left nut while *Black Magic* stormed away to the first mark. We never caught her. We'd lost the race in one absolutely dazzling act of match racing. Touché, Ace Gordon.

At the press conference that evening facing the dazzling lights, seated at the long table, pouring ice water, I bent into my microphone and mumbled answers to gleeful questions from grinning reporters from the *Herald* and the *Star*, as well as the rest. And, of course, the vivacious Claude La Luc, who asked me why I'd let *Black Magic* escape before I could sink her. If she were a man, I would have challenged her to a duel. I paid my homage to Ace Gordon and his crew for his amazing recovery. Ace thanked me for the opportunity to test his boat and crew more fully than they had been tested. The series now stood at four to two. I smelled a knighthood.

Race Seven

A sky-high blue day with one or two wisps of clouds that made it all seem possible. A cool morning, a fair breeze.

I had recovered, I think, from our stunning defeat the day before. Had I leveled off? Had I danced, laughed, drunk and made love too much during the lay-off week? I felt a bit down. Elizaphan and I had been arguing that morning. Aunt Pearl had changed just a bit. I had still not been able to make either one of them completely understand about the sinking. Or maybe it was me I couldn't make understand about it.

One more time, we were ready to go. Larry was present. When we got the sails on her and first heeled deeply, sailing full and by off the wind, we felt an Arctic chill in the air and, in the bow wave blowing the first scatters of spray back at us, we felt its ice. The foredeck crew had already been doused and were ready for a wintry afternoon of yachting. Winter in the middle of the New Zealand summer.

I yelled forward to my crew. *"Megwe?"*

"Megwe!" they answered fully almost together.

"A-bung?" I yelled.

"A-bung!" They answered.

I was trying to give them a lift, and I needed one myself. The pre-start dance was a good warm-up wake-up for the crew. They seemed to be feeling bad about the last non-race.

At the ten-minute gun. We didn't give *Black Magic* a thing. She took it. She swarmed all over us. Her rudders gave her the pre-start edge. She played that game better than we did as we circled each other; she flashed too close around us. Once again, I sensed her crew's anger, as well as their will power of steel. Once again, Ace Gordon seemed confident of winning. He had a lot to make up today; this race had to be his. He couldn't make one mistake. Match point. And the next match point and the next.

I didn't give a damn about the start: winning it or losing it. I just didn't want to be over the line early. I wasn't going to let the start decide the race today. So, *Black Magic* took the start from us. No, she *ripped* the start away from us and were gone while we were left staring at the words *Black Magic* written in gold across her black transom. I had made an early mistake and had sailed high too close to the committee boat, as I had in the last race when Ace Gordon had forced me either to ram the *Lady Anne,* or jibe. And I jibed quickly. Now, I don't know what Ace must have thought, but I could imagine the laughter on board the boats of the spectator fleet. Anyhow, she took the start from us by twelve seconds, a huge margin.

Larry Bayard tried to stick right by me, calling the shots even though he was on medication. Esperance helped me call the sails, and he had a very good eye for windshifts. As always, the course was set directly into the wind to the first mark, uphill all the way. The seas were moderate, coming at us three feet high with a fifteen knot wind behind them. Everyone was soaked; the decks awash with each surge. We were sailing well again. *Kinsman's* hull didn't mind head seas and took them lightly and well. We could catch *Black Magic.* This was going to be our first true, boat-for-boat test against *Black Magic.* I called for a trim. I'd gotten her to point slightly above her, maintaining our speed. We were taking the seas well. We seemed to be sailing better, pointing into the wind where the course lay. And because of a lift, maybe able to lay it on one tack.

I could see *Black Magic* burrowing, the waves burying her bow, her new bowsprit pulling her down. She was plunging. Plumes of white spray were obscuring her length.

We were outsailing her, sailing higher, better. We were gaining on her. We were definitely out-pointing her, and we slowly pulled up to her; then, to windward and inched past her and grabbed the lead as if it belonged to us. We gave them our own *Kinsman* written in black. It was uphill all the way to the mark, a surprisingly good sailing point for us that day, but we'd grabbed the windward edge after only a mile beating upwind. And we didn't give it back. We rounded the first mark ahead by two boat lengths.

Downwind was another story. Ace Gordon sent up a crowd of sails. Too much for the weather. He took risks and raised his big spinnaker, a sail the size of a tent at a country fair. It lifted *Magic's* bow, which was also being lifted by the Genoa jib he had set wing and wing. He had three sails set, all of them pulling. Downwind would be theirs today; upwind would be ours. Both boats were planing in the impulses that our keels gave us. The fastest point for both boats was before the wind, all sails out; we were reaching eighteen knots. A mile above the mark, *Black Magic* nipped us from behind and passed us close, shuffling our sails. Their crew ignored us. Ours, in their innocence, studied them as they went by.

At the fourth mark, we seemed to have caught her again, coming off the windward leg, but she got an overlap, barely a yard over our counter, and forced us off the mark. And we lost her again, and another two boat lengths on the next downwind leg. I tried to salvage the wing mark with sail changes. I even risked our double jib on the reach to the it. I narrowed the gap, and we stuck together pretty close all the way to the seventh mark. Surprisingly we were able to head her at the eighth.

Then *Magic* whipped around it in a tight U and grabbed a boat length's lead downwind. We jibed, but so did Gordon below us. And he wouldn't let us by. The line was coming up quickly. My crew sailed beautifully, jibing and jibing. But by late afternoon in the last two miles, wet, cold, and tired, the truth was clear. Ace wasn't going to let us pass. We were going to be beaten again; this time, outsailed.

And that's exactly what I told the enchanted press baying under glare of the television lights before I escaped the now gleeful, post-race news conference.

For the first time since we had raced against France at La Rochelle, I could feel my grip loosen and doubt take me over. My strings weren't taut. Something had rattled me. It was now four to three. There was no reason I could see that it couldn't become four to four by tomorrow evening. I asked for a lay day. Maybe twenty-four hours would change something. Aunt Pearl's words churned in my mind. "How dare you?" She had never wanted me to win the way I had against *Black Lion*. Maybe she felt *Magic*'s comeback was one of God's acts of reprisal.

⚑

Race Eight

Dead calm. Nothing stirred. The sea's surface was slick as the coating on an eyeball. The day seemed exhausted. By mid-morning, the air had been sucked out of it by the low barometric pressure. Not our weather. Not *Black Magic's* weather, either. In any inland town where the leaves on the trees in the town square stood motionless, it would have been a summer day like any other. But on the ocean and on the day of our race against New Zealand, it was a disaster. We were towed out to the start late, but it was no better offshore. Weather might have been on its way, but not today. If there was a sun, it was a white disk. At first I couldn't find the horizon; the sky had turned the sea grey, giving the surface a pale light. Wherever sea and sky met was a mystery.

"Unique, huh?" Larry said. I didn't answer. I still felt off my bearings. The lay day hadn't done a thing for me. The pre-start maneuver was a slow tango. A drifting match. The rule was simple. If the first boat could not complete the twenty-four-mile course in five hours, the race would be called. The Race Committee was going to wait and see.

We got across the line tailing *Black Magic*. This was the kind of weather where, if there were a breeze, it would be a fluky one; either boat could scoop the other: a puff here, a puff there. On the first leg, we got one and pulled ahead of the black boat; then we both got caught for long periods. I'd lost steerage completely and drifted off course so badly that *Kinsman's* bow was pointing directly at *Magic's* hull fifty yards across the water: a menacing sight considering our recent past.

Nothing. After four hours and some minutes, we crawled around the eighth mark and headed down on the run to the finish, two boats lengths ahead of *Black Magic*. Not a big lead if the wind came up, but a big lead if it didn't. We drifted away from each other and stood a tenth-of-a-mile apart. Now it was going to be anybody's race. Win or lose, it wouldn't be my doing. In another half-hour, the race would be called at this rate.

Then, it happened.

As if God had granted *Black Magic* a private audience, the surface of the water surrounding her rippled up into cat's paws, and the black started moving. She'd gotten a puff. I could see it on the water's surface where she was and not where we were. She kept moving away from us, ghosting, her sails out gathering in the zephyrs. Pulling away, soon she was a half-a-mile ahead of us.

Esperance watched her through binoculars. Was it too late for a reprieve? It could still happen for us, anytime; it was our turn. We could easily get a puff and catch her with the same luck, but we didn't. Time was running out. It was 4:52 p.m. At 5:00 p.m., the race would be called off. *Black Magic* was leading us by one mile, and she was still a mile from the finish line. She would start and stop, gliding from wind hole to wind hole. At 4:58 p.m., two minutes short of cancellation, we saw the puff of smoke, then heard the cannon. They had done it. They had crossed the finish line in the slowest, dullest, most sickening race I have ever sailed. The inconceivable was happening. We could hear the tooting from where we were.

As we were towed past *Black Magic's* tender, I saw Jocelyn. She was standing on the bridge and wearing a big hat, looking ahead. Then she turned toward us and smiled. It was not a good smile.

There would be no more lay days for us now; we had used up our allotment. It would be all over, this time tomorrow.

As they pulled alongside in Pearl's boat, Elizaphan blew me a kiss, and I blew her one back. But I could tell. I didn't see Pearl.

"Where is she?" I asked Saint.

"Not up to snuff."

"Her prayers have obviously kicked in." Saint didn't smile. He hardly looked at me as the power boat pulled away. Just the usual *rah rah* stuff that I had no use for. It was very depressing. I wanted to call Pearl and ask her to please stop praying for Ace Gordon, but I was too depressed. Even for humor.

Sometimes the line between winning and losing was as thin as this page. Sometimes it was a great distance. But it was simple. That day Ace Gordon had found one more way to win just like any true champion would.

⊱

Aunt Pearl

I was naked. I heard Elizaphan's voice. I was standing on a planked wood floor in the black. I didn't know why.

"The door!"

Someone was hitting the door. I was in our room.

"Mr. Routledge!" A woman's voice.

"Yes."

"You have a telephone call."

"Oh, yes. Thank you. I'm sorry."

Elizaphan was awake, lying down. She said it before I asked. "It's three fifteen."

"I'll be right back."

I wrapped a bath towel around my waist and took the stairs down two at a time thinking all sorts of dark thoughts. Half the guest house must have been awake by now. It was a wall phone and the receiver was dangling.

"Is this Charles Routledge?" I said it was. It was a woman with a New Zealand accent. "This is Mara at Mercy Hospital. I am very sorry to tell you that your Aunt Pearl has suffered a massive heart attack. Doctor Rose has arranged to pick you up from your dock. Would you be able to come over right now?"

"Yes," I heard my voice saying. "How is she?"

"She is not at all well, Mr. Routledge. It is critical. That's all we can tell you right now."

Elizaphan had begun to cry when I came back up to our room and told her. She was able to cry again. Like most Rwandans, her life had revolved around death. In the dark, we dressed instinctively without speaking and went downstairs and outside. There was no moon, and we did a bit of stumbling. By the time we'd trotted down to our camp, the boat was waiting for us.

Ba'ale was standing on the dock holding the bow line he had taken from the man driving her chartered boat. "Aunt Pearl," as the men called her, "she is very, very sick."

"I know Ba'ale. Stay by the telephone in the shed so you can hear it ring if I need to call you. If I do call, you might need to wake the men. They might want to come over to the hospital."

"Yes, Skipper."

When we entered the hospital, a man was running a floor waxer ahead of him. The waxed floors gleamed. Clean and light, it smelled like nothing else. I saw nothing. No one was on duty; no one waiting. I ran up the stairs to the second floor, Elizaphan behind me.

"Where is she?" I shouted to a nurse.

Aunt Pearl's room was at the end of a corridor on the third floor, the top floor. Through the glass aperture I could see inside. She was lying as if the hospital bed were part of her ensemble. Her eyes were closed.

A squirrel of a man came out of her room. Nervous, small. Doctor Rose.

"Are you Jibby?"

"Yes," I said. "Charles, actually." He seemed relieved.

"She has been asking for you, Charles."

Even then, I felt a wave of relief.

"How serious?" I felt the words bubble out of me.

"She is dying."

"Oh," I think I said. The words shoved me back. I held onto Elizaphan.

Doctor Rose said she would not last very long.

Elizaphan's body became rigid, then sagged. I caught her and helped her to the floor where she sat. I don't remember if we were crying then, but I remember that she reached up to me and helped me down. I was angry at the doctor.

"Why is she dying?"

"She has been a very naughty girl." He said that she had been very careless about her heart condition.

"What heart condition are you talking about?" I was blaming him.

"We only found out this night."

I couldn't speak. I sat crumpled on the floor. I saw his feet. He was waiting.

"Does she know she is . . . ?"

"Oh, my, yes. She does." He nodded forcefully. "I do not usually tell terminal patients right away, but she forced me."

She had probably offered him a new wing.

I'd always known Aunt Pearl would die, of course. But not then. This had been too sudden, as if she'd been hit by a meteor. She once told me that dying was as strange as birth. That it was all strange, everything about it. So many things that she'd said I remembered; they used to pass through my mind at odd times while I was sailing, leaving me to wonder what I'd do in case she did die. But then I'd see how alive she was, and it would go away. I hadn't known of her heart problems. I don't believe Saint Pierre did.

She was *not* dying. I was *certain* of that. But then I pushed the quiet door open and stood in the doorway. I knew that she was. It was over. I didn't need to be told again. Walking in, I could see that she had closed, that something had come up through her and burned her fires down to nothing. Elizaphan stayed back, weeping in the hall outside, afraid to see her or to be seen.

I entered her room without speaking. She was lying at attention. Her eyes were closed; her steel grey hair lay piled, fiercely awake. It was overwhelmingly true. A huge admission of our temporary stay here on earth. She knew all that she needed to know about our temporary stay here. Without opening her eyes, Pearl knew I was there.

"Jib, it's you. Good. I hated waking you." She looked at me slightly. Her eyes seemed grey that night. "How thoughty of you to come. Forgive me?"

"For what?"

"My snit."

She spoke softly. I couldn't answer her. I couldn't move. I stood in the doorway. When I was able to speak steadily I said, "Will you please promise to stop praying for them?" My joke.

Her eyes sparkled. "Come," she said.

I went over and sat, awed, trying not to touch the bed. I felt suddenly vivacious. But I had nothing to say. "Elizaphan is here," I said loudly. "She wants to say 'hello.'"

"Don't you mean 'goodbye?'"

"No, 'hello.'" I took her hand. It was like Limoges china. As if her bones had chilled.

"I am absolutely livid. As you can probably imagine."

She was very pale, transparent, not livid at all. I opened the door for Elizaphan, who entered and hung back.

"Didn't that little man even bother to tell you?" That she was dying. "I mean, at such an absurd moment. Can you imagine? A guest may come a bit late, that's understood. But never, *never* early. It's taboo."

Her guest was Death. Death had bad manners. Dying seemed less important to her than the outcome of the final race. She was going to miss it, and she hated that.

"Isn't it monstrous?" she whispered and answered herself. "I'll never know."

It was monstrous. What a dreadful feeling she must have. The Cup had become her own quest. And now, on the morning of the day it was going to be decided, this.

"One thing after another and now this. I am so glad I didn't drown."

She had always had an irrational fear of drowning. Her eyes closed. She seemed to doze off.

I excused myself and went down the hall. I phoned Ba'ale. He picked it up during the first ring. I told him the news. He took it badly. The men must be awakened and told and given the choice of coming or not coming. They would not need to wait for the first ferry. I would send Aunt Pearl's boat immediately. Ba'ale wanted to come, too, but I told him to stay and guard the camp. He refused. We would leave the camp unguarded at a bad time.

I went back in. Aunt Pearl was still dozing. I watched her for a minute or two. She awoke with a start. Then in a distant voice she said, "Now if you can believe it, I have just been dining with a flock of enormous crows."

Two of her fingers rose slightly toward the bed table. "Would you?"

There it was. Her black enameled necessaire. I clicked the gold clasp open. There were several unfiltered cigarettes.

"Would you light one for me?"

I did. The first puff tasted good. I passed it to her mouth. She sipped the smoke briefly. Her hand rose up and held it away like a wand.

"Three puffs," I said. "That's all you're allowed."

We smiled at my little poke at death. She held the cigarette drooping between her fingers still elegantly. She drew smoke in again. It looked strange; she was so frail and had smoke coming out of her.

"This is one voyage I have never had the slightest curiosity about."

There had never been anything I couldn't say to Aunt Pearl. She was capable of returning any serve. A duelist. She'd elected to become my mother when mine was no longer there, and she fulfilled a prophecy my father never could. And, of course, she had given me the trust I needed for the power to do what I was now trying to do in New Zealand. And what she had tried to do for that small African country was far better than all the gymnasiums and scholarships and the museum that bore the name Pearl Routledge Hood. She'd had a big chance at life and had taken more than anyone I knew could have taken from it. Her elegance came from her kindness. She was wise from saving lives. She was brave, virtuous, unorthodox from living well in the best sense of the word. Of her achievements, she wore no ribbons the way military people need to do.

"Would you read me that poem?"

"Which one?" I knew.

"The Dylan Thomas?"

"I don't remember it, Pearl."

"Yes, you do." I had recited it to her when Cap had died.

"I don't, Pearl, but I'll try."

"Yes. You jolly well try."

I wracked my memory and came up with only the most famous lines. I spoke them low, close to her ear, she closed her eyes.

> "Do not go gentle into that good night.
>   Old age should burn and rave at close of day —

Rage rage against the dying of the light.
And you the last wave by, singing the sun in flight
Have learned too late you grieved it on its way -
Rage rage against the dying of the light!"

She opened her eyes. They were moist.

"Several mistakes," she whispered. We both smiled. Her teeth were dark. All the years had risen through her face that night. Her brilliance had relaxed. Age surrounded her like a mob of cowards, beaten her up, and left her in an alley. There were pouches, lines, veins I hadn't ever seen, but her nose, a famous landmark, rose like the keel of a boat beached after a storm. She took her third puff and handed me the cigarette. I stubbed it out in a saucer.

"You will call dear Rut, won't you?"

"Of course."

Uncle Routledge had left Auckland for Newport after losing the challenge to us. She had offered, but he had refused to be driven by her to the airport. She told me he had never stopped using the words "treason" and "betrayal."

"Tell him how sorry I am, but that I honestly didn't think he had the chance of an ice swan in hell."

I laughed.

"The family's broken, Jib. Make peace. Will you try?"

A nurse entered and signaled me.

"The priest is outside," she whispered.

Pearl's eyes opened brightly. She had heard.

"Send him away," she said.

"She does not want a priest, nurse."

As to the final judgment Aunt Pearl had never been vague. She was Episcopalian, and for all her good works here on earth, she did not expect to be welcomed into the bosom of the Lord. She rolled her eyes heavenward.

"I just hope I don't run into Him."

She closed her eyes again. Then, as if she had just gotten a brilliant idea, she said, "I want to go swimming."

The men arrived all at once. They had never been inside a building such as this. They looked strong in their red t-shirts, but broken. Two and three came in at a time; half crouching, they entered the room and touched her. Mungo Katano. Isaaco Kayijaho. Leopold Cassel. Leon Champagne. Innocent Hatumaimana. Moses Mazimpaka. Kikongoro. Esperance Mukademezo. Josue Valence. Coco Joliecoeur. Mungo Kayijaho. Ba'ale Mukariogiro. There were tears. The great men of *Kinsman*. Ba'ale was sure she would run into Bujumbura and described him to her so she would recognize him.

She asked for water. I turned around. Elizaphan was lying curled on the floor facing away.

There was a long silence. I took her hand. She was trembling.

"Ironic, isn't it?" She was very angry about dying.

"I have never been a great fan of irony," I said. "Irony has always seemed to be nothing more than coincidence dressed up in white tie and tails."

She closed her eyes, waiting.

Suddenly she said, "It's raining, isn't it."

"No."

"Go look. It's raining. I'm sure it is."

It wasn't a question. I went to the window. Looking out over Hauraki Gulf to the horizon, the sky was making its first preparations for dawn. It was clear, starlit. The coming day would be perfect sailing. I sat by the bed and took her hand.

"Yes, Pearl, it is. It's a beautiful rain, not too hard, flattening the water."

"You see? I knew it was. I'm glad it's raining."

Her hand trembled horribly. As if it was taking electric shocks.

"I just hope it's not dull where I'm going. I have a great fear of long conversations with total strangers."

I wanted to tell her that wherever she went, she'd liven things up. But I couldn't. All I got out was, "I love you, Aunt Pearl." And it was not enough.

After a pause so long that I thought she had slipped away, she spoke. I could barely hear her.

"It has been fun, hasn't it, dear?"

She let go of my hand. She died then. Alone in the room with me and the crew and Elizaphan curled in the corner.

It was getting light outside when a nurse arrived with a pitcher of water. She entered the room as if she knew. She didn't speak. She folded Aunt Pearl's hands nicely and drew the sheet over her face. I had seen actors do this so many times in the movies that it seemed proper. But it wasn't. And after she'd covered her face, I could still see it, I imagined. Aunt Pearl would have hated it. Elizaphan had gotten to her feet and pushed the nurse out of the way. She pulled the sheet down and rearranged her hands so that her fingers were interlaced. Then she pulled the sheet up surrounding her face instead of hiding it. The nurse left. Then the men. We sat there at her bedside, Elizaphan and I holding hands, alone in the room with her now, in deep stunned shock, staring at Pearl as if she were still alive.

Eventually, I stood up and went back to the window. The sun was well above the horizon, flashing across Hauraki Gulf into the room, printing our shadows against the far wall. I could see way off in the distance where our triangular race course was set up. I couldn't see the buoys, just the area. In a sudden stab to my gut, it came back to me that I had a race to sail and win on that afternoon.

I left the room and hurried down the hall to inform the duty nurse of Aunt

Pearl's death. Elizaphan stayed in the room. I called Uncle Rut in Newport and left a message with Lume, who did not want to believe me. I repeated it several times. A maid took the phone from him and wrote the message down.

I put a call in to the Race Committee and left a taped message saying that *Kinsman* would be forced to forfeit the race that day unless we could be granted an emergency postponement. I mentioned Aunt Pearl's sudden dying and our crew's reaction to it. They were simply unable to sail. I asked the taped voice to contact Ace Gordon and to inform Jocelyn Ortion, a close friend of Pearl Routledge's. Aunt Pearl was well-known in New Zealand. Highly regarded. I repeated that, if the committee refused postponement, I would forfeit the America's Cup. I was holding the phone in the hall when Saint Pierre arrived.

"Saint. Where were you?" I couldn't say anything else.

"Jib, how terrible, how terrible."

"Yes." He had missed her dying.

"Has . . . ?" His eyebrows rose.

"Yes," I told him. It was all I could say.

"Oh, God," he said. "Oh my God." He had come too late. He hurried to her room as if he knew where it was. I followed him and watched him through the glass aperture in the door. He stood over her bed and said a prayer. A handsome man. He was wearing a dark suit, no shirt or tie, black shoes without socks. Even without a shirt under his jacket and socks above his shoes, he looked eminent. I watched him pray. The square, high head that made him seem taller. And though he was not bald, hair was not a factor; whenever baldness came to his head, it would come as a compliment

Saint was destroyed. Weeping like a girl, he sat beside Pearl as I had. He spoke words to her that I couldn't hear. They had loved each other dearly. He kissed her forehead, then her cheek. I had always hoped that they would end up together. After a few minutes, he came out.

"There's only one thing left that you can do for your Aunt Pearl and for that pint-sized country of yours. And you know what that is."

He was right. But I was hoping I didn't have to do it that afternoon.

Jocelyn came in at seven-thirty, slightly better-dressed than Saint, but not at all together. She'd thrown a cotton dress over her head and probably nothing else. She wore sandals. "Where is she?"

I told her she was too late. She sort of fainted, and I caught her.

In a moment, she said, "Tell me."

I had to say the words. And with my arm supporting her, I walked her down the hall to the room. In spite of everything, it felt good to be holding her again. Jocelyn went in and kissed Aunt Pearl on the forehead.

A little after eight, a man I didn't know, George, returned my call. The Race Committee would be generous. We had been granted two days.

A delay like this was unheard of but this was the nature of the Cup, one important aspect of it that remained, give way to good manners. Weren't there, after all, other considerations beside commercial pressures? One would hope. Ace Gordon had certainly been decisive in this. And Jocelyn had probably stood right beside him.

Now the sun was up.

Before he left the hospital, Saint Pierre said that so many people in New Zealand would want to pay their respects to Aunt Pearl that there would have to be a memorial service in Auckland and then another later in the month at her favorite cathedral, Saint Patrick's in Manhattan, and then another in Newport at her estate Rondelay. She would be interred at Ledges. While I was still at the hospital, he made a call to make arrangements for a local service.

The first reporter arrived at nine. All that day cables and calls came in. The early ones I read had beautiful words. Rave reviews, as if her life had been a great book or a hit play. I knew she had been thought of as a great lady, I hadn't realized how many people had thought that.

And so the boats would be idle for two days. They would swing idly at their docks killing time. It amazed me, these two boats both capable of such great power, their hulls and sails, both boats capable of bringing huge changes to their own small countries, swinging idly at their docks that morning.

⚑

The Service

I would miss her. Aunt Pearl.

We stayed close that day and the next, Elizaphan and I. Any worries she may have had about our future lives or *Kinsman* had been obliterated. I was still sort of crying when we left for the service. We walked from the guesthouse down to Pearl's boat docked at our camp. Elizaphan was through with her tears. It surprised me, but then I saw that something old had taken hold of her, the ebony shell that protected her from submitting to grief. Of course, she was devastated. She said again and again how her life had been ruined. Pearl had become an invisible home for Elizaphan to go to. A newfound mother. Not for the gifts she showered on her, but for her motherly, kind caring; for her interest in her mind, in her fears; for her humor, that she listened to her thoughts the way a girlfriend listens, and that she had approved of Elizaphan and I being together in spite of her youth. She had learned to love Aunt Pearl for all those things, and now she was not going to be there anymore; vanished, like everyone else in her life, and she felt vastly alone again, as she had felt when I met her. Aunt Pearl had been the only other Routledge who had appreciated her, or even understand her. Elizaphan was deeply hurt, but she felt sorry for Aunt Pearl, because she would miss so much of life.

There she was. *Kinsman.* Moored to her dock, moving slightly on the wind. In spite of her stern line and head line, spring lines, and breast lines binding her, she managed always to find a way to swing slightly, tugging at her lines, a thoroughbred in a stall. A leopard in a city zoo.

Ba'ale called me over to the shed. It was Mungo he said. Mungo was very bad. I went.

He was sitting on his hammock, crying and cursing. I think it was cursing. His right arm was swollen fat from an infected cut he'd gotten cleaning *Kinsman's* bottom underwater. The infection had reached his fingers, which resembled piglets. He was very sick. He couldn't get into his suit; the pain was severe. He was very upset that he wasn't well enough to come to the memorial service. His arm was useless, and it looked to me as if he wouldn't be well enough to crew the day after next. If so, we'd be a man short.

The sea was sparkling. Elizaphan and I rode over with the crew; all of them in their shiny black suits, me in a borrowed black jacket and tie from Mr. Prosser, Elizaphan wearing one of Aunt Pearl's flowered dresses. I was still sort of crying, off and on. I never knew when I wasn't. And what difference did it make? I was angry, and why shouldn't I be? As much out of self-pity for my being deprived of her company as I was that she'd been forced to leave before the end of the show.

No one expects to die. I wasn't ever going to. Neither was Elizaphan. I hadn't imagined the void that I saw Aunt Pearl's absence would carve out of our lives. We'd become very close over the last year. And even though I'd never planned to move back to Newport or probably New York, win or lose, I wouldn't have been seeing that much of her after the finals. My life had been drained. And she had been an instrument of religious magnitude to the crew; they worshipped her.

It was Aunt Pearl who had put *Kinsman* in the water, not me. I had made the spiderweb; she had turned it to gold. And now our beautiful *Kinsman* would finish without her.

Had *Kinsman* killed her? The stress? Doctor Rose said no. "Not at all," he said. It was irreversible decomposition of the arteries leading away from her heart. She had known about it. "She had been a very naughty girl," he said, and had refused to give up smoking.

I had dreamt of her that first night. A good dream, not a nightmare. I had dreamt of her alive. Of course, it was natural, Elizaphan told me. I would dream of her again many times. She knew.

Anyhow, as we walked through Auckland from the public dock to the chapel, I told Elizaphan the bad news: she'd have to crew on *Kinsman* in the final race. The good news was that she would never have to look at the water, because I needed her down in the sewer, handling sails with Kikongoro. They were all marked clearly. She was not excited.

Kinsman and *Black Magic* would be idle for another day. Both capable of power far beyond their measurements, hulls and sails; both boats capable of huge bounties. It amazed me, to combine beauty with salvation. Ours was a metaphor for survival, a dream, and a dream that might still come true. *Kinsman* would stir at her dock for another day, killing time.

After the simple memorial service at Saint Roc's Chapel, Saint Pierre told me that Aunt Pearl's body was to be cremated. I was surprised that had been her wish. He arranged a second memorial service; this one at Saint Patrick's Cathedral in Manhattan. Then, he said that after the service at Rondelay, she would be interred in the family vault at Uncle Rut's Ledges, which seemed the proper thing to do in the long run. He was her brother after all.

Carl Azima

After the memorial service, Saint Pierre told me that someone named Carl Azima wanted to get in touch with me and didn't know how. Something to do with Pearl. Saint gave him the number at Prosser's, and the next morning he called me at breakfast.

"Yes? Hello?"

A man's voice. I could never feel comfortable talking into the phone standing outside the dining room. He introduced himself.

"I'm Carl Azima."

"Yes?"

"I feel like I'm intruding."

"Yes?" You are. It's my day off.

"I'm calling from New York. It's an awfully bad time for you. May I call you Charles? But I felt I needed to call. We've become awfully excited by an idea here at Blankford Smith, you see your Aunt was such a beloved figure, one we must not soon forget."

"Yes?"

"Would you consider putting down your thoughts as a memoir of your Aunt Pearl and this exciting America's Cup business? We'd be delighted to publish such a book."

A memoir? That was what he was suggesting. Write a memoir. About this. Us. I'd never written anything longer than a term paper, but Carl said he knew by talking to Saint Pierre that I could easily do it. He'd assign me an assistant who'd take copious notes from what I told him and type them up. That's how it worked, he said.

"Well, if that's how it works."

"It is. You tell the story of this great collaboration with your aunt over the past two years, how you and she dreamed up this whole wonderful crazy plan to win the America's Cup for Rwanda."

"But what if we don't win it?" I asked him.

"Don't even think about that, Charles. Of course, it might be a little better if you did. But that doesn't matter. Why don't we come to that when we get to it and just see how things go."

"Okay," I said, trying not to sound unfriendly.

"Let me put Missy on the phone."

"We really ought to know by tomorrow night," I said, but I was on hold. Standing in the hallway, I waited for Missy.

Then, a Vassar arts major introduced herself as Missy.

"Now let's the three of discuss this," Carl said from another phone. "If we can agree in substance, we should get the ball started as soon as possible."

"I'm no writer," I said.

"No one is a writer until they write," he began.

"Exactly," Missy said.

She would fly down. She told me it would be a pleasure, unbelievably simple. That I should begin our story at the beginning when the idea was born. Not before and not later, but just at the moment this whole crazy thing had started.

"Remember details and put them down in sequence. Can you do that?"

"Yes," I said.

Carl said, "And if you can't remember, fudge a little."

"Exactly," Missy said.

"When can you start?"

"After we win the race, I guess." I laughed alone.

"Are you free after the race?" Missy asked.

"I hope so."

"Then you really need to get off by yourself for a while. I can come with you."

I told her that Elizaphan and I had planned to do just that. We had made vague plans. We had decided we needed time alone, away from everything, and would maybe take a slow boat to Cape Town or Durban or anywhere in South Africa that was accessible to the road back to Rwanda.

"Perfect," Missy said.

I told her that the trick would be to win. She didn't seem bothered by doubt. Or humor. If we did win the final race, I said, I had already told Ambassador Pierre Kagame that the men would begin preparations for the defense of the Cup in 2003, for Rwanda as host country, and for the races to be held on Lake Kivu, or if not, Lake Tanganyika. That, after all, had been our goal from the beginning, Aunt Pearl and I, to bring to Rwanda the world, jangling with its money.

"Perfect," they said more or less together. I could tell they were drooling.

Elizaphan would help me remember names and dates.

From the day I met her, she hadn't forgotten a thing. The beginning, I could remember. Driving innocently through Rwanda to catch up with Jocelyn. The costume party at Rondelay, our decisive lunch at Le Cirque when I told Aunt Pearl of my strange vision, our talk in her chapel, and how she brought in Saint Pierre to secure the plan.

"But what if we don't win today?" I asked again.

We all chuckled together in New York and Waiheke Island. He said we would still have a book, but to win anyway.

"How would I begin?"

"Make it an anecdote. Simply imagine a friend you admire whom you want to share it with. Someone you care about, maybe someone you love. Pick someone you can hear laughing, someone you can touch. Make it a letter to him if you want."

I picked Aunt Pearl.

"Well, that would be nice, Charles, but she already knows the story. I mean, sorry, but she started it with you, didn't she? So, you couldn't really tell her about it. You see?"

"I could write it to my son."

"He doesn't know the story?"

"No, he doesn't." I let it go at that. "Not yet."

"Excellent. Then you can write it to your son, something along the lines of, 'I want to tell you the story about how we won the America's Cup. You're going to love it, but I don't expect you to believe a word of it. You probably ought to, because it's true.' Like that, see what I mean?"

I said I saw. Anyhow, that's how this book I'm reading to you got started.

⚑

Lay Day

A long night of dreaming. Good dreams. Not of victory.

In my dream, both boats, sails set, were rigged, sails set, ready, the race about to start. Aunt Pearl standing high up on the bridge of her chartered boat, the bridge was higher than was possible. She was waving to us below, dressed entirely in black. In the cockpit with me were Elizaphan, Marcus, Esperance, Larry.

The ten-minute warning gun. During the pre-start, I'd been able to get on the black boat's tail, and she couldn't shake me off. It was unlikely that I could have pulled off this maneuver, but it was a dream, after all, and in it, I did.

At the five-minute gun, without thinking about it, I called for a fake tack followed by a quick jibe, and then with sails set, I powered through the black boat's lee and won the start from the leeward position. I had gambled on footing out ahead of her, pulling her down to cover me and even that had worked. I felt that if we had one point *Black Magic* didn't have, it was sailing full-and-by slightly off the wind, footing. The trick was to pull her down to a point off her course, and so we had. We held our slight lead and laid the first mark after a two-tack beat. We cut close around the mark, five seconds ahead and looking good. All was even now between the boats; we were hull to hull, our sails beautifully trimmed, lee rail awash, when I heard odd noises coming out of our hull.

At first, they seemed to be groaning sounds; then, they became guttural. Voices. Voices rising up from inside us below as if there were many sad voices. Closer to some deep, sad sort of music. As the voices rose out of our hull, singing this dire lament, *Kinsman*'s hull seemed to join the shape of the waves. They lifted her, the hull sailed high, and the helm became light in my fingers, I took my hands off the wheel and, without effort, we sailed ahead of the black boat. And so I woke up. I never knew the outcome of the race.

I woke in the darkness and lay there. It had been completely real. I was surprised to be dry. I tasted my arm to be sure. No sea salt. I was disturbed, even though we had been winning the race. I was troubled about it, the weird sounds. I wanted to go back to sleep and sail through to the finish, and finally I dozed off. But I never got back to it, and I woke up tired from sailing and with our room fragrant with the smell of flowers and of toasting bread from the kitchen below and of coffee, bacon and sausages. So, I got up. The room was full of Elizaphan's flowers living in tin cans.

Kinsman was not a dream, but in one way she was. Just as her power was untouchable, just as she would nevermore carry the power as well as she would carry the small Rwandan flag, win or lose, that afternoon.

It was the morning of the race. The dream had left me tired. I knew that by the ten-minute gun I'd be up for the race, but I was starting out the day badly, playing catch-up. Of course, I had dreamt of *Kinsman*, why not? She had been my life, good and bad, those two years; my growing up. My ripening.

Now I was ready, and I realized I wanted nothing. I was surprised to find out that I wanted only what I already had. What did I have? I had Elizaphan. I was alive. I was twenty-eight. Little else. Aunt Pearl had given me enough substance to live on as if I were a natural thing, a tree. And though I was prepared to lose the final race, maybe even on the verge of losing it, I was not preparing to lose it. But, unbelievably, I didn't give a damn.

⚑

Saint Pierre

I called Saint from the shed and told him about Carl Azima's call from New York.

"Will you do it?"

"Of course," I said.

Then he said, "What's your perception of this race?"

My perception? What the hell did *that* mean? I said something like, "My perception is that it's the most important race in the history of the world." I told him it was the race of a lifetime and, luckily, I was involved.

He laughed. "Aside from that."

"That it'll either go to one boat or the other."

"That's true, too. You're getting warm."

"Saint, just tell me what's on your mind." From the shed, I could see the tow boat backing toward our dock. We were taking *Kinsman* out for a spinnaker drill.

"You know this, Jib, but I must say it again. Match racing is like no other racing. You don't go to the mark; you stick with the other boat."

"Please, Saint." I didn't have time for this. I was late.

"Okay, Jib. Boat for boat, Ace Gordon has you beat. What do you think?"

"Possibly." Then I said, "Yeah."

"But he's only one or two seconds faster per mile. So take him for the ride of his life. He'll follow you. You be the driver. Wherever you go, he'll go. He has to cover you. He'll never let you alone. That's his style."

"I know that. I've done that. Tack tack, cover cover."

"What's your best point?"

"Funny you should ask. Footing."

"Then foot. Foot the hell out of him. Force him to foot, because you can."

"Good luck," we said to each other and, "Win it for Pearl." But now the stakes had been raised even higher, if that was possible. I *did* give a damn. The volume was turned up unbearably loud. I was worried. I was out of ideas. Footing? We'd dropped the last three races in a row. *Black Magic* could show us her stern once again. Why not? She was on a roll, and the roll could last another day. Until something changed. And we needed a change. But what? *Black Magic* wasn't going to start towing a bucket, and Ace Gordon wasn't going to become a moron. He had turned the series around. It had taken me a couple of days to realize how he'd done it.

It had started when he'd invited me over to lunch to inspect *Black Magic*. Showing me his secrets? No one does that. He was playing a game. He'd simply planted the seed in me that afternoon that whether I knew his secrets or not didn't matter to him; he was going to win. And he did, as advertised. He'd psyched me out so smoothly that I hadn't even felt it.

So I called him up and invited him over to our camp to inspect *Kinsman*, then lunch at the Mosquito Café. He'd only laughed. Nice try.

If he won the final race, afterwards, when it was all over, at the ceremony, he'd make an endearing speech. He would toast me, the losing skipper. With a kind smile, he would raise his glass to me. But in his other hand he'd be holding the America's Cup. In my right hand, I'd be holding my plane ticket; in the other hand, I'd be holding my dick.

☞

The Race

Seven had always been a good number for me. That morning Hauraki Gulf went from choppy to smooth, then back again to choppy with winds from eight to twenty knots. A good day for both our big sail areas, our sharp bows, our long lean hulls. It would be tight.

We got a tow out before New Zealand did. Elizaphan sat with me in the cockpit looking hurt, more nervous than I'd ever seen her. When Esperance took the wheel and we got some sail on her, we tacked back and forth off the wind, waiting. *Magic* finally came out, dropped her towline, and got her sails up. She looked formidable. What was different? She had a new mainsail, a translucent one like the one that had gone down with *Black Lion*. There was no ad on it, only the America's Cup cartouche. We were probably seeing her under sail for the last time.

Elizaphan kissed me before she slipped out of sight below decks.

The gun.

"Ten-minutes," Marcus said.

"Tack away!" Larry said.

I took the wheel. "Not this time, Larry."

Exactly as it had happened in my dream, I tried to tail *Black Magic* through the pre-start. She had twin knife-blade rudders, of course, so it was unlikely that I could pull this off, but it had worked in my dream, after all. And so without even thinking, I called for a faked tack, followed by a quick jibe, and with my sails flat, spun the wheel to weather, jibed, surprised her, and nipped her at the five-minute gun. It had worked. *Black Magic* seemed to have one slight weakness: she'd stall after a rapid maneuver. Her new main was slow to come over and fill. So I had her by the tail, and she couldn't get rid of me.

"Fifteen, fourteen, thirteen, twelve . . ." Esperance was saying. I fell off under *Black Magic* and powered through her lee, then started ahead of her in the safe leeward giving her my bad air, footing off the wind, drawing her down. So, to the amazement of the fleet, *Kinsman* won the start and the lead up the first leg. Larry and Marcus were as surprised as they were. But I wasn't. It was *déjà vu*. We gave *Black Magic* our lee bow. That is, we sailed just far enough ahead of her to screw up her wind. The wind had blown up and settled in at twenty. And we were able to starboard tack her and keep her under us all the way to the mark. Footing was our best point, and it was a wet ride to the mark.

Rounding it for the downwind run to the second mark four miles away, I called for our small, heavy duty spinnaker. And away we went, skiing, bow high. *Black Magic,* close on our tail, was trying to blanket us. Ace Gordon was better downwind than anyone I'd ever seen. We were both screaming, hitting windspeeds up to twenty, the fastest leg anyone aboard *Black Magic* had ever sailed, but we managed to hold her off, jibing downwind. And when we were a hundred yards above the second mark, I saw we'd be cutting it too close. Ace Gordon had finally been able to slip inside our angle, but was still half a boat length behind us. I thought we could round the mark safely ahead of him. Even if we led around the second mark by three seconds, that's all I would need. I could get *Kinsman* away quickly and have a good jump on *Black Magic* to the third mark and set a quick spinnaker. I didn't want Ace Gordon on my neck. The men were all set to jibe around the second mark. I'd be sailing in free wind and getting a lead *Magic* couldn't touch. It worked. We managed to hang onto a four-second lead to the wing mark and around. This was a race.

Ace Gordon made up time on the downwind leg to the fourth, and we were pretty even; he had the edge. To the fifth, Larry said I needed to go way out on a limb. I was going to lose this duel with Ace. The wind had dropped to eight, and Esperance was hunting for wind patches with his binoculars. He spotted one off to starboard at right angles to the fifth mark, and I decided to reach out on a starboard tack to where the ruffled water was breaking about half-a-mile west. I could see it over there. It would be a complete surprise. We'd be getting into free water.

But I wasn't going to get away from *Black Magic* that easily. Ace tailed me all the way to the fifth a boat length back, hugging me, and then back to the sixth. We were sailing beautifully downwind. I'd taken my eyes off *Magic* for a minute. I'd been focused on the fluorescent orange mark, an inflated pyramid bobbing two hundred yards ahead of us. Marcus had gone forward. Larry had been distracted. Then, I saw it in his face. Too late. He had caught us. She had us.

"Overlap, *Kinsman*," a calm voice spoke close by, as if it was *Magic*'s right to demand it. Then, just as calmly, "Sea room."

There she was, looming, the black bow was just under my armpit. We'd been making so much noise rattling and banging along, I hadn't heard her come up on us. But there she was, throwing our wash back at us dangerously close.

She had an overlap on us, and so she was asking us to step aside and give her the mark. I didn't have far to turn.

"Kinsman! Sea room!" Louder this time, more urgent.

I could do nothing, a few inches of her bow had gotten between our hull and the mark. Their bow was ahead of our stern. It was their right. They had become the inside boat sailing between us and the mark.

"Overlap," their bow man spoke directly to me, standing five yards away.

I saw it too late. I tried to turn away and give them the mark. I had to give it to her, but I had pinched too high to lay the mark. I couldn't go above my line. And so, as I was rounding up, I was forced to luff my sails. Then we caught a wave broadside and the tip of our boom grazed *Magic*'s side-stay. A touch. I heard the twang of our fairleader catching it. Very musical even in that wind. That's all it took. I was in the wrong. I knew it. I had clearly fouled *Black Magic*.

"Protest!"

I heard another voice say in a perfect New Zealand accent, "That's it, *Kinsman*. You're out."

I didn't see the red flag go up her backstay, but there it was, flapping nicely. The committee tender following us a hundred yards away had clearly seen it. A major infraction. After a brief consultation between the three nodding heads on board, one of them waved a black signal flag on a stick, wig-wag, wig-wag, back and forth. *Kinsman* was out.

Disqualified.

Ace Gordon had set me up. It was a perfectly-executed maneuver. Anyone watching would have thought it was my fault, but it was his bluff, his timing. He had punched *Magic*'s bowsprit up between *Kinsman* and the mark. So that's what it was for. It was surgical perfection. I had done my best, but he had done his better. I was no scrubber, but he was a world champion.

"You still got Rule 720, Jib," Larry said.

Without breaking her speed, *Black Magic* swept around the sixth mark, jibed, and still flying her protest flag sailed on to the seventh mark and an unprecedented comeback victory while we stood hove to, in irons. The committee tender came within speaking distance to make sure that I understood the gravity of their ruling.

"Hello, Kinsman. You have been disqualified from this race. Do you understand?" I do, thanks. It doesn't get any worse than that.

"Rule 720," I shouted to the official. He nodded.

"You are invoking Rule 720?"

"I am."

The other two nodded. And all the while, *Black Magic* was sailing hull down toward the horizon. They turned their bow away and stood by at a hundred yards to watch us fulfill Rule 720. It states that the offending boat, us, may be purified of our sin, by making two three-hundred-and-sixty-degree turns, one following the other. It's a good rule. It keeps two boats in the race, but that's about all. It's a devastating rule, because it puts one boat hopelessly behind and usually costs it the race. And it was probably too late for us, but it was the only way to absolve my foul: the ten Hail Marys of yacht racing. It was either Rule 720, or sail all the way back to Rwanda. I signaled the committee boat. I was ready.

We kept sailing. We fell away on a starboard tack. The wind had come up, blowing in gusts up over twenty knots, sheets of rain, wet on the deck, spray hitting me hard. I had immediately called for the sails to be sheeted home. When they were winched in, when the crew fore and aft were set and alert, I called for a jibe and down we turned, sails flat as knives, turning fast as I could. The lazy stays tightened. The taut stays released. The boom flopped over on its vang. We jibed around the mark and came out just about where we'd been. We did it again. It made no sense to the crew. Two flawless jibes around the fifth mark in good wind; we turned fast and got off at full speed after the final turn, but quick as we'd been, when we got underway again I could see that we'd been fatally gored.

Black Magic was showing us her butt, forty boat lengths ahead of us to the sixth mark. We'd clearly lost it at the fifth. I stared after *Black Magic*. She was sailing beautifully. It had been close, boat for boat, seconds apart, but now we'd never see her again. "*Lady Anne* can fire her little cannon now," I said. I was in a daze. After assuming victory was ours, coming all this way, forty-five races, I was about to lose the final. Even our crew realized.

How could I catch her? I wanted to call on sails I didn't have. My great-great-grandfather Hugh Routledge, who had skippered the *Staghound* from New York to San Francisco in twelve weeks, had a hold-full of sails to call upon. Above his mainsail, he could set a topsail; above the topsail, he could set a top gallant sail; above the top gallant sail, he could set a top royal; above the top royal, he could set a skysail; above the skysail, he could set a moonsail. All these sails were part of his treasury to lure the wind. I called for the only sail in my treasury, our golliwobbler, our huge light staysail, and a serious risk to our mast in this breeze. In a few moments, I saw Elizaphan's hand reach up out of the sewer holding the head of the sail. Moses grabbed it, clipped it to his halyard. Kikongoro began clipping its luff onto the twin headstay. It was a dangerous choice; the sail could drive us under.

In less than two minutes, up it went and down came the number three jib. I prayed the golliwobbler wouldn't split.

"*Hang on, men!*" I yelled.

We leapt forward, plunging, sailing hard lee rail awash, the crew clinging to the weather rail, our stays taut and humming. I knew how to sail. After a few minutes of this bone-busting, as fast as we were moving, we didn't seem to be gaining noticeably. Or, if we were, we'd never gain enough over three marks. In another two minutes, *Black Magic* would round the seventh and head for the eighth, then turn downwind after the eighth for the finish line. Eight miles to go. Ace Gordon had one job left, and that was to keep *Black Magic* between us and the finish line, a relatively easy task at this distance. We needed a spell of black magic of our own.

⚑

The Chant

It was between the brutal rattling, the crackling of the hull, the rush of sea water, and the wind shushing my ears that I heard it. The sounds from my dream. Moaning sounds, strange, rising from below the hull; guttural sounds that turned into music. They sounded like a dire lament, as if there were many sad voices. Then, nothing. The racketing of the hull. Had I heard them at all?

In any weather, the hull of a Twelve makes a racket, all sorts of cacophony. It is not a wooden hull, it is full of inventions, fabulous substitutes. But in heavier weather, it becomes huge, banging with every wave, rattling, creaking, groaning with stress. Below decks, it is as empty as the inside of a huge lyre and just as dark, but a lot less comfortable. The ideal sound box for clamor.

It was chanting. A deep rhythmic lament, a powerful dirge. Up out of the hull. It was blowing high and low on the wind. When he heard the wailing coming up through the deck, Larry perked up.

"The fuck is that?"

"Esperance, go see." He went forward and poked his head down into the sewer. When he came aft he said, "Ba'ale. He is singing with Elizaphan and Mungo."

"Some kind of memorial to Aunt Pearl?" I said.

Ba'ale was our lead singer. He'd always wanted to come on a race. This was the last one, so I'd invited him to sit beside me as a passenger. He was pretty useless on board with his teakwood right hand. I hadn't noticed it, but during the protest he had slipped down to the sewer. I knew he had started the chant and was down there leading it. He had the best voice of the crew, full of longing, crooning.

"Get them up here so we can hear them." We didn't need a sail change until the eight mark. "Tell them to bring lifelines."

The three climbed up the aluminum ladder, Ba'ale and Mungo still singing. And then Elizaphan came up smiling, seasick, singing, and clipped herself off to a sidestay. Ba'ale kept the chant going. On the foredeck, the men around him picked it up. The sheetmen aft joined them, a dozen voices. The crew was on its feet, clipped off to lifelines. Their hands were free between marks; they picked up the rhythm perfectly. The deck came to life, and everything became a percussion instrument. Winch handles struck the mast; palms pounded the deck. The stays became bass guitar strings. The foredeck itself became our drums. I was amazed by the men's force and their unity. Whenever a crewman tightened a winch or worked a line, he kept his part of the chant going. It was indescribable. They had done this so many nights, two years of nights, rehearsing for this performance. In the cockpit, Esperance stood up and joined in, I was on my feet at the wheel. Marcus behind me in the fourteenth seat joined in. I heard Larry making dreadful crooning sounds. That made it unanimous; we had a full choir. It was exciting be part of it. *Kinsman* had become a twenty-ton, high speed musical instrument.

After twenty minutes of chanting and hard sailing under the golliwobbler, Marcus put down his one-eyed electronic tachometer and came aft. He had been watching *Black Magic*. He kicked my leg and said very quietly, the way you do when you don't want to break a mood, "We're gaining on them." I tried to see what he meant, but I couldn't.

I shrugged, "Right."

"We are, Charles," he only mouthed the words.

He was right, of course. His toys didn't lie.

"Why'd you call me Charles?"

"Because I wouldn't want to see 'Jibby' engraved on the Cup."

I kicked him a little too hard.

But he was right. Even I could tell. Esperance saw it, too, and signaled me excitedly. We were gaining. We were gaining and chanting and gaining, chanting and gaining. It was getting crazy.

By the time we'd rounded the seventh mark, the chanting hadn't died and wasn't going to. It had warmed up; it was cooking, ready to go on all night. I could imagine Moses lighting a fire on the foredeck, having a cookout. We had gained. We had been a minute-twenty behind at the seventh mark and, by the time we rounded the eighth, that was down to forty-eight seconds. Now we were on a run, all sails out before us, wing and wing, upwind of *Black Magic*, but still too far back; they had not heard us yet.

Once we'd set the spinnaker and a jib below it for the final downwind run, the foredeck was open, the boat had leveled off. The crew was free to chant and dance on a flat deck. They'd been dancing, more or less, in a circle and chanting for themselves. Now I asked them to get it in a line, as they had in the evenings, and to stand facing forward and to sing *Black Magic* out of the water. The chant blew down on them, rising and falling from behind. I could see the moment it reached the first crewman's ears. He was standing at the backstay when he suddenly jerked his head up and squinted back at us. Then Turlington turned his head; then Ace. What the hell is going on back there? They were curious, sneaking looks. Then the rest of the crew began turning back to see where the chanting was coming from. Its source. They'd have to go to Central Africa to find its source. They could hear the deep, rhythmic, foreign sounds, unlike anything they'd ever heard, bearing down upon them from behind.

Later, McKinlay told me it was "terrifying." That was his word. He said he could actually feel us songing after him over the water. Bucky Ryder, main sheetman, and Ian Reilly, sailing as captain of the foredeck, both said it had been ominous, the scariest thing they'd ever heard, like a deep African spell. Very few New Zealanders had ever heard African music. We sounded like a yacht from very Hell itself.

We gained.

As we gained, the chanting rose, the beat quickened.

We were singing them down. *Magic* was now twelve boat lengths directly in front of us. She had fallen into a wind hole that she wasn't going to be getting out of right away. She could only glide forward, sails drooped, and listen to us, whether she wanted to or not.

And on we came, charging down on her, filling, rising, cresting, sweeping full, toward the nearly becalmed black boat. Ten boat lengths. Nine. Eight. Seven. Aboard *Magic*, Gordon helplessly watched us coming up on him. Then I was close enough to hear him call out, *"Sail change!"* Up from his sewer came a third sail, a huge jib to wing out inside the spinnaker. It was quick. With the three sails set, he picked up speed. But it didn't matter. We had the wind where we were, and we had the chanting.

⚑

The Jibe of God

The wind came with us. We were catching them from behind. With a mile to the finish, they weren't more than four boat lengths ahead of us.

Larry called for a jibe. We swung out to port. Ace jibed under us, heading us off. We jibed again; he jibed again, under us. We went back on port, so did *Magic*. He was quick to react; he wouldn't let us pass. He had trapped us above him, staying between us and the finish line, doing all he needed to do, turning twisting snaking, predicting each jibe we were going to make. With each jibe, heading us off. He could keep that up all the way to the gun. He was good. He was never going to let us by. One boat to beat, and we couldn't beat it.

We were quickly running out of real estate. And ideas, too. There were only so many.

"I need help, Larry," I said.

"We're in trouble," he said.

"Great," I turned to Marcus. "Your thoughts."

"We are."

"That's it?"

"Well, you could try a triple fake jibe. Not counting the fourth one, which isn't fake. I've heard of it tried, but I've never heard of it done successfully. But we could give it a shot."

"Yeah. We could always do that." I'd never heard of it. It was talk. Any maneuver looked good to me now, however risky, even one that was out of reach. Half-a-mile. We'd cover half-a-mile in two minutes.

"Esperance. We must try. Jibe three times quick quick quick. Fourth jibe real. Got it? Fake-fake-fake-real. Marcus take the wheel. Esperance come." We ran forward. The men were standing, facing forward, chanting. "Moses. Tell your crew to listen up." He got their attention, the chanting stopped.

Esperance translated. "We fake three times, jibes quick as you can. Jibe,

jibe, jibe, jibe. We pull jibe off in five seconds, one at a time. All over in thirty seconds; three fake jibes and one more."

They understood, nodding. We would head downwind, jibe, release stays, haul in stays, unclip pole, swing it in, clip other end, swap guy and sheet, fill spinnaker, head *Kinsman* upwind on new tack, quick turn back down, jibe, release stays, haul in stays, unclip pole, swing it in, clip it, swap guy and sheet, and do it again, three times at top speed. All stays let out and tightened in perfect sequence. All clicked in perfectly or mast goes down.

It was dangerous. If it didn't work *Black Magic* would sprint ahead as she already had, unmolested, on the opposite tack, and we'd be left holding a pole and a backed spinnaker. End of race seven. On the other hand, if *Magic* fell for it, we'd slip by her and shoot the steep end of the line. The pin end.

I ran aft to the cockpit.

"Moses catch your signals from Esperance. Watch him. Men ready forward?" The men jumped to their posts and grabbed the pole and lines.

"Men ready, Skipper."

"Men ready aft?" The men put their hands on winches and lines.

"We ready, Skipper."

Esperance ran aft.

"When?" Moses called back.

"Get ready. First jibe in thirty seconds. Watch Esperance. Good luck."

My hands were wide on the wheel. I was set to steer four swerves, major changes of direction. We had a good big rudder. If we pulled three off without a hitch, the fourth would put us back on the course we were sailing then.

We'd be free of *Black Magic* and sailing clear for the steep end of the finish line. It was all up to Moses' crew and Isaaco's aft how well we carried it off. One slip and it was over. I was betting the mast on their skill.

I could feel Tommy Tarlington's fox eyes watching us. He didn't need binoculars anymore. It was his job to spot us. He knew we were going to jibe; he just didn't know when. *Black Magic* was on alert to mirror us. Tarlington watched Kikongoro holding the spinnaker pole for movement. Jacob had taken in the lazy stay as much as he could, keeping light tension on it so that when we jibed the mast wouldn't go. Tarlington watched Isaaco free the lazy sheet and tighten it. Just so. Josue and Isaaco stood by to release the taut stay and the spinnaker guy.

"Hang on," I said to Marcus and Larry. I took a deep breath. "Ten," I said.

A thousand yards to finish. Esperance watched me. Moses watched Esperance.

"Four. Three. Two. One."

This was it.

At "one," Esperance banged the deck with his winch and called *"Trip!"* forward to Moses, sending the men into action. He grabbed hold of the spinnaker pole, tripped it and with two men clinging to it, flew it around the headstay. The mainsail flopped over; the jib cracked. Perfect. Of course, *Black Magic* heard it and saw it. They were supposed to.

Tarlington had already said the right words to Ace Gordon. The black boat had turned sharply downwind and had begun her jibe with ours. They mirrored us, swooped up nicely cutting us off again from the line. They were quicker to jibe, even a bit ahead of us jibing to port, keeping their boat between us and the line. But we had begun our second jibe, by the time they'd filled away to port, Moses had already released our pole. I could hear Tarlington's voice *"Fake! Fake!"* Another voice yelled, *"Jibe, jibe!"* They were sharp. They doused their spinnaker. Its sheet ran, sending the sail way out forward, their main boom crossed over, their jib popped, their sails filled out on starboard tack. Standard maneuvers of a quick jibe. But by the time their sails filled out to starboard, I'd spun the wheel again, swerving *Kinsman* downwind, Isaaco had hauled in our main, Moses had unclipped our pole, our spinnaker had flown around our forestay. *Magic* was a second late.

"Fake!" Ace Gordon yelled. *"Jibe her! Jibe her!"*

They were locked in on starboard tack for another three seconds. Too long. When they went into their second jibe, I'd already spun the wheel, sending *Kinsman* down. Isaaco had already crossed the mainsail, and Moses had freed the pole. We'd begun our third jibe. *Magic* tried to follow.

As I spun the wheel again for the fourth jibe, I saw that she couldn't do it. She'd lost it. A line had blown free, a sheet or a guy; she couldn't stay with us. Now she was too late. We charged past *Black Magic* under her stern, toward the open water between us and the finish line. Perfect. Again. Perfect. Again. She could no longer intercept us. Nothing stood between us and the line.

And there we were with a bagful of wind in our sails, sailing our own course in free air on starboard tack, directly toward the finish line with *Black Magic* sailing off on a port tack to hell and gone, or to Samoa, whichever landfall came first.

The chanting that had faded during the dicey maneuver, started up again and grew strong. I could hear Elizaphan's voice above the others. I was breathless. Larry was pale. Marcus was ecstatic.

"Yo ho ho, we did it!"

Three hundred yards from the line. I thought the damage to *Magic* was terminal, that Ace Gordon wasn't going to make it, but he wasn't finished with us. It took him five long seconds to recover. He was able to jibe her back onto port tack on his final lunge; he tried to shoot back up, trying to cross our bow and knock us off course. He ended up behind us. He was on top of us now in an impossible position to come between us and the line, but he was threatening our wind. It was all he could do. Our sails had filled;

so had his. He shot up to weather of us, with his three sails nicely set, and he was back on our tail, on top of us, taking our wind, trying to cover us now. He had his wind and a piece of ours. Our sails fell. He was definitely gaining. He had a chance. It was boat for boat. We came down the last hundred yards to the line, bow to bow. Anybody's race. I could see that our mast was ahead of *Magic's*, but hers was set further aft; we could have been even. It was that close.

She was sailing alongside us just a few yards away, both boats even, our crew chanting directly at theirs. Our crew dancing in line on the foredeck, in a ragged line facing *Magic's* crew, moving back and forth, some arm-in-arm, chanting directly at them. Their crew was silent, grimjawed, each crewman lying prone on deck, hearing us, staring straight ahead, willing their boat forward. I glanced at Ace Gordon, crouched at the helm, chin on deck, holding his tiller above his head. I caught his eye. It all gets down to this, doesn't it. The pale furious eyes glanced directly at me and darted away. It was all slipping away from him. He could not show me his disbelief, but what he could show me was his anger. A triple fake jibe.

The finish line came up. As we crossed it, there was a breath between us. Our bows crossed together. The gun was for us; the puff of smoke was ours. Ours had crossed first. The closest finish in the history of the America's Cup. We won we won we won, the men knew. The chant rose and fell.

The End of My Story

Elizaphan unclipped herself and ran aft. She wrung me like a tin bell. I was in tears. I have to say that. I went down on the deck.

"Don't, Charles. It's over, it's over."

"Not the race," I was able to say. I realized what it was. "Her. She's really dead isn't she? She's really dead."

Aunt Pearl's death had struck me down. I wept for her, sobbing out of control. I couldn't cry enough. Elizaphan grabbed me.

"Please stop, Charles. Don't, or I will, too."

She kissed everyone, even Larry Bayard. She settled beside me in the cockpit. It was tears and laughter. Marcus Cape was waving the big Rwandan flag.

Kinsman had been forgotten. We'd gotten the sails down and were moving on her bare bones, being steered by Larry Bayard, the only man off his feet.

Black Magic passed us sailing under her main. Ace Gordon was slumped forward, head down, always to remain this one instant away from immortality. His foredeck crew folded like crumpled napkins after dinner, two of them sat with their heads bent between their arms, but not close to the hurt they would feel tomorrow and remember throughout their lifetimes. The wind had lightened. *Black Magic* was no longer being sailed; she had been abandoned by her crew. Her mainsail had been let to run out over the water; the spinnaker hung slack on a lazy sheet. The great Dacron jib hung like a bedsheet on a line. The afterdeck sheetmen, the trimmers and grinders and tailers sat dazed, exhausted, aching, stupid from defeat. But it was their afterguard who had lost the race, not their crew. They sat stunned, overwhelmed, baffled, lost, beaten, amazed. It was a boat of misery and despair.

It had been the hardest-fought race I'd ever sailed. I read later that the lead had changed thirty-two times. And we had pulled off a soon-to-be famous bluff. No one could believe that we had beaten Ace Gordon in the last thirty seconds by out-maneuvering him without divine help. So when the *Auckland Star* called it the "Jibe of God," it became the "Jibe of God."

At the moment we crossed the line, my crew had not been aware that the puff of smoke was ours, that the horn was for the other boat, that we'd won. They'd looked back at my face. When they saw that I'd taken my hands off the helm and picked up Esperance and was hugging him and then Marcus, they knew. Their reaction was different than any I'd ever seen. Instead of slapping each other's palms in high fives, they simply picked up their beat from dirge to happiness and laughter. The incredible line of dancing men, their rhythm was gleeful, without Elizaphan there were eleven in the line, dancing in pretty much identical movements, back and forth, as they had been; moving back and forth from the headstay to the mast. The joy came from their bodies, a deeper joy. A fabulous sight. I'd never watched anything as emotional. I had never heard such exhilarating music; music more inspiring than any spiritual. They'd won everything. They could go home and begin again with hope.

Larry kept *Kinsman* barely moving on course amid the quiet spectator fleet of devastated onlookers. It was hard to believe that, in this country at this time, a few boats did pick up our crew's beat and blew out their various honks and tweets on our behalf. We had gotten so used to silence at the finish line that it was startling to hear anything coming from them after our victory. The tow boat threw us its line. The Cup was waiting at City Dock, not ours.

We eased alongside it. Saint Pierre had gotten in ahead of us, took our bow line, and made it off. He looked exhausted, faint, smiling. "You did it."

Yes.

The highly-polished Cup stood on a pedestal surrounded by officials who were formal in greeting us, who wore the same blazers and didn't seem to want to give it to us. None of them knew us, or we them. I did recognize the official who had disqualified us earlier that day. It was all pretty subdued. Elizaphan couldn't let go of me. The photographers and reporters were kept caged behind a rope. The Cup seemed smaller than it had before. More frail. The late afternoon sun glanced off its voluptuous curves. I never realized how absurdly feminine it was.

Kinsman's crew hadn't changed and still wore their red t-shirts. They stood in a knot waiting for *Black Magic's* crew to come over from their dock. The attention had now been turned up to one hundred percent, and it was overwhelming them. It was new; they were very embarrassed. I hadn't predicted that. Mungo was there with his fat arm in a sling. Kikonburo had somehow gotten a broken nose; I hadn't found out how yet. Other men had wire cuts and rope burns. The photographers asked them to pass the Cup from man to man, holding it by its wood base. They did rather quickly. No one seemed to want to hold it for longer than he had to. It didn't weigh anything.

Twenty minutes went by. It was rude. The men stuck to what they knew and drank the local ale, not Saint Pierre's Champagne. Luckily, they didn't feel like spraying either one on each other, which was a relief, and they were very good about not pushing their skipper off the dock. I'd had enough seawater for one afternoon.

I did spot someone who might benefit from a chilly douche. Claude La Luc. I went over and engaged her in conversation. She must have lost her footing or been standing too close to the edge of the dock, because somehow she slipped and started to fall backwards into the water. I reached out to grab her, but . . . Too late. There was nothing I could do. She made a great splash. When she was eventually raised to the dock, she promised to *attaque* me, which Saint told me was the French word for *sue*.

We stood waiting for the New Zealand crew. My men were patient, each with his bottle of ale, all smiles and bandages. They were thinking about the long trip home now and the rewards awaiting them. The new tools and livestock and land that they would be able to buy. The Kinsmen Committee. It had meant so much to Aunt Pearl, and it would now come true.

Black Magic's uniformed crew arrived in an open navy gig and formally walked onto the dock and stood together. They weren't a bad bunch, just hard losers. It was all they could do to show up I found out later. They looked powerful, blond, tanned. They looked beaten. Standing on the dock in their black shirts and white caps, man for man, they towered over our crew, each New Zealander stronger than his counterpart on *Kinsman*. They could have easily whipped us at rugby, and they looked like they were ready to, then and there.

Finally, the officials got the crews to line up and shake hands with each other, their line passing ours, which everyone hated. It all photographed well, but didn't feel good. It felt rotten. Only Ace Gordon was good. His afterguard shook hands with each of us. Tommy Tarlington, Corny Bone, Billy Shields, and all the others. I had met Dick Smallet, Bucky Ryder, MacKinlay Fogge, Ian Reilly, but not the others, I didn't know most of her crew. Good men who'd go back Monday morning to their jobs as near-heroes, who would stand for the rest of their lives on the brink of legend. Jocelyn Ortion did not even show up.

One by one, our crew had slipped onto *Kinsman* and had gone below decks to wait for this Cup business to blow over. I sent Esperance to wave our tow boat in.

When it came, Ace Gordon picked up the Cup and formally handed it to me. He said one word, "Champion." He used it as an adjective. I hugged him; he stood with his arms at his side. I stepped aboard *Kinsman* and waved "goodbye." As we pulled away into the darkness for our final tow to Waiheke Island, I watched the people on the dock grow small under the lights. I think I knew then that it had been my last race.

There was a phone message waiting for me at Mrs. Prosser's. Uncle Rut. I called him back. Six am. He wished me congratulations and told me he would see me in Rwanda for the next Cup races.

I closed the door to our room. It had been a long day. Finally, it was silent. We made love. Afterward, neither one of us could sleep. The air was breathless. Everything was good, everything was over, everything was new. We lay side-by-side and talked to the ceiling. It was a night for promises. Promises that would be easily kept.

We would go to Aunt Pearl's memorial service at Rondelay. We would go to my apartment in Greenwich Village and pack. We would learn how the tiger cat felt about traveling to Rwanda with us. We would be married there. Bishop Demaseine with his hippo face would marry us under the eyes of God, the same God who had thrived there on injustice. We would build a white cinderblock house on Lake Kivu, where the compound used to be. It would be a big house with a long verandah and rooms upstairs for children, and a balcony off the rooms overlooking the lake.

Elizaphan's breath came soft and easy, as waves sliding up on a beach. And before sleep came to me, in her measured breathing, I heard it again, the magnificent chanting of that afternoon. How ancient it had sounded. Centuries ago, had the sailors aboard the slave ships heard this deep lament rising from below their decks? The chanting of a ruined people, their unfathomable sadness, men and women being sailed out of Africa, away from their natural lives, their birthland, sailing on ships loaded to the gunwales with flesh, alive, their bones and blood chained foot-to-head aboard the great yachts of the slave traders sailing west out of their yacht clubs in Nigeria and the Ivory Coast.

It wasn't until morning when we walked out and down to the camp and to *Kinsman's* dock that Elizaphan noticed a change in the boat. It was her name. Written in black across her red transom, one letter in KINSMAN had been painted over; the A was now an E: KINSMEN. Not one kinsman, but all kinsmen, everywhere. I never knew who did it, and no one ever came forward. I think it was Ba'ale who started the rumor: "The name changed itself." Word spread among the men. "These things happen," they said. I liked that explanation. I still believe it.

Anyway, that's my story. As I told you at the beginning, I really don't expect you to believe it. But you probably ought to, because it's true.

Fin.

⚑

About the Author

Gardner McKay was born in Manhattan, NYC. His early years were spent in France, New York, Connecticut and Kentucky. As a child, Gardner learned to sail. He loved the ocean; sailing was in his blood. His great-great-grandfather was Donald McKay, the builder of clipper ships.

At age fifteen, Gardner published his first story. His plays have been performed in every state and internationally. His novel *Toyer* won critical acclaim upon its release in 1998 and is currently in pre-production for a major motion film. He had been a professional skipper, sculptor, photographer, college teacher, and actor, as well as a drama critic for the *Los Angeles Herald Tribune*. In addition to all that, he had raised African lions.

In 1980, Gardner met and married Madeleine, his one and only wife; in 2001, he succumbed to cancer at their home in Honolulu, Hawaii. During his final year, Gardner wrote his memoir, *Journey Without A Map*, which was published posthumously in 2009. *The Kinsman* was written shortly before his death.

Made in the USA
Middletown, DE
05 December 2014